THE LAST MAN IN BERLIN

A NOVEL

BY GAYLORD DOLD

SOURCEBOOKS LANDMARK
An Imprint of Sourcebooks, Inc.®
Naperville, Illinois

Published by Sourcebooks, Inc.
P.O. Box 4410, Naperville, Illinois 60567-4410
(630) 961-3900
FAX: (630) 961-2168
www.sourcebooks.com

Library of Congress Cataloging-in-Publication Data

Dold, Gaylord.
Last man in Berlin / by Gaylord Dold.
   p. cm.
ISBN 1-4022-0124-9 (alk. paper)
1. Berlin (Germany)—Fiction. I. Title.
PS3554.O436L37 2003
813'.54—dc21

                                                          2003007007

Printed and bound in the United States of America
QW 10 9 8 7 6 5 4 3 2 1

FIRST EDITION

ACKNOWLEDGMENTS

I wish to thank my editor at Sourcebooks, Hillel Black.
His support for this book, and his persistent enthusiasm,
have made all the difference.

ALSO BY GAYLORD DOLD

HISTORICAL NOTE

During the years 1930–1933, the Berlin Metropolitan Police was considered one of the most progressive and best-organized forces in Europe. It consisted of twenty-one thousand personnel, of which there were fourteen thousand uniformed beat officers, three thousand detectives, and some four hundred political spies. Headquartered at Alexanderplatz on the eastern edge of central Berlin, the force was divided into four "divisions."

Schupo (*Schutzpolizei*), the blue-uniformed beat cops.

Orpo (*Ordnungspolitzei*), special "order" units who lived in barracks and were used for crowd control and other emergencies.

Stapo (*Staatspolizei*), political police who spied on and infiltrated antigovernment organizations and parties.

Kripo (*Kriminalpolizei*), the plainclothes detective force.

Kripo was further organized into four departments, of which the most important were Department IA (political crime) and Department IV, the detectives. Department IV had nine inspectorates (e.g., Department IVA were the homicide detectives).

The central nervous system of the force, as opposed to its administrative officers (at Alexanderplatz), was called Schupo Kommando. This unit was located at Oberwallstrasse 56, and was referred to as "Berlin Mitte," which can be loosely translated as the "central office."

Subsequent to January 30, 1933, when Hitler was appointed presidential chancellor by Hindenburg, the Berlin Police were headed by Göring. Göring departed to become a warlord, but by that time, the Berlin police had lost its independence and had become a tool of the National Socialist Party.

BERLIN POLITICS, 1930–1933

KPD—The German Communist Party, the dominant political movement in the northern and eastern parts of the city.

SPD—The German Socialist Party, in democratic control of the Prussian state and Berlin city governments.

NSDAP—The National Socialist German Worker's Party, or Nazis. Goebbels led the party in Berlin.

Red Flag Fighters (Röte Fahne)—The paramilitary militia wing of the Communist Party which conducted running battles with other paramilitary wings, especially the Brown Shirts of the Nazi party. Also called the "Red Front."

Reichsbanner—The paramilitary militia of the socialist party.

Stürmabteilung (SA)—The paramilitary wing of the Nazi party, known as "Brown Shirts" after their famous uniform.

Karl Liebknecht House—A bulky brick building not far from police headquarters at Alexanderplatz, center for the well-organized Communist Party in Berlin.

Hedemanstrasse HQ—Nazi headquarters located in central Berlin, very near the Reichstag (Legislature).

Reichswehr—The German Army, restricted by the Versailles Treaty to one hundred thousand men.

Freicorps—Militias who roamed the countryside in the early 1920s. Opposed to Bolshevism.

PART ONE

AUTUMN 1930

"Within me there is a struggle between the delight of the blooming apple tree and the horror of a Hitler speech. But only the latter forces me to my desk."
—Berthold Brecht

1

The body lay face up in a dark cul-de-sac, eight meters off the Hirrenstrasse. The area—near Alexanderplatz police headquarters— was a communist neighborhood of brick tenements and wooden slums. Barlach would never have noticed the corpse had he not stepped away from the street to piss.

It had been a blustery fall day, followed by an unseasonably cold night. A Baltic front had crossed Berlin, and the first star-shaped chestnut leaves began to scissor down from the trees along Prenzlauerstrasse where Oberwachtmeister Fritz Barlach was on patrol. Barlach had been a beat-cop for six years, most of them on the streets of Scheunenviertel, a tough working-class precinct dominated by Marxists and unemployed thugs.

He had waited out the rain under a tobacconist's awning on Prenzlauer. Wearing the blue woolen uniform of a Schupo, a faded blue lightweight raincoat, and black boots with heavy gum soles, he lit a cigarette and cursed himself for running low on tobacco. For the thousandth time in six years, he surveyed the grim street. A tram passed, its rows of pale green leather seats illuminated by a shower of overhead sparks. In the gloom at the end of the block, a group of working men huddled together in front of a pub. Barlach could hear them laughing quietly, tipping up their steins of beer while cigar and cigarette smoke stemmed upward. In the rain, the cobbled street glistened and the air smelled faintly of coal dust.

As a Schupo, Barlach carried a standard police-issue 9mm "08" revolver and a sixteen-inch truncheon made from black walnut wrapped with a cowhide grip. From the dark, he conducted a quick census of the communist drinkers, counting perhaps twenty. Unbuttoning his raincoat, he showed the drinkers his black leather holster and the pistol grip inside. Some of the drinking men had put down their steins on outdoor tables and were glaring at the cop. The sound of polka music seeped from the pub.

"Schupo swine," someone called.

"Come join us for a drink, Schupo!"

"Puppet of the Republic!"

"Fascist bootlick!"

Barlach maintained his pace. He studied these men, cataloguing their faces in the dark—rough-looking factory hands, welders, plumbers and carpenters, truck drivers, unemployed stevedores and steel-workers. "Shit eater!" one of the men shouted. "Come drink with us, Schupo! While your mother fucks a rich man!"

He walked west into the Hirrenstrasse, testing shop doors and peeping into windows. Barlach paused at the entrance of a cul-de-sac. In the darkness, he could see three steel warehouse doors, a stack of packing crates, garbage cans, and litter. Turning his back to the street, he faced a wall and unbuttoned his fly, then let loose a stream of urine into a storm drain. He detected the approach of a tram, the clang of its bell and the hiss of electrical sparks on wet pavement. And just then, in a trick of light, Barlach saw the body in reflected glare.

He paced off eight meters, kneeled beside the body, and felt the neck for a pulse. His heart skipped several beats and he didn't know quite what to think. She was a delicate and fine-boned girl, immaculately groomed with a perfect cup of black hair cut squarely around her sharp-featured face. She wore a sequined evening dress of shimmering black material, silk stockings, and two-toned black-and-white heels. Her face was perfectly made up and near white with powder, spots of red rouge on each cheek, deep crimson lipstick, and dark kohl eye shadow. He placed his ear near the woman's mouth and detected no breath.

Barlach stood and studied the body again: jet-black imitation fingernails, tiny ankles and slim wrists, the well developed leg muscles of a dancer or gymnast. Her eyebrows had been plucked and painted over in black. On each finger was a ring. Barlach sat down on a packing crate. He shined his torch on the woman's bruised neck, noticed how her lipstick had been smeared at the right corner of her mouth. "What's a beauty like you doing in Scheunenviertel?" he said to himself.

He found a police call-box on the Hirrenstrasse and telephoned Alexanderplatz headquarters. When he returned to the cul-de-sac, he sat down again on a packing crate. It looked to Barlach as if she'd been through the rain shower two hours before. He took out his pocket watch and checked the time. Ten o'clock. He lit a cigarette, waiting for whatever bigwig inspector Alexanderplatz would dispatch.

— —

Kriminal Kommissar Harry Wulff sat on a marble windowsill where he could look down three stories to Alexanderplatz. A stream of trams came and went as commuters exited the Bahnhof where one could hear the scream and screech of arriving trains. News vendors hawked their late editions, and even from three stories high Wulff could hear a barrel organ.

An orderly named Krause had escorted Wulff down a long corridor to the outer alcove of the deputy commissioner's office and had offered him a seat in a high-back wing chair, along with a cup of hot tea. Wulff declined both the seat and the tea, taking instead a seat on cold marble so that he could observe Alexanderplatz and its ceaseless drama. That evening, there had been a surprise rainstorm. Wulff had taxied from his flat in Zimmerstrasse to headquarters at Alexanderplatz. He was wearing a gray serge suit and English-made brown brogues.

A janitor broomed Wulff's way. The man was hulking in a subnormal way, wearing gray work clothes with red dust rags stuffed in both back pockets. The janitor stopped for a moment as if surprised by the presence of Wulff sitting in the windowsill, then pulled one of the dust rags from his pocket and idly polished the surface of a mahogany end table.

"You must be here to see the little Jew," he said to Wulff.

"I'm here to see Weiss," Wulff said, annoyed. In the corridor, chandeliers caught and reflected the reddish light of the square below.

"It's late, isn't it?" the janitor said mysteriously.

Harry Wulff looked at his pocket watch, an expensive Swiss timepiece given to him by his father. Just near ten o'clock. The janitor wadded a red rag into his pocket.

"You work all night?" Wulff asked, making conversation.

"I've just now come on duty," the other replied.

Wulff half-turned and looked down at the square, hoping to end this tête-à-tête. He thought about smoking but saw no ashtray. The janitor leaned on his broom. "I've seen you here before, haven't I?"

"I'm a detective inspector," Wulff said.

"An inspector," the janitor repeated.

The Anhalter Bahnhof tram skidded to a stop on the square in a flower of sparks. The janitor spent time wrapping dust rags around his broom, then pinning them together. From the left, Krause passed through a gilded door. "The commissioner will see you now," Krause said officiously. Wulff stood and followed the orderly through a door. The office of the deputy police commissioner was vast, library shelves cluttered with books on one side, two desks piled high with papers, a coal fire guttering in one corner. Behind the desks, a huge fireplace smelled of damp ashes. Directly ahead sat Bernhard Weiss, who rose and offered Wulff a chair.

"I'm sorry this is such a late meeting," Weiss said. Wulff stood at least a head taller than the deputy commissioner. "I know it is late. I suppose you've heard about the riots in Wedding? Another communist scrape."

Wulff said he'd heard. Elections to the Reichstag had been scheduled, and street battles were common. In this particular skirmish, there had been no deaths.

Weiss played with time, peering at Wulff through thick bottle-bottom lenses. The deputy commissioner had a huge nose, bulbous ears, and a narrow, wedge-shaped head. He opened a manila dossier and studied it while Wulff waited in the near-dark of the office. The windows behind Wulff jumped with articulate red images, department-store neon, orange street lamps.

"You support the Republic, Wulff?" Weiss asked suddenly. The coal fire hissed and sputtered. Despite the fire and the carpeted floor, Wulff was chilled to the bone. "Perhaps you find this question provocative and strange?" he continued.

"I am for the Republic," Wulff said.

"As much as any man, I suppose?"

"As much as any man," Wulff said calmly.

"I thought so," Weiss said. "I believe we've met on other occasions, haven't we?"

Wulff thought back. "At the opening of the new police academy," he said. As a member of the criminal investigation team called

Kripo, Wulff had few reasons to meet Bernhard Weiss, the chief of Berlin's metropolitan political unit called Stapo, a branch of the police that kept tabs on subversive activities. "And I believe," Wulff continued, "we spoke briefly at the funeral of Foreign Minister Stresseman."

"So we did," Weiss said. "I've been looking at your dossier."

"It makes boring reading, I'm certain," Wulff said.

"Not at all," Weiss said. "You have an enviable record. But I wonder if you belong to a political party?"

"I vote my conscience," Wulff temporized.

"I see you've graduated from Berlin University with a degree in philosophy and history. You were made a detective at age twenty-three, then a detective inspector at age thirty. Most impressive advancement in Department IV. You'll have your own Ober-kommisarriat if you're not careful!"

"I've been most fortunate," Wulff said.

"And your father was on Ludendorff's staff during the Great War?"

Wulff paused, aware of being tested. He knew that Weiss had received the Iron Cross First Class in the Great War. The deputy commissioner had returned to Germany with a nasty shoulder wound and several pieces of shrapnel in his head. "You knew my father?" he asked finally.

"Only *of* him," Weiss replied. "Yes, you've compiled an impressive record." Weiss took off his spectacles and wiped them with a white handkerchief. "But I'm curious about something," he continued. "You do not investigate political crimes. It would seem you prefer the everyday to the historical. I wonder why a man of your talent is not of more use to the Republic? I must ask where this predilection for the ordinary comes from?"

"If it's a predilection, it is come by honestly," Wulff said.

"But of course," Weiss smiled. Two brass lamps lit his desk. His sleek brown hair was thickly pomaded and glistened in the light. "Do you know of Dr. Goebbels?"

"Certainly," Wulff said. "I know of him."

"You are aware of his campaign of slander against me?"

"Dimly at best," Wulff said.

"For two years Goebbels has waged literary war against me through the vehicle of his party-sponsored tabloid. He's a man who has made anti-Semitism and the death of the Republic his special province. His divine mission."

Wulff had seen the newssheet titled *Der Angriff*, a twice-weekly publication stocked with odious anti-Jewish slime, caricature, sexual innuendo, political bombast, and gossip. Wulff was aware that Weiss had fought back with lawsuits and arrests, closures of the press, even raids at Nazi Party headquarters, all in a losing battle.

"What has this to do with me?" Wulff asked.

"Yes, we come to the point," Weiss said. "I need a man like you in Department I. I want you to come to work for the Republic as part of the political police. You must believe me when I aver that the Republic is on its last legs."

"No doubt it is," Wulff said.

Weiss reached into his desk drawer and withdrew a thick sheaf of typewritten documents. "I've prepared a report about the Nazis and their Storm Troop for the Reich attorney," he said. "This is the report in my hand. If you read this report, you might find yourself educated to a certain grim reality. Perhaps you will agree with me that the current political struggle requires a policeman of your talent."

Weiss pushed the report toward Wulff. On the wall behind Weiss hung a portrait of Hindenberg, the old president in stiff white moustache and braided collar.

"Surely others are more suited to the job," Wulff said.

"Perhaps, Detective Inspector," Weiss mused. "The facts of the matter speak otherwise." He fixed Wulff with a piercing stare. "There are now twenty-one thousand officers on the Berlin Metropolitan force. Of those, perhaps three hundred are Stapo political police and of those perhaps fifty have the intelligence required to report on subversive activity with any acuity and foresight." Weiss walked to the coal fire and stood, warming his hands. "But you, my dear Wulff, you are different. I want you to organize a cadre of devoted specialists who will not only observe and report, but infiltrate the parties involved, actually becoming members! I've spoken with Oberkommissar Bruckmann. As your captain of criminal police, he will release you from your duties for a special assignment."

"I mean no offense," Wulff said. "But I'm Kripo to the core."

"And this core means what?" Weiss said dismissively, waving a hand as though he were swatting an imaginary fly. "There is no human core. You are an aristocrat and you've lost two brothers in the war and you've a Jewish lover. She is a medical doctor, I believe. Hundreds of thousands of Jews fought for Germany in the war and yet they are afraid to build a synagogue with its doors facing the streets. If this goes on, what will be the fate of our country?"

"You seem to know a great deal about me."

"I'm sorry, Wulff," Weiss said. "Even as we speak there are spies inside this headquarters building. I make it my business to know the nature of my staff."

"Including their personal lives?" Wulff asked.

Weiss shrugged. "You think anonymity is the birthright of a Kripo? How do you think a democracy fights perversion of this nature?"

Wulff saw no need to respond.

"Let me tell you something," Weiss continued. "The two most dangerous men in Berlin are Gauleiter Goebbels and Storm Troop 33 Führer Dieter Rom. Without inside information on their behavior and programs, this government is powerless to combat the planned revolution. I hoped you would join the fight."

"And as for my Jewish lover?" Wulff said.

"I have offended you," Weiss said. "You must forgive me, Detective Inspector. I am a man with thick skin. Goebbels vilifies me every day. My caricature is in print. He defiles my wife and my family. Now that the elections are upon us, it grows worse. Once, I, too, believed in absolute privacy. But these days, privacy is a luxury the Republic cannot afford."

"Is there anything else, sir?" Wulff said.

"Please," Weiss said, "give some thought to my request. And think about something else, too. As I've explained, a Nazi spy works somewhere in this building. Last week my men executed a surprise raid on the offices of Storm Troop 33. We found that all its papers and documents either had been removed or destroyed in advance of the raid. As you know, Storm 33 is responsible for many riots and murders. They knew of our plan in advance, Wulff. And when they know of our plans in advance, how can they be defeated? And, when I say the fate of Europe hangs in the balance, do you think I am being melodramatic?"

A telephone rang. Weiss picked up the receiver and spoke quietly for a minute. "Yes, yes, I see," the deputy commissioner said at last. He put down the phone and said, "There's been a murder in the Hirrenstrasse."

Wulff leaned forward, hands on knees. "Under what circumstances?"

"Not political," Weiss said.

"Hirrenstrasse isn't far," Wulff said.

"That was the night duty officer," Weiss continued. "He saw you sign the entry book downstairs. The Schupo wondered if you'd consent to investigate. Knowing you, you'll probably want to go."

"Where, exactly?"

"Scheunenviertel, near Prenzlauerstrasse. On the scene is a first sergeant named Barlach. Do you have an automobile?"

"I took a taxi here."

"Take an Opel from the garage."

"Barlach, he's from the Seventh?"

"You know the precincts well," Weiss said admiringly.

"A communist neighborhood."

Weiss rose from his chair. "Won't you promise to read a copy of my report?"

"Of course, sir," Wulff agreed, reluctantly picking up the massive folder.

Wulff left the office hurriedly and was escorted down a long corridor by the orderly Krause. At the end of the corridor, Wulff descended a wide marble staircase to the first landing where he saw the janitor dusting his way downstairs. Wulff brushed by the man.

"They say there's been a murder," the janitor said, his voice echoing in the vast chamber of the foyer.

"You're well informed," Wulff replied. He turned and made his way to the police garage, a warehouse compound near Alexanderplatz Bahnhof.

The Bahnhof tower clock tolled eleven. At that late hour, the crowds of Alexanderplatz had disappeared, abandoning the square to homeless and unemployed men who lurked in the entrances of the station and cadged pfennigs from late passersby. The red neon Wertheim sign had been turned off, plunging the huge department store into a mausoleum-like dark. Wulff was driving a tiny two-seater police Opel with the thick Weiss report on the cushion beside him.

Wulff drove north, winding across the Alexanderplatz roundabout and then found Hirrenstrasse, where he saw a small crowd of pub drinkers gathered on the sidewalk at the end of the block. In the near dark, Wulff spotted a police van parked half-on and half-off the sidewalk, its yellow dome-light revolving in periodic gloom as two white-smocked medical orderlies smoked cigarettes nearby. Wulff got out of the car and put on his raincoat. It had become very cold.

A large Schupo with blocky features and disheveled red hair approached Wulff from within the confines of a cul-de-sac just off Hirrenstrasse proper. "Oberwachtmeister Barlach," the Schupo reported, saluting.

"Very well, Barlach," Wulff acknowledged. "I'm Detective Inspector Wulff, Berlin Mitte." Wulff noted the sergeant's large size, square shoulders, and resolute eyes.

"She's in the alley," Barlach reported.

The medical orderlies had erected wooden barricades at the entrance to the cul-de-sac, placing several more in the middle of the Hirrenstrasse to hold back any crowd. The group of pub drinkers stood behind the barricade, gawking at the crime scene.

"You found her, Barlach?" Wulff asked.

"I stopped to take a piss down the storm drain here and I saw her just like this."

"Just like this?"

"Nothing has been touched. Absolutely nothing."

"Absolutely nothing?"

"I placed a finger on her throat to test a pulse and put my head near her breast. Other than that, nothing has been touched."

Wulff took a deep breath and studied the Hirrenstrasse. It was a typical working-class district at night: shops, a millinery, a bakery, one pub at the end of the block at the entrance to Prenzlauerstrasse. To the northwest was Grenadierstrasse, where there was a Catholic church and beyond that a tram stop, then more acres of Hinterhof. Wulff turned back, looking toward Prenzlauerstrasse again, a wide avenue that was the main thoroughfare of the Scheunenviertel, an axis to Alexanderplatz and the West End of Berlin. Just two hours before, Prenzlauer would have been jammed with traffic.

"Where's Stapo now?" Wulff asked the sergeant.

"I've sent patrolmen to interview concierges on each side of the Hirrenstrasse."

"They'll talk to you?" Wulff asked.

"They have in the past," Barlach told him.

Their combined breath created steam which escaped upward.

"How well do you know this street?" Wulff asked. Barlach stood just off his right shoulder.

"I know it quite well," Barlach answered. "Shopkeepers and the unemployed. Some workers still are employed at chemical plants, a few tanners who do seasonal jobs. There were some steel men until the Depression. Now many do nothing."

"Those gathered behind the barricade?"

"From the Red Rooster."

"Communists?"

"Most of them," Barlach said. "They can be talked to if you know how."

"Would they volunteer?"

"Not likely," Barlach said.

"So nobody has come forward."

Barlach shook his head. "They won't. But they might speak if they knew what was going on."

Wulff buckled his raincoat. "Let's take a look at her," he said. Barlach followed Wulff into the cul-de-sac.

"She's eight meters in," Barlach said.

Wulff saw her clearly. He shined his torch on the body which was on its back, eyes open.

"Sir," Barlach said. "I touched the dress to see if it was wet. There was a rain shower at eight o'clock tonight."

"And was it wet?"

"Damp, yes," Barlach said.

Wulff performed an inventory: black sequined dress hemmed three inches below the knee; a black sweater with an imitation ermine collar thrown over the shoulders; black hair with short sharp bangs; kohl eye shadow and dark red lipstick. He studied the stylish two-tone high-heeled shoes and noted a lack of wear on their heels and soles. Barlach switched on his own torch, throwing a second beam. In life, Wulff concluded, this woman might have looked beautifully cadaverous.

"She's tiny," Wulff said.

"A meter and a half."

Wulff called back for the orderlies to turn on the van headlights.

"About fifty kilos," Barlach concluded.

"Not more," Wulff said.

"She doesn't belong here," Wulff said.

"That's what I told myself too," Barlach replied.

"I assume you don't know her from the neighborhood?"

"Not here. Not anywhere."

Wulff stood thinking for a long moment. "Where do you suppose she was coming from? Where do you suppose she was going?"

Barlach remained silent. The van had been turned, and its lights suddenly exploded into the cul-de-sac. Wulff saw the sequined purse. "She carried a purse," Wulff said quietly, "but no raincoat and only a sweater around her shoulders for warmth. Her dress is slightly damp. I should think her hair is wet as well." Wulff kneeled and touched the dress, then the silk stockings. The skin of her face was warm, and he could now see faint traces of lividity on the backs of her arms and legs. "There is no rigor," Wulff said.

"Do you mind if I smoke?" Barlach asked.

Wulff gave his permission. "She has a bruise on the neck," Wulff said. "There are ruptured vessels under the thyroid bone."

"And look at the eyes," Barlach said.

Wulff put a light on them—black centers, pale purple iris, tiny blotched red edges. He moved the beam down her torso and examined the shoes again. "These shoes have hardly been worn," he said. Barlach kneeled down and beamed his torch. "There are scuffs on each heel. It's as though she'd been dragged partway into this alley from near Hirrenstrasse."

"So she has," Barlach agreed.

"She was strangled or attacked on the street and then dragged into the cul-de-sac. The killer finished his work here where it was dark."

"That's how it seems to me, Inspector," Barlach agreed again.

"And what time was the rain?"

"Eight o'clock."

"So she was killed just before then. Her skin is warm. It can't have been much before the rain, otherwise her skin would be cooler to the touch. And she went out without a raincoat, so she didn't expect the rain."

"Her lipstick is smudged, sir," Barlach offered.

"So it is," Wulff agreed. On the upper lip was a tick of misplaced red. "It's certain she didn't leave her house looking like that. Perhaps the lipstick was smudged in whatever struggle she put up."

"I'd wager she's been kissed," Barlach said.

Wulff sat on his haunches above the body. "Let's find out who she is," he said, putting on a pair of leather gloves. He opened the purse. Inside were five slim black cigars, a box of common wooden matches manufactured in Berlin, sixteen mark notes, and a few pfennig coins along with two tram tokens. A small compartment inside the purse contained a bottle of cheap spray lilac scent, eyeliner, lipstick, and tissues.

"No identity papers?" Barlach asked.

Wulff searched the pockets of the cheap sweater but found nothing. "A ring on every finger, Barlach," Wulff said. "But no identity papers. What do you make of it?"

Barlach exhaled cigarette smoke. "I haven't made up my mind yet, sir."

Wulff studied the rings. "Cut glass, rhinestone, and zirconia," he said. "Is there prostitution in this precinct?"

"Only around the Bahnhof," Barlach said. "There isn't money here for women." He threw down his cigarette, making certain it dropped into a storm drain. "This woman wasn't working the Scheunenviertel. I know the prostitutes around Alexanderplatz, and she wasn't one of them."

"Go and see if our communist friends recognize her," Wulff instructed. "Bring them by in single file, one by one. I'll wait over in the Opel so as not to cause a fuss."

Wulff retreated to the Opel and smoked while Barlach led a few men one at a time into the alley. Wulff pondered the street again, its shops and pubs, its many tenement windows overlooking the scene. It was perhaps one hundred meters corner to corner, one tram stop just northwest, then a church. Ten minutes passed before Barlach approached the Opel where Wulff had just finished his second cigarette.

"They couldn't wait to get a gander at her," Barlach said. "One minute they're screaming political insults at me and the next they're slobbering over themselves to have a look."

"Did anyone recognize her?"

"Not a soul," Barlach replied. "And I think they'd tell me if they did. They'd be too excited not to say anything."

"Barlach—" Wulff began.

"Sir?"

"Listen to me," Wulff whispered. "Hirrenstrasse connects two urban tram stops, doesn't it? There is a tram stop in the Grenadierstrasse and another in the Prenzlauer. Coming from the east, one going to Berlin makes the connection, and leaving from Berlin one makes the same connection in the opposite direction. Perhaps our victim was walking between two tram stops. She doesn't live around here. You've never seen her here before and the men in the pub have never seen her before. She has tram tokens in her purse. Perhaps she was leaving Berlin for the suburbs, or commuting to Berlin from the suburbs."

"But why no identification, sir?"

"I don't know, Barlach," he said.

"Perhaps she was walking with a man?"

"Or met someone. But why was she killed?"

"A man would have to be strong," Barlach said. "Drag her into this alley and strangle her without a peep."

"He'd be strong all right," Wulff agreed.

"Do you think she was, well—" Barlach stopped in mid-sentence.

"Raped," Wulff said.

"I'd thought of it," Barlach said.

Wulff headed back to the street with Barlach following. He instructed the orderlies to back their van away from the entrance to the alley and douse its lights. Wulff walked to the body, kneeled, and lifted the sequined black dress above the waist.

"Barlach—" Wulff said quietly.

"Sir?"

"She isn't a woman," Wulff said.

"Sir?"

"She's not a woman, Barlach."

"Not a woman?"

"She's a he. She's a man."

"She's a man, sir?" Barlach said, shocked.

— —

Wulff drove from the Hirrenstrasse to the edge of the Tiergarten, then parked opposite a row of imposing stone apartment buildings fronted by an ornate iron fence. He climbed the stairs to Apartment 15 and stood looking for his keys in front of a heavy oaken door on which a brass plaque read: JOHANNA DAVIDOV, M.D., PSYCHO-ANALYSIS. Once inside, he stood in a narrow hallway, allowing his eyes to adjust to the dark. On his right was a dusty philodendron. Straight ahead lay a large room piled high with newspapers, journals, books, and porcelain figures. Its interior walls were decorated with African art, masks, spears, and totems. Wulff advanced a few steps and eased open the bathroom door on his left. In the tub Johanna lay sleeping, an empty bottle of schnapps on the tile floor. Wulff took off his raincoat and sat beside the tub on a footstool. He studied Johanna's naked body and gently kissed her forehead.

"Oh Harry," Johanna murmured.

"You've been drinking schnapps, darling," Wulff chided her.

"I must have been." She lifted her knees. "Don't be cross with me, Harry."

Wulff immersed a hand in the tepid water and caressed her leg.

"I'm not cross with you," he said. "I'm sorry I'm late. There's been a murder in the Hirrenstrasse and before that I had a meeting with Deputy Commissioner Weiss at Alexanderplatz."

Johanna draped an arm around his neck as Wulff lifted her from the tub. He managed her to the bedroom where he wrapped her in a blanket and deposited her under the sheets. After closing the drapes to the French doors, Wulff returned and sat beside Johanna.

"Stay with me, Harry," she said softly. "Perhaps tonight we'll hear the lions in the zoo. They are perfectly marvelous at night."

"I imagine they are," Wulff said.

"What did Weiss want?"

"I can't tell you, dear," Wulff replied. "It was political. Dr. Goebbels."

"Oh, not Dr. Goebbels," Johanna said.

"Have you eaten?" Wulff asked, changing the subject.

"I don't recall," Johanna laughed. "But I'm not hungry now."

When Johanna asked him the time, Wulff told her midnight. He told her the weather had changed and that the poplars were losing their leaves. Johanna held Wulff's head and kissed him hard on the mouth. "Goebbels would not approve of you and me," she growled.

"Let's not seek his approval then," Wulff whispered.

"Take off your holster, Harry, and come to bed."

"I should go home, dear," Wulff protested. "There's been a murder and I've an early meeting at Alexanderplatz."

"You can do whatever you wish with me. Won't that be fun?"

"We'll have all weekend, darling," Wulff said.

"Fuck me tonight, Harry. You'll be my succubus and later we'll listen for the lions."

Wulff let her fall asleep that way, wrapped in a blanket. It was after one o'clock when he finally let himself out.

The janitor masturbated himself to orgasm.

In the single stall of the washroom toilet he sat with closed eyes. Suddenly relaxed, he looked at his slack penis, wiped it clean with a newspaper, and fought an urge to scream. He pulled on his work pants, flushed the toilet, then walked to the sink and stood looking into a mirror just above the basin. From the pocket of his pants he took a single tube of lipstick and applied two thin strips to both lips. Leaning forward, he touched his lips to the mirror image of himself. Closing his eyes again, he imagined a merry-go-round world of never-worry and carnival rides, organdy orange clouds and pale lustrous sunsets. Standing back from the mirror, he wiped lipstick from the glass with a dust rag, then from his mouth.

He left the washroom at Alexanderplatz basement, momentarily rid of the thing that entailed him to the devil's work.

3

The day's *Der Angriff*—a scurrilous political attack sheet edited by Goebbels and published by the Gau of the Berlin Nazi party—featured a caricature of Bernhard Weiss as the eternal vermin Jew, a misshapen rat with twitching ears and pointed nose, whiskers dripping with the blood of Germany's working class. FOUR MILLION UNEMPLOYED, screamed the headline, and the Jewish-Bolshevik-November criminals responsible for every lost job and every German humiliation.

Wulff dropped the newspaper onto a wooden table and sipped his morning coffee. He had ordered a boiled egg and toasted roll in the commissary of police headquarters. Its high ceilings and glass windows reverberated with traffic noise. Wulff ate a bite of egg and picked up the *Frankfurter Zeitung,* reading yet another presidential decree concerning weapons, demonstrations in the street, the banning of marches by either Storm Troops or Red Flag Fighters within four hundred meters of the Berlin city-center.

Wulff drained the weak coffee and lit his first cigarette of the morning. He spotted Barlach plodding through a tide of petty bureaucrats, police officials, secretaries, and Schupo administrators. The sergeant raised a hand in greeting and smiled nervously.

"This area is for criminal investigators," Barlach said cautiously.

"Don't stand on ceremony," Wulff joked.

Barlach sat reluctantly. He told Wulff he'd eaten breakfast at home and didn't wish to smoke in an officer mess area.

"And your canvass of the neighborhood?" Wulff asked.

"I've finished my questioning," Barlach explained to Wulff. "I pulled teeth, but nobody saw anything along the street last night at about the time of the murder. I'm convinced there was no noticeable scream. Earlier than seven, the street would have been somewhat crowded. From seven o'clock on, less so. Whoever killed the victim could have pulled her into the cul-de-sac quick as a snake."

"Just so," Wulff agreed. Wulff glanced down to the headline in *Vorwärts*, the socialist daily paper. FASCISTS RIOT AGAINST THE REPUBLIC. Barlach tugged at the collar of his heavy uniform jacket and adjusted the leather shako he wore. Wulff unfolded a copy of the *Berliner Zeitung*, a popular tabloid owned by the magnate Hugenberg, a capitalist media-mogul allegedly cozy with Hitler. On its glossy cover was a photo of Max Schmeling, the German boxing champion of the world. "So tell me, Barlach," Wulff continued, "doesn't it seem odd that this murder took place so quickly and efficiently?"

"I've thought about attempted rape, sir," Barlach said. "Or perhaps a ruffian on the street wanted a kiss but became enraged when he discovered the woman was a man."

"Yes, it could have been so," Wulff said.

Barlach shrugged, shook his head ambiguously. On the Bahnhof pediment outside, a flock of pigeons had settled. The sky was brilliantly blue.

"What shall we do then, sir?" Barlach asked finally. There was a hammerlock of silence.

Wulff gathered together his newspapers and tossed them aside. Rising at dawn, he'd read most of the Weiss report on Nazi subversion. "If it *was* a kiss," Wulff mused. Wulff closed his eyes and pictured it. "If this was a kiss, Barlach, as you insist, then we must assume our stranger believed his victim was a woman."

"The killer was a street ruffian, sir?" Barlach asked.

Wulff restrained a smile. He realized he'd been indulging in metaphysics. He picked up his black leather coat in one hand and cradled it. "Simply to say," Wulff said, "that I think we have a woman being murdered here. Not a man dressed as a woman. Not a transvestite either. If our killer realized his mistake, he realized it only at the moment of the kiss. Perhaps this is a minor distinction, but it may prove important to the investigation." Wulff stood and donned his leather coat. "If we can discover the victim's identity, perhaps we can cobble together a case."

Barlach grunted affably. He presented his collected notes and diagrams in a small folder. "I've thought of something," Barlach said. "Last night I assumed the victim was traveling from Prenzlauer to the Grenadier tram stop. It seemed logical to think that she was leaving Berlin and going home to the suburbs. Perhaps now I think he was commuting from the suburbs toward Berlin."

Wulff dropped a knuckle on the wooden surface of the table. "You're a born detective," he said. "She was a woman going out for the night!"

"But without her identity papers," Barlach cautioned.

"Of course!" Wulff said. "Don't you see, Barlach? She had no identity as a woman."

"Yes, sir."

"Wouldn't you like a cigarette, Barlach?" Wulff asked, proffering a silver cigarette case that Johanna had given him. Barlach hesitated, then smiled and took a cigarette.

"I don't mind if I do," Barlach said.

— ◆ —

Wulff would always remember the blood-red orchid stain on the pathologist's smock.

He and Barlach had walked down a flight of marble stairs to the half-basement of Alexanderplatz headquarters and entered a corridor with windows at shoulder level, its beveled stone walls interrupted at intervals by sculpted imperial eagles. When Wulff pulled open the door to the morgue lab, Aaron Levitt greeted him in a white working smock smeared with a blot of blood in the compelling shape of an orchid.

"You're late," growled Levitt, a grizzled Jew with a bright glabrous scalp and a fringe of fuzzy white hair. "I've been waiting ten minutes to get started on your corpse."

The pathologist turned, walked to a zinc washbasin, and began to bathe his hands in soapy water, then applied an alcohol spritz and antiseptic solution. He pulled on a set of yellow rubber gloves after dropping talcum into each finger hole. The room they were in was fifteen meters square and contained four metal operating tables, shelves of examining trays and collecting buckets, glass cases for needles, tools, jars, tubes, beakers, and ornate paraphernalia. On one metal table lay the fully clothed victim.

Levitt snapped his rubber gloves. "I was up late last night taking readings," Levitt said. "I got his temperature. I also had the photographer come down and take his picture with clothes on as you directed." Levitt led the way to the operating table where they spent a moment studying the corpse. "I've had a good look at the injuries, and there was no sexual assault," Levitt said.

"The body temperature last night?" Wulff asked.

"Only two degrees below normal," Levitt said. "My preliminary opinion is based on temperature and on the degree of rigor present when he was brought in about eleven, and also on the lividity in the arms and legs. The condition of the eyes was a factor. Insect activity was negligible. I'd say he'd been dead only three hours when he was brought in, perhaps an hour or so either way." Levitt paused. "Yes, four hours at the most, which places the death at around seven o'clock."

"I want all the pathology you can give me on this one," Wulff said. "I include in that toxicology, stomach contents. And we don't know his identity. See if you can give me some clue to that. And please make a dental examination."

Levitt picked up a paper towel and dabbed at his face. "Ach!" he said suddenly as Barlach started. "Wulff, Wulff! How many times have we autopsied these bodies? You tell me, how many times?"

"Old man, you'll have to admit that we don't often have a problem with identity."

"Even so, have my autopsies ever been less then first rate?" Levitt leaned over and spit a glob of phlegm into a blood bucket near the operating table. "And here you bring me a man dressed as a woman!"

"I hardly choose my cases, Levitt."

"These matters of identity!" Levitt laughed heartily. "Am I not a Jew pretending to be a German?"

"Tell me what you know, old man," Wulff said.

"All right, all right," Levitt grumbled. "I can tell you a few things about this strange hybrid woman already."

Barlach rounded the head of the table and stood half-distracted, staring down at the corpse from a distance of one meter.

"Look at the eyes, gentlemen," Levitt said. He plucked up an eyelid. "There are tiny *petechia* in the mucous linings." Wulff leaned in to see disorganized red splotches under the eyelids, broken vessels that had flooded the cornea. "And, of course," Levitt whispered dramatically, "there is significant bruising to both dorsal and ventral aspects of the neck." Levitt touched the neck with an index finger. "It is possible the hyoid bone is fractured. Certainly there is significant injury to the thyroid cartilage. And if you look carefully you can see a partial outlined thumbprint just right of the carotid itself."

Wulff recognized the print immediately, a dark brown lozenge bruise in the shape of a human thumb. At the end of the bruise was a fractional laceration, perhaps caused by a fingernail.

"I'm no genius, of course," Levitt said, thumping his head hard with a right palm. "A Jew yes, but a genius no! This victim was strangled. Are we clear on that?"

"May I wait outside, sir?" Barlach said. Wulff nodded and Barlach left hurriedly.

When the morgue door had shut, Levitt said, "Your Oberwachtmeister is having stomach trouble, Wulff."

Wulff smiled. "You are a rare bird, Levitt," he said.

Levitt said, "There is something else about your victim. This smudge of lipstick on the edge of the right lip."

"What do you conclude?"

Levitt shrugged exaggeratedly. He flicked off the penlight.

"A last kiss," Levitt said.

Wulff circled the table indulging in a last glimpse of the corpse before its clothes were taken off and the torso gutted by a Y-incision, before the scalp was peeled over the face and the brain extracted.

"Killed about seven o'clock?" Wulff asked seriously.

"Not a bad guess, I'd say," Levitt told him. "In this case I think we're correct. The autopsy will be more precise, but nothing is likely to change much either way. You have your time of death and your method." Levitt used a towel to wipe a track of makeup off the corpse. "There are red splotches on the epidermis," he said. "Poor fellow was strangled all right. Who is he?"

"I was really hoping you could tell me," Wulff said. He buttoned his black leather coat. "Send the fingerprints upstairs." Wulff walked partway to the door and turned. "What time will the preliminary report be ready?"

"Early tonight," Levitt said. "I'll leave a copy here if I'm gone. I can't stay here all night waiting for you, can I?"

The detective inspector found Barlach leaning heavily against a marble water fountain in the hall. Around him fans of sunshine spread on the tile floor from each shoulder-level window. Barlach snapped to weary attention and looked at Wulff shame-facedly.

"Don't worry about it, Barlach," Wulff told him. "Now we have to go upstairs to the Records Section and gather photos of this dead man-woman. I want you to circulate the photo to shops and pubs in the neighborhood. And I want you to show the photo to tram conductors on both the Prenzlauer and Grenadier lines. If they recognize her, report it to me at once. Later tonight, they'll have photos of the "male" version of this victim, and you can circulate those as well tomorrow. If what we think is correct, this woman should have left the Grenadier tram around seven o'clock and begun to walk down the Hirrenstrasse to catch the Prenzlauer tram on to Berlin. She was quite beautiful in a certain way. Surely a tram conductor will remember her. Perhaps we will be lucky, Barlach."

Barlach saluted. "It would be my honor to assist you, Detective Inspector."

"We'll talk soon, sergeant, either by telephone or in person."

"May I ask why you've chosen me to assist with this investigation?"

Wulff was in the process of lighting a cigarette. He pondered the lack of motive for this murder. "Perhaps it is your devotion to duty," he told Barlach.

Barlach nodded sheepishly and trudged up the marble stairs just ahead of Wulff. Wulff erased an image of the victim's face from his mind, though he knew he would long remember the blood orchid on Levitt's smock.

━ ━

Again Wulff was led into the deputy commissioner's office by Krause. Once inside he was surprised to see his own captain, Oberkommissar Bruckmann standing near the windows that looked down at Alexanderplatz, one hand cupping a black cigar. Wulff blinked in surprise, then stood to attention and nodded quickly at Bruckmann who returned the gesture. Wulff saluted Weiss, who was seated behind his monumental desk in front of the fireplace. The deputy commissioner seemed dwarfed by stacks of reports, documents, photographs, and journals.

"No need for formality," Weiss said. "We're just having a little chat. Please come in and sit down."

Wulff shook hands with Bruckmann, a stiffly ramrod man who had gone through the Great War on the Western Front. He had lost his right eye to shrapnel and walked with a slight limp. It was said that a British shell had pierced the bunker in which six men had been sitting, breakfasting on rat. The shell had killed five of them, sending Bruckmann to the hospital for six days. As a result, Bruckmann wore an eye patch and a neat scar on his cheek. Wulff sat down and exchanged a few meaningless pleasantries with the captain, whose short-cropped gray hair and conically shaped head gave one the impression of a bullet. Wulff declined Bruckmann's offer of a cigar. Wulff was carrying the Weiss report, which he laid carefully amid the disastrous clutter.

"Hitler is with his entourage at the Kaiserhof Hotel," Weiss said.

"He's come up in the world," Bruckmann remarked tonelessly. "He even drives a new supercharged black Mercedes. Or his chauffeur drives it for him." Bruckmann grunted. "And to think only seven years ago this corporal led a failed revolution in Munich!"

Wulff nudged the report toward Weiss. Bruckmann let a tipple of ash float indecorously to the carpet.

"I see you've returned my report on the Nazi threat to our government," Weiss said to Wulff. "Did you read it?"

"I read it last night," Wulff said. "And I finished it this morning in the commissary along with *Der Angriff*.

"You enjoyed the caricature of me?"

"It is disgusting," Wulff said.

Weiss smiled wistfully. "I am quite used to it by now. Although the same cannot be said for my wife and children." Weiss rose and walked to the window and stood beside a heavy purple brocade drape.

"You should get some rest," Bruckmann interjected to Wulff, putting an avuncular arm on his shoulder.

"Rest is for the weary," Wulff said.

"But what of the wicked?" Weiss joked. "What rest is there for the wicked?"

"If you mean the report," Wulff said, "then surely the Reich state attorney will act."

"He has refused already," Weiss said tartly. "The report is now in the hands of the Prussian Ministry of Interior. You have read my conclusion. Unless there is an absolute ban on both the Communist and the Nazi parties, this Republic is doomed. Do you not agree with me, Wulff?"

Bruckmann turned suddenly to the window. "Oh, Wulff," he said, "you have my permission to speak of political matters."

"I'm sorry, Deputy Commissioner, but these matters are not for the criminal investigators of Kripo."

"But if the Right gains power," Weiss said slowly, "your new police commissioner will be Hermann Göring."

"Think, Wulff, think!" Bruckmann laughed. "The socialist Grzenski or the Nazi Göring!" Bruckmann stomped a foot. "Which is it to be?"

"Göring is an oaf," Wulff said.

"An oaf!" Bruckmann grunted. "Did you hear yourself, Wulff? You've called Göring an oaf!"

Weiss returned to his desk and sat again. "No, Wulff," he said. "Göring is not an oaf. None of these Nazis is an oaf. Nor are they blind worms and white mice."

"But what can I do?" Wulff said.

"We must prosecute these Nazis as traitors and political criminals."

"But I am Kripo," Wulff protested. "It is a job for the political operatives of Stapo."

"You refuse—" Weiss said. "Of course, you have the right to refuse. But I've brought your captain here today to tell you that he'll excuse you from Department IV if you should wish to take up my offer of reassignment."

"I'm sorry, Deputy Commissioner," Wulff said. "But it is not a job for me. I am not political."

"Quite so," Weiss said. "All right, Wulff, but I've told you there is a security problem here at Alexanderplatz HQ. Won't you at least look into that for me? In this way you could be of service to the Republic as well. After the elections, we plan raids on both the Communist and Nazi party headquarters. If the plans for these raids are not secure, they will be futile."

Bruckmann stepped toward Wulff and shrugged as if to offer sympathy—What can one do?

"I have cases," Wulff said.

"Bruckmann here will ease your load," Weiss said. "My orderly Krause can provide you with all the information you will need to search for this termite. Krause has the exact location of every document involved in Stapo planning, its chain of custody, and the names of men involved in development and execution. Somewhere in the chain is a weak link."

"I suppose I could make some inquiries," Wulff said reluctantly.

"Good then," Weiss said. "And you may utilize another officer to assist you if you wish. Chief Grzenski and I have authorized a secret budget to pay your assistant, say fifteen marks each week. Lamentably for you, your reward is the knowledge that the government appreciates your efforts."

"I report to you directly?" Wulff asked.

"To me directly, Inspector."

"I'll try, sir," Wulff said.

Weiss rose and circled his desk, offering his hand to Wulff and Bruckmann. They shook, then Wulff followed Bruckmann through huge ornate doors to an outer alcove where Krause had a desk and waiting area. They stood together in bright sunshine.

Bruckmann clapped Wulff hard on the back. "So, so," Bruckmann said in his gravel voice. "The impudent Jew trapped you in his web?" Bruckmann smiled, revealing his tiny sharp teeth.

"Perhaps we are all trapped," Wulff said.

"You should have declined," Bruckmann said. "I told him you would. I was prepared to back you. He wants more from you, Wulff. This is only the beginning of your involvement with Weiss, I warn you. And I must sadly advise you that your career is in danger if you consort with this Jew and his staff of Stapo socialists."

"I'll be careful," Wulff said.

"A second German revolution is in the air," Bruckmann said. "We must place ourselves on the winning side if at all possible." Bruckmann had worn a gray tunic to the meeting. He tossed it over his right shoulder. "I expect you to keep me fully informed about your activities for Weiss. And I wouldn't be too quick to locate this termite. Weiss the kike will impale you and drink your blood if you're not careful."

"I'll keep you informed, captain," Wulff lied.

"And this assistant, do you have someone in mind?"

"Not as yet," Wulff lied again.

4

The fourth floor of Alexanderplatz HQ housed Department ED, Records Section for the metropolitan police force. Wulff met with orderlies and clerks filing directives to circulate a fact sheet on the Hirrenstrasse murder. He spoke to technicians in charge of the fingerprint bureau, instructing them to deliver the victim's prints to every police department in the German federal states. He wrote a bulletin about a missing male to be sent along with the fingerprints. Finally, he directed the chief forensic photographer to deliver a packet of photos of the dead victim—both male and female versions—to all the same departments and states.

Wulff hiked to the fifth floor, presented his credentials to an officious Prussian personnel director in the municipal department, and delivered a signed and witnessed request for access to all files on department employees, along with a statement of all those with permission to enter the building at any time. Wulff requested the logs of duty officers charged with signing in and out all visitors, citizens, police, and politicians. The Prussian official, eyeing him with characteristic disdain, told Wulff that it would take at least a week, if not more, to compile such lists, logs, and information. Wulff told him to take three days, on orders from Deputy Commissioner Weiss. Before leaving, Wulff telephoned the duty officer at Precinct Seven, learning that Police Oberwachtmeister Barlach was scheduled to report for official duty at four o'clock that afternoon. It was his weekend on call, one of every fourth.

Out on Alexanderplatz, Wulff hailed a taxi. He got into the back seat and opened a window as the taxi sped past Red Town Hall. Wulff was fighting a sense of unease at his new assignment working for Weiss. When the taxi halted, he crossed the wide street and used a key to enter Johanna's apartment building, then climbed four flights of carpeted stairs to the hallway. Johanna opened the door in a flowing red-velvet robe, her face drowsy with recent sleep, her jet-black hair tangled in a ribbon and comb. Wulff kissed her, walked into the parlor, and dropped like a rock into her Egyptian-style ottoman.

Johanna circled him and threw open the drapes, filling the room with autumn light. She busied herself in the kitchen, then brought Wulff fresh coffee, poured him a cup, and sat curled on the sofa.

"You were here last night, weren't you, Harry?" she asked. "Did we do anything immoral?"

"You were too sleepy," Wulff told her.

Johanna's flat was clamorous with art. Dominating the bookshelves were oriental brush prints and psychoanalytical journals. The African art had been collected by Johanna's father, who had worked in the Côte d'Ivoire. "Harry, did we speak of Goebbels last night?" Johanna asked.

"Don't think of Goebbels, dear," he told her.

"I know we talked about Goebbels, Harry, and I know you told me there'd been a murder in the Hirrenstrasse. How terrible, how really terrible."

"My god, Johanna, you are amazing."

"You should talk to me, darling," she said.

"Psychoanalysis again," Wulff said. "You think talk is the answer to the world's problems."

It was warm in the room, and Harry was growing somnolent. "Not to the problems of the world, dear," Johanna said. "Just to the problems of the individual."

"Yes then, dear," Wulff agreed. "There's been a murder in the Hirrenstrasse."

"And what about Goebbels?"

"Weiss asked me to assume a special assignment."

"My poor Harry," she said. "You can't tell me about it, can you? It's a secret, isn't it?"

"The Goebbels part is secret, yes," Wulff told her. "You know I can't tell you."

"This is the path to neurosis," Johanna said.

"You are my only neurosis," he said.

"Does it worry you, Harry?" she asked him. "Loving a Jew and working for one, too?"

"Don't, Johanna, please," he said. He put down his cup and saucer. "It isn't like that."

"Have I put my mark on you?"

"Don't say these things," Wulff told her. "Weiss asked me to infiltrate the Nazi party and investigate Goebbels. But that isn't part of my Kripo duty. That isn't my job. I shouldn't tell you these things, but I want you to know how it is for me. I am going to do something for Weiss, but I'm afraid it is much more prosaic than undercover work. It is paperwork more than anything. And it isn't strictly political."

"Oh my dear sweet Harry," Johanna sighed. "You are so very naive, have I told you that before?" Before he could answer, Wulff felt himself being nuzzled, Johanna's nose against his neck. She opened his pants and played with him until at last Wulff dissolved in a shudder, knocking over a cup and saucer. For a long time he lay on the ottoman with her black hair as his shawl.

"I love you," Wulff said.

"Would you like to confide in me?" she whispered.

"About what? Weiss?"

"Weiss, Goebbels, Hirrenstrasse?"

"I shouldn't," Wulff said, his heart still pounding. "Weiss believes that the Republic is coming to an end politically. He's done considerable research on the Nazis and the Communists. He thinks that both parties should be banned. He wants to outlaw their pubs and their meetings and their fighting groups. He believes the Nazis are political criminals, and that harboring them in a democratic parliamentary system is contradictory. But his own organization is riddled with Nazis and spies. And he meets constant anti-Semitism. I suppose he thinks I'm somebody he can trust."

Johanna looked up at Wulff. "He singled you out because you have a Jewish lover?"

Harry Wulff felt perplexed. "Perhaps he trusts me because I am Kripo to the core," Wulff said.

A tram went by four stories below, then the clip-clip of a horse-drawn milk dray.

Johanna said, "You know I've been writing a psychological monograph on Goebbels, don't you, Harry?"

"Yes, I know, dear," he said. "Only I wish you wouldn't continue.

I wish you'd give it up, and I certainly wish you wouldn't publish it. These people are dangerous."

"Of course!" Johanna cried. "They are dangerous, Harry! That's the whole point!" Johanna reached up and took his face in her hands, kissing him delicately on the mouth. "Do you know what Brecht said? Do you know, Harry? Do you know what Brecht said about these people?"

They touched, forehead to forehead. "Tell me what Brecht said," Harry Wulff replied.

"Brecht said, 'Within me there is a struggle between the delight of the blooming apple tree and the horror of a Hitler speech. But only the latter forces me to my desk.'" Johanna kissed him softly again, no more than a breath. "And Goebbels has forced me to my desk."

"You are an amazing woman," Wulff said. "But I'm afraid for you."

"What can we do?"

"We can flee," Wulff said. "We can run away together and be married in Switzerland."

"But we are Germans, Harry," she told him. "And the elections are next week! Shall we not carry placards through the streets, signs supporting the Republic and the socialists, the democracy? Shall we not convince the communists to participate in government on a constructive basis? Shall we not replace old Hindenberg and feed the four million unemployed? Please tell me, Harry, where in Europe can we hide from the future?"

Wulff sighed. "Let's not talk politics again," he said.

"All right," Johanna conceded. "And tomorrow, let's go to Luna Park and swim. I want to watch the ducks and ride the roller coaster and the Ferris wheel and listen to a band concert beside that fabulously absurd papier-mâché mountain."

"Johanna dear," Wulff said wistfully, "I have to work today. Tonight I am taking the train to Lubeck. My father is ill and I've got to spend a Sunday with him. I've been so busy I forgot to tell you. I hope you aren't disappointed in me."

"Oh no, my darling," Johanna told him, placing a finger on his lips.

"Someday I want you to meet my father."

"We've had this discussion before," Johanna said. "Your father does not want to meet your Jewish whore."

"*Please* don't talk like that," Wulff scolded.

"Darling, darling—" she whispered to Wulff, who had thrown his arms around her in exasperation.

"My father would like you," Wulff said, indulging in a non-sequitur.

"Harry, your father carries a schoolboy dueling scar that runs down his right cheek and he used to dine with General Ludendorff on Sunday afternoons. I am certain he is a dear man, but he was on the General Staff."

"All right," Wulff conceded. "I can't win this argument. For now you're much too beautiful to scold."

"You always say nearly the right thing, darling. And you've had a terrible murder in the Hirrenstrasse."

"It was a transvestite," he said.

"How interesting for you, Harry."

"Perhaps you can help me with it," he said. "The dead transvestite was probably a homosexual prostitute, am I right?"

Johanna tossed her head back and laughed throatily. She hugged Wulff and teased his eyelids with her tongue.

"Oh, my dear Harry," she said. "I should instruct you in the complexities of human sexuality sometime!"

"The victim wore women's clothes and was artfully made-up, down to false eyelashes and plucked eyebrows and a dainty sweater with a false ermine collar."

"Harry my dear," she said. "Berlin is filled with men who wear women's clothes."

"Fascinating," he said.

"If you had only studied psychology as assiduously as you studied philosophy," she said.

Wulff smiled. "This does help my thinking, actually," he said.

"Matters of sex and gender are complex," Johanna continued. "Don't allow cultural habits to mislead you, dear. Your victim could have been anything and anybody. I'm thinking about a particular cultural legend descending from the Tarahumara Indians of the Mexican Sierra Madre. In their stories, there are three genders! Men possess one soul and women two, but the homosexual possesses seven souls, Harry. Think of having seven souls!"

"Do you have more coffee?" Wulff laughed.

— —

Wulff slept for three hours, covered by Johanna's robe. He dreamed of violet space, of windswept trees and a white-faced corpse tumbling madly through the tunnel of his mind. When he woke, he felt surprised at the lightness and splendid color of the room. He washed, then had a lunch of bread, cheese, and some salad. He kissed Johanna good-bye, then taxied across central Berlin to the seventh precinct headquarters on Bülow Platz, two kilometers north and west of Alexanderplatz Bahnhof.

The station house was a narrow granite structure that had once housed a local fire company. Wulff walked inside and spoke with the duty officer, finding Barlach at the back of the building in a washroom and locker area. Barlach was on a wooden bench, half-in and half-out of his Schupo uniform, smoking a cigar and holding a tin cup of apple cider. When he saw Wulff, the sergeant struggled to his feet, attempting to pull on his woolen trousers, balance the cup of cider, and salute.

"Don't worry, Sergeant Barlach," Wulff told him. "I wanted to speak with you alone before your shift."

"Yes, sir, all right, sir," Barlach said, sitting again, but clearly discomfited by Wulff's presence in a Schupo changing room. "You caught me by surprise is all, sir," Barlach said, pulling on his pants.

"I want you to work with me on the Hirrenstrasse murder," Wulff said, coming to the point. "Would you agree to that?"

"Investigation, sir, I'd like that."

"I've cleared it with your captain," Wulff said. "Right now photos are being prepared of the victim in male and female formats. When you show the photos, determine if any of the conductors recognize the man or woman. Perhaps our victim rode the tram regularly. Perhaps you can even learn where he got on the tram that night. Or perhaps the male version of our victim is a regular passenger. I think you understand what I'm driving at."

"I'll go to Alexanderplatz and pick up the photographs," Barlach said.

"It's Saturday, Barlach," Wulff said. "There's no need to begin until Monday morning. I suspect our victim will turn up in missing persons this weekend."

"I'll do my best, sir," Barlach said. "I'm honored for the chance to work with you, Inspector Wulff."

"There's nothing extra in it for you, Barlach."

"I don't mind the work. It's better than patrol."

Barlach laced his black boots and buttoned his woolen Schupo shirt to its neck.

"Perhaps we'll have some luck," Wulff said. "Perhaps our killer was on the same tram Friday night. Perhaps our killer is a regular passenger as well. This thought occurred to me this morning. And so perhaps one of our weekday conductors will connect the killer and our victim. If not, then we must assume that our killer met his victim in the Hirrenstrasse, and met her by chance."

"I'll work all day," Barlach said.

Wulff sat down on a wooden bench and lit a cigarette. He offered a match for Barlach's cigar, which had gone out. "Barlach, I want to ask you something," Wulff said.

"Of course, sir," Barlach replied.

"Are you for the Republic?"

Barlach smoked for a moment. He crossed the room and crushed his cigar against the dirty porcelain of a sink. He looked at himself in the mirror. "I don't know what to say, sir," he said to Wulff.

"It isn't a trick question."

"As much as any man," Barlach said.

Wulff chuckled to himself. "As am I," he said. "Barlach, I'll come to the point. There is a Nazi termite in operation at Alexanderplatz. Deputy Commissioner Weiss has asked me to locate this leak if it is possible. He has authorized me to take on an assistant. I'd like that assistant to be you."

"I'd not be able to tell my wife?"

"No, Barlach, your wife may not know." Wulff crushed out his smoke. "Do you object to working for a Jew?"

"It isn't that, sir," Barlach said.

"What is it then?"

"Just the times, sir," Barlach said.

"I know how you feel."

"Do you think I can do the job?"

"I wouldn't ask otherwise," Wulff said.

"If you think so then," Barlach said.

Wulff stood, aware that Barlach's hesitation had nothing to do with either courage or fear. He and Barlach were worlds apart, Wulff from the aristocratic Baltic, Barlach from the working-class slums of Berlin. Yet both suffered the same uncertainty.

It was the times.

— —

Alexanderplatz HQ was deserted as Wulff passed through the preliminary Reichswehr checkpoint at the entrance. The evening sky above the Bahnhof had turned buff-orange and smelled of diesel exhaust. Two heavily armed corporals checked Wulff's identify papers at the front gate, and two more checked him at the top of the marble staircase before he went inside. Wulff presented himself to the duty officer who sat stiffly at a table in the foyer. The duty officer entered his name in a log, then waved him through. Wulff walked down the basement stairs to the lower level and let himself inside the pathologist's office. Levitt sat stooped over a pile of reports at his desk. He was smoking absent-mindedly, scribbling with a pen.

"Ah, Wulff," Levitt growled in mock annoyance. "I said *tonight*, Inspector! And it isn't night, but you come anyway. Please look outside if you will!" Levitt gestured to the half-windows of his office, painted black.

"Come on, old man, I've a train to catch at Lehrter Bahnhof in two hours."

Levitt grunted, then broke into a wide grin that revealed his crooked teeth. He swivelled on his chair to face Wulff, then motioned for the inspector to take a seat opposite him on a stool.

"Suppose I summarize my findings then," Levitt said. "This victim of yours is very interesting," he said. "To the particulars! One meter and twenty-six centimeters in height, fifty-five kilos in weight, and well-confirmed without diseases. Not particularly well-nourished, but nobody in Berlin is particularly well-nourished these days. You are looking at a fine specimen, Inspector Wulff, very fine. About twenty-six years of age. This will come as no surprise, but the official cause of death is to be listed as asphyxiation through strangulation by hand. It is to be classified as a homicide. In addition to the evidence we observed together this morning, there is edema in the mouth tissues. And a clear thumb print on the right side of the neck. Your murderer was very strong and probably right-handed."

"Now I have only three million suspects," Wulff said.

"More or less," Levitt said. "The brain and internal organs are all quite normal."

"Anything unusual?" Wulff asked.

"*He* has some unusual characteristics," Levitt continued. "I manually examined the epidermis as I always do. The tips of every finger of the left hand are heavily calloused. The callouses are too thick and specific for this man to have been a typist or stenographer. Besides, men rarely do this sort of work for a living." Levitt leaned toward Wulff now. "I'd say a violin or guitar player."

"Very good," Wulff said.

"Ach, there's more," Levitt said. "The two upper wisdom teeth of this victim have been recently extracted. It is a somewhat hurried and clumsy job. The stitches were removed only in the last few days. Your victim has just seen his dentist."

"This may add up to something," Wulff told Levitt.

"The rest is rather drab, I'm afraid. The toxicology is normal for drugs and alcohol. The blood work is incomplete, but I don't expect anything to appear out of the ordinary. I'll telephone you if I'm wrong. For what it's worth, there is a tiny abrasion on the back of the head where the killer pushed it against a stone wall. Perhaps you will use a black light or laminal at the crime scene to pick up traces of blood, as if that would help."

"It was a rainy night. The walls are stone."

"Too bad for you then, Wulff," Levitt said. "There is one thing of possibly remote importance. The victim wore false fingernails.

Scrapings were taken from them. We found skin of course, but something else as well."

"Something else?"

"Evidence of a glue," Levitt said. "Strange, no?"

"Glue, what do you mean?"

"It is a light petroleum-based resinous substance. Forensics has it now. It will be thoroughly analyzed."

"But glue, what does it mean?"

"You are the investigator," Levitt said. "I merely observe and catalogue."

"And your written report?"

"It will be ready tomorrow or perhaps Monday at the latest."

"I'll be anxious to read it," Wulff said.

Levitt stood, and the two men shook hands. "You look tired, Wulff. You should get some rest. Instead, you are making a journey."

"My father is ill," Wulff told the pathologist.

"I wish him the best," Levitt said.

＞－

In a frosty light, the janitor woke to find himself curled like a shrimp on the hard, narrow bed in his rented room. For a split second he was unable to decide if it was morning, afternoon, or approaching night, if the day was beginning or ending. Around him, the crumbling suburban villa in Lichtenberg seemed to tremble and quake.

The carpet was thick with dust. The paper dolls he made lined the shelves above his head and fixed him with astonished gazes. There were hundreds of them in the room, glossy creations that he had fashioned from movie magazine photos. The dolls lined his two bookshelves and perched on windowsills. They dangled from the ceiling on strings and were tacked to the walls.

The janitor sat up suddenly, pulled on a pair of dirty socks, and scanned his territory. For a moment, he opened his memory to a liquid space in which his mother hovered. He recalled her on the porch of their hovel near Juprelle in Belgium. In his memory, he was dressed in crinoline and lace, his long curly hair falling around his shoulders. His mother was caressing it.

He heated some tea. Around him was vast suburban silence. In this part of Lichtenberg stood rows and rows of detached stone houses, then row upon row of semi-detached wooden houses, and after that the inevitable shops and pubs, old farmhouses lost in the crush of urbanity, miles of scrub, abandoned apple orchards, open fields meandering into open country. He listened keenly as his tea boiled, but he heard nothing of the war widow who lived downstairs. When the tea was brewed, he carried a cup to the dresser where he had carefully erected a kind of shrine made from candles and dolls, then sat in front of the mirror. There were six small bulbs on each side of the mirror, an extravagance he could hardly afford. He turned on the lights and immediately felt X-rayed by the bulbs. He began to spread cream base on his fingertips, then massaged the makeup onto his face. He pressed the cream deeply into his shoulders, his neck, and rubbed at the dark circles under his eyes. He picked up one of many brushes from the dressing table, dabbed it in his makeup kit, and pressed powder onto the cream base. He spread the makeup on thickly. When he finished, there would be a new self, powdered and rouged, with two red new lips in a shade of lipstick called Apple. He puckered his lips, arched himself toward the mirror, and kissed the image of his lips. A shudder passed through him. At last he stood, picked up a short blond wig, and put it on, dabbing theatrical glue on his temples. Slipping on a pair of cotton panties, he moved away from the mirror.

He walked to his closet, opened its door, and examined the few dresses and skirts hanging inside. He closed the door in a sweaty panic, searching his magazines for a head that resembled the head of the woman who had just seduced him. He remembered watching her as she caught a tram at the Kohlberg stop, how she had structured each female movement into a flirtatious spiral. From among the many tabloids and pictorials, he found a head, an almost perfect likeness. Later, he found a shiny black sequined dress and two silk-clad legs.

He cut cardboard into a perfect shape, then began to glue a head, torso, dress, legs, onto the cardboard. All he lacked was a pair of shoes, but he vowed to find the right pair, black-and-white, high-heeled.

Ahead of him lay an afternoon of nothingness, a progression of hours, another vacant Saturday. Carefully he glued the doll's head to its cardboard backing.

"You're in for a big disappointment," the dead woman had told him.

5

The Schwabing whore laughed as police captain Bruckmann struck her on the ass. He was wielding a rhinoceros-hide whip, erecting tiny red crescents of puckered skin on her legs and inner thighs. Bruckmann had fucked her once already, and now he was rinsing off in a wash basin at the rented room of a hotel in Alt-Köln. Bruckmann turned, sweating heavily, and struck the whore on her buttocks again. He stood back suddenly and wiped himself with a hotel towel, paused to look at his image in the hotel room mirror, then pulled up his uniform trousers. Leaning down, he bit the whore on her neck.

"Ooooh *liebchin*," the whore moaned in mock pleasure. "Such a playmate!" She tossed her slack hair over one shoulder.

"Put something on," Bruckmann demanded. A blue chemise barely covered her back. Bruckmann had been told she was a bohemian from Munich.

The whore stood and adjusted the chemise so that it covered her. She walked to the basin and washed her face, then left the room for her own down the hall. Bruckmann toweled off, shaved, then put on a clean white shirt and his gray police sweater. When he had finished, he walked downstairs to the hotel bar where Dieter Rom was sitting at a corner table drinking a small glass of brandy. Bruckmann took a seat opposite Rom, leader of Storm Troop 33, one of the most active and notorious Brown Shirt cadres in central Berlin. The table at the far end of the bar sat amid a clutter of perhaps a dozen others. In late evening, the bar was deserted of customers, save for Bruckmann and Rom who were being served by a beefy Pomeranian bartender in a white smock.

"Where did you discover this disgusting bitch?" Bruckmann asked Rom, pouring himself a glass of brandy. "She's an amusement, I agree, but she looks as though she's been attacked by rats."

"She has," Rom said. "She's a Schwabing sow. Probably a communist at heart. But I've heard she's willing to put up with anything."

"She's talented, I agree," Bruckmann said.

Bruckmann put the glass rim to his lips and breathed alcohol fumes. Across the table, Rom sat motionless, a square-featured man with short-cropped blond hair and dead-blue eyes. He was wearing a black pinstripe suit and red tie.

"Her talent is her silence," Rom suggested.

"Her talent is her availability," Bruckmann countered.

"Ah, but then," Rom said, shrugging, "we're not here to discuss the whore, are we?" Rom lifted his glass in a pretend toast. "Accept her as a gift from Storm 33. Let's leave it at that."

"From Hitler himself?" Bruckmann said cynically.

"Not quite so high up. I thought a Munich whore might amuse you, Bruckmann."

"Perhaps if I were her first. Am I?" Bruckmann made a spider imitation with his fingers.

Rom grunted in amusement. "Forgive me the allusion, but Hitler would turn a blind eye."

"Perhaps Hitler has fucked her, too," Bruckmann suggested.

"Ah, but Herr Hitler is at the Kaiserhof, isn't he? Not some dingy guesthouse in the Alt-Köln."

"Is he too busy with party doctrine to dirty his cock?"

Rom sipped his brandy. "You shouldn't joke about such matters, Bruckmann. Really."

Bruckmann tossed back a brandy. "Do you have my money?" he asked.

Rom extracted a plain envelope from his suit-coat pocket and slid it across the rough wooden surface of the table. Bruckmann slit open the envelope with a fingernail and counted the paper marks one at a time.

"One hundred marks," Rom said when Bruckmann was finished.

Bruckmann tucked the money inside his sweater pocket. He nodded his bullet-shaped head side to side, yawned deeply, then adjusted his eye patch. "It is no longer enough money," he said.

Rom pondered the situation. "Is this something you've decided for yourself, or has your termite had a hand in formulating this demand?"

"Let me explain," Bruckmann replied. "For more than a year you've been getting reports on the daily Stapo work plan. This is direct from the office of the deputy commissioner. My termite has gone to extraordinary lengths to provide you with advance warning of several raids on Nazi headquarters, and on your Storm 33 local pub. He takes grave risks. It is a grave risk for me to pass this information to you, what with me a captain of Kripo. And I'm certain you've passed this information along to your superior Storm Führer Maikowski and the Charlottenburg Group. In this guise you have become something of a hero to the group I'm sure." Bruckmann paused for effect. He had meticulously planned this speech, though the whore had delayed its delivery. "And now comes the famous Weiss report requesting a criminalization of the party and the Storm Troop. This would criminalize Goebbels and Hitler, if you will. I'm told the Prussian Ministry of Interior may take this suggestion seriously."

"A pretty speech," Rom said. "Word has it that the Weiss report has been rejected by the Reich attorney."

"Even so—" Bruckmann said, spreading his hands, working them like spiders again. "You have to admit the atmosphere is growing dangerous. Every day the pressure increases."

"On the street perhaps," Rom agreed. "But we know of the report. We will not pay extra to read it."

"I'm not speaking of the report," Bruckmann said. "Listen to me—the Jew, Weiss, has engaged a criminal inspector from Kripo to investigate the leak in his office. This raises the ante, so to speak."

Rom raised an eyebrow, tapping a knuckle on the wooden table. Bruckmann had finished his brandy and Rom signaled for another carafe. "How do you know this?" he asked.

"It is a threatening development, isn't it? My termite will now be in constant danger."

"How do you know this?" Rom demanded.

"I was there!" Bruckmann announced with enjoyment. Bruckmann pondered his luck. Weiss wrote a daily diary, not much more than a memorandum of memories meant for his own files and not the official chain of command. His termite could sneak into the office, catch a glimpse of these files, and sometimes important information about police plans. "I am the Kriminal Oberkommissar, am I not?" The bartender delivered a small carafe of bad brandy. Bruckmann poured himself a glass.

"And who is this Kripo investigator?" Rom asked.

"I can only tell you he is very competent," Bruckmann said. Bruckmann had been afflicted with asthma as a child. The dust-laden room was giving him a headache.

"The extra money you want? Is it to be used to corrupt this investigator?"

"He is not corruptible," Bruckmann said. "He's a Kripo. But I'm told he fucks a Jewess."

Harry Wulff, Rom thought, who had made a study of the Kripo infrastructure. "Not such a great crime," he said. "The Romans fucked their slaves. Americans fucked *their* slaves. Even you Bruckmann, you fuck a Schwabing communist!"

"One more thing," Bruckmann said. "My termite knows of his Kripo nemesis. He knows this is now a much more dangerous game. And the Kripo has been authorized to hire an assistant. A greater risk calls for a higher payment of compensation."

"Compensation is geared to results," Rom said.

"And difficulty," Bruckmann countered.

"Then by all means be careful."

"Piss on this!" Bruckmann shouted. "What about the money?" An elderly couple walked into the bar and took a seat at the table in the opposite corner. "We must have the money," he demanded angrily.

"And I thought your motives were nationalistic," Rom said.

"Oh, but they are," Bruckmann said. "But then there are times when I think of Goebbels in his luxury apartment on the Reichkanzlerplatz, his mahogany furniture and fine paintings, his luxurious suits and party expense account. There are times when I think of Hitler himself and his new black supercharged Mercedes. I think, yes! What of nationalism? What of self-sacrifice for Germany? But I am always drawn back to the shining black Mercedes, and I think—what about the money?"

"Please be careful, Bruckmann," Rom warned. "Your humor may one day hang you." Rom looked down at his immaculately manicured hands. "I'll take up the matter with my SA colleague Maikowski," he said.

"Soon," Bruckmann urged. "Before next weekend."

"That is very soon," Rom countered.

"It will cost you. Triple."

"Three hundred? Don't be stupid."

"Three hundred," Bruckmann said. He rose, adjusted his gray sweater. "Please give my regards to Maikowski and the Aryan cabal."

Rom looked away, fighting an angry impulse. He watched the old couple drinking their two steins of beer silently, red-faced.

Bruckmann left the table, walked upstairs, and found the whore in her room at the end of a dusty corridor. She was lounging on the bed, still in her pale blue chemise. She had washed her hair. "I thought I'd seen the last of you," the whore said.

The hotel room was a brown square, decorated by alpine scenes, with a chest of drawers, one closet with no door, a single wooden chair in one corner. It smelled of ant powder and sausage. Bruckmann unloosed his Kripo belt and looped it around his right hand.

"Do you mind?" he asked politely. He was half-erect, his heart beating.

"Be gentle with me, lover," the whore said.

— —

For hours the janitor Theodor Loos wandered Jagerstrasse, lost in its mill. Music assaulted him from dozens of bars, casinos, cabarets, and nightclubs. He had dressed in a baggy brown suit, a bulky black overcoat, and a watchcap.

At the entrance to the Club El Dorado he paused, caught up in its bright neon embrace. Gathering his courage, he broke through a beaded curtain and was engulfed in din, smoke, song, and clamor. On a faraway stage, barely visible from where Loos stood in the entryway surrounded by other customers, a line of female impersonators danced in lewd tandem, balloons aloft, prancing like ostriches. Loos paid a five-mark entry fee to a hatcheck girl behind a busy counter. He was handed a black mask which he put on, covering his eyes and nose, then wandered out onto the dance floor, which was densely packed. In minutes he had found a corner table near the back of the hall. To his right was the stage, still far away. He ordered an apple brandy.

The walls were mirrored, the ceiling draped with imitation red velvet. On the table before him sat a single black telephone. When the waiter delivered his apple brandy, Loos lifted the glass and looked at the dancers through the medium of its liquid, swimming throngs in masks, black suits, and ball gowns. He sipped the brandy, fumes exploding inside his head like fireworks. Through dense smoke he tried to watch the dancers on stage, perhaps twenty in skimpy costumes, a rich tabloid of exhibitionist cross-dressing.

When the telephone rang, he picked up the receiver and listened. "Ah, how terrible to be lonely," a voice told him.

"Who are you?" Loos asked. "Where are you?"

"Slowly, slowly," the voice said. "You ask two questions at a time, too many."

Loos scanned the room, desperate to make contact with his interrogator. He exchanged glances with several whose gaze moved on. He felt hot inside his bulky overcoat, his forehead slick with sweat.

"Who are you?" Loos asked again. He took off his coat and flung it across the back of a chair. The crowd had surged around him, then parted.

"Call me Uli," the voice said. On stage the female impersonators were playing a ludicrous game of sodomistic hopscotch. "How are you called?"

"Call me Siegfried," Loos said breathlessly.

"Oooh, my mighty Siegfried," Uli said. "You've never been to the El Dorado before, have you Siegfried?"

"Will you drink with me, Uli?" Loos asked, gaining courage with each passing second. "Let me buy you a drink."

"But of course," Uli said gayly. "Why not?"

Loos put down the receiver and scanned the dance floor, the overhanging balcony packed with drinkers, couples struggling for kisses, men and women smoking distractedly. All around, men were speaking feverishly into telephones. Loos summoned a waiter, a tiny fellow dressed as a Grimm character.

"Please, a drink for Uli," Loos stuttered. "You know Uli?"

"Everybody knows Uli," the waiter answered.

A single female impersonator dominated the stage now. Standing haughtily in a bright halo of light, she wore a black dress, a pink feather boa, and a shimmering blond wig. The audience fell silent as the performer began a filthy ballad.

"A drink for Uli then," Loos said.

"Uli drinks only Sekt and crème de menthe," the waiter said. "Two marks please."

Loos searched his pocket, found a gold mark and dropped it on the table. The waiter coughed in surprise, then quickly snatched the coin. A few minutes later, he returned carrying a tray on which was balanced a fluted glass of sparkling wine tinted green by liqueur. The waiter fluttered three paper marks to the table, then darted swiftly between dancing couples on the floor and disappeared. When he reemerged, Loos caught sight of him in the darkened balcony depositing his order before a creature dressed in black. The creature scooped up the drink, cuddled it in her black-gloved hand, and parted her pink lips. She floated Loos a bright wide smile. Uli was wearing a white wig that framed her pert face, a face onto which she'd dabbed white makeup, arched eyebrows, and three narrow whiskers on each cheek. Loos picked up the receiver and listened.

"It's lovely, my Siegfried," Uli said.

"So, you're a cat?"

The crowded room was rapt as the singer panted her filthy ballad, a satire of Nazi sex involving Hitler, Goebbels, and Göring. A ripple of laughter infected the audience.

"I'm your very own pussy," Uli said. "You like pussy, don't you Siegfried?"

Suddenly and without warning, the cabaret floor exploded into a kaleidoscope of light, shards and petals and facets of color wheeling on the mirrored walls. Loos ducked, then turned and saw himself in a mirror. "Where do you live?" Loos said impulsively into the phone. He realized the stupid clumsiness of his question the moment it left his lips.

"Slowly, my darling Siegfried," Uli purred. "We've only just met. There is so much to talk about, so much to experience together. Don't you agree?"

"I have money," Loos said.

"A gold mark!" Uli laughed. "You must be very prosperous, Siegfried. Berlin has become such a dull and moralistic place. But here you have paid with a gold mark! How wonderful and decadent."

Loos saw his cat-woman clearly now. She had stood, revealing her apple blossom white dress, black gloves, and white wig. Loos was becoming physically disoriented. Feeling nauseated, he threw on his topcoat and fled, leaving the mask behind.

On the Jagerstrasse, he caught his breath. He blinked in an effort to dematerialize the monsters in his head. Had he been stupid enough to spend a gold mark? Hadn't Bruckmann warned him against ostentation? He moved north, flowing with crowds headed for Unter den Linden. At the Adlon Hotel tram stop, he revisited the image of Uli, her cat-face and bright white wig. Here, on the most famous boulevard in all Europe, Theodor Loos sensed that he had discovered the dramatic potential of existence.

⁓ ⁓

Storm Troop 33 Führer Dieter Rom opened the hotel room door, slipping inside as the latch clicked shut. The Schwabing whore was examining her body and blood-spotted chemise in a mirror. Rom watched the whore, the two of them exchanging reflected smiles.

"He's a politician, I suppose," the whore said. A pouty scowl crossed her face.

Rom grunted, amused that the whore hadn't recognized Bruckmann's police uniform. Even for a whore, this one looked underfed. Rom was aware of her morphine habit. She was applying lipstick and eyeliner now, discovering her neck wounds.

"I just suppose he's a fucking politician," she said. "That's just what I'd expect."

"He's not a politician," Rom said. "But he could be, I suppose. They all could be politicians. He got a bit rough?"

"Does that surprise you?" the whore said. She cupped her hands and drank from a tap.

"I'm pleased. Was he pleased?"

"He's easy to please," the whore said. "He likes to hurt and he likes to be hurt."

"I want you to see him again, Eva," Rom told her, arms folded now. He took out a small wad of marks from his jacket pocket and tossed them on the bed. From another pocket he found four gold marks and jingled them in his hand.

Eva raised an eyebrow.

"Let him hurt you, Eva, next time," Rom said.

"Oh, I think so," she said.

"And we'll want photos," Rom said.

"I wondered why the gold marks."

"You'll be staying in Berlin for a few days. I've reserved this room for you. You've enough money for meals."

"You'll be sending up some Storm Troops?"

"Nothing so blatant as that, Eva," Rom told her.

"Oh, then I'm getting a go at Hitler himself," she said, snapping a garter. "He looks as though he might enjoy being hurt. But I don't imagine he'd want to show his cock. It might be embarrassing."

"You're quite amusing, Eva," Rom said. "But I wouldn't talk like that, even to me. Let's just focus on Bruckmann for now."

Rom walked to the door and opened it. "Order your meals from the bartender downstairs. I'm not confining you to quarters, Eva, but don't have too much fun. I need you to be close by in case of emergencies. We'll see Bruckmann soon enough as it is."

"What's he done to you?" the whore asked.

Rom closed the door softly.

— —

At dawn, Wulff was on the foredeck of a small ferry, sitting behind empty passenger quarters amid rows of wooden benches, the galley over his right shoulder where he and his brothers had often eaten sausages and eggs on their frequent trips to and from the island. His brother Peter had been at Tannenberg with General Ludendorff. After a particularly brutal charge, he'd been lost in the carnage, his body never recovered amid the mud and confusion, the smoke and masses of severed arms and legs. His other brother, Rolf, had been lost in France during the first battle of the Marne. Now Wulff's father lived alone in an old house which resembled a Gothic hunting lodge.

Wulff stepped off the ferry at the Kirchdorf pier and walked through the gray, rain-stunned town. Wulff could hear strains of organ music from the Lutheran church, the muffled voices of a choir practicing hymns. He walked two miles in mist carrying only an overnight case. The lodge stood fifty meters from a cliff overlooking the sea.

Wulff mounted the porch and greeted his father who was relaxing in a canvas deck chair. Covered by a green wool blanket and smoking a cigarette, the German army colonel seemed a shadow of his former self to Wulff. Having climbed the steps, he sat in a chair beside his father.

"You look tired, Harry," his father said.

Wulff lit a cigarette. A servant brought them coffee in huge mugs.

"How are you, Father?" Wulff asked. "Please tell me how you really are."

"Don't worry about me, Harry," his father said. He eyed his son and smiled. The old man was wearing a green Loden jacket and his iron gray hair was brushed back stiffly over a widow's peak. "Old age is an inevitability. Nothing much to worry about."

"I wish you wouldn't talk so fatalistically," Wulff said.

"I'm not entirely humorless, Harry," Gunter Wulff replied. "One does manage finally to see the irony."

"It isn't irony that concerns me," Wulff said.

Gunter Wulff waved off the implication. "But what about *you*," he said. "You haven't written for a long time."

"Berlin is in an uproar," Wulff said. "There were six hundred political murders in Germany last year. Many of them were in Berlin. This year promises to be worse."

Gunter Wulff crushed his cigarette in a pewter bowl. "Life in Berlin makes one wary," he said. "I hate to see a man becoming wary, especially a young man like yourself. It's best to face life on a horse."

Wulff laughed and drank some coffee. He looked at the distant Baltic. "This isn't wariness," Wulff said. "It's just honest German realism."

"Ah, yes," Gunter Wulff said. "We blame all our troubles on Germany. On history. We've done it all our lives haven't we?" The father smiled and adjusted his blanket. Wulff closed his eyes and toured the place in his imagination, its two stories smelling of must and leather, a boar's head above the stone fireplace, a portrait of the Kaiser, guns and swords in cases and on racks.

"There's more," Wulff told his father.

"This is about your woman friend?"

Wulff looked up in surprise. "Yes, it's about my woman friend. You're still very good at anticipating the movements of troops." His father nodded. "She's Jewish," Wulff said. Gunter Wulff ran his tongue along his lips as he gazed out at miles of sandy waste, tulle grass, and lichen-covered boulders. Wulff finished his cigarette and tamped it out in the pewter bowl. The silence had run two minutes. "And I'm doing political work for Bernhard Weiss," Wulff told his father.

"Is that necessary?" his father asked.

"Not necessary," Wulff said. "But I've agreed to do it nonetheless."

"You are on the losing side," Gunter Wulff said.

"And which is the winning side?" he asked his father.

Gunter Wulff underwent a coughing spasm. "There is no winning side," he said at last.

Wulff drained the last of his coffee, feeling the effect of two straight nights with little sleep and a long train ride through northern Germany. Now he wanted a good breakfast and a walk along the cliffs with his father.

"You know Erik Bruckmann, don't you, Father?" Wulff asked.

"Erik Bruckmann—"

"A captain of intelligence in Belgium during the War."

"Ah, Erik Bruckmann."

"I work under him at Kripo. He's a Kriminal Oberkommissar."

"He's a Prussian," Gunter Wulff said. "Isn't that the one? With one eye and a nasty scar."

"That's the one," Wulff laughed.

"Yes, Harry. I know him."

"Bruckmann advised me against working for Weiss."

"Probably good advice," Gunter said. "Please, Harry. Don't think I'm anxious about you or question your judgment. But Jews are definitely on the losing side. If it is not possible to win, Harry, then at least avoid losing. If you choose Weiss, you choose a weak ally."

"And your opinion of Bruckmann?"

"I don't have one. He's a total opportunist. What more can one say?"

"A total opportunist!" Wulff scoffed.

Gunter Wulff stood and threw down the blanket that had covered him. "And what of your Jewess?" he asked.

"Johanna," Wulff said. "She's unique. And she's no opportunist."

"Is she beautiful?"

"Very beautiful."

"You are infatuated, Harry," Gunter Wulff said.

"I love her, Father," Wulff protested.

The old man took his son's arm. "There are fried eggs and bread in the kitchen. Andrew has some blackberry jam. We've even managed to find bacon in the village."

They went to breakfast. Perhaps later they could walk the beach at low tide. Wulff had done that with his brothers when the future held nothing but promise.

▬ ▬

Wulff woke to village bells. He lay on a pallet bed in his older brother's attic room, the low-ceilinged "rabbit hutch" that had been off-limits to Harry when he was a child. Crowded together was a single hand-hewn bed, several chairs, and a writing desk. On the wall were family photographs, newspaper clippings, athletic and riding ribbons. Wulff had slept with the window open, and he could smell the sea and fresh coffee. Dressing hurriedly, he discovered his father on the porch polishing a pair of army field glasses. The binoculars were large Danish 8x, made before the war.

"You've had a good sleep," Gunter Wulff said. "Andrew will make us lunch."

"What about a walk?" Wulff suggested.

They hiked the cliff trail, leading from the house south to the beach. Above them a flock of eider geese rose and followed, twenty animals with white bellies and black heads.

"I've become a birdwatcher," Gunter Wulff told his son. "We should not have fought the English in the last war. We are too much alike. We become birdwatchers in old age."

Wulff laughed. "Nudists in youth, birdwatchers in old age."

The eiders dispersed according to their own laws. The surface of the Baltic was hard-ice blue.

"I told Johanna you were ill," Wulff said. "I wanted to come here alone."

"You *are* troubled," Gunter said. He put his field glasses in a leather case and continued on. He was walking with the aid of a cane. "Is it about Weiss?"

"There is a termite in Alexanderplatz," Wulff said.

"There are termites everywhere, Harry. If it weren't for termites, everything would collapse."

"Now who's being cynical?"

The old man managed a smile. "Ach, yes," he said. "You've an outsider at headquarters who reveals plans?"

"Precisely."

"Which faction benefits?"

"The Nazis, certainly," Wulff said.

"Others?"

"I don't know." Wulff helped his father scramble over a boulder. They neared a sheltered cove where Wulff had played and camped as a boy.

"So this is your not-too-political job for Weiss? This is why you are troubled?"

"I am glad to see *you*," Wulff said.

The old man halted, placed an arm on his son's shoulder. "Such work jeopardizes your career," he said. "You yourself told me that the election results are in doubt. Who knows which party will emerge holding the reins of government? I read the papers, Harry. I know that the Reich disfavors this Prussian government of socialists and

Jews. If you align yourself with them, you are in an exposed position. You must always defend your flanks, Harry." From a hundred meters, they could hear Andrew calling them to lunch.

"I've come to ask if the army could have a termite in place there as well."

Gunter Wulff had been with Ludendorff on the General Staff, responsible as intelligence liaison on the eastern front, then acted as special courier between the army and the Prussian government. He had contacts and friends. He had a sterling reputation as a German patriot. He was owed debts on which not even the interest had been paid.

"You're thinking Bruckmann, aren't you?" Gunter Wulff asked.

"Bruckmann—I don't know. I asked about him only to learn his political sympathies."

"He has none. I told you, Harry. But if he had, they would certainly not be with the Republic."

Wulff helped his father back up the path, through heavy sand and gorse.

"Bruckmann has his one good eye on me," Wulff joked.

"This Bruckmann," Gunter said. "He might have been a brave soldier for the Empire, I don't know. But after the war, I know he sold himself to the highest bidder, which was the Freicorps. There are rumors he ran a torture camp in Belgium. That he organized a fifth column."

"Help me, Father," Wulff said. "If the army has a termite in Alexanderplatz, I'd like to know. Perhaps someone in the veterans organizations will talk." Wulff held his father's free arm.

"The Reichswehr would not sell information to the Nazi party," Gunter Wulff said.

"I know," Wulff replied. "But an army spy might help me uncover this Nazi mole."

They sat together on the porch, Wulff smoking a cigarette, his father gazing at the cliffs.

6

From a backless wooden bench high in the third balcony of the monumental Sportpalast, Wulff and Johanna listened to Hitler's election campaign speech. The sports stadium was surrounded by SA cadres. Orpo had cordoned off wide sections of street, still enforcing the presidential ban on demonstrations in central Berlin. Backup squads of Schupo kept to alleys, or were massed on buses parked in the shadows of monuments and diplomatic buildings where there were reinforcements of armored cars. Wulff had attended boxing and bicycle races at the Sportpalast many times. But he had never heard Hitler, never been tempted by the atmosphere of sweaty adulation. At the arena, the floor was crowded with hastily arranged wooden chairs, a specially roped-in section for newspaper reporters and film cameras, party officials, and workers from Berlin's central and northern suburbs. A contingent of armed SA guarded the stage.

Wulff estimated the crowd at twelve thousand. By the start of welcoming speeches, perhaps another thousand had drifted in. Smoke sifted toward the ceiling rafters and there was an air of nervous expectation. Nearly thirty minutes late, Göring commenced a bombastic harangue against the German enemies of rearmament, against peacemongering and Versailles. For an hour, he waved his arms and strutted his corpulent body on the stage, whipping the crowd into paroxysms of laughter and derision. Following a tremendous cheer, Goebbels took the podium dressed in a tight black suit, his hair freshly pomaded and combed back to reveal an ovoid head. His diatribe was against the Jews.

To the left, laconic and self-composed, Hitler sat attending to his notes, fixing the audience with an occasional stare. When he finally took the podium, the crowd rose in a tremendous cheer as he began his speech quietly, building by the minute, until an hour later he was fairly frothing at the mouth. In the midst of the tumult, Wulff and Johanna managed to leave by a side exit.

They walked hurriedly down the Avenue of the Puppets, beneath statues of Hohenzollern kings. Even now, SA men lined the street, hawking cigarettes, razor blades, and ersatz margarine to raise money for the Cause. Wulff buttoned his coat and put his arm around Johanna.

"I'm thirsty, Harry," she said.

They crossed the Spree on a stone bridge walkway, then hurried down Friedrich Ebert Strasse toward the Reichstag.

"We should have gone to a Dietrich film," Wulff told her. "It would have been better to have seen a Dietrich film. I'm sorry about all this, dear."

"It's all right, darling," Johanna said. "I've heard all this before. Remember?" She looped her arm through his and they continued down Friedrich Ebert Strasse amid trim government buildings and department stores, past the Lufthansa office and film studio executive suites, down a broad boulevard of smart shops and galleries. "It's amazing how widespread all this filth is getting," Johanna added.

They walked to the Adlon Hotel near Brandenburg Gate, a long way in mist and cold. The Adlon was one of the most elegant hotels in Berlin, an institution of high culture. With its marble floor, polished glass chandeliers, and vases of fresh flowers on every table, the hotel was a gathering spot for Berlin's elite. Wulff deposited their coats and hats at the hatcheck counter in the lobby, and the couple strode into the crowded bar near the ballroom. Wulff saw Erwin Kisch, a journalist who'd gained his reputation on the barricades in Austria, engaged in a heated conversation with an aristocratic-looking man in a tuxedo. Kisch—dressed in complete bohemian regalia—a flowered silk shirt, bright orange cashmere sweater, ski pants, and beret, was a little drunk already, though it was just past ten o'clock. Johanna took off her hat and unpinned her hair.

"Johanna, Johanna," Kisch called, rising from his place at the bar with a big smile. "Tell me you've been to hear Hitler! Can you imagine! If I'd have gone they would have lynched me on the spot! You must be exhausted by all that nonsense!" Kisch circled the table, gave Johanna a big hug, and shook Wulff's hand.

"Anything different this time?" Kisch asked. They all took seats.

"From Goebbels?" Johanna said. She ordered a snifter of brandy. "Let me think," she continued. "Goebbels likened the Jews to tuberculosis. The Jews are a new scourge on Germany's lungs. Yes! As if this clubfooted little dwarf were in perfect health."

"The fucking clubfoot," Kisch howled. "Pardon me, Johanna."

"He claims Germany's Jews are a national disease," Johanna said. Her brandy was delivered and she drank some of it. The bar beyond was crowded two deep with drinkers, men and women in fancy dress. Wulff ordered brandy as well. "According to Goebbels, surgery must be performed on the German body politic and the Jews must be removed. The clubfoot is interested in the health of Germany."

"Rubbish, rubbish!" Kisch shouted. He raised his glass in a mock salute and finished the schnapps in one gulp. "As a Viennese Marxist and atheist, I reserve the right to speak, and to demand an apology from this Goebbels coward! Where is this demented little prick? I shall slap his face and demand satisfaction!" Kisch slammed his glass on the table. "The little runt claims to have been wounded in the war. He never even saw the front, never wore a uniform!"

A group of tuxedoed men had come into the bar and stood at its entrance, surveying the scene. Wulff noticed Louis Adlon among them, the hotel owner accompanying a crowd from the opera. Adlon caught Wulff's eye, nodded and smiled.

"An interesting observation," Johanna said. "Perhaps we must psychoanalyze these brutes. Are they not cases of arrested development? Do they not love to march and sing and hike and build fires? Do they not love to live in barracks like teenagers on a great adventure? Do they not love uniforms and martial music? Are they not as sentimental as old women?"

Kisch seemed to think for a moment, red-faced and sweating. "These Nazis are political criminals. Nothing more and nothing less."

"And they have their lovely symbols," Johanna said calmly. "One must examine the swastika, the brown shirt. They have appropriated the color brown. Imagine, devotion to brown!"

"Piss on these symbols," Kisch said. "Do you know where their mystical brown comes from? Do you?" Kisch was wide-eyed. "When the SA was first established in Munich they had almost no money. They searched for army surplus and finally discovered a cache of brown-colored shirts belonging to the Kaiser's Colonial Service. They purchased thousands of these surplus shirts and wore them because they were cheap. So much for their mystical devotion to brown!" Kisch shrugged and licked his lips. His eyes were shiny with schnapps. "Don't tell me you believe in this mystical appeal to white, red, and black, the revolution, the ancient German *volk*?"

"There is a depth of appeal at work here," Johanna said quietly. "You should not underestimate it."

"And the swastika? What about the swastika? This is an ancient decoration that does not belong solely to the Germans. What do you make of this bit of symbolism?"

"It's sexual, isn't it?" Johanna said suddenly. "You have left out the sexual component of this movement, haven't you?"

"I should have known, Johanna!" Kisch squealed in delight. "Sex must be involved somehow!"

Wulff sniffed his brandy and said, "There is a primitive sort of satisfaction in it. The simple fact is that the crowd could not take their eyes from the speakers tonight. They were mesmerized, hypnotized almost. I would wager that a doctor might find some interesting things if he were able to take the blood pressure and pulse of every member of that crowd at the Sportpalast. It was not alcohol that stimulated them, that caused them to breathe heavily, roll their eyes, and sweat. They were in the throes of something. What, I don't know." Wulff sneaked a look at Johanna who was gazing at him with tenderness. He drank some brandy.

"And your conclusion, Harry?" Johanna asked.

"I know only that Göring looked exactly like lithographs I've seen of the Emperor Nero. There was a spit curl in the middle of his forehead. His face was fat and red. His hands were small and feminine." Wulff paused, suddenly self-aware.

"Nero! How marvelous!" Kisch laughed.

"We always return to sex," Johanna suggested. "Harry is right. Göring is very feminine in appearance. And the swastika is said to represent the primitive whirl of sexual chaos, the yin and the yang, two bodies in an orgiastic perpetuity of coupling."

"They'll make brood mares of you women," Kisch said gauntly. "Lock you in hutches and breed you like rabbits."

Johanna glanced up at Wulff, who stood beside the table holding his brandy snifter. "Harry, how many people would you say attended Hitler's speech tonight at the Sportpalast?"

"Twelve thousand, more or less," he said.

Kisch licked his lips but remained silent. From a corner of the ballroom they could hear a violin.

"More than half the audience was female," Johanna said sternly. "I watched them. They sat listening to all these speeches by men in rapt attention. They were, as Harry says, spellbound. You could almost say they were sexually transported."

"Mesmerized—really, Johanna," Kisch countered.

Johanna half-rose from the table, then sat back. "But my dear Kisch, you must account for the numbers of women in Hitler's audiences. You must account for the fact that female celebrities, actresses of film and stage, opera singers, all of them appear in Goebbel's entourage or attend his parties. Hitler is pursued by rich patronesses of all types. You simply must account for the sexual appeal of these men!"

"Surely—" Kisch began, then stopped. The idea seemed to stun him.

"Yes, Erwin," Johanna continued in a soothing voice. "The Nazis are a party of men, a kind of band or tribe. Their leaders are nomadic in their lifestyles, all save for Goebbels and Göring, who pretend to be family men. The rest are rootless roamers, without kinship ties or societal roots. There is something profoundly appealing to women about this type of man."

Louis Adlon, a tall man in an impeccably maintained tuxedo, eased himself alongside Wulff. He had a full head of white hair, a thin moustache.

"They are quite wound up again," Adlon whispered to Wulff, dragging him bodily to one side. "But it is my favorite roundtable, despite the dangerous political talk."

Johanna raised her glass, toasted Adlon silently, and offered him a broad smile. Adlon ordered a glass of champagne from a passing waiter. Wulff's father had known Adlon in the old days, and Wulff himself had sat on Adlon's knee during fancy dress dinners at the

Adlon apartment. Adlon was served the champagne in a fluted crystal glass. "And so ladies and gentlemen," he said, toasting the group at the table, "you are gazing into your crystal balls and deciding the future of Germany?"

"Our topic is sex," Kisch said.

"Sex!" Adlon laughed. "How very delightful."

"Perhaps you can help us, Louis," Kisch asked. "Is there a sexual component in the Nazi party, one which defines its appeal?"

Adlon rubbed his chin in mock concentration. He raised his glass, contemplated the wine, then put it to his lips and drank. "Hitler has many female admirers," Adlon said. "In Munich he is adored by Helene Bechstein, wife of the famous piano manufacturer. One must never underestimate the allure of a renegade political figure for certain females."

"Hitler screwed his niece and murdered her," Kisch said flatly.

Adlon touched Wulff's elbow and led him away from the table a few paces.

"How is your father?" Adlon said quietly to Wulff.

"Well enough, thank you," Wulff said.

"Please give him my best," Adlon said. He leaned close to Wulff, speaking in confidential tones. "Germans like your father are disappearing fast. Not to put too fine a point on it, but the same is happening to me."

"Nonsense," Wulff said. "You appear quite formidable."

Adlon shook his head and smiled. "We have new Germans now, Harry." Wulff was watching Johanna in the bar mirror. "These new Germans even now come into my hotel. You must speak with Johanna about the future, Harry. Do it soon."

"She won't leave," Wulff said.

"She can live in Switzerland. She was educated there. She has friends."

"Surely things can't be that bad, in your opinion," Wulff said.

"Don't deceive yourself," Adlon said. A wave of laughter swept the bar. A joke had been told about a monkey and a Catholic priest. Adlon said, "Göring eats every night at the Hocher's Restaurant and comes here afterward for a drink. As I've overheard your conversations and those of your friends, Harry, I've overheard his, and those of *his* friends. These Nazis are monsters, Harry, waiting for the doors of their cages to open."

Johanna rose, stood behind Adlon, and gave him a friendly hug. "I want to go home," she whispered in Wulff's ear.

Wulff finished his brandy. He helped Johanna with her sweater, and they walked through the lobby to the Unter den Linden. She put her head on his shoulder in the cold night air.

"Stay with me tonight, Harry?" she asked.

They caught a taxi along Unter den Linden. There were people at the tram stops now, crowds at the outdoor cafés.

"I must go back to Alexanderplatz," Wulff said.

"You're working?" Johanna said, disappointed.

"I'm sorry, but it's important."

They arrived at the Tiergarten. The taxi swerved into Lennestrasse.

"How will it end, Harry? What did Louis tell you?"

"Adlon wants you to leave Germany now."

"And what about you, Harry? What do you want?"

"I'm afraid," Wulff said. "Adlon says he is afraid of these new Germans. I am too."

"New Germans!" Johanna laughed. "Like the ones we saw tonight, Harry? You know what they say. As blond as Hitler, as tall as Goebbels, as thin as Göring!"

～ ～

Wulff waved to Barlach, who was just inside a barbed-wire checkpoint manned by two Reichswehr corporals at the entrance to Alexanderplatz HQ. Wulff pulled out his ID and flashed it at the armed corporal, who raised his carbine to let the inspector pass.

"Let's sit for a while," Wulff suggested, realizing that Barlach would stand all day in Wulff's presence unless ordered to do otherwise. When they were seated on a marble visitor's bench, Wulff lit a cigarette and offered one to Barlach, who refused. "What about the tram lines?" Wulff asked.

"I've interviewed the tram conductor. He recognized the photo of the victim in male clothing and made an absolutely positive identification. The victim got on the tram every morning around ten o'clock at stop 69 near Marzahn carrying a violin case. The conductor had never seen him wearing women's clothing before."

"So our victim lives in Prenzlauer or Friedrichshain or Lichtenberg?" Wulff concluded.

"If he wanted to walk to the tram stop."

"We'll check the Lichtenberg dentists tomorrow. We might get lucky."

"I'll make the rounds?" Barlach asked.

"You do that," Wulff said. "How was the Hirrenstrasse on election night?" he asked.

"Torches, flags, and fires. Red Flag Fighters spoiling to give you their opinions."

"I saw a Hitler speech tonight," Wulff said.

"Yes, sir," Barlach replied.

"Have you ever seen Hitler?"

"No, sir, I haven't," Barlach said.

"It's just as well," Wulff told him.

Wulff led the way to the morgue. Inside the lab, a legless corpse lay on one of the metal tables, one of many drunks run over by a tram. Levitt sat hunched over a pile of documents.

"You've got our report?" Wulff asked.

Levitt tapped a file. "In here," he said. "But there isn't much new. Maybe one thing."

"One thing?" Wulff asked curiously.

"I told you we found scrapings of glue under the victim's false fingernails? Well, it was theatrical glue. And there were traces of other substances as well."

"Probably blood and skin, yes?" Wulff asked.

"No blood, Wulff," Levitt told him. "But your victim did touch the killer's face. Perhaps scratched him slightly, though not enough to break the skin. What we found under the victim's fingernails was a quantity of cream base and face powder."

Wulff frowned. "Cream base and face powder? You mean makeup?"

"You're a Kripo genius," Levitt said. Levitt nodded his head up and down furiously.

"Could a chemist positively identify these substances?" Wulff asked.

Levitt shook his head. "Wulff, Wulff, you ask too much of science. There are thousands of these compounds on the market. I would be surprised if one could specify the exact brand. There are many, and they have the same chemical composition. If women only knew!" Levitt handed over the formal autopsy. "You're free to study it," he said. "I'll file the death certificate tomorrow morning." He shrugged again. "But you know as much about the poor wretch as I do."

Wulff thanked the pathologist and led Barlach to the outer hall. They were alone save for a janitor sweeping their way from the darkness.

"What do you make of this cream base and powder?" Barlach asked.

"When I first heard about the glue, I thought perhaps we were dealing with a hairpiece or toupee. Now I'm not so sure."

"The kiss they shared," Barlach murmured. "There's something strange in it."

They walked upstairs and stood in the empty foyer.

"I'll find the dentist tomorrow," Barlach said confidently.

"I've just thought of something," Wulff said.

"Sir?"

"The *man* who rode the Grenadier line got on at the Precinct 69 stop every morning. But he was not recognized on the Prenzlauer line. That means that every working day this victim rode from the suburbs to the Grenadier stop, then got off and walked somewhere nearby with his violin case."

"Yes, of course," Barlach said.

"Where did he go? Carrying a violin case."

"I don't follow."

"He was poor," Wulff said. "Levitt says he was undernourished. He may have been an immigrant, don't you see? He earned little enough money, but he has earned some. Enough to have his wisdom teeth pulled."

"Sir?"

"I think he was a street musician," Wulff said. "There are dozens of them in Alexanderplatz near the station. There are barrel organs and hurdy-gurdies. And there are violinists!"

"Of course!" Barlach laughed. "I'll show the photographs around the square tomorrow morning."

Wulff leaned over and whispered, "You must keep the fact that you work for me a secret. Confidentiality is very important."

They said good night on the front stairs. It was after midnight when Wulff arrived at his small flat.

— —

The janitor stood at a supply room door, watching the two police. Before coming to work, he had counted his money twice—twenty marks, and a single gold mark given to him by Bruckmann after the last report. A single gold mark for reporting the daily diary of the deputy commissioner!

He felt a slipstream of fear. Detective Inspector Harry Wulff was investigating the Hirrenstrasse murder. For a moment he relished his fear, and then it became a starburst in his chest. Perhaps tonight he would open the morgue door and read the official autopsy report. It would be like reliving the crime.

He touched the tube of lipstick he carried in his pocket. He thrilled to its touch, the same hard rush of sexual ardor he sensed when he looked at Harry Wulff.

7

Wulff cleaned the Walther pistol he often carried. When he finished, he stowed the cleaning kit, loaded the weapon with fresh ammunition, then put the gun into a leather holster on his desk. He stared down to the street from his third-story perch near the Interior Ministry. It was a standard weekday of traffic, trams, buses, and a few Charabancs carrying tourists. Wulff turned his back to the window, and his eye fell on a massive headline in the *Berlin Tagebuch*: NAZIS GRAB HUGE ELECTION WINDFALL. Wulff buckled the Walther under his left arm and walked down a corridor and knocked on the office door of the Kriminal Oberkommissar of Berlin Mitte, Erik Bruckmann.

Bruckmann opened the door, explaining that his clerk was on an errand. Wulff followed his captain through a reception area and into a corner office that overlooked Berlin's neoclassical French Gymnasium. Bruckmann sat down behind a plain wooden desk while Wulff remained at the window.

"Our Nazi friends did quite well," Bruckmann said.

"It seems that way," Wulff agreed.

"Your Jewish deputy is trembling in his boots, no doubt," Bruckmann said.

"But then we're not here to talk politics," Wulff said.

Bruckmann smiled edgily. A pure autumn light flooded the office. The scar on Bruckmann's throat was bone-white. "I want to know about your inquiries for Weiss," he said. "I told you I expected a complete report on all your activities. You still work for me."

"I'm examining personnel files and duty rosters," Wulff said. The files had been delivered to his office only that morning, one stack of paper more than a meter high. There were three hundred and fifteen active officials, bureaucrats, and clerks at Alexanderplatz HQ, along with dozens of Reichswehr and civil guards, maintenance men, and visitors. Wulff was having fingerprint sets made to match the files and dossiers, as well as sheets of photos and investigative memos. "It's mostly a paper task," he said.

"And how will you proceed?" Bruckmann asked.

"Narrow down the list."

Bruckmann grunted in disdain. "And you have an assistant in all this?"

"Not as yet," Wulff lied. "I don't know it would do any good to work with someone I neither know nor trust."

"And Weiss? You've met with him recently?" Bruckmann fingered his scar. "Has Weiss suggested a protocol?"

"I'm on my own," Wulff said. "The deputy commissioner has his hands full with other matters."

"Do you wish to be relieved of other duties?"

"I have only one case," Wulff said.

"Ah, this stupid murder in the Hirrenstrasse," Bruckmann said.

"The victim is not yet identified."

"Perhaps you'd like to transfer it away to another inspector. It seems a pity to waste your talent on a transvestite."

"I'll pursue it," Wulff said. "It interests me."

"Mark it in your weekly report," Bruckmann said. When Wulff nodded, Bruckmann said, "You're very clever, aren't you, Wulff? With these election results, you've outsmarted yourself by this relationship with Weiss. You've laid your chip on the wrong color."

Wulff said he was mindful of the political wind, then excused himself and left Berlin Mitte in his police Opel.

He drove down Unter den Linden in heavy traffic, crossed to the Lustgarten, then curled around the Imperial Palace. North up the Konigstrasse, he turned at the edge of Red Town Hall amid the hawkers, organ grinders, and peddlers. On every street corner, bedraggled men and women had set up temporary stalls made of tin or plywood, selling ersatz coffee and margarine, hocked jewelry, books, tools, scrap iron and soap, pipes, used clothing, and black-market tobacco. Wulff counted forty beggars as he sat becalmed in traffic.

He parked in a bus zone on Alexanderstrasse where two jugglers were tossing colored balls back and forth for handout pfennigs. Barlach was crossing the square in a blizzard of flying coattails and leaves. Wulff got out of the Opel and stood beside it.

"He worked here!" Barlach shouted, fifteen meters from Wulff, huffing and puffing. "You were right, sir! He worked here."

"Good, Barlach," Wulff said.

"Yes, in Alexanderplatz. Right under our noses. And that isn't all. The other musicians remember him clearly. In fact, he's quite well known for his skill. Apparently, he played beautifully."

"And who is this mystery violinist?"

Barlach was wearing the same creased blue suit and brown shoes he'd worn the day before. "They call him Timkin," Barlach said. "That's all they know. He would come about ten in the morning and set up his violin, open the case, and play for whatever pfennigs came his way. He'd become quite popular with the train and tram riders."

"So, going home he walked up Prenzlauer and caught the Grenadier tram for the ride to Lichtenberg."

"That's not all," Barlach said. "There are only two dentists in the vicinity of Precinct 69 in Lichtenberg. I telephoned them both this morning, and the second one did Timkin's dental work. The victim is known by the name of Timkin Mueller, and the dentist extracted two upper wisdom teeth last week. He took out two stitches on Wednesday. I even have Mueller's address!"

"Excellent work, Barlach," Wulff said.

Barlach handed Wulff a piece of note paper on which he'd written an obscure address off the suburban tram line, halfway to the train stop at Marzahn. Wulff recalled that these suburbs were composed of detached and semi-detached villas and apartments, failing businesses, and abandoned factories.

"Timkin is not a German name," Barlach said.

Wulff got inside the Opel and opened the passenger door. Barlach circled the small car, then hauled his huge body into its tiny seat. "Polish?" Wulff guessed. "Galician?"

"An immigrant, surely," Barlach said. Barlach looked at the jugglers. "Have you read the election results?" he asked Wulff.

"Yes, I've read them," he answered. "The Nazis promise to relieve the immigrant problem. Do you believe them, Barlach? Goebbels wishes to relocate the Jews. Is this the answer to all our problems, sergeant?"

"I don't know, sir," Barlach replied.

Wulff lit a cigarette, realizing that he shouldn't engage in political discussions with subordinates. "Let's take a drive out to Lichtenberg and see Mueller's room. It may tell us everything we need to know."

— —

Bruckmann found an isolated seat on the second balcony of the Capitol Cinema on Auguste-Viktoria Platz. On a gigantic silver screen far below, Greta Garbo was engulfed in smoke escaping the engine of a train. At two o'clock, he left his seat and walked to the mezzanine restroom. He washed his hands, ran some water on his face, and studied himself in the mirror. A moment later, Theodor Loos pushed open the washroom door and silently stood staring at Bruckmann with dead eyes.

"Theodor, my friend," Bruckmann said, toweling his hands.

"How much money have you got for me?" Loos asked, coming inside, taking a position near the urinals.

"Do you like the movie?" Bruckmann asked. Bruckmann had discovered the teenage Loos in a refugee detention camp in Luxembourg, just over the Belgian border where he had been assigned to single out collaborators and traitors to create a fifth column. In those days, Loos was only eighteen or nineteen, already keen to betray his fellow prisoners. At first, Bruckmann offered the boy scraps of bread and cheese to spy on French prisoners. Bruckmann soon discovered that Loos cultivated an absurd fondness for torture and strangulation. In time, the boy's skills at lock-picking would come in handy as well.

Bruckmann fondled a wad of marks. He stepped toward Loos and extended the bundle of money. Loos snatched it away and counted the notes twice.

"Twenty-five marks," Loos said. "We should have more money, Bruckmann."

"Theodor, Theodor," Bruckmann said gently, "you wish more money from our Nazi friends? I am trying as best I can."

Loos strode to the door and stood with his back to it, blocking the way. "We stopped the raid on Hedemannstrasse Nazi HQ, didn't we? Surely that must be worth more than fifty marks a week?"

"I'll see what I can do," Bruckmann said. "I am working against great odds. But for now we have other business."

"What other business?" Loos said.

"Weiss has assigned a Kriminal Kommissar to investigate leaks at Alexanderplatz."

"Who is this man?"

"Harry Wulff."

"I've seen him several times," Loos said. He recalled the thin saturnine man with sharp aquiline features and a cold blue gaze.

"You've seen him?"

"I've even spoken to him," Loos said.

"Don't be a fool," Bruckmann warned. "Harry Wulff is very clever. We can't take any chances with him. He is being paid to inaugurate a security plan for Alexanderplatz HQ. This means he will be examining personnel records and political dossiers. There will probably be some kind of trap laid."

"What kind of trap?"

"This interests you now, eh?"

"Keep talking," Loos said coldly.

"I'm guessing, mind you," Bruckmann told him. "But you must keep a very low profile. No more conversations with Kriminal Kommissar Wulff, please."

"He works for the Jew?"

Bruckmann nodded.

"And my money?"

"The Nazis will pay. I'm working on it."

"I must have gold marks," Loos said.

"Are you hoarding gold now, Theodor?"

"Shut up, Bruckmann," Loos snapped.

"Relax, my friend," Bruckmann said. Bruckmann handed over two gold marks. Loos took them eagerly. "A gift from me," Bruckmann said.

Loos studied the coins. "Wulff is investigating a murder in Hirrenstrasse?" he asked.

"The murder of a transvestite," Bruckmann said. "But how did you know?"

"Simple," Loos said. "I am an expert with locks."

"It is his only case," Bruckmann said.

"Does he have a suspect?"

"It is unimportant," Bruckmann answered wearily. He had tired of the conversation. "Just try to read the daily memos and report to me. But don't take any chances, and inform me of the plans of Weiss in regard to criminalizing the Nazis. Don't do anything stupid while Wulff is around. He's like a bloodhound."

"You'll see to my money?"

"Yes, Theodor, yes."

"I want gold marks," Loos said.

Bruckmann neared the door cautiously and gave Loos a solid clap on the back. Edging around the huge man, he emerged into the deserted lobby. For a moment he stood, listening to the voices of Greta Garbo and John Gilbert, remembering the pleasure Loos took in the garrote.

⌐ ⌐

Sitting in the cramped Opel, Wulff and Barlach smoked. On a dark evening, storm clouds had gathered on the northern horizon. They had searched the house for an hour, finding nothing but scraps of Mueller's clothes and a few sheets of violin music stamped with the logo of a shop in Danzig. The war widow who owned the house already had sold Mueller's violin and placed a "to let" sign in the window.

"Do we contact Danzig authorities?" Barlach asked.

"I'll send a wire," Wulff said. "We'll try to find some of Mueller's family. But we won't discover anything useful in his past. And he may have been alone in the world."

"What *did* happen to him?"

"My guess is that he rode the tram with his killer alongside. Some unknown man from Lichtenberg. The murderer is here somewhere in these suburbs." Wulff gestured to the rows of houses, villas, the blighted trees.

"That doesn't help much, does it?" Barlach said.

"Not much," Wulff agreed. "I think the murderer was a stranger to Mueller. That makes our job very difficult."

Wulff sat quietly as a flock of crows fought the wind. Smokestacks and overhead electric wires cluttered the horizon. Barlach finished his cigarette as Wulff started the engine and accelerated them down a lane between rows of brick villas. In the dark, a bent man was chopping at an elm, breaking it up for firewood.

8

Wulff watched an October storm from his third-floor office at Berlin Mitte. For an hour he had been sorting photographs of HQ employees, counting noses, and organizing faces. Meanwhile, he'd hit a brick wall in the Hirrenstrasse murder investigation.

For the past two days, the Nazis had rampaged through the streets of central Berlin, explicitly defying a presidential decree banning them from the area. Gangs of SA in brown shirts roamed between the Reichstag and Potsdamerplatz on the hunt for Jews, waving flags and banners, breaking shop windows, cursing down the Republic in slogan and song, and painting swastikas on Jewish shops. Schupo units had tried closing the busy Friedrich Ebert Strasse to funnel the Nazis east and west away from the central city. They had erected barricades and roadblocks, but the Nazis had cleverly escaped into side streets, reformed, and emerged energized in different spots, outflanking the bulky Orpo details. On the floor of Parliament, Nazis wore their brown shirts, again defying a Hindenberg edict prohibiting paramilitary garb. Göring was installed as president of the Reichstag.

Wulff put down a file folder and looked out at the street again, at its gray light and granite facades, the barren trees on the grounds of the Ministry. A Mitte messenger opened his door after a soft tap and dropped a brown paper package on his desk. Wulff crushed out a cigarette, cut the string with his knife, and tore open the wrapping paper. Inside was a small, oblong white box. He popped open the box and discovered a cardboard figure pasted over with a glossy magazine face, black dress, black-and-white high-heeled shoes, and a wig. Across the face someone had drawn an *X*.

Wulff dropped the doll and examined the wrapping paper and the box. It had been mailed from Central Berlin Post, perhaps eight hundred yards up the Konigstrasse from where Wulff was presently sitting in his office. Wulff looked down at the doll on his desk, the face taunting him, its over-white makeup, ruby lips, and high cheekbones. There was no mistaking the likeness to Timkin Mueller. After ten minutes, Wulff rewrapped the doll and carefully put it back inside its white box. He locked his office and left for Alexanderplatz HQ.

— —

Weiss put down the telephone and looked hard at Inspector Harry Wulff. The Kriminal Kommissar had delivered his weekly report. A report about nothing, containing nothing. Weiss sat at his desk, scribbling notes on a pad, perusing Wulff's thin report. A harsh north wind was banging at the window glass, ruffling the chestnut trees outside. Weiss heaved a big sigh. "At least I am temporarily not a subject of caricature for Goebbels," he said. "Now that he's in the Reichstag, he has ample opportunity to attack others in person."

"But you still have a termite here," Wulff said.

"I'm sorry, Kriminal Kommissar," Weiss said. "Sometimes I think it hardly matters." He paused, blushed. "I'm not proud of being discouraged. In reality, this HQ is probably crawling with spies, counterspies, and counter-counterspies. It is the nature of the game."

"I'm continuing my work," Wulff said.

"Please," Weiss said quietly.

Wulff thought of the doll.

Weiss took off his thick glasses and polished the lenses distractedly. Nazi rampages in the Alt Köln had resulted in dozens of beatings of elderly Jews, left-socialists, and communists, and the vandalization of Jewish businesses. Pressure had fallen on Stapo and Orpo to halt the depredation, and Weiss looked as though he hadn't slept in a month.

"We assume the termite is in Alexanderplatz," Wulff said. "Could it be with Schupo-Kommando?"

"Only if the Polizei-Oberst himself is disloyal, which I doubt. Some precinct captains and some of their men are Nazis, but surely not Schupo-Kommando."

"Right now," Wulff said, "I have three hundred and fifteen political and personnel files on every administrative officer in this building. There are another thirty dossiers on Reichswehr and maintenance staff. If one includes the heads of Schupo, Stapo, and all the secretaries and clerks, there are four hundred suspects."

"It is ridiculous, I suppose."

"Could we issue a false order? Perhaps issue an order for a raid on the Goebbels' personal apartment? Something totally outrageous. See if it leaks, time its leaking, and pin down the source that way?"

"I can't do that now," Weiss said. "Goebbels is a member of Parliament. To issue such an order, even a false one, would be political suicide. And I have no wish to commit suicide. Not at the moment, anyway!"

"What about an oral order?"

"I'm prohibited by the chief from directing officers by oral order. I don't wish to leave you without options, but my hands are tied by the regulations. There must be a written record of every executive action. And you can see why. The result of oral orders from an executive would be constant interpretation and misinterpretation of such orders."

"Perhaps a dual set of orders," Wulff suggested.

Weiss turned over an hourglass on his desk. They were silent for a time, both men anticipating nothing.

"I'm sorry, Wulff," Weiss said. "I've been so distracted by the violence. Do you think our termite is working for the political cadres of Stapo?"

"It would be logical," Wulff said. "Somebody high up. I'm doing background on police colonels and captains now to take care of Schupo. I'll begin combing through your Stapo staff. Any one of them could be your termite, I suppose."

Weiss left his desk and stood with his back to the coal fire. "Goebbels is a heartbeat from controlling the Berlin police. He must be stopped."

"Issue a written order for his arrest," Wulff said. "Make only the necessary copies. Countermand it immediately. We'll see if the news reaches Goebbels himself through Nazi party channels. It's an experiment."

"I don't wish to do that," Weiss said. "If news got out, I'd look foolish or worse."

"What choice is there?"

Weiss rubbed his hands together, warming them. "Tomorrow," Weiss said, "on Shabbat I'll dictate an order to Krause in writing. It will go nowhere. On Monday, I'll circulate it to my Stapo chiefs. Then I will countermand it thirty minutes later. That's the best I can do."

Wulff shook hands with Weiss, who had crossed the room, joining him at the window above the square. Wulff left and made his way downstairs and through the Reichswehr checkpoints. When Wulff had gone, Weiss made notes of their conversation in his personal daybook.

➤ ➤

At a Jewish grocery on Fischerstrasse, Wulff bought a packet of stale dates and figs, three overripe black bananas, and a can of herbal tea. The Nazi rampages had not reached this part of Alt-Köln, its narrow winding streets and overhanging medieval buildings. Even so, some of the shop windows were boarded.

Wulff taxied to Lennestrasse and let himself into Johanna's flat. She met him in the hallway wearing a luxuriant gold-and-green caftan. Wulff took off his shoes and sat tiredly on the ottoman. He offered her his package of food. While Wulff relaxed, Johanna made tea. He found himself recalling the first time he'd met Johanna at the Adlon Hotel, a glittering evening after he and his father had attended a performance of Parsifal at the Kroll Opera House. Wulff remembered being dressed in a tuxedo with a ridiculous red cummerbund, standing beneath a glaze of chandelier light in the hotel bar holding a fluted glass of sparkling Sekt, when through the refracted glare of smoke, bubbles, and light, he'd seen a marvelous female across the room. In the ballroom, an orchestra was playing Strauss.

Johanna brought their tea on a silver tray and poured two cups. She had lit two Shabbat candles. "I haven't left the room for two days," Johanna told Wulff. Her clients had canceled appointments. She'd heard gunfire from the direction of the Reichstag, and tear-gas canisters had burst on the cobbled streets nearby. She'd read that an elderly *Ostjud* had lost an eye to a beating.

Wulff sipped his tea. Johanna had sliced the two bananas and put them on a plate. "Would you like to leave Berlin for a while?" Wulff asked. "It can be arranged. My father would put you up."

Johanna sat cross-legged on the opposite end of the ottoman. "I'm a Berliner," she said. "Why should I be driven from my home?"

"You're not being driven," Wulff said. "Go for a vacation to Vienna or Basil or Zurich."

Johanna ate a fig. "The Austrians are worse anti-Semites than the Germans," she said at last. "They harass Freud and burn his books. The *völkish* papers attack him personally in print." She lifted her teacup and looked sadly at Wulff. It was dark in the apartment. The heavy drapes had been pulled. "Must we talk of this tonight, Harry? I feel I should be going to synagogue. But I'm too afraid. Isn't that terrible, Harry? Isn't that just terrible?"

"I could take you," Wulff suggested.

"Thank you, darling. But—no."

"I'm not worried about my career, you know," he said.

"You're already besmirched," Johanna told him. "Consorting with Jews, psychoanalysts, and a communist journalist! You're acting very irresponsibly."

Wulff picked up the leather satchel he'd brought from work. It contained hundreds of photographs of Alexanderplatz officials, workers, police. It also contained the doll. He opened a white box, and unwrapped the doll from its tissue.

"What is this?" Johanna asked.

"I want your professional help," Wulff said.

"You're playing with dolls now, darling?" Johanna laughed.

"Not yet," Wulff told her.

Wulff tasted a rubbery date. "Do you remember the Hirrenstrasse murder?" he asked.

"Yes, I do. Very sad," Johanna replied. "A man dressed as a woman. The woman who'd been kissed."

Wulff lifted the doll. "I received this at the office just today. It was mailed from Central Post, delivered just six hours later. No return address, of course. Everything quite anonymous."

Johanna studied the doll, a piece of flat cardboard with ribbed backing, magazine photos carefully glued to its surface. It was clearly a representation of the woman in a sequined black dress, her white face obliterated by an *X*.

"It's the murdered man," Wulff said. "Exact in every particular. The perspective is off, of course. But it is the victim."

"Harry—" Johanna said. "The killer sent this to you? Is that what you think?"

"What else could it be?"

"How—compelling," Johanna said, eating another stale fig, placing a finger on the doll while studying it. "Fascinating," she said. "Frightening."

"It's a perfect likeness of the dead man," Wulff said. "And the doll isn't sloppily made. Each magazine photo was carefully chosen to accurately represent parts of the man dressed as a woman. It must have taken days to complete. Finding the right magazine photos would have been a chore. Whoever did this was meticulous."

"You never told me the name of the victim."

"A Danziger named Timkin Mueller. He lived alone in Lichtenberg and worked as a street musician in Alexanderplatz. Mueller had only one female outfit and he was wearing it the Friday night he was killed. I have no idea why he was killed or what he was doing going to central Berlin that night."

"Oh, Harry," Johanna said in surprise. "It just occurs to me! That Friday night was the night of the huge Transvestite Ball. It's a yearly event, attended by thousands. It's in the Jagerstrasse district. I'm surprised we hadn't thought of it before."

"It makes sense now," Wulff said. "Mueller was taking a late tram from his rented room in Lichtenberg, heading for central Berlin. His one big night in costume."

"Poor fellow," Johanna said. "But how demented."

"Demented?" Wulff said.

"There's a maniac at work here, Harry," she said.

"I thought it might interest you," Wulff said. "I've concluded that Mueller didn't know his killer. There may have been a shared kiss. We've found traces of cream base, powder, and theatrical glue under the victim's fingernails."

Johanna sat thinking and sipping tea. The candles guttered gloomily. She had pinned back her hair and was freshly bathed. "Do you think the killer was wearing makeup too?"

"It is entirely possible."

"Did you want my professional opinion, Harry? That's what you said, isn't it?"

"There's nothing I'd like better," Wulff said.

"How can I help you, Harry?"

"I'm still analyzing my victim," Wulff said. "He owned one female dress, quite an expense for him. Probably cost him most of what he made in six months of playing the violin at Alexanderplatz. Yet he seemed to have only one life. I doubt if we'll find a secret existence for him. He seemed to come and go like clockwork during the week. Any ideas?"

"I really suspect your victim was not a professional cross-dresser. Nor was he a prostitute. He may have been somewhat effeminate, or just enjoyed dressing up for one night in women's clothes. Perhaps he did it in private for personal amusement or pleasure. We're likely never to know. But I can tell you the Transvestite Ball every year is attended by people you'd pass by on the street in a suit or lederhosen and never give a second thought. The killer is dangerous."

"I'm certain of that."

"More than dangerous," Johanna said. "When one looks at the doll, one imagines the hours spent collecting these split images, assembling them from magazines and tabloids. Imagine how he must have poured over them in his room, reliving the murder again and again, daring his own behavior to repeat itself. This demonstrates an obvious obsessive-compulsive quality, Harry, attention to absurd detail that borders on the hallucinatory. In this case, the obsession is probably a reverse fascination with the mother."

"And what about the kiss?"

"A key ambivalent event," Johanna told him. "The outer-killer approached a beautiful woman and tried to kiss her. The inner-killer knew secretly that this person was a man dressed as a woman. He knew there had been a gender transformation and was both fascinated and repelled by it. In his outer fantasy, he was simply being an aggressive male on the street. On the other hand, this kiss burst his inward self into a million pieces."

"Please," Wulff said.

"Harry, your killer transferred his anger to the man beneath the woman's clothes."

"For God's sake," Wulff laughed quietly. "He was kissing his mother but killing his father?" Wulff finished his cup of tea. "Just who the hell am I looking for?" he asked.

"This is no figure from a Greek tragedy," Johanna said. "He's probably approaching early middle age. His psychological conflict has taken time to mature. When he was young, your killer was probably somewhat sadistic, mean-tempered, aloof in a halting sense, and socially inferior. If you want a guess, I'd say he's a wanderer or someone with a menial position in society. He is not well-educated. Most people who are educated become socialized. Their worst instincts are filtered out. In youth, I suspect this man was easily manipulated, learning that social relations have no value except as means to an end. He is filled with self-loathing, but has convinced himself that he is somehow superior. In reality, he is probably irritable, suspicious, and confused. But he is also devious and clever. As you can tell, he is deft with his hands. He may have studied a craft. But his intelligence is more and more being taken over by his mania."

"And the mania?"

"It is a delusion," Johanna said. "His delusion is his gender confusion."

"Does he cross-dress?"

"Oh absolutely, Harry," Johanna said. "You have evidence that he uses a cream base and face powder, and that somewhere along the line he's worn a wig. I suspect he's toyed with the idea of cross-dressing for a long time. Perhaps since youth. Only now, as he gets older, he sees the possibility of presenting himself to society as a woman. He processes his mother and sees himself. Some of these neuroses may have a deeply religious base." Johanna touched Wulff's arm. "But remember, these guesses are not based strictly on science. They represent a hypothesis only."

"And what does our killer do now? How does he earn his living in Berlin?"

"It's only speculation, Harry," Johanna said.

"Be my beautiful guest."

"All right," she said. "Perhaps the doll itself is a clue. This man is good with his hands. He's meticulous in an obsessive way. And most obsessives are very meticulous. You'll find them in jobs where they are alone a lot of the time, where dealing with people or interacting with society is minimal at best. And Harry, the doll probably isn't the only one he's ever made. Making this doll is another ritual act of murder. The *X* across the face relocates the murder to the doll."

"Does he want to do it again?"

"Oh, I think so, Harry," Johanna sighed. "He's probably on slow boil right now."

"But he's capable of employment?"

"If it isn't too stressful."

"Is he a homosexual?" Wulff asked. "Does he practice that life?"

"No, I don't think so, Harry," Johanna said. "Most cross-dressers aren't strictly speaking homosexual. In fact, most are engaged in harmless play. They're toying with their inner impulses. Nothing harmful ever comes from it. Many marry, raise families, and pursue careers. They just find they enjoy slipping into women's panties from time to time. Their wives may know of their pleasures, and some may even share in it. It approximates any kind of other sexual happiness. But in your killer's case it shadows deeper troubles. Unfortunately, we don't know about his childhood."

"A loner who works with his hands," Wulff said. "Someone angry, guilt ridden, and complex." Across nameless distances, the killer was speaking to Wulff, imparting messages to him through the medium of the doll. They were in *contact*. "Why would he send me the doll?" Wulff asked Johanna finally.

Johanna crawled forward on the ottoman, curled around Wulff. Against the windows was a lush murmur of rain. "I'm frightened, Harry," she said.

"It's the times," he told her, not half-believing it himself.

"I'm not talking about my general fears," she said. "Whoever killed Timkin Mueller has picked you as a special figure. You are his distant authority. His totem. He sees you as sexually competent while he himself feels shamed in your presence. He is freighted with your authority and wishes to challenge it."

"You take this Oedipal analysis seriously?"

"Of course I do, Harry."

"But how could it matter?"

"You represent his father, Harry," she said. "You're the father he wishes to kill."

Loos wandered the dance floor. He changed tables three times in all until finally he achieved the view he wanted—Uli in the balcony wearing a skin-tight, cream-white gown concentrically hemmed at waist, knee, and ankle, a boa of ostrich feathers around her neck. She had stylized her cat-face with heavily painted whiskers on each cheek, her great wide eyes outlined by kohl. She puckered her tight, pink mouth and smiled insouciantly at Loos. In the hot cabaret and wearing his overcoat and watchcap, Loos sweated and drank apple brandy. There were several hundred people in the room. Loos tried to ignore the stage show, which featured a lewdly dressed man in a gray Reichswehr uniform with its buttock portion cut out.

The telephone on his table rang.

"You're back on the Matzstrasse," Uli said into the telephone receiver.

Loos locked onto her gaze. She sat at a table in the balcony smoking a cigarette fixed in her teeth with a black holder. Loos gulped a mouthful of apple brandy. "May I buy you a drink?" he asked.

The noise in the cabaret was overwhelming—men and women babbling into phones, laughter, bawdy songs from the stage.

"Sekt and crème de menthe," Uli said. "You know that's my favorite drink. I love green, don't you?"

Loos leaned forward as a strange lucidity came over him. He felt as though he could overhear every conversation on the dance floor, each whispered endearment, every chance joke. It recalled to him the closeness of the hut in Juprelle where his earnest mother would light dozens of candles and place them in front of her Virgin shrines, then force him into one of the little-girl dresses she had made for him so that they could kneel and pray together.

Loos ordered the Sekt and crème de menthe. The waiter carried it across the room on a tray above his head. When Uli received the drink, she raised her glass and saluted Loos. "Do you know who you are, Siegfried?" she asked him.

"I begin to—" Loos said haltingly.

Loos signaled for a waiter and asked him to deliver her two gold marks. When she opened the envelope, Loos watched her smile broadly and lick her lips. She puckered her pink mouth at him and purred.

"You are such a man of the world, my Siegfried," Uli said happily. "And so very rich! So important!"

"I have more money," he said.

"In time—" she told him.

Breathless now. "Yes, of course," Loos forced himself to say.

He dropped the receiver into its cradle. The cat-woman held the receiver to her ear, listened, nodded imperceptibly, then put it down. Loos buttoned his overcoat and left the cabaret, glad to catch a breath of night air. He walked a block down from the El Dorado to Jaegerstrasse, stopped on a corner opposite the Deutsche Bank, and bought a dozen glossy tabloids from a vendor. On Unter den Linden, he caught a tram and transferred at Grendadier for Lichtenberg.

Thirty minutes later, he was in his rented room. Downstairs, the widowed landlady was listening to a comedy on the radio. Loos sat in the half-dark of candlelight, leafing through magazine after magazine, searching for the right dress, the right wig, the proper boa, something white with blue highlights.

He lit a dozen candles. As long as he could, he resisted the urge to paint his face, to waste time staring at himself in the mirror. When he could stand the urge no longer, he delivered himself to its creative side, making himself up with arched eyebrows, thin whiskers, taut pink mouth, and kohled eyes. He purred into the mirror, his face touching the glass. Below, the widow played her radio. Loos leaned forward and kissed the cat-woman.

⏤ ⏤

Johanna left him sleeping under goose down, the French windows open to rain and the hum of trees.

She sat in the kitchen and drank a glass of milk, thinking of Harry, the first time she'd seen him in his tuxedo and red cummerbund, a tall and elegantly slim young man conversing with Louis Adlon in the hotel bar where she'd gone for drinks with her circle. At first, he'd seemed almost too blond, too Nordic for words, Harry Wulff supporting a tulip-shaped glass of Sekt in one hand while smoking a cigarette with the other. Then she noticed his stare, the rudeness of the man fixing her with his locked-in blue eyes. And then she found it amusing, almost titillating.

What had she worn that night? Someday she'd have to ask Harry if he remembered. She recalled being half-drunk under the glare of the chandeliers while a small orchestra played waltzes in the ballroom. Then, as if in a dream, he'd appeared suddenly at her table flashing a little-boy smile that charmed her in spite of herself.

"May I introduce myself?" he had asked. "My name is Harry Wulff." She had laughed self-consciously, tipping up her glass of wine in an effort to mask a flush of embarrassment, sneaking another glance at him through the medium of her liquor.

Johanna walked a glass of milk to the bedroom and placed it on a night stand. To please Harry, the room was cold. As a boy, he'd often slept outside in the most frightful weather. He'd hiked in the Alps and gone sailing in the Baltic. She pictured Harry again, glamorous in the bar of the Adlon Hotel. He told her he'd been to see Parsifal at the Kroll. Bashful, almost nonplussed, he had searched for something to say.

"You're a diplomat?" Johanna had asked, leading him out of the dead-end of his torment.

"A policeman," he told her.

His answer had come as an unexpected but pleasant surprise. At that moment, she liked him enormously.

PART
Two

1931

"Goebbels is the master of the blindworms and white mice."
—*Vossische Zeitung* (a Berlin daily)

9

Storm Führer Dieter Rom had heard all the Maikowski stories—
Maikowski in uniform leading Storm Troops on a rampage through a
communist pub in Wedding, stabbing one KPD thug in the eye with
his knife, another in the thigh after a bear-hug wrestling match, in
bloody confusion Maikowski pumping round after round from his pistol into massed Stapo cadres, scattering them like autumn leaves in a
thunderstorm. Rom had heard three different versions of how
Maikowski had seduced the Prussian government into allowing SA uniforms to be worn at a political rally in Schloss Kaserne, then orches-
trated a monstrous riot, a free-for-all that killed three and wounded
forty-one, just the kind of sport the SA loved and the government
despised, abhorred, was embarrassed by. Through gossip and innuendo,
Rom had even heard about some of Maikowski's tastier sexual proclivi-
ties and peccadilloes, tidbits of sexual drool that dribbled down the
party grapevine of secretaries, backbiters, and Gau leaders, reaching
Rom through the dappled sunlight and jalousied windows of rumor.

They were in a private booth at the Kaiserhof, Maikowski just in
from Munich on the early train, rushing from a general staff meeting
to plan SA strategy. Rom had picked him up at the south Bahnhof in
an SA Opel Landauer, Rom fresh in a dark blue business suit,
Maikowski in the dress brown of the SA captain. Maikowski was rail
thin, a bantam rooster kind of man with sinister bluish eyes, a long
horse face, and a prancing manner. He betrayed a slight tick in the
corner of his mouth, especially in times of stress, and sometimes
lapsed into a nascent stutter that was one-third sneer and two-thirds
bombast. In some ways, Rom admired the man's curious manner, his
brutal honesty in matters of SA policy, his wit and feeling in questions of cruelty, his ideological adroitness. Maikowski copied Hitler's
furious outbursts, his unwillingness to listen, the shuffling walk
through crowds without being afflicted by self-consciousness.
Whenever they talked, Rom got the impression that Maikowski had
an answer to every situation or problem. He would arch an eyebrow
to answer a complicated question.

Maikowski raised a cup of genuine oolong tea, available now only in expensive hotels like the Kaiserhof and Adlon. "You are to be congratulated," he told Rom, savoring the rich aroma of real tea. He abandoned his sneer for a brief moment, allowing Rom a stare of profundity. "The SA leadership appreciates your campaign against the defeatist Jewish film, its Jewish exhibitors."

For two weeks, Rom had led Storm 33 in a series of demonstrations against the commercial showing of *All Quiet on the Western Front*. Day after day, they massed in front of the Capitol Cinema and other Westend theaters, intimidating potential customers. Later, they'd exploded stink bombs in the building, let loose hundreds of white mice, frightened women, and caused a panic, a minor stampede in which dozens were slightly injured. Culminating the campaign, Rom led a march through the streets and warrens of Alt-Köln, the medieval Jewish quarter, breaking windows as they went, chasing Jews, and beating those caught. Rom had been quoted as claiming victory over the November criminals, the Jews, and degenerate modern art.

Rom watched out of the corner of his eye as several beautiful women gathered at the bar, ordering champagne and caviar. "The film campaign was child's play," Rom told Maikowski. "A mere bagatelle. The struggle continues." Rom glanced at the women, admiring their fine clothes.

"I couldn't agree more," Maikowski said. "But driving the Jewish film from Berlin deserves credit."

The Kaiserhof bar was cherry wood with mahogany wainscot. Its upper rooms contained a Hitler residence, his home away from his Munich home, housing Hitler and his entourage when the Führer was attending party conferences, planning sessions, or giving speeches. Now, on a blustery evening ripe with the threat of spring rain, snow in the Tiergarten almost entirely melted, Berliners were contemplating warmer weather. But Rom was drinking tea, contemplating not the weather but his own string of successes in the struggle, a bombastic attack on a KPD social club in Eden Palast in which two communists were badly beaten up and the club itself firebombed and destroyed. On New Year's Eve, Storm 33 had murdered two

Reichsbanner men in the Hafenlandstrasse. Word was circulating that Rom and his men were tough and incorruptible; the same word had gotten around to that effect when Maikowski had led them. Perhaps someday he would travel to Munich and hobnob with Röhm, Hitler, and Heydrich, play with Hitler's German shepherds at the Brown House or lunch with the leader at Berchtesgaden.

"Even so—" Maikowski was saying. "Every struggle has its minor battles. These too must be won. They are important. Fear and confusion emanates from our middle classes. We can turn the bourgeois into a mass that can be manipulated. We can lead them anywhere. Remember, the first principle is to declass the bourgeois. Strip a man of his class and his work, and he becomes no more than clay." Maikowski dropped his eyes to the rich brown tea, its china cup with a delicate filigree of cornflowers.

Rom nodded. He'd heard these ideological musings more times than he could count. Rom said nothing as a matter of course. He drank mineral water in deference to Hitler's asceticism.

"I'm here to talk about Bruckmann," Maikowski said. "You've told me about their new demand for funds. Your termite is an interesting case." For two years, Rom had been paying Bruckmann one hundred marks a week. On more than one occasion, his information had proved quite valuable, both to the SA and the party.

"He has produced steadily if not spectacularly," Rom said.

"But he's an expense," Maikowski replied. Like Stalin, Maikowski could hone a topic. Rom was aware of an imbalance, a range of dissonance that passed through the air like an electric arc.

"A hundred marks," Rom said noncommitally. He studied Maikowski as the man lifted his teacup. "It's little enough. Certainly the party leadership lives well with its fancy Mercedes cars, its mountain villas, its rooms in exquisite hotels." One could never go wrong extolling the virtues of SA frugality while emphasizing party lavishness. Rom paused to sip some of his mineral water. "You may recall our cadres bunked in pubs, sleeping on wooden cots, selling cigarettes in the streets."

"Ach, Rom, how could I forget?" Maikowski laughed mildly. "But don't tell me you begrudge Goebbels his apartment in Stieglitz and his bevy of actresses? You're jealous, aren't you, Rom? You're envious of the cripple's success with beautiful women!"

Rom felt his face redden, the spread more of chagrin than anger. "My grudge is against the Jews and Bolsheviks," Rom said, reverting to platitudes.

"Of course, yes, good," Maikowski said. "But I must tell you something about Bruckmann. He sells information to the Reichswehr as well. He's being paid by the SA and he is being paid by the army for the same information. A nice racket, no?"

Rom was honestly shocked. He looked up from his mineral water and said, "Are you certain of this?"

"Oh—absolutely," Maikowski said dryly. A tic appeared in the corner of his mouth. "And as we all know, the termite is not Bruckmann himself. Bruckmann is merely the conduit. Bruckmann has placed someone inside Alexanderplatz. And now the SA leadership wishes to know who that someone is, wishes to learn the true identity of the termite. It has been decided that this effort should be carried out by you, Rom."

Rom was pleased again. He forgot his momentary chagrin. "I can do this," Rom said. "I've been waiting for the chance. Frankly, I'm tired of Bruckmann and his demand for more money. He's a former army captain, so his loyalty, if he has any, is probably to the army. And besides, it would be better if we ran this termite ourselves."

"Ye—ye—ye, yes," Maikowski stuttered. Rom had the sudden sensation of being observed by the beautiful women from the bar. An object of pity, ridicule, admiration? "Bruckmann has only his calculations, and no loyalty to anyone. But I do think he calculates his chances as better with the army than with the SA. You must find a way to deal directly with the termite at Alexanderplatz. If you cannot do so, I will recommend that we end the relationship. And I would prefer not to do that. I simply feel that unless we eliminate Bruckmann, the operation is no longer secure. For one thing, we will face constant demands for more payments to Bruckmann and his termite. And there is the possibility of blackmail."

"I have a way," Rom said. "I was merely waiting for an order from leadership to execute it." He smiled expansively.

"Would you care to inform me?" Maikowski asked.

"It involves a Schwabing whore."

"You are a practical man," Maikowski said, finishing his tea and folding his arms on the table. "You must understand that the struggle against Reichswehr influence in Prussia is critical to our takeover of government. Army Chief of Staff von Bloomberg views the SA with disdain. He sees us as the chief army adversary in the political struggle. Schleicher at the Reich Ministry of War belittles our organization." Maikowski began to whisper, a snake-like hiss. "We must *own* the Prussian police. They must lick our boots and assholes! Please understand that Bruckmann is capable of selling us false information as well. It is an important task."

"You can rely on me," Rom said. "I'll eliminate Bruckmann. It will be a pleasure."

"Keep your mind clear," Maikowski snapped. He folded his hands, ready to pontificate. "This is the clear and true path: we create the Jewish question. We create the question of Bolshevik revolution to influence mass politics in Germany. We create a mass of declassed bourgeois, a mass we control. Next, we sweep away the bourgeois parliament with its rules and votes. Clear your mind to these objectives."

"My mind is clear," Rom said, secretly bored. He was thinking of his mistress named Bibi, her pendulous tits and powerful legs. He was thinking of the whore named Eva from Schwabing, her shaved pussy and blue-veined legs. He could put Eva on the night train from Munich that very evening with the promise of morphine and a warm place to sleep. He liked the simplicity of dealing with Eva.

"Crush Bruckmann like a bug," Maikowski said.

"Give me two weeks."

Maikowski stood and brushed his SA trousers, pressing the creases between two fingers. His face twitched once, and he walked from the bar without another word.

━ ━

Gunter Wulff insisted on walking from the lodge to the village for Easter services. A night rain had muddied the road. The two of them were daunted by the sullenness of the plain, its ominous wind and clouds that threatened more storms. Wulff followed his father through the mud and the new weeds, pausing to light a cigarette as the old man caught his breath. In the village church, they attended a Lutheran service, then hired a carriage for the return.

After church, they sat on the porch smoking, talking about old days, Wulff constantly reminded by some inner voice that he'd encountered a brick wall in his investigation of the Alexanderplatz termite. These days, Barlach prowled the halls of HQ while Wulff spent his time investigating security personnel, Reichswehr guards, and running down rumors with the help of his newspaper contacts. Wulff had circulated a few false stories to journalists, hoping that a sudden change in plan could be plotted on duty rosters, any subtle response by a police or Stapo captain that could be registered. In conference with Deputy Commissioner Weiss, Wulff learned that information was still leaking, tidbits here and there. In addition to the disappointments at Alexanderplatz, Wulff had reached an absolute dead end in his investigation of the Hirrenstrasse murder. He'd contacted every major police department in Germany, circulated accounts of the murder and a psychological profile of the killer, but had received nothing in return to indicate similar crimes elsewhere in the Reich. He had spent hours delving into sex crimes, but had found nothing of particular interest. Experts at Alexanderplatz subjected the doll to dozens of chemical tests, had dusted it for fingerprints, finding nothing. He had learned that the dress for the doll had been cut from the *Berlin Lokalanzeiger*, one of many Ullstein fashion magazines published in Berlin and distributed by the hundreds of thousands all over Germany at shops, department stores, outdoor kiosks, newsstands, and bookshops.

Gunter Wulff finished his afternoon nap and came downstairs, making his way slowly with a cane carved from black walnut. They sat in the brightly lighted kitchen at the back of the house. The servant Andrew had set out big bowls of rabbit stew, glasses of fresh cow's milk, freshly baked black bread, and pickled beets from the garden.

"How is Berlin now?" the old man asked. "I hardly even read a newspaper these days."

"From bad to worse."

"It is the unemployed," Gunter Wulff sighed. "It is the unemployed and their idleness."

"That and the violence," Wulff agreed.

"You continue to work for Weiss, no?"

"Uh, yes. I'm studying that problem," Wulff replied at last.

"You've made no progress, uh?" his father said. "I can see from the look on your face."

"Essentially," Wulff answered hesitantly. "It's that easy to see?"

"But you won't surrender."

"I never surrender," Wulff said.

"And Johanna?"

Hearing her name from his father's lips stunned him. He tried to imagine another world he could inhabit if only for a brief amount of time. "I'm in love with her," Wulff said.

"I *am* sympathetic, you know," Gunter Wulff told him. "As I grow older, certain prejudices mean less and less to me. An old man can ignore the opinions of others. I've just attended church with my trousers flaked by mud." He paused, listening to the first plink of a raindrop on the roof. "But I am old now. For a young man, what others think is often critical."

"I'm aware of what they think," Wulff said.

"You are a stubborn boy."

"I wonder where I came by it?"

Gunter Wulff smiled. "Your mother, no doubt!" he laughed. "Harry, I may have been a colonel in the German army, but she ruled the house. Make no mistake."

Wulff dunked a chunk of black bread into the stew and savored its smell. He chewed the bread and washed it down with milk. The day outside was leaden.

"I'm leaving early," Wulff said.

The old man closed his eyes, thinking. "Then I must tell you something important. I have made some subtle inquiries with the staff at Reichswehr Intelligence."

Wulff raised an eyebrow. "You have?"

"I still have many friends there," Gunter Wulff continued. "Former colleagues. I have given and received many favors in my day. But I have granted far more favors than I have received."

"It must be quite difficult for you to ask," Wulff said. "I'm sorry to put you through it."

"No, no—you must understand," Gunter Wulff protested. "Perhaps I can help you after all. I have learned that the Reichswehr does have a source inside Alexanderplatz. But I am not certain that my information can help you find this termite. Apparently the source of the army's information is outside your HQ and only receives it from a conduit. The army pays a small price to this conduit each week. Even the highest levels of intelligence don't know the identity of the actual termite. Only the identity of the conduit."

"But there *is* a conduit."

"Yes, Harry. I have located the conduit."

"Can you tell me his name?"

"Yes, Harry," Gunter Wulff said. "But I think you are going to be disappointed. The conduit who is selling information about confidential police activity at Alexanderplatz HQ is Kriminal Oberkommissar Erik Bruckmann from your office at Berlin Mitte. I'm told the information itself is sparse, but some of it is useful. Bruckmann claims to be a loyal army man, but the army is certain he isn't. They think he sells this information to other bidders. But they do know he gets his information from inside. For now, the Reichswehr does not know the identity of this termite."

Wulff felt betrayed, part of an elaborate charade. He thought suddenly of Johanna, the two of them strolling peacefully through bird-thronged space in the Tiergarten, oblivious to the surrounding metropolis. The doll crossed his mind, its terrible significance. "I've examined Bruckmann's dossier," Gunter Wulff said. "Bruckmann began his army career in the cavalry corps. He advanced into Belgium and was wounded severely." Gunter Wulff lifted a spoonful of rabbit stew. "He formed a fifth column of Flemish traitors, Belgian prisoners of war who were tortured to force them to inform on their own staffs. In return, they received sensitive positions in the refugee administration."

"I'm told Bruckmann was useful in the war," Gunter Wulff said. "I had a rough idea of his duties." Gunter Wulff dabbed the corner of his mouth with a linen napkin and pushed away from the table. He grabbed his cane, and Wulff followed his father outside to the porch where they sat in identical wooden deck chairs. The brownish moors stretched away on every side. A single car passed on the road far away. "Bruckmann used torture," Gunter Wulff said. "I once disbelieved the rumors of army complicity in his activities. I believed they were propaganda from the English. My own men were honorable to a fault. But I think Bruckmann was not so honorable. You must push forward your inquiry. I have made my own inquiry and asked my question. There are sure to be rumors on the staff. Some may reach the command's ear, and your termite may disappear. Or some rumors may reach Bruckmann."

"Bruckmann already knows. He was there when I discussed this assignment with Weiss."

"Ah, then it is a game, Harry," Gunter Wulff said. "The Reichswehr watches the SA and the SA watches the army. The police watch the SA and the SA watches the police, and the Reichswehr also watches the police. All three spy on one another regularly. Perhaps this is the definition of modern democracy!"

"Parliament is not to blame," Wulff said. "What has this inquiry cost you, Father?"

"You mean—?" Gunter Wulff asked, haltingly. "Ah, will someone come to my door and shoot me between the eyes with a Mauser?" He laughed. "No, son, nobody will come to my door with a gun and shoot me between the eyes. But the Reichswehr knows that my son is a police officer. Intelligence would not have told me about Bruckmann unless they meant you to know as well. I assume Bruckmann sells his information to the SA as well, and that it proves much more useful to the SA than it proves to the army. If this weren't so, I would not have been told. I am a conduit to you, just as Bruckmann is a conduit to the SA. Isn't it amusing, Harry, how few secrets there are in a secretive country like ours?"

Wulff had to smile. "I'll watch Bruckmann carefully," he said. "He'll lead me to his termite."

"Soon, I trust."

Wulff smoked another cigarette. Wild weather was coming. He'd have to catch his ferry before it hit. "Why don't you come to Berlin?

We could go to the opera. Perhaps you'd like to let an apartment as well. I could watch out for your health. The winters here are bad."

"Watch out for me!" Gunter Wulff laughed. "For that I have Andrew."

"What about the opera? Your old city friends? Louis Adlon asks about you often."

"Those days are over, Harry," Gunter Wulff said.

"They don't have to be."

"Oh yes, Harry, they do."

Wulff wanted to argue, but knew it was useless.

"Old age suits me, Harry," Gunter Wulff said. "The present instability of the world hardly matters. Its flux is nothing." He shrugged and struggled up, cane in hand. "But for someone young it must be a madhouse of torment."

— ‐ —

At seven o'clock, Barlach signed out with the duty officer at Alexanderplatz HQ. He was numb from hours poring over personnel files, a chronological ordering of directives from Weiss, he and Wulff looking for anomalies, correspondence, backgrounds, oddities. He paused on the steps of HQ and buttoned his overcoat, then walked down the marble staircase. Barlach crossed the square, and skirted its subway construction. The sun had set and the evening was blustery, the sky darkly blue. By now, most commuters had caught their trams and buses, and the streets were growing quiet. In front of local pubs, groups of the unemployed gathered to drink and discuss politics.

At the end of Hirrenstrasse, Barlach watched a tram offload its few passengers coming in from the suburbs. One of them, a tall stoop-shouldered man wearing an overcoat and watchcap, walked with a slow gait toward Barlach, looking as though he'd trudged down Hirrenstrasse for centuries, hands in pockets, barely looking up as he paced the brick street. Barlach paused near a grocery and watched the man with a growing sense of déjà vu. As the man approached, Barlach met his eyes, exchanged what passed for a look of recognition, a momentary inkblot of psychological connection. Barlach waited for him to pass, then crossed the street and fell into line behind the man, who approached the Alexanderplatz, walking faster now. Barlach halted at the edge of the square, observing as the man ascended HQ's marble stairs, passed through the first Reichswehr checkpoint, then signed in with the duty officer just inside the heavy glass doors.

Barlach frowned inwardly, concentrating on whatever it was that had captured his attention. The man? Something in his own memory? He made a mental note to check the personnel files for a photograph and history. It was Monday, and Wulff would be returning from his Easter visit to the Baltic. Barlach decided that this chance encounter on the Hirrenstrasse was something that should be mentioned to the Kriminal Kommissar.

Barlach glanced up at the Bahnhof clock tower. It was late. His wife would be worried. Such a life! Grubbing for termites!

— —

The red Wertheim department store sign went dark suddenly. The square plunged into black, a distinct moon glow outlining each building, the shadows of the chestnut trees, beggars wrapped in thin cloth coats. Loos stood in shadow, exploring the haunted feelings that tormented him, a sense of being observed from a great distance. A nagging fear came over him as he remembered his mother lifting him onto a wooden bench in their hut as she examined him like a microbe before dressing him in the Virgin's clothes—a blue hand-stitched mantle and white head-cloth. He took off his overcoat, threw it over his shoulder, and cradled the watchcap under an arm. Two Reichswehr guards looked at him curiously. There had been a dozen people in the square as Loos crossed. Which one had been watching him?

During the Great War, he had been sent to a displaced persons camp, suffering from severe head lice and malnutrition. One day, Bruckmann had come to the tumble-down barracks where the prisoners were housed and had offered him a cup of corn gruel with ersatz sausages, even a gristle of burnt beef. Something in their mutual glance revealed itself immediately, a shared intimacy without words. Above the wooden cot he slept on had been a sign, hand-lettered: EDGAR BRAUN, displaced person. Belgian national.

Bruckmann assigned a nurse to Braun, singling him out for special treatment, medical attention, regular food rations, and thorough delousing by a medical unit attached to German cavalry. In two weeks, Bruckmann arranged for Braun to be transferred to another camp in Germany, this time for Belgian prisoners of war, almost all of them officers. Braun's career began in earnest then, a short test period of spying on the officers, reporting their conversations, passing on gossip to higher authority. He cajoled them with his penchant for self-deprecation. And then he would report to Bruckmann. Almost at once, he enjoyed his position, his specialized role as traitor and spy, a former vagabond and locksmith now in charge of miscommunication, falsehood, and deceit. Later, at a camp in the Ypres salient, Bruck-mann had taught his young protégé the art of the garrote, how one could wind a corded noose around a man's neck, tighten it slowly, release it just at the point of unconsciousness, then repeat the process over and over again until a confession poured from an exhausted pris-oner like hymns from a true believer. What was Edgar Braun besides the sum total of all the pain he'd ever experienced?

The end of the old days—he recalled it, a gray day late in 1923. It was raining, and leaves were blowing against the windshield of an armored vehicle. In front sat Edgar Braun with Bruckmann driving, both wearing muddy field uniforms. Braun was ill with the flu, his skin damp to the touch. Bruckmann had given him some black-market penicillin. They sat outside a clinic, mud smearing the windshield.

"The game is over," Bruckmann had said to Braun. "I'm going to Berlin."

"And what about me?" Braun asked. "I've worked for Germany," he said.

"They'll kill you in Belgium," Bruckmann replied.

"Fucking idiot!" Braun cried. "Of course they'll kill me in Belgium. That's what I'm talking about."

"I've made an arrangement," Bruckmann said, smiling slowly, drawing out the suspense.

A body of nuns surrounded their muddy vehicle, glancing at them furtively.

"This arrangement," Braun said. "It benefits me?"

"Come to Berlin," Bruckmann said. "There is an arrangement there which might be of some benefit to you."

"And what is this arrangement?"

"See up there," Bruckmann said, gesturing to a second-story window. "This is a clinic. Once it was a Jesuit boys' school. Behind that window is a boy named Theodor Loos. He is precisely your age, Edgar. Precisely." Bruckmann lifted his gaze, a comprehending gesture that revealed the scar on his neck. "He is said to be dying of influenza. On the other hand, there is a chance he will recover. This boy is not only your age, but very similar in physical characteristics. One can only ponder his chances of recovery. Are they any better than fifty-fifty?"

"You tell me," Braun growled.

"I would say much less than fifty-fifty."

The nuns had gone. Now the muddy street was deserted, swept by a relentless rain. One could smell the bitterness of winter.

"There is more?" Braun asked.

"Oh, much more. This fellow Loos is a German national. His father is a good German and his mother a Belgian from the upper middle class. Think of it, Edgar! Up there a boy who looks like you and is just your age lies dying. He speaks Flemish and German just as you speak Flemish and German."

"What about the nuns?" Braun asked.

"They fear the Freicorps," Bruckmann said. "They believe me when I tell them Theodor Loos is one of ours."

"They fear us," Braun repeated.

"I have his papers and documents," Bruckmann said. "His older brother is in the camps. They are separated in age by twenty years. And the parents are both dead. Is this not a marvelous circumstance, Edgar?"

They left the vehicle and walked upstairs through cold stone halls. In one high-ceilinged room were thirty cots, fifteen on each side. The dying were behind temporary partitions.

The sick boy's face was flushed and damp with sweat. He had a pencil-thin moustache and a head of wavy black hair. The nuns had covered him with an army-issue gray blanket pulled to his neck. Bruckmann handed Braun an envelope. "His passport, birth certificate, military discharge," Bruckmann said.

Braun studied the passport photo, a passable likeness of himself. One thumbprint.

"What about the print?" Braun asked.

"Nothing is perfect," Bruckmann told him quietly.

"Who is he?"

"In another life, he worked on boilers. He had studied civil engineering for two years at Lille. You could learn about boilers, couldn't you Edgar?"

"A glorified janitor," Braun said.

"They say everyday life is worse than war."

"And what is this everyday life I'm joining?"

"I'm becoming a policeman," Bruckmann said. "The way for me has been paved by politicians in Berlin. If you wish to follow me there, I can place you in one of the ministries as a maintenance man."

Braun picked up a pillow. Loos had opened his eyes and was staring vacantly at his visitors. Braun placed the pillow over the sick man's face.

"You are a rare creature," Bruckmann said.

Braun looked up. "He does not struggle," Braun said.

"I wish you much profit from your new identity, Theodor," Bruckmann said.

Braun increased the pressure. He sensed himself becoming Theodor Loos, suddenly catapulted into a new life by strength of will. The real Loos lifted a shaky hand, but soon let it drop.

In that way, Edgar Braun became Theodor Loos.

10

Spring's sudden brightness pleased Wulff. After four days of implacable Baltic gray, the brilliant blue sky and lucid yellow sunshine presented another world to him, a different planet in a new solar system. In some ways, it could have been a bygone and more colorful Germany, where at any moment the Kaiser and his entourage might round a corner, the King on his Belgian stud at the head of the Imperial guard, legions of adoring city folk admiring its precision, waving handkerchiefs, small Reich flags, and banners with patriotic slogans.

Wulff looked up from his reverie as Barlach tossed a crumb of bread to a squadron of head-ducking pigeons. They were sitting on a bench in the Tiergarten, not far from a busy news kiosk beneath the Brandenburg Gate. Wulff had bought a copy of the *Frankfurter Zeitung*, which he considered the best paper in Germany. There was news of the financial crisis and an American depression that was driving foreign investment out of Germany, banks calling international loans.

"May I inquire about your father's health?" Barlach asked tentatively.

"My father is quite well, thank you," Wulff told him.

On the Chausee edge stood a young girl with a homemade sign around her neck on a string. On it, she'd printed in careful German script: IN NEED OF WORK. CAN DO STENOGRAPHY, TYPING. OF EXCELLENT CHARACTER. PLEASE HELP ME. Wulff studied her sad face, its pronounced longing. Wulff folded the newspaper and stuck it in his coat pocket. "According to the newspaper, we'll all be poverty-stricken soon," he said, then added, "I've made a break in the case."

Barlach raised his head in surprise. The Charlottenburg tram passed, every seat empty. The municipal government had raised fares for passengers and lowered salaries for employees, conductors, and drivers. Trade unions had demonstrated, but were ignored. A saying had circulated among the workers that only pigeons could afford to ride the trams. Goebbels had toured the city, accusing Jewish financiers of causing the banking and labor crisis. Broadsheets were filled with anti-Semitic invective.

"You've made a break?" Barlach asked. "We've missed something in all this work?"

"No. I've received inside information from the army. This must be kept in strictest confidence. There is no excuse to tell anyone, not your wife, not your captain."

"You can trust me, Kriminal Kommissar."

"Our Alexanderplatz termite has an outside conduit."

"A conduit, sir?"

"A handler, if you will."

"And do you know who this is?"

"Kriminal Oberkommissar Bruckmann," Wulff said.

Barlach blanched. "A member of Department IV?"

"I have it on authority."

"How could such a thing happen?"

Wulff shook his head. "Bruckmann is a veteran of the Reichswehr. I know his past."

"You've seen his dossier?"

"I haven't," Wulff said. "But I know what it contains."

"I understand," Barlach said.

"At any rate, Bruckmann has old loyalties to the army. Perhaps they are not loyalties, but at least they are connections. For several years, he has been selling inside police information to Intelligence. His information includes deployment plans for Stapo and Orpo cadres, as well as long-range strategic political goals."

"But how did you discover this?"

Wulff clapped his hands softly. "Never mind that," Wulff said. "But Bruckmann sells the same information to the Nazis and the SA. The Reichswehr has lost patience with this situation." Wulff watched some mountain jays cavort in the pines and firs of the Tiergarten. They were massive birds with fluffy blue breasts and sharp gray beaks. In tandem, they issued sharp cries.

"Why would he sell information to the SA?"

"For money. Nothing else."

"What shall we do?" Barlach asked. "Should we follow him and discover his contact?"

"*You'll* follow him," Wulff said. "Of course, he'd spot me in a moment. But you he won't recognize. And I've told him nothing about my assistant. So, unless your own Schupo captain has told him, your identity is still secret."

"There are only rumors in my unit," Barlach said. "I have been away from duty for months now. But my captain is solidly behind me on this."

"All right then," Wulff said. "In this we have no choice. I want you to begin your surveillance of Bruckmann."

"Immediately, sir?"

Wulff had made some condensed notes on Bruckmann, his habits, his address, and his duties at Mitte. He handed them to Barlach, who tucked the small sheet of note paper in his pocket after studying it. In truth, Wulff knew little of Bruckmann's personal life beyond his home address, license tag number, and hours of work. He would allow Barlach the pleasure of discovering Bruckmann's inner nature.

"Here's what we'll do," Wulff said. "I'll keep an eye on Bruckmann during the days, his hours at Mitte. You be prepared to follow him after he leaves the office every afternoon, and during his lunches. I'll get you an extra stipend so that you can take taxis when he drives. If he takes a meal, take one yourself at a discreet distance. I don't think Bruckmann would meet his termite during working hours, but he might. Anything is possible. When Bruckmann retires for the night, I'll take over the surveillance. That way you can go home and get some sleep. We'll have his movements covered twenty-four hours a day."

Wulff stood and buckled his leather coat. The jays were making a frightful racket. He had read that they feasted on pigeon's eggs and the live young of other species.

Barlach crossed Wulff's path. "About the Hirrenstrasse murder," he said. They began a slow walk in the direction of the Charlottenburg Chausee. "I'm wondering if you've made any progress, sir?"

"Every department in Germany has my bulletin," Wulff answered. "There are no similar crimes." Wulff had not told Barlach about the doll.

"I've seen a man—" Barlach said quietly.

They passed the stenographer with her homemade placard. They could see her skin now, its unhealthy pallor, and her red-rimmed eyes. She fixed Wulff with a hopeful smile. Wulff, sick inside, felt anger at the fate of Germany's young girls.

"You were saying?" Wulff asked, distracted.

"I was on the Hirrenstrasse, and I saw a man getting off the inbound Grenadier tram at seven o'clock in the evening on a work day. Last Friday night in fact. I think because it was Friday night I thought about it, what with the murder occurring on that night and all."

"Just a man?"

"He looked familiar," Barlach said. "I thought I recognized him. Perhaps it was just a feeling. But it seemed to me he hurried on."

"A feeling, you say?" Wulff was trying to concentrate, but his attention kept wandering to the unemployed secretary.

"I was leaving Alexanderplatz," Barlach said. "It was early evening, and most people were leaving the city for the suburbs. On Grenadier, there must have been twenty people waiting to get on the tram, but only a handful got off. The ones who got off scattered to the wind, and only one of them came down the Hirrenstrasse toward me. That's probably why I noticed. It was Friday, and the murder occurred at about that time. I thought it was strange. It had a uniqueness that settled in my head. I'm being ridiculous."

"Not at all," Wulff said encouragingly. "Do you have a hypothesis to go with this observation?"

"This man looked at me for an instant. I stood beneath a tobacconist's awning, and he looked at me. I followed him down the street to the square. He crossed the square."

"And who is this man?"

"I don't know, sir. He was a large man, stoop-shouldered and wearing an overcoat and watchcap. Workingman's clothing. He went up the steps of HQ."

"An employee of the Metropolitan Police?"

"It looks that way," Barlach said. "I thought I might review some photographs."

"Let me know what you learn," Wulff said.

They reached Sieges Alee, where the Charlottenburg Chausee bordered the Tiergarten. Idle carriages were waiting for nonexistent tourists. The horses stood steaming, harried and haggard-looking with their noses down. Wulff clapped Barlach on the shoulder. "Did you choose this new suit yourself?" he laughed.

"My wife, sir," Barlach said. "I wouldn't know tweed from velvet."

"Now you look like a real detective," Wulff told him.

Barlach glanced down at his suit pants, spreading his hands on the material. He beamed ashamedly, caught himself, and looked up again. An open charabanc passed them with two passengers in a van built for thirty or more tourists. Here now—Wulff thought—was Berlin as it should be, a cold salty wind in the trees, blue sky, leafing chestnuts, and a heavy dose of spruce in the air. Wulff wondered if these two tourists would notice the stenographer, a placard hanging around her neck like an accusation. He wondered if they would pity the starving horses or fear the Brown Shirts hawking cigarettes at the base of the Brandenburg gate.

━ ━

Johanna wore a cream-beige skirt with a white silk blouse buttoned to her neck and a pale lilac-colored sweater thrown over her shoulders. They were sitting at an outdoor table at the Café Schön on Unter den Linden. The weather was chilly, and there were only a few customers. Johanna ordered spinach and radishes, and a plate of country mushrooms neither of them could afford. Wulff was drinking an Alsatian beer.

"Oh darling, the banks are closing," Johanna said. Her eyes were bright and brimming. Before lunch, they'd made feverish and hurried love standing up in the hallway of Johanna's Lennestrasse apartment. "Do you think all the banks will close?" she asked him.

"You mustn't worry, dear," he told her soothingly. "There is nothing to do about it."

"They've closed the banks in America," she said. The waiter brought their spinach and radishes, a small yellow plate lined by morels. "If the banks close in America, the banks will close in Germany."

Wulff had spent an early morning delving into Bruckmann's Reichswehr career. He was sorting for clues, poking through the moral rubble of a life in the Freicorps, bringing his captain into focus. He was on the verge of asking his father to ferret out the actual Freicorps material, something that the army considered its darkest secret. It seemed reckless to ask his father for another favor, but he pondered his choices.

"Shall we withdraw our savings after lunch?" Wulff teased. Wulff was having corn soup. Two Schupo wandered by, twirling truncheons and staring innocently at the deserted café. Wulff remembered meeting Johanna at the Schön when they were first lovers. One could hardly find a table. Now the place was empty, waiters lurking in dark corners. The café had struck down its prices and fired staff. "I want to ask you something," he said. "Do you remember our Hirrenstrasse murder?"

"How could I forget?"

"I've made no progress since we talked," Wulff said. "I've sent bulletins all over Germany. Nothing is coming back. It makes me think our killer is unique."

"I think I told you that," Johanna scolded him.

"I'm still rather surprised."

"I wish I could help you more," Johanna said. "But without knowing the specifics of his childhood and running some written tests, I can't say much. It may be that this crime is his first and that it was a chance occurrence. Perhaps he has committed crimes before, but this one seems to articulate a special pain. Of course, I'm just guessing."

"I tend to agree now. But I don't understand."

"It was unplanned, Harry," Johanna said. "But in some ways this crime bubbled up from somewhere deep in this man's subconscious. In a sense, it was formulated long ago."

"Planned in a sense, only unconsciously."

"I would think so," Johanna said. "After all, there is no such thing as an accident for the unconscious mind."

"And he will kill again."

"Oh I think so, Harry, if he has the chance. The doll is proof that he's proud of his accomplishment. He'll try to work himself up to another similar murder. It is possible it could take years for him to find a suitable target, something that fits the pattern of his childhood memories. You yourself know that he is likely to be arrested for some other crime and spend time in jail with no opportunity to kill again. But if he has the chance, he will."

"Could he be drawn out?"

"Drawn out? How do you mean, dear?"

"You've told me he's only now reaching his potential as a killer. When he kissed that transvestite, something in his head was released into the real world. Now, it's back in hiding temporarily. I want to do something to provoke him, bring him out before he's ready. Perhaps he'll make a mistake. Do you think he could be drawn out in this way?"

"Provoke him how?" Johanna asked. "This could be a very dangerous thing. This strangulation is a kind of metaphor isn't it? The choking of something that tries to come out into the world."

"He chokes bad messages," Wulff said.

"Something like that."

"So, perhaps his anger could be channeled at *me*."

Johanna stiffened. "*Please* don't continue, dear."

"Listen, Johanna, please," Wulff said, touching her hand across the white linen tablecloth. She turned away, pretending to watch the avenue, its trams and idle carriages. "The doll was sent to *me*," Wulff continued. "If you're right about the reason, then the killer's anger may be against an absent father, the one who didn't protect him from danger, the one he resents. The father who abandoned him to a mother with some kind of illness. This father must be exorcized."

"These are only guesses, Harry," Johanna said. "They are not clinical observations. They are not *scientific*. I wish you wouldn't take my ramblings so seriously. I certainly don't."

"But can I bait him? Make him focus on me?"

"Too dangerous. For you both."

"I want to stop him before he kills another innocent person. If baiting transfers his anger to me, then why couldn't it work?"

Johanna fixed him with a forced smile. "I'm not a frivolous person, Harry," she said. "But I have to tell you that you are spoiling a perfectly lovely lunch. I was going to tell you about my two neurotic

Jewish housewife patients. They've come back to treatment, Harry, no longer afraid to walk the streets. Besides, their husbands own banks that are about to close for a week. I wonder what will happen to these ladies when the banks close?"

"We've changed the subject?" Wulff said.

Johanna stabbed a radish and crunched it angrily in her teeth. "His rage would be hard to direct," she said finally. "This killer is probably already fixed on someone else. Perhaps a cross-dresser or transvestite. It is someone who represents deep trauma in his past." She put down her fork and contemplated the spring day. "Precisely what are you thinking of doing, dear?"

"A planted newspaper article," Wulff said. "Our friend Kisch would put something in if I asked."

"You'd call out a killer? You'd force this man into an open contest?"

"It's a thought," Wulff smiled.

"Use his fear of homosexuality?"

"It occurred to me."

"Focus his rage on you? The investigator?"

Wulff put on a mock frown. "I think you get the idea," he said. He could tell that a change of mood had come over her, something beyond this discussion of the killer. Far from alienating him, Johanna's moods fascinated Wulff, affording him an opportunity for deeper intuition into the forces which moved her. He shrugged and touched her hand. "It may mean nothing," Wulff said.

"This is dangerous, Harry," Johanna said.

"But could it be done?"

"I'd hate to theorize," she said.

"Does that mean you think it is a bad idea?" Wulff put down his spoon. "What I want to know is this. If I antagonize our killer in the press, will this increase the danger to others?"

Johanna smiled. "I'm a coward on your behalf, Harry darling," she said.

At that moment, a mother and daughter approached Wulff asking for money. The little girl was pale with skinny stick arms and legs, a dirty face, her hair plastered down and unwashed. Such a thing had never happened on Unter den Linden within Wulff's memory. He gave them each a mark and watched helplessly as they shuffled off toward the Brandenburg Gate.

— ⁓

Barlach sat uncomfortably on a marble bench near the Berlin Mitte entrance, just off the courtyard of the Interior Ministry, where he had a clear view north and south of Department IV. If he strained, he could see Bruckmann's blue police Opel parked in a space near Wilhelmstrasse. For most of the morning, Barlach had been buried in the bowels of Alexanderplatz HQ, looking at photographs of employees, trying to locate a face he'd recognized from the Hirrenstrasse. He was looking for a large man with prominent ears, narrow-set eyes, and black disheveled hair that needed to be cut. Of course, Barlach knew, he could have been a visitor to headquarters, one of the many who came and went during the course of any business day. Barlach knew he could check the duty roster, but he didn't want to speak to the guards until he'd run out of options.

Just at three o'clock, when Barlach was about to leave his observation perch, Bruckmann strode out the front door of the Mitte offices and walked up the Wilhelmstrasse, almost catching Barlach's eye as he passed. Barlach let him go, then followed half a block behind, both men walking past the French Embassy and Gymnasium, the facades of consular offices, buildings with gray granite walls and yellow shutters on huge French windows, shiny black cars in parking spaces out front. It was cloudless and sunny and a bit chilly, and Barlach had broken a sweat of anticipation.

Barlach was a bit surprised when Bruckmann left the Spree bridge overpass and walked down the quay steps toward the river itself. Barlach waited up top, leaning an elbow on the granite support, watching as Bruckmann descended down toward the water. Fifty meters down the embankment, Barlach saw Bruckmann purchase a ticket at the kiosk, stride over the gangplank of one of the glass-topped tour boats that plied the river in spring and summer, then take a seat in the stern away from the cabin and other passengers. He waited for five minutes until the tour boat pulled away from its mooring and chugged upriver toward the cathedral.

Barlach watched the shallow-draft motor launch cruise through a slipstream of wake, bouncing over the brick-colored river water. Why would Bruckmann take a tour boat during the middle of the day? And Bruckmann had arrived at one of its many stops just in time to hop aboard and depart, indicating that he'd known the schedule in advance. Barlach knew that the tour boat made a dozen stops on its journey upriver through Berlin, heading east, then southeast toward the Monbijou Palace and grounds, the Comic Opera, Imperial Palace, and finally the Kaiser Wilhelm Cathedral. Passengers could embark and disembark at any of those stopping points. Nevertheless, the tour boat was not a commuter vessel. Its prices were much too steep, its journey much too slow, and accompanied by a constant running commentary on Berlin's points of interest.

The boat rounded a riverbend and was gone. Barlach cursed his luck in not having the four-mark fare. His appropriation from Weiss had not come through.

Loos bought a ticket at the Lustgarten stop. He crossed the temporary gangplank and walked to the stern of the vessel, sitting two seats away from Bruckmann. Bruckmann got up and leaned against the wooden railing, studying the spires of the cathedral. There were a dozen or so English tourists on the boat, most of them on bench-seats under the glass-topped roof toward the bow.

"Good afternoon, Theodor," Bruckmann said, his back turned. A tour guide was intoning facts about the cathedral through a bullhorn. Geese sat on the embankment. "Do you have something for me?"

"The Jew Weiss is preparing to present a plan to the Reichstag through the Prussian Ministry of Interior. This plan will propose breaking the rule of immunity for Reichstag members. He harbors dreams of arresting the Nazi members who create turmoil on the floor of the Parliament."

Bruckmann turned, leaning back against the rail as he followed a flock of pigeons with his eyes. "This is very good, Theodor," he said. "This will please our Nazi friends enormously."

"What about the money?" Loos said. "I'm tired of taking these risks for twenty-five marks a week."

Bruckmann left the rail and sat down a row ahead of Loos. He handed him a tourist brochure into which he'd stuffed twenty-five marks. Loos took the brochure and put it in the pocket of his overcoat. "I've always wondered how you manage to assemble these bits of information," he asked Loos.

"My business," Loos growled. He locked Bruckmann with a harsh stare. "And I want a hundred marks."

"Twenty-five is what they pay," Bruckmann said. Of course, he had been receiving two hundred a week from the Reichswehr and SA combined, a tidy profit from the risk of Loos. "I can ask for more, and I have. They are contemplating this request. But we mustn't kill our golden goose, Theodor."

"Not so golden if you had to take the risk," Loos said.

"Twenty-five marks is a fortune these days, Theodor," Bruckmann said. "Tell me you don't have fun with your money?"

The boat halted in front of the Palace. Tourists fled to starboard, clicking their cameras. A child wandered to the stern and stood looking at the two seated men. He grinned wickedly, stuck out his tongue, and smiled. It was an English child with bad teeth from too much chocolate.

"Piss on your twenty-five marks," Loos said angrily.

"You must be patient," Bruckmann insisted. "There is another revolution in the air, Theodor. Either the Reichswehr or the SA will be the victor. When it comes, we will be on the winning side." Bruckmann turned, offering his puppet a winning smile of encouragement. "I'll ask the SA again when I deliver this information. It could save their deputies in Parliament a lot of trouble."

"Be certain you do," Loos said.

Bruckmann left the boat at the Palace stop. He walked up the steps of the quay and onto the edge of Schlossplatz in heavy pedestrian traffic. As usual, Loos would ride the boat back to the Reichstag bridge, then take a tram home to Lichtenberg.

11

Bruckmann walked to the Fisherhof in Alt-Köln, a tottering wood-and-brick hotel in the medieval quarter, making his way through the narrow streets with a keen sense of alertness. He found the lobby of the hotel dusty and deserted, a clerk drowsing in the midday silence, and in the bar, only Rom and a beefy bartender who was toweling a glass with bored distraction. Rom turned from his table in the corner, the SA leader sitting by himself in a patch of sunshine near a window, over his shoulder a box full of neglected geraniums. As usual, Rom was not wearing his SA uniform, preferring instead a crisp double-breasted blue suit with a single pink carnation in its lapel. As a meeting place, this old hotel in the Jewish section was Rom's private joke.

"You're early," Bruckmann said. "I suppose you tried to follow me, or have me followed."

"Nonsense," Rom said. He was sipping a cup of sweet black Russian tea.

Bruckmann sat down opposite Rom, who had his back to the fly-specked window.

"Just don't ever try it," Bruckmann warned.

"You're a born paranoid," Rom said, smiling. "I've brought you a present. She's upstairs now, soaping her pussy."

Bruckmann laughed quietly and glanced back at the bartender, who was still wiping glasses. "You are a mind-reader, my friend," Bruckmann said.

"It isn't your mind I read," Rom told him. "And I would never have you followed. It wouldn't be worth it. I want us to trust one another."

"Our termite is very protective of his identity," Bruckmann said. Prevarication had become a second skin, as natural to him as water to a duck. "He will stop working for you at one word from me."

"You've made this clear," Rom said. "I'm not certain I understand your current hostility, old friend. Have we not been partners in business for several years now? Do we not trust one another after all this time?" Rom touched his teacup, pursued its half-moonish areas of color with his eyes. "Remember, when the movement gains power, people like you and me will benefit."

The bartender approached, a dirty towel draped over one arm. "Gentlemen?" he said.

"You'll have a schnapps, won't you?" Rom said. "Bring the gentleman a schnapps. And not that filthy stuff you sell the Jews and communists."

Bruckmann nodded at Rom, amused. When the bartender had gone, Bruckmann said, "I have something special for you."

"A pleasant beginning," Rom said.

"Ah, but we must make a new agreement."

"This new agreement," Rom said coldly. "I assume it's the one we've talked about before. Based on the seriousness of the risk." Rom was reasonably certain that Bruckmann was selling his information to the army as well as the SA, something Rom might have done himself had their positions been reversed.

"And?" Bruckmann said simply.

"One hundred marks a week is a substantial sum," Rom said. He was amusing himself, cat-and-mousing the situation.

"Have we not spared Goebbels himself considerable embarrassment?"

"On occasion," Rom admitted.

"Now I must have more money."

"Times are hard," Rom protested. In fact, the SA was flush with cash from its insurance and protection schemes, its cigarette-peddling rackets, the selling of soap, margarine, ersatz coffee, kickbacks from shop owners, politicians, construction unions, and tradesmen. Some SA units even ran prostitutes through local pubs. "The banks are closing as we speak," Rom said.

"Rumor has it that Goebbels is fucking Magda Quandt," Bruckmann said. "She is a wealthy woman."

"But Goebbels is not SA," Rom said. "Surely we are talking about the SA now. Poor as church mice."

"Piss on Goebbels then," Bruckmann said, gesticulating. "And piss on your precious party and piss on your precious SA. I want twice as much each week. The risk is enormous. And the information is juicy this week. You won't be sorry."

"Blackmail, Bruckmann? Please."

Bruckmann had warmed to his task. When the bartender brought the schnapps in a small, gold-rimmed glass, Bruckmann lifted it and examined it thoughtfully in the light, tilted back his head, and downed the contents in one gulp.

"I'll speak with Maikowski again. But I think you can count on two hundred," Rom said.

"Talk to him then," Bruckmann said. "I should have thought you'd have talked to him before now."

"He's been away on business. Perhaps you could impart your new information now as a matter of trust between old business partners. I promise you that you will receive your two hundred."

Bruckmann turned, signaling for the bartender. The balding man poured another schnapps and delivered it to Bruckmann, who cupped it greedily in both hands. "The Jew has written a memorandum," he said. "Weiss is proposing to arrest the Nazi leadership in Parliament for wearing their brown shirts on the floor in contravention of the Prussian edict. He will present this proposal to Hindenburg through the Interior Ministry."

"Our nemesis Jew," Rom said.

Bruckmann drank half of his schnapps. Rom had concluded that this policeman already had turned his mind's attention to the Schwabing whore upstairs, her shaved pubis and stringy blond hair. "Worth two hundred and more, isn't it?" Bruckmann said.

"The Prussian government will never carry it off," Rom said.

"Even so—" Bruckmann shrugged. "It is an interesting idea to arrest the Nazis on the floor of the Reichstag."

"And what of the immunity law?"

Bruckmann waved impatiently. "I told you I wanted two hundred marks. You'd best speak to Maikowski."

"You say Weiss is *contemplating* arrests?"

"I've made myself quite clear."

"Why only contemplating?" Rom asked, dragging the conversation out for strategic reasons, toying with Bruckmann, filling the void between them with implications. "You're not speaking of issued orders are you? And how do you get these choice pieces of information?"

"I am being accurate," Bruckmann said impatiently. "Never mind how my termite learns this."

"An accurate truth!" Rom laughed.

"And further," Bruckmann said, feeling both annoyed and belittled, "Weiss proposes to station Orpo armored units around the Reichstag during those arrests, which will be carried out by the criminal police of Kripo. It would make for an interesting political drama."

"You're saying these arrests are merely for show?"

"I don't know," Bruckmann said. "Immunity can be waived only on order from the president."

"Hindenburg will never oblige this socialist Prussian government and its Jewish Deputy Police Commissioner."

Bruckmann and Rom laughed, sharing a tension-lifting joke. Bruckmann contemplated a nearby window, its intricate pattern of fingerprints and squashed flies. He felt a cloud forming in his head, something that was shutting off the sunlight to his brain.

"Are you quite all right, Bruckmann?" Rom asked.

"Yes, quite all right," Bruckmann insisted. He licked his lips, which had grown unnaturally dry. "I feel a bit light-headed is all. I'm presuming that Goebbels will marry his rich society whore." He coughed once and touched his forehead. "Actually, she's quite attractive, a true Aryan specimen. I wonder what she sees in that club-footed dwarf?"

"You mustn't say such things, Bruckmann," Rom laughed. "One day that dwarf may run this city."

"Run this city!" Bruckmann laughed recklessly. "During the war, I served my country while the dwarf was hiding at the university composing his failed novel."

"It isn't a bad novel," Rom said.

"Hitler a painter, Goebbels a novelist!"

"You'd best keep your voice down," Rom cautioned.

"Talk to Maikowski," Bruckmann demanded again, leaning into Rom with a whisper.

Rom could see beads of sweat on Bruckmann's forehead. He nodded to the bartender, who left the room. "She's waiting for you, Bruckmann," Rom said theatrically. "I'm sure I can get you two hundred, so let's stop worrying the topic. For now, you'd best go upstairs. You remember the room, don't you? She's in the same room as last time."

Bruckmann took a deep breath. A stone lay on his breast, crushing him with its invisible weight. Even his fingers felt numb. Standing from the table, he staggered and then caught his balance, adjusted his tie, swallowed once deeply, and cast a glance through the windows out onto the narrow street where some Eastern Jews were passing, men in black with long white beards and curled side locks under black felt hats. Filthy swine! Bruckmann blinked and made his way upstairs to the whore.

— —

From behind his desk, Deputy Weiss greeted Wulff with an enthusiastic nod and smile. He looked as though he hadn't slept in days, a huge purple bag suspended beneath each eye. And despite the fact that the day outside was warm, Weiss chose to keep the French windows tightly closed and a coal fire smoldering in the corner stove. "Please make yourself comfortable, Kommissar," he told Wulff. "I'm just finishing up some Orpo requisitions," Weiss said, scribbling away with a pen. "I'll be right with you."

Wulff pondered the day. He tried to consolidate the many hours he'd spent attempting to isolate the termite inside Alexanderplatz HQ. Now, he'd come a full step closer to achieving his goal.

"There now," Weiss said, affixing his signature to a final document. "I'm hoping we can talk without interruption today."

"I've made some progress," Wulff said.

"I'm delighted to hear it," Weiss replied.

"I have the name of someone who sells information to the SA."

"A name?" Weiss said in surprise. He began to pace the room in nervous excitement, five steps to the fireplace mantle, a glance up at President Hindenburg's portrait, five steps back to the window near Wulff where he stood rubbing his hands together in anticipation.

"You have a name?" Weiss said.

"Erik Bruckmann," Wulff said.

Weiss frowned and looked away in shock. "A Kriminal Oberkommissar is selling confidential information to the SA?"

"He's a conduit," Weiss said.

"He is an operator?"

"Precisely. He operates a termite inside HQ."

"You're certain of this?" Wulff said.

"Reasonably so."

"Whom does he operate?"

"I don't know that yet," Wulff admitted.

Weiss returned to his desk and sat wearily. He covered his face with the cup of one hand and began to tap a knuckle on the desk. "This is a critical time," he said. "How do they manage it?" he asked Wulff.

"I don't know that either," Wulff said. "I'm having Bruckmann followed. We'll catch our termite in days."

"You can isolate him?"

"It's being done."

"You have a man on him?"

"As we speak. But I'll need a few marks for taxis."

"Beyond the twenty-five you give your assistant?"

"Well beyond," Wulff said.

Weiss breathed a disappointed sigh. "Indeed," he said, distractedly. Weiss returned to the window, opened the drapes, and stood looking down at the beautiful spring day. Near the Wertheim department store, a balloon-seller strolled beneath his wares. "Shall we say two hundred marks for two weeks' full-time surveillance? Would this be satisfactory?"

"Yes, certainly."

"And the Reichswehr records regarding Bruckmann," Weiss said. "I can go to Army Intelligence. Perhaps I can strike a deal."

"What is the chance?" Wulff replied, knowing Weiss had no chance at all.

"I'm afraid Reichswehr Intelligence and the socialist government of Prussia are not on good terms. Nor do they think kindly of this particular Jewish policeman." Weiss laughed a bemused little laugh.

"And, of course, the chief of police is a socialist and former trade unionist!"

"But in the interest of state security?"

"They must be offered something in return," Weiss said. "It is always give and take." Weiss opened the window latch and pushed its frame forward. From below came organ music and a heady aroma of lime trees and lilacs in bloom. "I never notice the cold in this room," Weiss said. "Here it is April, and you're wearing a leather coat."

"It's a lovely day," Wulff said.

"I'll think of something to offer them," Weiss said. "Perhaps an information-sharing agreement as to communists. We'll see."

"I've examined the duty rosters," Wulff said. "Bruckmann doesn't visit Alexanderplatz that often. Still, I'd like to see his intelligence file. If he is to be prosecuted for treason, we'll need evidence."

"Follow him. Keep me fully informed."

"We'll have our termite," Wulff promised. "We're very close now. If we follow Bruckmann for a week, we'll probably nab him."

Weiss placed a hand on the window glass. "With his immunity, Goebbels can attack me and my family without fear of prosecution. I cannot even file a personal libel suit. I have a wife and children who see this filth."

"It will stop soon I hope, sir," Wulff said. There was a saying in Germany for men like Weiss: *A man on the street, a Jew at home.* "I do wish us luck," Wulff added. At that moment, Wulff knew that he would have to ask his father for assistance with Bruckmann's intelligence file. What choice did he have?

They shook hands, and Wulff left Alexanderplatz in search of Barlach.

An odor of boiled cabbage permeated the passageway. The smell nauseated Bruckmann, who had a headache already, perhaps from bad schnapps or dust in the air. In the hall he paused, supporting himself with a hand on the wall, then continued in a halting gait toward the room. When he reached the door he paused again, took another deep breath, and opened the door slowly. The whore was washing herself in a bidet, soaping her recently shaved pubis, looking up at Bruckmann with a perfidious smile on her face. She grabbed a yellow towel and began to dab herself dry. Bruckmann stood silently, watching her work, trying to focus his way through the murky hotel room light.

"Come in, honey," the whore said cheerfully. "Don't just stand there so everyone can see!"

Bruckmann took note of her dyed hair, its metallic quality, hair she'd combed back from her forehead and tied with a pink ribbon.

"Come in, honey, don't just stand there!" she said again.

Bruckmann pulled shut the door and tossed his jacket coat on the bed. He remembered the room, its drab brownness, the peeling wallpaper and water-stained carpet. While he stood wavering, the whore closed a set of dusty drapes and plunged the room into murky half-tones. She was wearing cheap stockings that revealed her varicose veins and knobby knees. Bruckmann collapsed on the bed, feeling as though he'd just climbed a mountain.

"You look a little pale, honey," the whore said. "But I've got something to cheer you up." She lifted her camisole and squatted rudely in front of Bruckmann, showing him her horsey-teeth and bruised neck, the stubble between her legs.

Bruckmann smiled, picked up the rhinoceros-hide riding crop he carried, and snapped it against the bed. The sound seemed to lift his spirits. Already he was anticipating a pleasurable session with this Schwabing pig. Unbidden, the whore was unbuttoning his trousers, untying his shoes, stripping off his black socks. Bruckmann held her head in his hands and stepped unsteadily out of his pants. Pain ripped his head open like a melon and he sat down heavily, underwear around his ankles. The whore crawled onto the bed and sat beside Bruckmann for a moment, caressed his brow, then pushed herself up on hands and knees, lifting her ass so that it nearly struck him in the face. He picked up the riding crop and snapped it once lightly against her paper-white skin. She meowed with pleasure, then twirled her ass as Bruckmann slapped her hard again on the lower legs.

"I've still got bruises from our last session," the whore said. "You bit me on the neck. Do you remember that, honey?" Bruckmann struck her softly, tapping her on the shoulder, thigh, and calf. Sitting on the bed in his tangled underwear, he felt overcome with other-worldliness, a sense of stepping outside his own existence. "Do you want to get on top of me and hurt me, honey?" she asked him.

Bruckmann fought a wave of nausea. With effort, he managed to turn onto one side and put two knees on the bed. The whore wiggled her ass in his face as Bruckmann tried to mount her from behind. He dropped his face onto her back and tried to bite. On his knees, he balanced against her, holding himself in thin air like a tightrope walker in the circus, his skin damp and slick, a perfectly dreadful newsreel of images contorting his vision. He felt the crop drop onto her back and make a wet snap.

Bruckmann turned when he heard the door click open. Rom stood in the entry in his perfectly tailored blue suit, the pink carnation like a spot of watery blood on his breast. He blinked his cold blue eyes at Bruckmann and let out a sigh. Behind Rom was a beefy man who resembled the Fisherhof bartender, holding a large photographic camera in one hand. Bruckmann tried to lift away from the whore, catching himself in a half-fall with his underwear tangled now between his feet. The whore put her hand on his face and shoved him stiffly away, and Bruckmann tumbled from the bed, landing on the floor face-up. Bruckmann sensed a burble of puke in the corner of his mouth just as the room exploded into a fantasy of brilliant light. The whore pulled off his underwear and Bruckmann looked at the brown nub of his penis as the room went bright again.

Bruckmann was lifted by two sets of arms. He flopped heavily on a chair near the bed, riding crop in one hand, underwear at his feet on the floor. The weight of something fantastic pressed against his skull. The whore was sitting on his lap, licking his ear, allowing a drop of spittle to drop from her mouth and land on his forehead as the room exploded again and again. Bruckmann tried to rise, bur-bling a noise of protest as he felt the riding crop strike him on the shoulder. He tumbled off the chair, landing on his hands and knees. A bubble of vomit hit the floor in front of his face.

The whore laughed and placed her bare foot on Bruckmann's neck, forcing down his head. He felt a lash on his back, the tingle of the rhinoceros hide, his face descending into the filthy nap of the carpet, its smell of cabbage and cat piss. He felt himself growing heavier and heavier as the sounds above him receded. A wicked whore's laugh, an echo of snaps, the taste of blood. The whore raised the crop, brought it down hard three times on Bruckmann's bare ass, drawing blood, raising a triple line of parallel welts. She straddled him and smiled at the camera, her shaved pussy riding Bruckmann's head as flashes filled the room.

Bruckmann could see Rom's freshly polished black shoes in front of his face. "Go clean yourself up, Eva," Rom said.

A door opened. Closed. Bruckmann felt his head nudged by an object. "You're quite a mess, Kriminal Oberkommissar." Rom lifted Bruckmann's head just off the floor with the toe of his shoe.

"I'm sick, Rom," Bruckmann said.

"You should feel sick," Rom said. "You fucking perverted bastard." Rom leaned over and picked up the riding crop. He raised it, snapped it in the air once, then brought it down on Bruckmann's right cheek, lacerating the skin.

"Oh no," Bruckmann muttered, touching the wound.

"Your appetites are thoroughly disgusting," Rom laughed. "Fortunately, we have documented them. When your superiors at Alexanderplatz see these, your career will be finished. I'd say good riddance, wouldn't you?"

"Rom—" Bruckmann said. His vision had doubled, four black shoes, an army of carpet stains. The room was drowned in swimming pools and halos of color, an avalanche of confusion. "Rom, for God's sake."

"Rom, for God's sake!" Rom shouted. He snapped the crop onto the carpet in front of Bruckmann's doubled gaze.

"You can't do this," Bruckmann said.

"But I already have," Rom said. "The charade is over, my dear Bruckmann. I want the name of your termite at Alexanderplatz. I want it now. Give us his name and you can keep your position as a policeman. Otherwise, these photographs go directly to the chief of detectives at Department IV, and another set to the socialists in charge of Alexanderplatz itself. You'll be lucky to walk the streets in Fisher-Kietz where the communists will lick your ass with their truncheons. Think of it, Bruckmann! No job, no pension, no salary! A reputation as a masochist who allows Schwabing whores to tickle his ass with a rhinoceros-hide riding crop. Can you imagine losing your job in times like these? Becoming a pariah?"

Bruckmann managed to pull on his underwear, hiding his limp penis. He was too sick to bother with the trousers.

"What was it?" he asked.

"Chloral hydrate, you fuck," Rom told him

"You'll never operate my termite," Bruckmann said. "I'll ruin him first."

"Have it your way," Rom said.

Bruckmann tried to swallow. His throat was thick with something wet and slick. "All right," he muttered between deep breaths. "You may as well know."

"Good Bruckmann! Good!" Rom tapped Bruckmann on the head with his crop. "I assure you these terrible photographs will never see the light of day."

"And the negatives?"

"Our guarantee, Bruckmann," Rom laughed.

"He's a janitor," Bruckmann said.

"Don't play games."

"A janitor is my termite," Bruckmann said. "His name is Theodor Loos. He works at night in the basement tending the boilers and sweeping the floors."

"Very good, Herr Kriminal Oberkommissar!"

The whore opened the bathroom door. She had put on a cheap sheath skirt and slip-on shoes. She eased her way around Bruckmann,who had found his trouser legs and was pulling them up.

"Go downstairs and wait for me," Rom told the whore.

"You damn bitch," Bruckmann muttered.

The whore crossed the room, opened the door, and stood giving Bruckmann a cruel smile.

"Lie down for thirty minutes, you fool," Rom said to Bruckmann. "You'll feel better. Then clean yourself and get on with your business. Say nothing to anybody about this or the photographs will be submitted to the police. It would give me great pleasure to see you exposed. However, I trust you will deprive me of that pleasure by cooperating through silence. If not, the party will publish these. The great Bruckmann being beaten by a common whore. Squatting on his head. The great Bruckmann groveling in his own vomit with a pussy as a hat. You will be the absolute sensation of Berlin!"

"Piss off," Bruckmann said.

Rom left the room and went downstairs to the bar, delivering to the barman two hundred marks. He walked into the lobby and looked outside at the narrow streets of Alt-Köln to where a seven-seat open Landauer touring car was parked, a car belonging to the local Gau of the Nazi party. In the back, Maikowski sat, wearing a formal SA uniform and smoking a black cigar.

Rom opened the car door and sat down in back beside Maikowski. "It's done," he said. "His contact is a janitor at Alexanderplatz named Theodor Loos."

"How delightful," Maikowski said. "A janitor!" Maikowski tapped the chauffeur on the shoulder and the big car growled to life. They pulled into the street and rumbled over its cobbles. Maikowski stuffed the cigar in his mouth and puffed smoke, then began to hum a tune. It was the "Song of the Storm Columns." Maikowski whispered the first words of the song, slightly off key: *Only when the Jews are bleeding, only then shall we be free.*

They were in view of the Kaiser Wilhelm Cathedral. Rom remarked on the loveliness of the day.

Wulff answered the door of his flat wearing a sweater and corduroy pants. Barlach stood in the hall holding his own jacket and cap. Wulff had been home only an hour. He'd managed to take off his suit, wash his face, slip into some comfortable pants, and read two pages of the newspaper while drinking a glass of mineral water. Barlach looked at Wulff with a sheepish smile, then apologized for calling so late in the day.

"Come in Barlach," Wulff said. He led the way to a cluttered small parlor where there were two chairs, a couch, and many scattered books. Wulff had spread boxes of documents throughout his apartment, a mess of dossiers, folders, and files.

"Sorry to bother you, sir," Barlach said. "But I thought I should report to you immediately about Bruckmann."

"You must be tired," Wulff said.

"It's all right, sir."

"You saw something? Someone?"

"Not exactly, sir," Barlach said.

Wulff offered the sergeant a glass of milk or some tea, but he declined both.

"You saw the termite?" Wulff asked excitedly.

"I could have," Barlach said. "I saw the Oberkommissar come out of Mitte this afternoon. I was sitting on a bench and he was in plain sight. He walked to the river and bought a ticket for the Spree tour boat going upstream. I couldn't follow because I didn't have the four-mark fare. But I thought you should know."

"The Spree tour? That is unusual."

"I would say so," Barlach said.

"I saw Weiss today. Your stipend is two hundred marks for two weeks. Twenty-four-hour surveillance. That means you will be doing only the work of four men!"

"We're close, aren't we?" Barlach said.

"I should think," Wulff replied. "I wouldn't have thought Bruckmann would meet his contact in the middle of the day. It's a pity. I should have given you some money. Starting tomorrow, you take an early shift. Get some rest tonight and watch Bruckmann's apartment at dawn. I'll watch his office during the day with you out-side the Mitte entrance in case he leaves again. I'll take over the sur-veillance at night. I'll watch his house and movements after dark, say, from ten o'clock. Telephone me in the early afternoon and tell me where you are every day."

"Very good, sir," Barlach said. "But there's something I meant to tell you."

"What is it, Barlach?"

"Do you remember that I reported seeing a man get off the Grenadier tram at Hirrenstrasse? It was last Friday at about the time of the murder."

"I remember. What about it?"

"I've learned his identity. His name is Theodor Loos. His photo is in personnel records at Alexanderplatz. He's a janitor. I've seen to it that his file is available to you."

"He's your suspect?"

Barlach shrugged. "He may as well be."

"I guess he may," Wulff said.

They shook hands at the door, and Wulff watched Barlach walk tiredly down the carpeted hallway. Wulff returned to his parlor and listened to Louis Armstrong records and drank Alsatian beer for an hour. He telephoned Johanna to wish her a good night, then spent nearly forty minutes with her on the phone.

It was after midnight when Wulff went to bed. He tossed and turned and finally fell into a fitful, dream-filled sleep.

12

Rom's chauffeur had been lost for twenty minutes in the suburban maze of Lichtenberg. They meandered down dead-end lanes where there was row upon row of identical dilapidated villas, semi-detached houses constructed of pebbled stone with black slate roofs. There were crumbling upper-class detached houses and occasional parks with untended poplars and elms. At Ulm Alee they parked across from an address Rom had gotten through Bruckmann, a two-story detached villa made of crushed rock with mullioned windows set at regular intervals, a flagstone walk winding through untended trellis roses, and a few lilacs and hydrangeas.

They waited thirty minutes in twilight, Rom smoking in the back seat, oblivious to the evening. At dusk, as the sky colored pink through green and opalescent, Loos walked out of the front door and down the flagstone path. He was wearing an overcoat, coveralls, and a torn denim jacket. His lanky black hair hung down in curls, and he walked with a shuffling gait. Rom watched him pass through what remained of an iron step.

Rom sat up in the open car. Loos stepped onto the sidewalk, adjusted his watchcap, looking up at the nearly cloudless evening sky as though searching for some planet in another solar system. He began walking down Ulm Alee toward a tram stop Rom knew was half a kilometer away. Rom tapped the chauffeur lightly on the shoulder. The chauffeur pulled the huge vehicle forward slowly.

"Theodor Loos," Rom called as they pulled parallel to the walking man. There was not a soul on the street. A brisk wind had risen from the west and one could smell coal dust in the air. Newsprint was being blown down the street. "Theodor Loos," Rom called again.

Loos halted and hunched his shoulders. "Who are you?" he asked suspiciously. His voice contained a voltage that connected itself to Rom immediately. "What do you want? Are you following me?"

Rom admired this cruel face, its inscrutable frown and patient anger, the prognathous brow and jug ears, the narrow set eyes which were remarkable in both their depth and lack of depth.

"Please relax," Rom said. "I just want the chance to talk to you a moment." Rom leaned over the passenger compartment, one hand on the door. "I only want a moment. Please."

"Who the fuck are you?" Loos said quietly. He spat contemptuously on the pavement and stared at the chauffeur. "Tell me immediately."

"My name is Dieter Rom. I'm a Storm Führer. Perhaps you've heard of Storm 33?"

"Dieter Rom?" Loos repeated in accented German. He had halted and was standing in the growing dark, hands at his sides.

"You've heard of us?" Rom asked. "You've heard of us, haven't you?"

Loos looked back at the widow's villa thirty meters away across a yard of weeds, a stump of elm. "You are Dieter Rom?" Loos said at last.

"Would you mind coming over here?" Rom asked him. The chauffeur inched his vehicle forward. A housewife down the street was calling for invisible children. On the gleaming horizon were the ghostly outlines of smokestacks. "I'd like to talk to you. That's all. Just a talk."

"Talk about what?" Loos said.

Rom had worn his SA uniform, its freshly laundered, crisp brown shirt ironed into sharp angles and creases, dark brown worsted pants, heavy black leather boots polished to a mirror shine, a crisscross of leather belts on his chest and waist, one over the shoulder, and a large red swastika armband and kepi-style hat. Rom gathered himself, stood and bowed slightly, allowing Loos to see the uniform in its full glory.

"Please—Herr Loos," Rom said, bowing slightly in false deference, "we are alone here, yes? I'd like to speak to you for a moment about a matter of some importance to both of us."

Loos glanced around, three hundred and sixty degrees of circumspection.

Like luring a frightened dog, Rom thought. "Would you like a cigarette?" he asked.

Hands on hips Loos said, "You're the leader of Storm 33?"

Stars studded the eastern horizon now, a sprinkle of points amid the smokestacks. To the southwest, central Berlin glowed orange. Now that the sun had set, it was cool in the open air. Rom nodded, produced a gold cigarette case, and extended it toward Loos, who took one of the cigarettes and allowed Rom to light it with a gold lighter. Loos drew smoke deeply into his lungs and held it there for an uncommonly long time, then sucked the exhalations back through his nose.

"English cigarettes," Loos said.

"Good, aren't they?"

"They're all right," Loos replied.

Rom waited for something to happen. "I'm acquainted with Bruckmann," he said finally.

Loos allowed the cigarette to burn, its red tip a tiny anchor in the gathering night. In blue clothes and a dark denim jacket, Loos himself was disappearing from sight like an apparition. Now, only a malignant smile and the burning tip of the cigarette presented themselves to Rom.

"What do you want of me?" Loos asked pointedly. The cigarette smouldered unsmoked. "Why do you stop me in the street like this?"

"Because we belong together, my friend," Rom said.

"We belong together—" Loos hissed. "I'm going to work now, please." He moved off a step or two.

"But we're on the same side," Rom said. He felt the moment passing, the lifeline he'd extended falling short.

"What side would that be?" Loos said, moving slowly, the automobile in tandem just behind.

"The winning side," Rom said. "The side you've been fighting on since you joined the movement. The side you served in Belgium and the side you served in the Freicorps and the side you served when you were with Bruckmann and the Black Reichswehr. You remember Munich? You remember the pleasure you took in serving the movement by stamping out the communist menace in Bavaria?"

"You are a long-winded man," Loos said.

"Let me come to the point then," Rom said. "Your friend Bruckmann has been fucking you in the ass."

Loos stopped suddenly. "Where is Bruckmann?" he asked. "What about Bruckmann?"

Rom smiled, attempting to transform their confrontation into a conspiracy. "Herr Bruckmann is indisposed. He's suffered a sudden illness, shall we say."

"An illness? What kind of illness?"

"Please, why don't you get in the car? Let me drive you as far as Grenadier. I know you're on your way to work at Alexanderplatz. You may as well allow me to drive you that far at least. Surely that would be preferable to riding the stinking tram."

"Why should I?"

Rom cursed silently. Such sullen stupidity. It made him weary to think of it. "It would benefit you greatly," he said patiently.

Loos spat. There were thorny weeds in the cracks of the sidewalk. Chunks of asphalt had broken away from the curb. Tanks had passed this way during the revolution.

"Benefit me in what way?" Loos asked.

"Financially," Rom said flatly. "Financially, if nothing else. But perhaps you'd like a uniform. Share in the coming glory of the movement." Rom paused. "But financially at first."

Loos glanced back at the widow's house. His head ached suddenly. "Bruckmann. Fucking me?"

"Please, please," Rom said, opening the door. "Won't you at least let me drive you to Grenadier?"

The chauffeur touched an interior switch. The car exploded into a glow, allowing Loos to see its maroon leather seats and the pale yellow glow of dash instruments. Rom slid to one side. Loos stumbled forward and tumbled into the seat beside Rom, just as the vehicle began to move off.

"That's better, isn't it?" Rom said. He felt as though he were soothing a frightened child. He opened a gold cigarette case and placed it on the seat between them. "We'll just get you to Grenadier and then you can walk the rest of the way. Nobody will see us, I assure you."

"What do you want?" Loos asked.

Rom laughed good-naturedly. He found manipulation a richly rewarding game, one he practiced with the art of a bullfighter. Coax the bull, deploy distractions, sink the sword.

"Bruckmann has been fucking you for a long time," Rom said. "Right up your ass."

Loos was silent, watching the passage of anonymous row houses, shops, overhead electric wires. "Fucking me how?" he asked finally. His broad face was bloodless in the light of the Landauer. "Just how has Bruckmann been fucking me?"

"Take it easy," Rom said. "He's been fucking the SA as well. You're not the only one."

"Just *how* has he been fucking me?" Loos growled.

They drove southwest through chains of suburban Berlin, row houses, vacant lots, deserted tram stops, blocks of shops and pubs. "Do you know what the SA pays Bruckmann for his information each week?"

"Bruckmann has told you about me?"

"Fifty marks, you think?"

"Yes, fifty marks."

"The SA pays twice that, Theodor," Rom said.

"I was told fifty marks."

"Twice that, I'm afraid. For two years."

"Twice that?" Loos said.

Now, Rom thought, he becomes a robot.

"One hundred marks each week," Rom said. "That's what the SA has been paying Bruckmann every week. Did you know that, Herr Loos? And did you know that Bruckmann sells this same information to the army every week? I don't know what the army pays Bruckmann, but did you know that this was happening?"

Loos clenched his fists as the neighborhood rolled by. He felt a sudden urge to burn this stuffy world, to strangle its inhabitants as they fled their flaming structures. It was the world he hated, this collocation of Virgin Marys, bankers, and Jewish shopkeepers.

"Bruckmann gave me twenty-five marks," Loos said.

"There you have it!" Rom said. "Suppose we eliminate Bruckmann from this transaction, along with the army. And suppose you join the movement? Serve the movement?"

"Where is Bruckmann now?"

"He's—"

"Never mind," Loos said. "What do you want from me?"

"Nothing, my friend," Rom said. "I want nothing from you. I only want to give you what is rightfully yours, along with a chance to serve Germany. I want you to share in the spoils of victory. To the victor should go the spoils, no?"

"What spoils are these?"

"Only what belongs to us," Rom said. "Let's say that from now on you work only for the SA. You will share your rightful payment with nobody. After all, it is your risk. And your information will no longer go to the Reichswehr, which opposes the movement."

"You give me one hundred marks?"

"Ah—we have an agreement," Rom said calmly.

"What happens to Bruckmann?"

"Forget Bruckmann," Rom said. "He's insignificant. He stays on his police job." Bruckmann would be blackmailed for the rest of his life. "What is important is the movement and that you get your rightful share of its victory."

"You will pay me one hundred marks each week?"

"One hundred marks," Rom repeated.

The Landauer had stopped for traffic. Loos spat onto the pavement. They were in Scheunenviertel, about six blocks from Liebknecht House, communist headquarters for central Berlin. The buildings of this district were all brick tenements, Hinterhofs, blocks of stone blackened by decades of coal dust.

"We shall continue as usual," Rom said. "Only you will meet me and not Bruckmann."

"At the regular places," Loos said.

"And that would be?"

"On the Spree tour boat or at the second balcony washroom in Capitol Cinema during the day." Loos picked up a cigarette from the gold case and put it in the pocket of his denim jacket. "Friday afternoons at two o'clock. Next week on the Spree boat. Bring me my money."

"I'd be delighted," Rom said. "May I ask how you come by your information at Alexanderplatz?"

"No, you may not," Loos said. If they only knew, Loos thought to himself. Entry gained to the commissioner's office. He read Weiss's diary. It had nothing to do with elaborate safecracking, official orders, or duty lists. If Weiss was stupid enough to keep a diary, then Loos would continue to read it. "That is for me to know," Loos said.

"As you wish," Rom said.

"One other thing," Loos said. "I wish to speak with Bruckmann one last time."

"Surely that isn't necessary," Rom said. "We've taken good care of Bruckmann, I assure you."

"Please," Loos said. "Otherwise there is no deal. We are old comrades. I want to see him tomorrow at two o'clock at the Capitol Cinema. Send him there. Tell him to be at the same place at the same time. On the second balcony. In the washroom. He knows the place. Arrange this for me."

"I'm sure the Kriminal Oberkommissar will do as you ask," Rom said. "But are you certain you wish to do this? I know of no purpose it could serve. I'm telling you the absolute truth, you understand. Bruckmann has been neutralized. He won't be cheating anyone now."

"Tell him," Loos growled angrily. "And you and I will meet a week from Friday on the Spree tour boat. Get on near the French Embassy. I'll meet you upriver. Bring my money."

"As you wish, Theodor," Rom said. He took out a swastika pin from his shirt pocket and handed it to Loos, who held it in the palm of his right hand. "Welcome to the Storm Column, Theodor," Rom said. "We need men like you. Good men, good Aryans. Men who live for history. Men who live to clean Germany of dirt and disease and defeatism. You'll not be sorry you took this step."

They pulled to a stop at the corner of Grenadier. Loos took a second cigarette, paused, took a third. He opened the passenger door.

"Two thousand years from now they'll be talking about our movement," Rom said.

"Bruckmann tomorrow," Loos said. He got out of the vehicle and stood on the sidewalk, hands on hips.

Rom tapped the chauffeur, who inched the Landauer forward. When he looked back, Rom saw Loos standing in the dark street, staring down at the swastika pin Rom had given him.

— —

Wulff watched the rain from Johanna's ottoman. Thunderless spring rain, painting the French windows. He was conscious of being stared at by dozens of African masks, Yoruba and Ibo carvings, one Senegalese face etched into angles and prisms of dark wood. Working at Berlin Mitte all day, he had followed Bruckmann to his apartment in the dark suburb of Wilmersdorf. He'd waited outside in his police Opel while it began to rain, slumped there in his black leather coat, smoking cigarette after cigarette until four hours had passed and the windows of Bruckmann's apartment turned black. Back on Lennestrasse, Johanna had met him at her door, led him to the ottoman, and had taken off his shoes. She had gotten him a glass of beer, then sat at his shoulder while he watched the rain.

She kissed his ear playfully, stuck out her tongue and moistened his neck. Wulff closed his eyes and allowed himself to be push-pulled by sexual desire. Wulff took Johanna's black hair in his hand and smelled it as though it were fragrant dirt.

"My Jewish widow had a dream last night," Johanna said. "If I weren't such an ethical professional, I'd tell you about it. You'll have to use your imagination, dear. It involves a bucket of soapy water."

"I'm intrigued," Wulff said languidly. He buried his face further in her hair. In the distance was the steaming of a quiet city.

Johanna fluffed her hair, covering Wulff. "Her dream involves flying and fire."

Wulff laughed, muffled in hair. "I have a professional question for you," he said.

Johanna lifted the glass of beer to his lips. "Don't you want your beer?" she asked.

"A Kripo first sergeant is helping me with my investigations now," Wulff said. "He caught a glimpse of some chap walking down the Hirrenstrasse last Friday night. Just a coincidence, I suppose. This fellow had just gotten off the suburban Lichtenberg tram at the Grenadier stop. It was the same tram and the same time as the tram ridden by the murder victim in the Hirrenstrasse. My assistant found this man's photograph in the employee personnel files at Alexanderplatz."

"That's something, isn't it?" Johanna said.

"It's something, yes," Wulff said. "But I don't know what. Since the autopsy, we've had no real evidence that might lead to the killer. My inquiries to other departments have turned up absolutely nothing."

"Inquiring about sex murders won't help exactly," Johanna said.

"I understand, dear, but even so—" Wulff said.

"Your killer is not a sex murderer."

"And that's why I need your opinion."

"Yes, darling," Johanna said, biting her lip in mock supplication. She put her head on his chest. "When it rains, all I can think of is making love to you. Isn't that silly? A grown woman with infantile associations?"

"Please, darling," Wulff said. He picked up the glass of beer and drank a little. "This fellow who rides the tram to Grenadier and walks down Hirrenstrasse is named Theodor Loos. I wanted to ask you about his background, see what you think. See if anything clicks through that lovely psychoanalytic mind of yours."

"Take my opinions, dear," Johanna laughed softly. "Everything I have is yours!"

"I've studied the dossier of this Loos," Wulff told her. "He's thirty-three years old. According to the file, he isn't married. I'd suspect he's never been married, but I don't know for certain. His father is a German and his mother Belgian, with a French background. Loos has German citizenship, though he lived for many years in Lille while his father was a traveling customs inspector with the German railway system before the war. Then, as the war broke out, the father moved his whole family back to Freiburg, where they'd lived for some years prior. According to the records, Loos had a good education in a local Catholic seminary school, and then later at a public gymnasium. He spent his youth in and around Freiburg. When the war broke out, he tried to enlist, but the armistice came and he was mustered out almost as soon as he joined. In time, he spent two years at a technical school studying civil engineering, but became ill with a serious case of influenza at the end of 1923. He wasn't expected to survive, but he did, and came to Berlin for some reason. His work experience is with boilers and general maintenance. During the inflation, he found employment as a janitor in the ministry of interior for the Reich. Later, he found a better job at Alexanderplatz."

"Are his parents alive?" Johanna asked.

"Both of them are dead," Wulff said. "Loos was born to them very late in life. Apparently, he has an older brother whose whereabouts are unknown. Twenty years or so older than Loos. The father was a respected civil servant. After the war, the mother had a difficult time of it because of her foreign nationality, and was quite poor. Theirs was a happy marriage. That's about all there is."

"And you want my opinion about what?"

"Could this be our killer?" Wulff said. "Does this sound like the man you described to me? The man who hated his father and wishes to kill him in revenge? Does this sound like the background of a tormented soul?"

Johanna brushed back a lock of her hair. "These records are hardly the story of a life," she said. "But on this account, I'd have to say I don't think so, dear. Our killer should not have had a stable life, not even the shadow of one. Unmarried and living alone, that would describe him. But the stable family life and the education, no."

"That's what I thought, too," Wulff said.

"You must be disappointed," Johanna said.

"Yes, very," he said. "I thought Barlach had something."

"Could you follow Loos for a time?"

"Perhaps someday," Wulff told her. "Now there is neither the time, the manpower, nor the money to do so."

"I'm sorry, dear," Johanna whispered in his ear. She began to massage his temple. Wulff pulled her onto the ottoman and put his hands inside the caftan. Rain was running mad in the trees.

—◦—

Barlach remembered it dimly, as one remembers a bad dream. He recalled putting down the *Berliner Zeitung* at half past one. He had been sitting on a marble bench outside Berlin Mitte for an hour, and suffering hunger pangs. There on the corner of Dorotheenstrasse, his view of headquarters was excellent, straight on and unobstructed—two side exits, a main entrance, a view of the French Embassy and the Reich Ministry of the Interior, the first a pink granite monstrosity, the second a hulking sandstone edifice.

At the time, he thought himself stranded with nothing to do but wait. He wondered if it would be his fate to wait for as much as two weeks, perhaps longer. Months? Years? Decades? Standing, he stretched his bulky body and walked twenty paces to a pretzel vendor on the corner, bought a fresh pretzel, smeared it with mustard, then ate the whole thing in three large bites. When he got back to his marble bench, he spotted Bruckmann coming down the Mitte steps, hailing one of Berlin's black taxis.

Still chewing the last bite of pretzel, Barlach hailed his own cab. Capitalized by Alexanderplatz, Barlach could pay the fare. Wulff had told him to spare no expense. They traveled south across central Berlin, skirted the Spree embankment, caught occasionally in heavy midday traffic. They crawled their way toward the cathedral. Barlach knew that Bruckmann lived in a spacious apartment in Wilmersdorf, south and west of central Berlin, the opposite direction from where they were going.

Bruckmann left his taxi a block from the huge church. At Auguste-Viktoria Platz, there were fewer pedestrians and vehicles than on Dorotheenstrasse. Even so, there were street vendors, hawkers, businessmen, taxis, and busses in modest numbers. He paid his fare and lined up behind Bruckmann, who was striding briskly northward. Barlach remembered being surprised when Bruckmann went inside the gilt-and-chrome doors of the art-deco Capitol Cinema and bought a ticket at the kiosk.

Barlach waited outside, studying the marquee. A Greta Garbo: *Susan Lennox: Her Fall and Rise.* When he was certain Bruckmann had left the lobby, Barlach purchased an expensive loge seat, knowing he'd be able to see both the main floor and the balconies. After a few minutes, he found his way up some side stairs and took a seat, knowing that in the dark, Bruckmann would be there somewhere.

Barlach stared at the huge silver screen. Greta Garbo, sleek and eight meters tall, smoking one of her many filmic cigarettes, was engaged in seductive conversation with several gentlemen clad in tuxedos. When his eyes had adjusted to the dark, Barlach spotted Bruckmann high in the second balcony, about twenty rows up near the back of the theater. At this time of the afternoon, only a few people were in the audience, most of those scattered on the main floor. Barlach watched Garbo again, and when he glanced back a few minutes later, Bruckmann had gone.

It was two o'clock in the afternoon. Of that much Barlach was certain, but not much more. He remembered an illuminated clock face. He may have seen a coattail vanishing through red velvet curtains.

Barlach hurried up a set of carpeted stairs. Behind him, Garbo had begun to sing her torch song, a dirge of regret. As Barlach reached the upper mezzanine floor, he saw Bruckmann disappear through the washroom doors.

"Damn," Barlach said to himself. He couldn't follow Bruckmann into the washroom, he was certain of that. And then the thought crossed his mind that Bruckmann was perhaps simply slipping away from the demands of police work. He waited in shadow. Time passed, a few minutes, then five. He glanced at his watch. Six minutes after two. Then seven after two.

Barlach decided to enter the washroom, wash his hands, and leave. It seemed certain that Bruckmann wouldn't recognize him, probably wouldn't pay him any attention at all. Barlach would be just another of many Garbo fanatics escaping the horrors of everyday life. Barlach moved for the washroom door, prepared for anything. After that, he remembered nothing.

13

The man who became Theodor Loos had been introduced to the pleasures of the garrote by Erik Bruckmann. It quickly became a symbol of his own inner strengths, those he'd struggled to achieve despite an absent father and a bizarrely psychopathic mother, despite his own rootlessness and declassed ardor. For reasons wholly unknown to him, the garrote reminded Loos of his mother. She had come to him in bed, slipped herself into his body, surrounded him and suffocated him simultaneously. She would cover his tiny and feverish body with kisses. The things she did to him in the dark!

Now, this Loos-Braun composite leaned down and splashed water on his face. Standing before the mirror in a mezzanine washroom used by the patrons of the second balcony in the Capitol Cinema in Auguste-Viktoria Platz, he delivered himself to the hands of his own obsessive compulsions. According to his watch, it was two o'clock. He dried his face with a flimsy paper towel and scanned his features in the mirror. Backing into one of the commode stalls, he closed its door, taking the garrote from his overcoat pocket. He coiled the hemp into tight circles, then pulled a knot around the metal bar at one end. He closed the top of the toilet stool and sat down on its wooden lid.

The door to the washroom creaked open. Loos relaxed, feeling the garrote animate itself. There was a moment of silence until Loos stood, opened the stall door, and saw Bruckmann standing in front of a row of mirrors and sinks, the Kriminal Oberkommissar examining himself nervously, brushing a finger through his spare grayish hair. Bruckmann smiled at Loos, each of them exchanging a glance through the medium of images.

"Ah, my old friend," Bruckmann said. Loos was a pace behind now. With flashbulb speed, Loos garrotted Bruckmann, pulled the noose tight around his neck, and twisted the metal bar once. Bruckmann, a full head shorter than Loos, was brought instantly to his toes, emitting a short, spectacular grunt. Loos placed his knee in the small of Bruckmann's back, arching the man into a question mark position.

Loos backed the bucking Oberkommissar into the toilet stall, turned him, and kicked the door closed. He mounted the toilet lid and stood to his full height, bringing Bruckmann off his feet. Bruckmann clutched at the garrote furiously, trying to strike upward at Loos but failing. Loos twisted the metal bar again.

"I wish to ask you a question," Loos whispered.

Bruckmann said something that sounded like "please."

Loos turned the metal bar, loosening the garrote a bit.

"Please, you've got to let me talk," Bruckmann said in tortured tones.

"I wish for you to talk." He lowered Bruckmann back to his toes.

"Rom is lying," Bruckmann said. "Wasn't it I who transformed you from the lowly Edgar Braun into Theodor Loos? We have been together too long for this to happen." Bruckmann's gravelly voice had been reduced to a canary's twitter. Loos noticed that his scar had turned white. A circle of blood had begun to ooze from beneath the hemp.

"You cheated me," Loos said quietly.

"I can fix things," Bruckmann managed to say.

Bruckmann had broken a fingernail on the garrote. It charmed Loos. They'd discussed the garrote many times, how hopeless it was to claw. It was the merest reflex. Loos tightened the garrote again, Bruckmann going slack. His shoulders sagged and there was a faint rush of breath leaving the body. Loos lifted Bruckmann off his feet again and detected the smell of shit. Loos held him that way for several minutes. After a time, he loosed the garrote, put his arms under Bruckmann's shoulders, and lifted him toward the coat peg on the back of the stall door. Loos turned the man's collar and hung him there like a trophy.

Bruckmann was staring at him with one bright eye, slightly bluish. He had shit his pants, and there was the unmistakable odor of human waste in the stall. A dark, bloody smile on the neck.

"You mustn't underestimate me," Loos said to Bruckmann. "You've always underestimated me."

The door to the washroom opened again. Loos buttoned his overcoat and put his hand on the walnut truncheon he always carried in one pocket. He pulled down the watchcap over his forehead and stepped outside the stall, careful to shut the door quickly, holding it closed with his knee for a moment while he looked in the mirror to see who'd come inside. The man he saw looked familiar, a solidly built fellow about Loos's own height and weight, wearing a nicely tailored new tweed suit and carrying a raincoat over one arm. For a moment, this stranger and Loos were caught in an entanglement of confusion until Loos struck him hard in the middle of the forehead with a blow that landed with sickening precision. The stranger collapsed in a heap on the tile floor, striking his head with a second sickening thud. Loos stepped over the body and struck it again.

He went to the sink and splashed cold water on his face. He was alone with the mirror, recalling again the face of his mother, its horrid caricature of the Virgin Mary as beer-hall tart, the face that had led Loos in prayers so many times, had planted wet kisses on his navel, the face that had prodded and sucked and licked its way into his mind.

— ▬

Wulff had parked his police Opel near the cinema, around the corner from Auguste-Platz, then walked fifty paces to the blazing marquee which advertised the latest Garbo masterpiece, a potboiler of German expressionist romanticism. That afternoon, there had been a brief rain shower, and puddles remained on the cobblestones and pavement bricks, reservoirs of light from neon signs. Black cabs and red buses passed on the square, and evening commuters were filling the streets. Weiss was standing just beneath the marquee in his gray suit.

"They're upstairs with Schupo," he said.

"What about Barlach?" Wulff asked.

They went into the lobby where a small crowd of gawkers had gathered at one end of the carpeted foyer, along with two Schupo and a detective from Department IV. Weiss told Wulff that Schupo had been detailed to guard the exits of the theater. Others were in cars, blocking the alleys outside. Wulff had brought along a Department IV photographer and two forensic experts. All three were standing in the lobby smoking cigarettes.

"Barlach is in the police infirmary as we speak," Weiss said quietly. "He was taken there by ambulance. He's going to the hospital as soon as emergency treatment is given by the police doctor."

"How bad is it?"

"I honestly don't know," Weiss replied. "He'll be given the best care. I've given explicit instructions that he be given the best care."

"I want Levitt up here," Wulff said.

Weiss walked up to a Schupo and gave the instructions. He came back to Wulff and said, "Levitt is being notified. I've issued an explicit order that he come here sooner rather than later. He's on at Alexanderplatz. I suspect he'll come right away."

"I want to see Barlach later," Wulff said.

"I need you here for a time."

"He's bad, isn't he?"

"I think perhaps he is," Weiss admitted. "But I'm not a doctor and I haven't seen him. They say he's critical."

"What happened?" Wulff asked.

"I know only what these Schupo told me just before you arrived. It was about three o'clock when an usher on duty at the loge and upper balconies went into a second balcony washroom and discovered Barlach on the floor in a pool of blood. According to the ticket seller, Barlach purchased a single loge seat and went in about two o'clock. At three, the film ended, and as usual the usher went into the washroom to clean. Apparently, there is hardly any audience during the day. The usher said that Barlach seemed to be bleeding from the ears and nose. It didn't take long for the usher to find Bruckmann hanging from a hook in the first toilet stall. He ran downstairs to the manager's office, and the manager called Schupo. The local precinct sent two men, and they took a look at the scene, called for the ambulance, cordoned off the entrance, and telephoned Department IV. At the time the movie let out, there were thirty or so people in the audience, but most of them had gone already. There are about fifteen or so who remained. Schupo has interviewed them, and they're standing over there waiting to go home. Schupo has their names and addresses, but the others are gone for good. There is no way to get them back."

"It doesn't matter," Wulff said. "The murderer was gone before the film was over at three. He probably never even sat down in the theater."

"I quite agree," Weiss said.

Wulff went to his experts and gave them their instructions. He walked back to Weiss.

"Where is the ticket-taker?" he asked.

Weiss pointed out a skinny, sixtyish woman in a light blue cinema uniform. She was chewing gum.

Wulff went over. "Do you know who was sitting up in the second balcony?"

She looked at Wulff without interest. "I sell a lot of tickets. It's hard to remember."

"Try to do your best," Wulff said, placating her. He looked at the fifteen, those assembled in the lobby. Wulff asked the ticket taker to identify anybody among them who might have gone up to the balcony seats. Anybody unusual, anybody who looked like a killer.

"Not there," she said. "But there might have been a big lout of a fellow. Looked like a workman. Overcoat and hat. I'm just guessing, mind you."

"He was big?"

"He seemed big to me."

"And what did he look like?"

"Big."

"Think, damn it," Wulff said.

"He had big ears," she said. "They stuck out of his hat."

Wulff went back to Weiss, who was standing at the bottom of a flight of stairs that led to the balcony areas.

"I want to handle this as a political case on the Stapo side," Weiss said. "But I want you to be the chief investigator. Lead my team of men. Use Stapo for legwork. Can you live if we bypass Kripo?"

Wulff hesitated. He was reluctant to see this case politicized. "If you order it," he said grimly. He'd had quite enough of political cases. If he had deliberately set out to wreck his Kripo career, he couldn't have achieved the goal any better. "In that case," he said, "I want to have access to your best men. I want them to interrogate every patron here."

"I'll get you in touch with our best," Weiss said.

Wulff followed him up a narrow set of carpeted stairs that led to a foyer with entrances to the second balcony. On their right at the end of the lobby was a heavy oak door to the washroom. Inside they found four urinals along one wall, a row of sinks and mirrors, three toilet stalls with swinging doors. On the floor was a smear of blood. A stocky Schupo was standing in one corner with a shako in one hand.

"Do you know anything?" Wulff asked the Schupo.

"Nothing special," he answered. "I talked to the usher who found the bodies. He didn't have much to say. By then, the ambulance was on its way." *Bodies*. Wulff had flinched at the word. "The ticket-taker downstairs says she doesn't know anything. I'm guessing the killer went down the back stairs and took one of the darkened exits on the main floor. They open from inside and are locked outside. That's how he got out, I'd say."

"What about the usher? You grill him?"

"He doesn't know anything. He's on duty at the mezzanine level."

"You can go," Wulff told him. "I want your written report on my desk tomorrow morning, along with that of your partner." Wulff gave his name, departmental address. Wulff watched the policeman go, then stood quietly, looking at the rows of mirrors, the tiled whiteness, the bright smear of drying blood on the floor.

"Let's take a look," Wulff said.

They skirted the blood smear and opened a stall door. Bruckmann was on a hook, blue-faced and calm.

"That's as dead as it gets," Weiss said.

"He struggled a bit," Wulff commented. He was studying the body, Bruckmann's head at a cocked angle, the necklace of blood at his throat. Bruckmann's eyepatch had dropped, revealing a marbled, sightless eye. He looked almost apologetic in death.

"He's got broken fingernails," Wulff said.

"He tried to fight the garrote," Weiss agreed.

"He panicked and forgot what he should have been doing," Wulff said.

"How long did he last?"

"A few minutes at best. Probably less."

Wulff looked into the stall. There were a few drops of blood on the floor near the toilet bowl, a smear on the partition wall.

"The killer was strong enough to stand on the toilet, then lift this man off his feet. He toyed with him for a while."

Weiss leaned in, then retreated quickly. "There was something ritualistic in this don't you think?"

Wulff stepped out of the stall, and together he and Weiss went out into the carpeted lobby. They'd begun another showing of the film. Garbo was speaking in discreet but husky tones.

"I'll instruct the Stapo team," Wulff said. "But I'm going back in and search Bruckmann, make some notes before they take him away. There may be something in his pockets. But I doubt it."

"He was meeting his contact, wasn't he? His termite?"

"Probably so," Wulff said. I doubt that the SA would kill a police captain in cold blood, especially one sympathetic to their cause."

"But why would his termite kill him?"

Wulff had no answer.

— ~

At the end of the lobby, Wulff could see the forensic pathologist huffing up the last few stairs. He was smoking a cigar and had paused to catch his breath. He leaned down and spat into a marble waterfountain bowl. Wulff shook hands with Weiss, who walked through the lobby, spoke briefly with Levitt, then disappeared down the stairs. Wulff could smell popcorn, Levitt's cigar, the fresh aroma of clean carpet. He could hear Garbo's insouciant voice. Levitt approached and nodded his head sadly. They shook hands as orchestral music swelled from the film and Garbo began to sing.

"I'm sorry we meet like this," Levitt told Wulff.

"I'm sorry to call you out."

"Your friend, the sergeant?"

Wulff shrugged. "Not good," he said.

He led Levitt to the washroom. Beneath the stall door they could see a shoe with a spot of blood on one toe. Levitt straddled the puddle of blood on the floor, opened the stall door, and looked at Bruckmann. He studied the body on its hook, the blue face, bulging eyes, the cut-gash throat oozing dried blood.

"Who is he?" Levitt asked.

"Oberkommissar Bruckmann," Wulff said. "He's my captain."

"I knew it was a policeman," Levitt said. "But a captain." Levitt stepped carefully into the stall. "He's certainly a mess." He studied the face and hands, then placed a finger carefully on Bruckmann's neck. "Garrote," Levitt said quietly.

"It looks that way," Wulff agreed.

"Quiet, efficient, personal."

"Right-handed killer?" Wulff asked.

"I should think so," Levitt said. "All the standard indicia of slow strangulation. Neck tissue and muscular damage. Slow work too, perhaps five minutes or so. If you know what you are doing, you can kill almost instantly with the garrote. Or you can go slowly. I'll do a complete work-up at Alexanderplatz."

"I want the chemistry on Bruckmann."

"You'll get it," Levitt said. "But who uses a garrote?"

"Someone practiced."

"This will send you back to your files, won't it?" Levitt said. "Poor Bruckmann," Levitt said quietly. "He tried to struggle, but it was hopeless. He grabbed the cord around his neck like an amateur. I wonder why they always grab for the cord?"

"A reflex, I suppose."

"What is your training?"

"There are better responses than grabbing for the cord," Wulff said. "One must react instantaneously and without fear. Relax and place two hands on your attacker's head. Find his eye sockets and stick your thumbs in each. Tear out his eyes if you can. You have about thirty seconds."

Levitt smiled. "You are a remarkable man, Wulff," he said. "You actually receive training in such matters."

"Book learning," Wulff said.

Levitt chewed his cigar, studying Bruckmann, fascinated by the death throe and its putrid colors. "So what am I really doing here?" he asked finally. "You are perfectly capable of making a thorough forensic analysis of this scene. You knew Bruckmann was dragged in here, killed with a garrote, and slowly at that. You probably even know why. And you have Stapo forensic men downstairs. I saw them when I came in. So, just what am I doing here?"

"This case may be political," Wulff said. "I just wanted to have somebody on my side."

"You'll get your careful autopsy," Levitt said. He stepped out of the stall. "First you work with Weiss on a secret project. Now you're working this political murder at a cinema with Stapo forensic people. You will ruin your career, Wulff! Being seen so often with Jews and socialists!"

"Never mind that," Wulff laughed.

"Such a mensch," Levitt told him. "You are an enigma to me, Wulff. And you have not answered my question. You don't really need me on this crime scene. So what am I doing here?"

"Barlach is in bad shape, so I'm told," Wulff said. "He's at the police infirmary now. I know nothing beyond the fact that he came into this washroom and was struck with a blunt instrument on the head. That he's in serious condition. But I do know that you are one of the best medical men in Berlin. I'd like you to come to the infirmary with me and attend to Barlach. It would mean a great deal to me. I want Barlach to receive the best care and not be delivered to a silent ward somewhere to lie unattended. Will you do this for me, Levitt?"

"Ach, such a mensch," Levitt said. He swept past Wulff, saying, "Who would have thought it! Such a mensch!"

— —

Maikowski watched Rom enter the smoky Storm-local, one of a dozen pubs in Charlottenburg that catered to SA men and certain hard-core party officials. Rom was dressed in a natty blue suit with a pink carnation in one of its lapels. He paused here and there on his way toward Maikowski to speak with tough cadre members, party bigwigs, some unemployed who slept on wooden cots in the back. The pub smelled of cabbage and stale cigarette smoke. Maikowski kicked out a wooden chair, and Rom sat, breathed deeply, and sighed.

"What the fuck in hell have you done?" Maikowski asked him angrily.

"Nothing," Rom said.

Maikowski was nursing a cup of tea. "Bruckmann is dead, you idiot," he said maliciously.

"I didn't kill him, for fuck's sake," Rom growled. "Loos must have done it."

"The finger will point to us."

"We turn the finger to the army."

"Perhaps the army really did it," Maikowski said hopefully.

"Doubtful," Rom said. "What do we do about Loos?"

"Yes—what?"

"This Loos, he's crazy. We know next to nothing about him. He worked for Bruckmann as a termite. He's a goddamn janitor. He killed Bruckmann."

"What did you tell Loos?"

"I told him to forget Bruckmann. I told him we'd deal with Bruckmann, keep him on his police job, that he'd be useful in that position and could be blackmailed for years. Loos asked if he could meet the man one last time."

"And you agreed?"

"He gave me no choice."

Maikowski sipped his black tea. It was Russian tea, a fondness Maikowski enjoyed, a preserve of the old days. He tapped a knuckle on the table. "I trust Loos will have useful information for us. If he killed a police detective, there will be hell to pay. They will conduct an exhaustive investigation. No stone unturned and all that nonsense."

"I speak with Loos next week," Rom said. "He wishes to meet on the Spree boat."

"We *do* need his information," Maikowski said. "The Jew Weiss is trying to tighten the screws. God knows what he has up his filthy sleeve. This murder comes at a most unfortunate time. Hitler has declared a policy of legality."

"I couldn't agree more," Rom said blandly.

"Piss on that crazy, fucking janitor," Maikowski said.

Again, Rom agreed.

14

The police infirmary was a drab, two-story pile of soot-covered brick located three blocks from Alexanderplatz HQ on a busy corner of the Voltaire Magazine. Wulff drove there in his Opel and waited in a grimly lighted hall while Levitt examined X rays, consulted with the emergency physicians, and looked over the patient himself. Wulff smoked four cigarettes one after the other before Levitt emerged from a set of swinging doors carrying a metal tray of negatives. He was wearing a borrowed white smock, blue rubber gloves, and was chewing an unlit cigar. He looked at Wulff and shook his head, glancing down at the tray of X rays.

"A fractured skull," Levitt said.

"How bad is it?"

"I can't lie to you," Levitt said. "It is very bad." He shuffled the negatives distractedly, as though he thought he might find something new, holding one or two up to the poor light, confirming to himself those things he already understood.

"Can he speak?"

"He's in a deep coma," Levitt replied. "That's something to be thankful for in a way. There is a brain hemorrhage and the cortex has swollen. It is nature's way of protecting from further injury. Right now there is nothing to be done until the swelling goes down."

"What is the prognosis?" Wulff was pacing in tiny circles, around and around a two-meter circumference. "Is he going to live? And if he does, will he have a real life?"

"Live," Levitt intoned. "Come and sit down with me for a moment," he added gently, taking Wulff by the elbow and leading him down the hall toward a tiny waiting area.

"What is it?" Wulff asked when they got there.

"I told you he was bad, dear Wulff," Levitt sighed. He put a single hand on Wulff's shoulder, offering him a thin but generous smile. "There is something strange in all this, though. I must say."

"Strange?" Wulff asked. "Strange in what way?"

"I helped dress the head wounds just now. There were two serious contusions, one of considerable gravity on the forehead and another on the right temple. These were also compression wounds. Just what you'd expect from a blunt instrument. One can see the depressions clearly, conical in shape. I looked at one of the swabs very carefully, and some have been delivered to the forensic team at Alexanderplatz. But I could see minute particles under the microscope myself."

"What sorts of particles?"

"It appears to be wood. Black and heavily grained."

"What kind of wood?"

"My guess would be walnut."

Wulff thought. "The police use black walnut truncheons."

"Yes, of course," Levitt said. "That's why I thought it strange."

"But anyone could have a truncheon. They are sold openly as surplus."

"The SA uses a black walnut truncheon as well," Levitt said. "Cut in half, these can be concealed underneath a coat or jacket."

"The SA does that. Avoids the ban on weapons by concealing theirs."

"So I've heard," Levitt said.

Wulff was pacing in circles again, bitter tropes of worry. "Whoever killed Bruckmann struck Barlach when he walked into the washroom. He carried the truncheon under an overcoat or raincoat. Perhaps he's a policeman." This made sense to Wulff if it was the termite who killed Bruckmann. "Or perhaps he's a member of the SA, either openly or in sympathy with them."

"Please don't excite yourself," Levitt pleaded. "I know you like Barlach very much. We'll do our best for him, I assure you."

"Can we meet later?"

"I'll see to Barlach and then get down to work on Bruckmann. Come to the morgue late tonight." Levitt walked toward the hall, then paused. Down the hall, they had Barlach on a gurney covered by a white sheet, his head heavily bandaged. "Do you have any idea who did these terrible things?" Levitt asked before moving down the hall.

"A termite," Wulff said.

"A termite! Who is this termite?"

"It isn't important now," Wulff told him. When Levitt had gone, Wulff telephoned Erwin Kisch and arranged a midnight meeting at Johanna's apartment on Lennestrasse. For a free schnapps, Kisch would meet anyone, anywhere, anytime.

— —

Wulff led a three-hour briefing by Stapo's best forensic fingerprint analysts, scene reconstructors, and chemists, all gathered in a third-floor office at Alexanderplatz. There was a partial palm print in a spot of blood on the back wall of the toilet stall where Bruckmann had been garrotted, as if the killer had momentarily lost his balance and placed a hand on the wall for balance. It was a large hand, but the print itself was useless. Each theater patron—of those remaining at three o'clock the day of the killing—had been interviewed exhaustively, and a diagram made of where each had been seated in the theater. The general consensus was that there had been only a few people in the balconies at the time, and despite the ransacking of each patron's individual memory, nothing meaningful emerged from the team.

After the meeting, Wulff ate a sausage and roll, drank a cup of lukewarm tea, then walked down to the morgue in Alexanderplatz's half-basement. It was just after ten o'clock at night, and the hallways were empty save for a janitor who watched Wulff coming down the stairs, and then disappeared into the boiler room. Wulff found Levitt at his desk. On a metal table across the room lay the naked corpse of Oberkommissar Bruckmann, split in half like a butchered chicken, hands and feet pale cobalt blue under the harsh, bright glare of laboratory lamps.

"Ah, Wulff," Levitt said, "come in, come in." Wulff noticed two bodies on metal trays, both covered by sheets, in addition to Bruckmann. "I'm just finishing up the preliminary on Bruckmann."

"Anything new?" Wulff asked.

"Nothing much," Levitt answered. "Time of death, two o'clock." Wulff and Levitt exchanged a weary smile. "But then we knew all this before, didn't we?"

"And the black walnut wood?"

"I've sent samples to your forensic team as well. I think they'll agree with my analysis. I've compared some samples from Kripo truncheons I borrowed here, and they look almost exactly the same under a microscope. I can't be certain of course, which is where your Stapo team will come in handy." Levitt stood and stretched. "May I ask how Barlach is doing now?"

"The same," Wulff said sadly. Wulff had been on the phone to Wilmersdorf Hospital twice during his meeting.

"And the poor man's wife?"

"I spoke with her by phone," Wulff said. "She's not in very good shape. She's pregnant."

"Oh, my goodness," Levitt said.

"But you said there was one surprise," Wulff reminded Levitt.

"Yes, one minor surprise," Levitt said. "I ran a standard toxicology test on Bruckmann. Small amounts of chloral hydrate were found in his blood."

"Chloral hydrate?" Wulff said in surprise.

"Yes, odd isn't it?

"It's what?"

"Knockout drops, if you ask me," Levitt said.

"I wonder what it means," Wulff said. "He obviously wasn't drugged when he walked into the theater."

"It would have been a few days before. I can't think of any modern remedy that utilizes this compound. Perhaps you can search his flat and find out if he was on any medications."

Wulff sighed loudly, exhausted from a long, difficult day. He had decided to see the wife tonight, to drop by the hospital before going home to Johanna's flat. It was well out of the way, but it had to be done. Wilmersdorf Hospital was at the far southwestern edge of Berlin, an hour round trip by car, much more by tram. It would be close, getting back to Lennestrasse by midnight.

"Send the formal autopsy to my office tomorrow, please," Wulff said. "And thank you for seeing to Barlach."

Levitt nodded sadly. Wulff stood in the harsh glare of the lab lights, wishing for something that was just barely out of his reach. He had begun to hate Berlin, its teeming misery, its crime-ridden

Bahnhof districts, its pitiful Hinterhofs. He hated it and he pitied it and he lamented his affection for it.

"Are you quite all right, Wulff?" Levitt asked him.

"Yes," Wulff said, "I'm quite all right, thank you."

— ⌐

Johanna kissed him at the door. She was in a bathrobe and slippers, wearing a night-chignon. She led him to the bathroom where she'd run a tub of water, undressed him casually, then sat beside the tub as Wulff submerged himself.

"Kisch is coming here at midnight," Wulff told her. "I'm sorry." Wulff rested, the first time in what seemed like a full twenty-four hours. He'd spent forty minutes at the hospital conferring with night-staff and nurses, talking with Barlach's lovely wife, a small, compact woman who looked as though she'd been crying for most of the afternoon and evening.

"How is your friend?" Johanna asked, splashing soapy water on his chest. She ran a sponge across his arms and upper neck, rubbing his skin red. Wulff closed his eyes, imagining a waterfall on green jagged slopes. Johanna was there as well, a huge orange orchid in her hair.

"No change," Wulff said, his reverie ended. "The doctor says one can't predict the result of these head injuries. They may have to operate."

"I'm sorry, dear," she said. "Is it too late for us to run off to Switzerland tonight?"

Wulff smiled, eyes closed. She dabbed his face with the sponge, Wulff touching her wrist, kissing her hand, composing a love melody in his head. "Running away won't work now," he said.

"And the poor man's wife?"

"She's strong," Wulff said.

"And what on earth is Kisch coming here for?" She soaped his chest. "By the way, I've made you a tray of cheese and pickles if you want it. I thought you might be hungry when you got here. There may be a bottle of bad schnapps in there as well."

"I'll need time alone with Kisch," Wulff said.

Johanna affected a pout, her face shiny in the damp room. The tile walls dripped with moisture, tiny rivulets tracking down the grout. Wulff spent another ten minutes luxuriating in his bath, the water growing tepid. He dried himself, put on some old clothes he kept at the flat—a pair of woolen slacks, a white unstarched shirt, the gray sweater he wore when they stayed home and listened to jazz and drank vodka on winter evenings. In the parlor, Johanna had put on an Anita Berber record, the room filling with dreamy music, ballads that reminded one of slow-burning fires. Wulff went to the living room and ate a single pickle from the plate, his mind now worming its way toward Bruckmann. When there was a knock on the door, Wulff kissed Johanna. She went to the bedroom.

When Wulff opened the door, Kisch was standing with arms open in gesture of mock supplication, his face ruddy from drink and his hair wildly frizzled. Wulff could smell schnapps on his breath, and the wild-horse look in his eye told tales of an evening on Unter den Linden. He led the journalist to the parlor, where Kisch paced the floor, examined Johanna's African mask collection, then looked out at the Tiergarten, which was plunged into dark.

"Where's the party?" Kisch asked. "You've disappointed me. I expected dancing dervishes, a wild orgy!" Kisch laughed and imitated a belly dancer. "And I thought there would be cocaine!"

"A schnapps, perhaps," Wulff said. Kisch sat down on the ottoman as Wulff got the bottle. He poured a glass for Kisch, who drank it down.

"There—that's better," Kisch sighed. He smacked his lips suggestively. "Much better." He arranged himself dramatically on the ottoman, legs splayed and arms wide, a short barrel-chested man with salt-and-pepper hair and a bright set of puckish eyes. "So, where is the lovely Johanna tonight?" he asked Wulff. "Don't tell me you've evicted her from this lair of psychoanalytic sybaritism?" Kisch raised his empty glass. Wulff poured another schnapps. "You are a lucky dog, Wulff," Kisch laughed.

"She's sleeping," Wulff told him.

"Wulff, you're slipping," Kisch said. "What's all this about?"

"I wanted to talk to you alone."

"Alone? Wulff, you're losing your grip!"

Wulff pulled up a chair. "You've heard about the murder of the police captain named Bruckmann?"

"There's a rumor," Kisch said. "It will be front-page news tomorrow morning."

"Are you interested?"

Erwin Kisch had written freelance for all the socialist papers in Germany and Austria. Although not formally employed by any of them, he was recognized as the most serious and thoughtful writer of his crusading type. He was hated by the Right, mistrusted by the far Left for his uncompromising principle, and respected by almost everybody else.

Kisch clapped his hands. "Is it political? You're telling me this is political?"

"It might be," Wulff said quietly.

"Ah, then I'm interested," Kisch said. "I've been at the Café Megalomania all evening. You can't imagine the wild stories being circulated about Bruckmann's murder. Here we have an Oberkommissar of Department IV discovered dead in a bathroom at the Capitol Cinema on Auguste-Viktoria Platz—and in the middle of a work day! One can only speculate about the homosexual schemes, the wild cocaine parties, the subtleties of pederasty! Was he sucking an usher, Wulff? Ultimately, what is one to say about a captain found strangled in a washroom?"

"Not *merely* strangled," Wulff said.

"Not merely strangled, you say?"

"Garroted," Wulff said.

"How delightful!" Kisch squealed. "How fucking marvelous!"

"There's more," Wulff told him. He filled the schnapps glass. "He was found hanging from a coat hook in the stall."

Kisch slapped his knee in delight. He drained the schnapps and helped himself to another. The record had stopped. There was silence on the street except for an occasional tram bell.

"Is that why I'm here?" Kisch asked. "To discuss Bruckmann's death? To have a good laugh?"

"I want this meeting to remain our secret," Wulff said.

"I'm not being followed," Kisch said. "At least not yet. When the Nazis gain control, then I'll be followed."

"They'll not take over."

Kisch laughed cynically. "I hope you're right!" he exclaimed. "But it is best to be realistic, no?"

Kisch drank another glass of schnapps. Wulff had been with him at many parties and had seen his prodigious ability, the man finishing a bottle while remaining on his feet. His face would redden and his gestures become frantic and exuberant, but he never seemed to lose control. It amazed and astonished Wulff. "But really, dear Wulff, what am I doing here?" Kisch asked at last.

"Erwin, listen to me carefully," Wulff said. "I want to plant an article in the press. In some middlebrow paper that everybody reads and then uses to wrap fish heads. Can it be arranged?"

"I suppose it could," Kisch said, wrinkling a brow. "It isn't strictly ethical, you know."

"An article about Bruckmann. And perhaps another article about another murder as well."

Kisch put down his glass. He rubbed his chin reflectively and frowned. "And what is the nature of this first article?" he asked.

"That either the SA or army is responsible for Bruckmann's death," Wulff said. "It is a white lie, off center by perhaps millimeters only."

Kisch clapped his hands again. "But Wulff, this is incredible! Why would the SA kill Bruckmann? He's almost one of them!"

"Nevertheless," Wulff said.

"And I'm to float this story? What of my reputation? What of my long history of sober veracity and ethical behavior?" Kisch smiled knowingly, winking at Wulff.

"I have my reasons," Wulff said. "And I wouldn't even mention it unless it was important. Sowing the seeds of discontent, that sort of thing. I can keep you informed of all the pertinent details of the case when they become known. And I promise you the absolute truth after this one little slip. You will have an exclusive lead on this story. You can cover it as a political one and you'll be essentially correct."

"Not simple speculation? I won't be led down a garden path."

"Use your own byline."

"This has to be reasonably true," Kisch said.

"Always," Wulff promised.

Kisch thought for a moment, then poured a schnapps. "Why are you doing this?" he asked.

"You want the truth?" Wulff asked. "Or would you rather be officially in the dark?"

Kisch shrugged and sniffed the schnapps. It was cheap stuff, and Johanna had chilled it. Good schnapps was rare in Berlin, and very expensive. "Why not the truth? If I'm tortured, I'll hold out long enough to get you a message!"

"All right then," Wulff said. "I don't know if either the SA or army is behind this killing. I think perhaps they have some involvement, however slight. But the one that is absolutely innocent may have reason to cooperate with me and provide sensitive data."

Kisch smiled broadly. "How very ingenious, Wulff," he said.

"Plant it without attribution at first if you wish," Wulff said. "If it goes nowhere, you'll be off the hook. If it develops, you can have your scoop."

"Very funny, very funny," Kisch said. "But I think this could be dangerous for you. You are known as the lead investigator in this matter. People will know where this information comes from. You will be suspected immediately as a leak."

"Write an article for the *Berliner Zeitung* or for the *Weltbühne*. Bury it in the middle somewhere. Make it as hypothetical as you wish. It will be noticed. I'll supply you with juicy details. I *want* it known that there is a leak."

"You are quite remarkable," Kisch said. "And in return you give me an exclusive on the rest of the case? Top to bottom, Wulff, no holds barred. Nothing expurgated or censored. No getting cold feet. I'm tired of writing half-baked political shit. I want to write it the way it happens."

"No holds barred, Kisch," Wulff said.

"And this is all you ask? It can't be that important?"

"It goes somewhere else as well."

"And I don't need to know where?"

"That's right," Wulff said. "And there is a small quid pro quo."

"Ah, I'm so glad," Kisch laughed. "Otherwise, I would have to reconsider your reputation. I might have to reclassify you as one of the fools."

"There was a murder in the Hirrenstrasse last autumn," Wulff said. "I want you to plant a lengthy profile of the suspected murderer."

"But Wulff!" Kisch protested. "You know I don't do bourgeois crime stories! They are so bloody boring and repetitive. They are so— how shall I say it—heartrending!"

"Then ask one of your bourgeois colleagues to plant the story. I'll even write it for you!" Wulff sat forward, hands on knees. "Yes, that's it! I'll write the article in journalese, and you find a place for it in the bourgeois press. I'll make it somewhat sensational. I want it in tabloids where it will be read. Something with a wide circulation with the working class and petit bourgeois. I want clerks reading it on the way to work."

Kisch waved a hand. "I've never heard of this murder," he declaimed.

"I'll write the damn article!" Wulff laughed. "Surely you can call in a favor."

"And who is this murderer of yours?"

"I have no idea."

"Then how can there be a profile?"

"A profile is a shadow. Isn't that the definition of a profile?"

Kisch clucked his tongue. "I have it!" he shouted. "This is another of your stalking horses isn't it? You have an ulterior motive!"

"Do we have a deal?" Wulff asked.

Wulff watched Kisch think. He was known to be a man who took chances, a gambler and a tempter of fate.

"Ach, why not?" Kisch said. "Give me the information on Bruckmann and I'll write your article. I'll see to both projects. You can rely on me. Those bootlickers in the bourgeois press will print anything that stinks of death and scandal."

Wulff played more Anita Berber and poured two glasses of schnapps from the half-empty bottle. They drank schnapps and listened to music until almost one o'clock in the morning.

Wulff lay on his side listening to the beat of her heart. She was only half-asleep.

"I could hear you out there," Johanna whispered.

"That was Anita Berber," Wulff told her. "Go to sleep."

"Let's run away."

"I thought that was impossible."

"I mean for the weekend, silly."

"And get married?"

"Now you're silly a second time."

"I'm not being silly," Wulff said. He raised his head and looked at her.

"*Rassenschande*," Johanna said. "Marrying me would be a race crime. It would make you guilty."

"I don't want to hear this even in jest," Wulff said. He placed a hand on her stomach.

"It is the truth, even if it isn't said." She mussed his hair and sighed. "What were you doing out there with Kisch? He's quite crazy, you know."

"Never mind. Go back to sleep."

"Do you want to make love?"

"It's late. Go to sleep."

"In the morning, darling," she said. "But if you want to now, it is all right with me."

"I know," Wulff said.

He lay quietly then, investigating the silence. He thought of Poel Island, as he often did, the summers he spent there as a boy, the many nights he'd lain awake with his brothers regarding the violence and glamour of the Baltic night. Now in Berlin there was only the breath of his lover and the snick-snack of a breeze against lace curtains.

15

Wulff carried his favorite weapons—a non-issue Walther pistol, along with a standard police Parabellum 7.65, both in oiled leather holsters. Over one shoulder he had strapped his father's war-vintage Mauser and scope. They were walking in single file along a sandy path toward the cliffs and the beach below, Gunter Wulff cautiously picking his way through the bracken and wet ferns. Halfway down, Gunter Wulff sat down heavily on a boulder they'd excavated from the cliff-side years before. Early this morning, Wulff had come down by himself and set up paper targets on a cup-of-sand hill just sixty meters from the boulder. Wulff checked his Mauser, loaded it, then handed the weapon to his father who cradled it in one arm, touched the sight with a tip of his right thumb, then smiled to himself as though it were some instinctual mode of communication, man-to-gun.

Gunter Wulff fired, producing a sharp crack. He had hit the first target, slightly outside the bull's-eye and to the left, but for a man with a tender hip, failing eyesight, and a bad case of arthritis in the shoulder, it was an excellent shot.

"It's my eyes," Gunter Wulff lamented. "How long has it been since we've done this?"

Wulff didn't answer. It was a purely rhetorical question, a thinking-out-loud in the cloudburst of memories that hovered between them. Wulff checked his Walther, loaded it, then contemplated the wood and iron in his hand. He extended his arm and fired. Part of the paper target ripped and fluttered to earth. He'd been a couple of centimeters from center.

"Peter taught you well," his father said dryly.

"Both of you."

Gunter Wulff lifted the rifle, sighted, and fired another round. The whine of the bullet amazed Wulff as it always did. Wulff and his father were in a cove shelter from the wind, though on the cliff-top they could see firs swirling. There were whitecaps out on the Baltic, where a single sailboat braved rough seas. Gunter Wulff had scored a bull's-eye.

"How is Berlin now?" the old man asked. He shouldered the rifle, accepting its weight with a grimace.

"In chaos," Wulff told him.

In the weeks before his visit, Wulff had been spending most of his time combing through Bruckmann's available military records, interviewing associates and police officials, running down available leads. Weiss had informed him that the termite was still at work, an irritant at most. And as for the murderer of Timkin Mueller, Wulff was no closer than he'd been for months.

"Surely not in chaos," Gunter Wulff said. "It can't be that bad."

Wulff fired the Walther and pierced his target. "The communists killed a Schupo Oberwachtmeister named Kuhfeld this summer. They ambushed him near Bülow Platz and the Liebknecht HQ. The poor fellow was minding his own business and was shot in the dark. Supposedly, it was revenge for an arrest he'd made months before."

"You have suspects in custody?"

"Not yet," Wulff said. "Weiss has Stapo on the case. And then another Schupo named Zanhert was killed near the Seventy-second Precinct by communists. He was a Hauptmeister. Two Schupo murders in one summer."

"They've killed a sergeant and a master sergeant?" Gunter Wulff asked. "And nobody can stop them?"

"The Nazis are worse," Wulff said. "They cause riots, intimidate news vendors, and march constantly. They select KPD members who are out on the street alone and beat them to a bloody pulp. They harass the Jews of Alt-Köln. They raid communist pubs and set them on fire. They destroy newspaper kiosks if the vendors won't sell Nazi papers."

Wulff fired the Walther again. His shot tore clean through the bull's-eye. He was surprising himself, how he'd managed to maintain this level of skill with so little recent practice.

"I read the news sometimes," Gunter Wulff said. "It's almost more than I can bear. Even at my age!"

Wulff loaded and fired the Parabellum. He struck an outer ring, dissatisfied with the balance and weight of the heavy police weapon.

"I have something for you," Gunter Wulff said suddenly. There was a palpable silence. "I have something for you that is of great significance, son."

Wulff sat down on the boulder. The sun had broken a ring of high clouds again, shedding diaphanous light on the surface of the sea, crystals of color that dappled the surf.

"But Father—" Wulff said.

Gunter Wulff touched his son's shoulder, an affectionate gesture. He cradled the Mauser again, breached it, sent a shell flying. "I've been given a secret dossier on Bruckmann," he said. "You'd be surprised at how thick it is. Many pages of notes, memoranda, observations, along with some old photographs. The Reichswehr has had its eye on this fellow for a long time now, although he has been allowed to proceed through the police ranks unhindered on the theory that he might be of use some day, and that he was relatively harmless in his current position." Gunter Wulff paused and looked at the sea with one hand over his eyes. "But his career is fully documented."

"I don't know what to say," Wulff told his father.

"It is too late to say anything," Gunter Wulff said. "I believe the Reichswehr intelligence staff reads all the Berlin newspapers. They are aware that certain speculations place suspicion on them for the murder of Bruckmann. This is their way of saying they had no part in such activities. No part whatsoever."

"I planted the articles," Wulff admitted. "It was my intention that the Reichswehr come directly to me if they wished to deny their involvement. I did not want to involve you further, believe me. It is well known that I am the chief investigator on the Bruckmann case. I saw no reason why they should contact you."

"It is their way of closing the books on my deficit account for favors," Gunter Wulff said. "After this, they owe me nothing further. And by implication, they owe you nothing either."

"I meant for them to come to me," Wulff said, suddenly ashamed of involving his father.

"Ah, but they trust me, Harry," the old man said. "I take it you never really believed the army was involved?"

"Never," Wulff said.

"These documents have come with a proviso," Gunter Wulff said.

"Of course."

"The army wishes that these documents never leave Poel Island. I've given my word on this to former colleagues. So, you see why I invited you on this urgent visit. Why I feigned my little illness."

"And you mentioned target practice," Wulff said.

"That part was true."

"Have you looked at the dossier?"

"I have looked at the inventory, Harry," Gunter Wulff said. "Only to exercise my responsibility for all the documents. I must account to the army for each one and return them. I have given my solemn word on this, Harry."

"I'll not disappoint you, Father."

Gunter Wulff laughed gently. "Of course you won't," he said. "And I suppose the Reichswehr prefers even the Prussian police as allies over the SA."

"It is because the SA wishes to replace the army as Germany's military arm."

"Yes, this is doggerel of the worst sort," Gunter Wulff said.

"How long do I have with the dossier?"

"This weekend and no longer. You have tonight and you have all day tomorrow. Then I must return it intact. You may make no copies and no photographs of photographs. You will rely on your memory or your own notes, but nothing verbatim. And even these notes must be unsigned and uninitialed." Gunter Wulff looked out to sea again, then back to his son. "And my word is your word."

"As always," Wulff agreed.

Wulff wiped down the Walther with an oilcloth, then holstered it. He reloaded the Parabellum, emptying it at a paper target with little luck. Father and son sat together in the sun for a long time, talking about the old days. They walked back to the lodge for a lunch of boiled pork and fresh beans and drank two Dutch beers Gunter Wulff had been saving for a special occasion.

━ ━

Dieter Rom entered the Storm-local where Maikowski had been drinking schnapps for an hour, shot after shot of liquor chased by lager. In the doorway, he paused to adjust his eyes to the semi-dark, then walked directly to Maikowski's table in back.

"You're late," Maikowski growled, staring into his glass.

Rom contemplated the thousand and one annoying Maikowskis, his surly moods, his attenuated drunkenness, the barking of official orders from a mouth fouled by coarse epithets and obscenities. Rom himself preferred the pretty drolleries of party officials, men he could manipulate with humor and intellect, the playful wellsprings of his offbeat sadism. He believed that the infliction of pain without irony was an empty exercise, a practice fit only for dullards. Unless one derived ironic satisfaction from pain, what was its use in life? He truly believed Maikowski to be a man who derived no true satisfaction from the infliction of pain, neither pleasure nor intellectual stimulation.

"And you're drunk," Rom said.

"Not so fucking drunk as you are late," Maikowski told him.

Rom withstood a malevolent grin, one which showed Maikowski's bad teeth. In some ways, these exchanges amused both men, satisfying their curiosity and framing their bond.

"We're wasting time," Rom said.

Maikowski looked at Rom, his eyes shiny with alcohol. "Piss on it then," he said.

"I just delivered one hundred marks to our termite," Rom said. "We met on the Spree tour boat. I'm changing our meeting place. There are no tourists in Berlin now and the boat is conspicuously empty. Two men sitting together on a tour boat in summer. How ridiculous!"

"Change it then."

"Where would you suggest?"

"Try the White Mouse in Franzosischenstrasse."

"Ah, that's perfect," Rom said. "A cabaret filled with prancing queers."

Maikowski drank some beer and licked froth from his lips. "You're not a secret prancing queer, are you?"

Rom ignored the insult. "We have a problem with the termite," he said.

"I'm aware."

"The *Berliner Zeitung* is speculating that the death of Bruckmann was caused somehow by the SA. It has been implied that our termite is the killer and that we in the SA are his sponsor. Now we're paying one hundred marks a week to the man who killed Bruckmann. He is becoming as much a liability as an asset."

"And what do you suggest?"

"Perhaps we survey him for a time."

Maikowski lit a cigar and motioned to a waiter who was standing in a corner of the room, arms folded. The waiter delivered another schnapps to Maikowski who sipped it with obvious relish. "Do you have any other suggestions?" Maikowski asked.

"Only an observation," Rom said. "I think our termite is crazy in the head."

"I'm shocked!" Maikowski roared. "A killer, a traitor, a Freicorps freebooter, and you tell me he is crazy in his head! Rom you're a master psychologist!"

"Piss off," Rom said.

"Shall we kill this termite of ours?"

"Let's give him a few months," Rom said. "I'll control him for now, but sooner or later he's going to become a complete liability. Besides, we now have more and more loyal party members in every police precinct in Berlin. In time, we'll control the force and have no need for this termite of ours. The Jew Weiss is already hiring party members and he doesn't even know it. We'll shove the SA up his ass."

"Oh, I quite agree," Maikowski said. "So watch this janitor closely. Perhaps this newspaper attack on the SA will die out in time. There are enough political murders to distract even the closest of attention spans. Even a sow like Kisch will go away sooner or later."

"But this man, Wulff—"

"Yes, he's quite a danger."

"He has his finger on this termite."

"Perhaps Wulff will do our dirty work for us."

The pale blues of twilight surrounded Wulff. He looked up from his reading—the Bruckmann dossier—and recalled his mother's face. In the distance, dogs were barking. There had been a funeral at the village church and summer fog had begun to blanket the coast.

Wulff read about Bruckmann during his army career on the battlefields of Belgium, the terrible face and neck wounds that had altered his appearance and cost him an eye, wounds that had transformed him from a soldier to a spy. He had run internment camps for civilian officials, bureaucrats, foreign nationals, town mayors, and petty politicians. Later, he'd commanded prisoner-of-war camps, still organizing traitors and spies who groveled for food from their German captors. He found the names of informers organized into cells run by Bruckmann and his colleagues and henchmen. He followed Bruckmann's Freicorps cadres through campaigns after the war, rampaging through the defeated countryside like so many dirty condottiere. There were reports of torture, murder, wantonness, mayhem committed for sport and in the name of German nationalism.

In the dim light, Wulff held up four badly yellowed photographs from those days. In one, Bruckmann stood full front and on his right a man named Braun—Edgar Braun, with a face obscured by other faces, a heavy woolen cap pulled down over a pugnacious face, a busy head of dark curly hair, a patch of bright sun on one arm. And then Edgar Braun had dropped out of sight in Freiburg late in 1923 during a particularly bad epidemic of influenza. In every photo, it was Braun just to the right of Bruckmann, a kind of Judas figure.

Wulff put down the dossiers and lit a cigarette. It was nearly ten o'clock. On the horizon there was a faint glow, as though somewhere the forest was burning. Ships were passing in the strait. He could hear them, the faint rumble of their engines, an occasional foghorn. Wulff had isolated perhaps a dozen close associates of Bruckmann from his early days, but most of them were presently accounted for, either dead or enlisted in the army, men occupying places of responsibility in the judiciary or civil bureaucracy. Only Edgar Braun was missing.

Wulff put down his work and greeted his father, who had walked out onto the porch. Wulff had been studying the reports for six hours, a long stretch.

"Is any of it useful?" Gunter Wulff asked.

"It is very complete."

"I'm not surprised," Gunter Wulff said. "I was on the staff at Intelligence. The Reichswehr spends considerable time gathering information. In some ways it is quite ridiculous. And in other ways, it is surprising what a little information can do for one's sense of well-being."

"There is one man in particular," Wulff said. "I have no reason to worry about him, except that he seems to have disappeared from the record in 1923. Most of Bruckmann's other associates turn up here and there in places of authority. Or they are dead. But nine years ago, this fellow Braun just disappeared. It was during an influenza epidemic, so perhaps he died."

"And his background?"

"He's Belgian. From the village of Juprelle just north of Liège. I have the name of his mother, but there is no mention of the father. It is strange, a Belgian becoming involved in the German Freicorps movement. Apparently he did most of Bruckmann's dirty work during the Ruhr uprisings and particularly in Munich during the Soviet."

"It is a very slender thread," Gunter Wulff said.

"But it is more than I had before."

"And have you finished?"

"I'm only halfway through the reports."

"You return to Berlin tomorrow night?"

"I'll stay up late. Work all day tomorrow."

"Please stay, Harry. Stay as long as you wish."

"I must return," Wulff said.

"Will you be promoted?"

"Into Bruckmann's position?" Wulff said. "I'm being considered."

"I am proud of you, son," Gunter Wulff said.

"I know you are, Father."

"And what about Johanna?"

"I'd like you to meet her."

"Perhaps."

The servant Andrew had put on a recording of English music hall fluff and was listening to it in his quarters at the back of the house.

"I want to marry her," Wulff said.

Gunter Wulff sat down in a rocker. He looked out at the fog. "You have asked her?" he said.

"I've asked."

"And she says?"

"She avoids the subject. She says it would be foolish. She jokes that it is a race crime."

"Perhaps she is right to avoid the subject."

"Father."

"Don't be angry," Gunter Wulff said quickly. "We both know there is no such thing as a race crime. But it does affect people. It enters their minds in subtle ways. It graces the table every time one sits down. It would end your career, and you would be unhappy, and she would be blamed. You would suffer from resentment."

Wulff crushed out his cigarette. "I don't want to talk about it," he said.

"You're angry," Gunter Wulff said.

"I'm angry that your views represent the majority opinion," Wulff said.

Gunter Wulff stood. "Yes, perhaps you're right," he said.

Wulff stayed up late reading by the light of kerosene lamps. At midnight, he came across a scribbled note made by a Freicorps mole at Intelligence. Edgar Braun's specialty was the garrote.

— —

The Sunday papers were in a pile on the floor. Wulff was in pajamas. Johanna was wearing a velvet nightdress, perched in bare feet at the opposite end of the ottoman while Wulff smoked, easing back from two days of pouring over the Bruckmann dossiers.

He opened the *Frankfurter Zeitung*. GERMAN BANKS CLOSED in black letters. Foreign exchange was fleeing Germany, exports had dried to a trickle, the Central Bank was lending its reserves to float credit for necessities like heating oil, coal, and food. Loans for provincial banks were nonexistent. The *Berliner Zeitung*: BANK SHUTDOWN ORDERED. QUIET CHAOS.

Wulff drank half a glass of milk. He touched one foot to Johanna's knee. They exchanged a smile.

"My practice is now two Jewish housewives," Johanna lamented. "And how is your father?"

"We went shooting," Wulff said. "We walked down to the beach and shot for the first time in years. It isn't easy for him to climb down the cliffs. He's seventy-six and a little crippled in the hip."

"Did you talk about us?"

Wulff studied the headlines. Disaster, ruin, violence. A generation doomed. Instead of answering her, he shrugged and smiled weakly.

"Will you be promoted?" she asked.

"I'm being considered. The final decision rests with the Assistant Kommissar for Department IV. But Weiss is influential, and I think he's recommending me."

"I have something wonderful to tell you," Johanna whispered. "It's a surprise!"

"We could use good tidings."

"Your friend Barlach is conscious."

Wulff sat up. "That *is* wonderful."

"A duty nurse called here. You'd left this number, and she left a message with me."

"Did she tell you anything else?"

"Just that he was awake and eating," Johanna answered. "I knew you'd be pleased. He seems to mean something to you."

"Oh yes," Wulff said.

"You like him, don't you?"

Wulff nodded. "Marry me, darling," he said.

Johanna looked startled. She bit her lip, and a tear pearled the corner of her right eye. "Oh please dear, not now."

"Why not now?"

"The country is so sick," she said. "One can't just ignore it, pretend one can marry and raise children."

"Germany stands in our way?" Wulff asked.

"I'm a Jew, Harry," Johanna said. "And you come from an aristocratic Schleswig family known for its attachments to the army. You have a position in the police that is becoming more political every day. If you marry me, it will be like committing suicide."

"You ascribe to realism," Wulff said. "Life without you would be a form of suicide."

Johanna smiled weakly. "Darling, listen to me," she said. "The banks in Germany are closed. According to the papers, there have been three hundred political murders in Germany so far this year. The clothes in my closet are falling apart thread by thread because the material is ersatz. We drink ersatz milk made from powder and we eat ersatz cheese and there is no toilet paper in the stores. My aunt sends me pickles from her farm and we rejoice. Jews are beaten in the streets of Berlin. Is this an atmosphere in which you wish to make a gamble with everything?"

Wulff had heard it all before, dozens of times. The whys and why-nots were driving him mad. "In sickness and in health. For richer and for poorer. For better and for worse. I believe in the power of human love."

Johanna put her head in his lap. "Of course you do," she said. "And I love you more than you can know."

Wulff stroked her hair. He loved its texture, its tones, and its abundance. "We could run away. Abandon ship."

"And what would we do for money?"

Wulff had his salary and nothing more. His father had the Poel lodge and a small pension. The rest had gone in the inflation or had been depleted by his mother's lengthy illness.

"You're so practical," Wulff said. "I can work."

"And I'll take in ironing!" Johanna said.

"I'm not joking," Wulff said.

"And where would we go?"

"France? Austria?"

"The Jews are hated in those countries more than they are hated in Germany."

It was true. They both knew it was true. Europe had become a deep vessel of hate. A sewer. Wulff leaned over and kissed her ear as two large teardrops rolled down her cheeks. "Let's talk about something else, darling," she said. "Are you making progress in the Bruckmann investigation?"

Wulff dried her tears with a handkerchief. "Yes, a little," he said. He would live on the moon with Johanna if it were possible. He would roam its dry craters.

"I almost forgot, darling!" Johanna said suddenly. She left the room, then returned carrying a small paper package tied with brown string. "For you," she said, handing him the package. "The postman delivered it here Saturday after you'd left for Poel. I thought it strange that you'd receive mail here, but I decided it was from a close friend. Open it!"

Wulff held the package, testing its weight, contemplating its surprises. There was no return address, only his own name printed in block letters with a pen. The postmark was Central Berlin.

"It isn't from my father," Wulff said. He snapped the string and peeled back two layers of brown paper. Johanna leaned over expectantly. Inside the package was a paper doll on flat cardboard with fashion magazine photographs pasted onto the backing. Wulff examined its face—a fashion-model smile, slinky evening dress, long shoulder-length gloves. Its blonde hair was trimmed short in the modern style, hair that cupped a round face with arched eyebrows, the unmistakable whiskers of a cat, a small pinkish mouth. Kohl-rimmed eyes and white makeup.

"Another doll," Wulff muttered. "You say it came here Saturday after I'd gone?"

Johanna said, "What does it mean?"

Wulff held the doll and studied it, contemplated its silent testimony. "It's a message," he said. "It's a warning and a challenge."

"But darling—"

Wulff rewrapped the doll in tissue and covered it with brown paper, then retied the string. "I'm afraid we're too late," he said.

"Too late dear? What's it all about?"

Wulff felt cold. "If this is a message, then it is telling me that there's been another murder. Perhaps on Saturday this victim was still alive."

"But why send the doll *here*?" Johanna said.

"You've seen the series of articles Kisch placed in the *Zeitung?*"

"The ones about the Hirrenstrasse murderer? Yes, I've seen those, dear. I told you it was a dangerous game."

"The killer has read them too. This proves it. He wants to challenge me directly. He wants me to know that he's been watching. That he knows my personal life. In a way, it is a correlative of my investigations of him. He's answering me, Johanna. I can smell him."

"I thought this might happen," Johanna said.

"Perhaps he hasn't killed yet," Wulff said. "I think I should go to the office."

"But it's Sunday night. You're exhausted. It's too late to do anything, isn't it?"

Wulff knew she was right. It was too late. It was always too late.

"You're right," Wulff said. "And besides, I'm worried for you now. If he knows about you and me, he's had his eye on this apartment. We're going to have to be very careful, dear."

"I'm afraid," Johanna said.

Wulff shared her fear. But he was angry as well. He hated bringing Johanna so close to a killer.

PART
THREE

SUMMER–WINTER 1931

"When someone speaks to me of culture, I reach for my revolver."
—Hermann Göring

16

He had spent Saturday afternoon spying on the Jewish woman and Harry Wulff, watching them wander the Tiergarten, feeding pigeons and throwing peanuts to hungry squirrels. Later, he'd gone to Mauerstrasse, in heavy evening traffic, where the crowds were thick, despite a depressed economy. On Jagerstrasse, he had turned east, walking toward the El Dorado with his heart pounding. He went inside the nightclub without stopping to take off his topcoat, sat at his usual table, and picked up the heavy black telephone. He was momentarily startled to come eye to eye with Uli and her cat face. And then, thank God, Uli was on the phone, caressing him with the soft meticulous cadences of her cat-voice.

"Meow, meow," Uli cooed.

Loos stared up at her, suffocating his senses with the purple dress that clung to her body like spring rain. "Uli," he stammered ingloriously. He felt out of breath, stunned and running knee-deep in streams of blood. "I have money, Uli," he said stupidly.

When the waiter came, he ordered champagne and crème de menthe for the woman, and an apple brandy for himself. From his corner table in the crowded nightclub, a table where he'd sat for night after surreal night, he could see her in full view, Uli at her table in the balcony directly across the dance floor. Before him, the checked black-and-white tablecloth, the ceramic ashtrays, the black candle burning in its holder, all seemed to waver and distort. Tiny star bulbs on the ceiling cast a dim glow on Uli. A grainy pall of cigar smoke hung in the room.

Loos watched as the waiter delivered his proffered drink, Uli smiling, touching the fluted glass, her lips glistening and offering Loos a smile for his two marks. Her gloved hand caressed a breast, cupping it gingerly.

"I have money," Loos stammered again, flushed now with the nearness of his future. "I have money and I want to take you home. I want to go home with you, Uli."

"All right, my little dear," Uli breathed over the line. "But later, please, dear. After the evening is over. Uli has work."

"Now, now," Loos shouted petulantly. "I've waited so long. It has been such a long wait."

Uli put down the fluted glass and adjusted her gloves. The small house orchestra had stopped playing, and dancers were returning to their tables. Loos was wearing his black mask, the one given him at the door by a distracted hostess. Uli settled her gaze on him. He felt fixed in its radiance.

"I have one hundred marks," Loos said calmly. He felt suddenly in control.

"But I must work, my darling," Uli protested. "Come back late tonight. Come back at midnight. I'll leave the club a little early for my Siegfried!"

"Now, now," Loos protested again.

Uli was silent, watching the dancers. "But darling, can you give me another twenty-five marks for the waiter and the bartender? They depend on me, upon my tips. It would be unfair to leave them in the middle of the evening unless I can compensate them." She licked her cat lips. "You've been very patient, haven't you, Siegfried?" She sipped champagne and crème de menthe, torturing the moment with silence. "Just leave twenty-five marks on the table. I'll tell the waiter."

Loos counted out the amount in gold and stacked it in plain sight on the table, a pile of money just tawnier than his apple brandy. Uli stood, watching as Loos counted out the marks, admiring their symmetry and allure. Loos felt a gust of pride tease his body. Uli stood and dropped a rabbit stole. There were bare patches on the stole where the fur had fallen out. "Meet me outside at the corner of Mauerstrasse," Uli said, hanging up the phone.

Loos left the table and made his way through the crowd. He tossed his mask at the doorman, then fled into the night, finding himself on Jagerstrasse, sniffing the warm exhaust-riddled summer night. He passed under the marquee of the Mickey Mouse Review, which advertised naked women who pranced like rodents, tail to tail, rat noses touching rat asses. Waiting impatiently at the corner of Mauerstrasse, he watched the whores parading in their summer best.

Just then Uli touched his shoulder, and a bolt of electricity passed through him. A hottish breeze ruffled her stole. Up close, Loos thought she appeared older, her skin cracked under its layers of white makeup. There were creases in her forehead, lines that reminded him of his landlady, the one who waited up for him on weekend nights when he'd roam the clubs and bars.

"You're quite a big boy," Uli said.

A group of sailors was engaged in laughter. The night sky seemed to reflect neon.

"Do you have a place for us?" Uli asked nonchalantly.

"It is too far. Just a room."

"I have a place," she said. "But it is far, too. But we could go there if you like."

"Please, let's go to your place," Loos said, calming himself by secretly touching the garrote in his overcoat pocket. Uli put an arm through his, as lovers might, Loos stealing a glance at the sky, hoping to call comfort from its immensity. "Your place, yes," Loos murmured. "Let's go to your place. I can pay for a taxi."

Uli hailed a cab, both of them riding in back, with Loos on the left behind the driver. As they heaved into traffic, Uli placed a hand on his thigh, then moved it up and down suggestively as Loos closed his eyes. He rolled down a window and breathed the night air as the cab sped past the Potsdamer Bahnhof, skirting an edge of the Tiergarten where Loos only that afternoon had sat observing the apartment of the Jewess and her police lover. Flanking railroad tracks led toward the suburbs of Charlottenburg. The chestnuts were shedding white blossoms that fell like summer snow.

She touched his penis through thick trousers. He felt as though his skeleton might shatter and collapse into a helpless pile of sticks. She kissed his ear and he smelled her sweet, crème de menthe breath. "Shall I fix you in the taxi while we ride through the night?" Uli asked.

"Please, later," he found himself answering.

"You *are* a shy one!" she whispered.

"Give us a kiss then," Uli sighed coyly. "Give Uli a kiss for the long ride home."

Loos received her mouth, her lips lighting on his like a moth. When he opened his eyes again, he could see that they'd come to the slums of a communist neighborhood called Little Wedding, row upon row of brick houses and shops, dreary little pubs with a few tables still out front. Then the taxi slowed, the driver creeping along, seeking some address or another that Uli had given him. She whispered a phrase Loos failed to decipher. Uli traced his penis with one hand. "I can hardly wait for that big cock," she said in mock breathlessness.

Loos paid the cabbie three marks. They walked in single-file down a dark alley, then up a flight of wooden stairs to a narrow-roofed landing where Uli fumbled in her purse for keys, Loos with his back to a drop-off of three stories.

Down a hallway, the apartment had two rooms, a bed that fed away from the wall, a three-ring burner in one corner. She had partitioned the main room with a shower curtain assembly. Loos was told he could wash in the sink, that he was free to soap his body if he wished. For one hundred gold marks he could do whatever he wished…within reason.

Loos remained standing in his ridiculous hat and coat, unable to take off either. Uli stripped off her cheap wig, revealing a head of nearly smooth stubble. In the light, he noticed gaps in her teeth, and in the mirror, a smear of lipstick on his face where she'd kissed his lips.

"We have all night, don't we?" Uli said. "You might as well make yourself comfortable. Would you like a drink, dearie? Maybe you need a drink to loosen up and have fun? Is that it? Or what did you have in mind?"

Loos only nodded.

Suddenly and without warning, Uli lifted the dress over her head, letting it drop to the floor. She had wound cloth strips over her genitals, securing the ends around her waist. She possessed bicyclist's legs, smooth shaven and well-muscled. Turning, she ran a hand over her chest. "I'm all yours, darling," she said. "Do you want me in the ass?"

"That drink," Loos said.

Uli turned, smiling with hands on hips. Loos looked at her hairless chest, the cheap bra stuffed with rags. A narrow boy's waist. He imagined himself in the chapel of the Catholic church in Juprelle, the congregation turned to view him and his mother as she dragged him down the aisle in girl's clothes.

"Edgar," he said to Uli. "My name is Edgar."

"I'm Vincent," Uli told him. "This is your first time, isn't it, Edgar? I can tell. You look white as a sheet. But don't worry. We'll go slow. You'll see. That is, unless you like it fast."

"The drink, please," Loos replied.

Uli pulled down the day bed and fluffed its coverlet. The floor was complexly carpeted in a flower pattern, worn by age and stinking of cat shit. She had piled dishes in one corner of the small kitchen compartment, a rumple of tea bags, stale bread, and green cheese. Uli walked to the compartment and opened an overhead cabinet. Loos took the garotte from his pocket and looped it once. While Uli poured him a schnapps, Loos studied her boyish buttocks, her hairless back, and fine-boned shoulders.

Ruthlessly he tightened the garotte around her neck and arched her upward as she upset the schnapps bottle, which tumbled to the floor. A circle of liquor spread around their feet as Loos lifted Uli from her feet, Uli grasping the garrote with both hands. Loos heard a pop, a tiny child's balloon exploding in her throat as he let her down gently. She lay on the floor on her back, looking up at him in brilliant surprise. The struggle had smeared one of her smallish whiskers. Loos folded the garrote back into his pocket and sat down heavily on the day bed. His heart was pounding and there was a nightmarish vacuum in his head.

⚊ ⚊

Wulff studied the Wilmersdorfer trees, massive chestnuts with sheeting white crowns and rows of delicate filigreed lindens. Now that the nurse had opened a window blind, the room was flooded with a blinding white light. Everything smelled of freshly laundered sheets, strong lye soap, and lilies. Barlach lay under a blue hospital blanket, his eyes fluttering open and shut at random. Sores had formed at the corners of his mouth, and his arms were thin.

"Don't talk," Wulff whispered.

"I must talk," Barlach said.

"All right then," Wulff said. "Tell me what you remember. I'll listen and you can talk."

"I remember going to the cinema," Barlach said. "I remember buying a ticket. I remember an old man taking my ticket. I remember the smell of popping corn."

"You were following Bruckmann," Wulff said. "Do you remember following Bruckmann?"

"Yes, I think so," Barlach said. Wulff fluffed a pillow and propped up Barlach's head. The man had lost at least thirty pounds. "There was a marble water fountain. I think I drank from it."

"Just go easy," Wulff said.

"I see lights flashing in my face. I see something dark and then a sudden flash."

"Do you remember going into the washroom on the mezzanine?"

"Washroom?"

"Never mind now," Wulff said quietly.

Sunshine ticked through the chestnuts outside, the huge parasols of Wilmersdorf. Gray stone walls hid rambling houses, the bourgeois silence of suburban Berlin. Wulff knew that Bruckmann kept an apartment in Wilmersdorf, three rooms in the upstairs half of an older manor house, not far from the hospital. Below, ladies were walking their Pomeranians and dark cabs trailed bursts of sunshine.

"Have you found the Hirrenstrasse killer yet?" Barlach asked, spooking Wulff from a daydream.

Wulff smiled. Once a Schupo, always a Schupo.

"The bastard sent me another doll," Wulff complained. "Last Saturday morning."

"It's Monday now?"

"You were in your sleep."

"He's near you? He knows where you live?"

"He knows where Johanna lives."

Barlach coughed.

"He's near us now," Wulff said. "You'll be in the hospital another week. Get out of here and get back to work!"

Barlach smiled weakly. "Where is Bruckmann?" he asked.

"Dead," Wulff said calmly. "The man who hit you on the head also killed Bruckmann. This happened in the balcony washroom of the Capitol Cinema."

"I don't remember," Barlach. "My head aches."

"Can you stay awake a moment?" Wulff asked. Barlach nodded, eyes closed. "The other doll looks like a man made up with the face of a woman who's made up to look like a cat. Do you understand me? A painted face with whiskers and arched eyebrows. Straight hair with bangs, long gloves, and an evening dress. This is a very elegant person in a strange sort of way."

"I can hear you," Barlach said.

"I believe the doll represents one of the transvestite actors on Jagerstrasse. Perhaps a prostitute or chorine. Does Vukoch still head the Jagerstrasse Verein?"

"Yes, talk to Paul Vukoch," Barlach said. "His gang operates the Goldene Spinne on Jagerstrasse. Do you think this doll represents someone who works on Jagerstrasse?"

"Get some sleep, my friend," Wulff said. Suddenly Barlach seemed far away, passing through oceans. Sun licked the clean hospital sheets, striping them, beams landing lightly on the sick man's face. His skin radiated illness.

"My new suit is ruined," Barlach muttered.

"You'll have another," Wulff told him.

— ⁃

Bruckmann's apartment lay on the western edge of Wilmersdorf, near the Kurfurstendamm and the Halensee Bahnhof. Wulff had ordered the landlord to maintain the premises as unlet and had sealed it with special police tape. Inside the simple three-room flat, there was little sunlight, its windows looking north over trees and more apartment buildings. The walls were bare of ornament, just a few sticks of Bruckmann's tubular steel furniture here and there, an ashtray full of cigar butts, some bath towels, shirts, shoes, and liquor bottles. Wulff sat in the midst of half-packed boxes looking at the labels he'd affixed himself: LETTERS. STATEMENTS. PHOTOS. PERSONAL EFFECTS.

Wulff was in shadow, smoking a cigarette while the shape of something dithered inside his head. Did everyone dream while wide awake? Wulff looked at one of Bruckmann's black boots, its muddy sole. He had piled some suits in one corner of the living room, along with overcoats, sweaters, trousers, and underwear. Amid the clutter, Wulff thought again of Johanna. The whole weekend he'd found himself driving by her apartment at all hours. He telephoned her five, six, even seven times a day, just to hear her voice. "Don't worry about me, darling Harry!" she would chirp, feigning annoyance when he interrupted one of her Saturday sessions.

With his penknife, Wulff slit open one of the boxes labeled PHOTOS. He dug through a pile of yellowed photographs. Some were moldy, some stuck together and useless, and some were too yellowed to be recognized. In one, a group of half a dozen men hunkered near a pile of rubble. Wulff recognized a younger Bruckmann, short, stern-looking, and rough, with an eye patch and wearing a black beret. Behind him and just left stood another man in fuzzy profile, taller and sharp-boned, with broad shoulders, jug ears, and a long raincoat that reached almost to the ankles of his muddy combat boots. Wulff flipped over the photo and read a list of names lettered in pencil: *Kruger, Phaltz, Rieger, Stein,* then a blank for the man who stood just to the left of Bruckmann, a figure with a shaved head and black goatee, his face a half-leer of laconic cruelty as a curlicue of smoke escaped the photo in its upper right corner. Who were these men—Wulff wondered—these men standing amid the abysmal clutter of war with wooded hills in the near background?

Wulff turned the photo back over and studied the cruel face of the shaven-headed man. Too indistinct to be of much use. Wulff thought back to the day he'd spent on Poel Island, studying Bruckmann's dossier. It was the same man! Longer hair then, no goatee, but the same man! The thing haunting Wulff was pregnant now, colored by substance, an orange burst of recognition. *Edgar Braun*, his arm raised over Bruckmann's shoulder, the man holding something corded.

A garrote?

The nightclubs and dance halls of Jagerstrasse were closed, the streets eerily empty. It was nearly ten o'clock in the morning, and earlier Wulff had driven past Johanna's apartment on Lennestrasse. Unable to stop himself, he had gone upstairs and interrupted one of her sessions just to see her face.

At the intersection of Mauerstrasse, Wulff found the Goldene Spinne, its double doors with dual frosted porthole windows, a gold gyroscope embossed just above each gold door handle. He knocked a few times, got no answer, then walked around to a side alley where he could see a kitchen entrance. Inside were two dishwashers and a cook preparing food. He tapped once on the screen, asked for Vukoch, and was directed down a short hallway to a large cork-lined room that contained a round wooden table, one sofa against a wall, and some scattered metal chairs. A chalkboard covered by indecipherable scribbles hung on one of the walls, probably race results and football scores. On another wall hung photos of racehorses, jockeys, boxers, bicycle riders, and a skier or two.

Vukoch was at the wooden table, sitting with a short pug-faced man Wulff recognized from the sports tabloids, a boxer who had once enjoyed a brief reign of popularity in Berlin. Vukoch he'd never met, but he would have been hard to miss in a crowd, a tall, lean man wearing an immaculately dark-blue, double-breasted suit, a pearl-white dress shirt worn open-collared, rings on each finger, and a chocolate-brown spider tattoo on his left wrist. Vukoch put down his coffee cup and smiled vaguely at Wulff, who had introduced himself on the way in. Wulff recalled the club now from police reports he'd read. Its clientele were "sportsmen," boxers, jockeys, and gamblers. There had been rumors of cocaine dealings, and Department E had kept the club under surveillance one summer during the twenties.

"So you're the famous Wulff," Vukoch said amiably, extending his right hand and offering another smile, this one brighter. Wulff studied the spider tattoo, its eight legs spread toward the forearm. Wulff had telephoned ahead and was told to come. Cops were always welcome at the Goldene Spinne.

The two men shook hands. "I won't take much of your time," Wulff said.

"I'm always glad to help Kripo," Vukoch said.

Wulff remained standing as the boxer picked up a half-finished cup of coffee, rose, then disappeared behind a beaded curtain. Wulff declined an offer of real coffee. "I'm looking for someone," Wulff said.

"By last count, there are fourteen thousand policemen in Berlin. Why come to me?"

"It's a special someone."

"Well then."

"Someone I thought you might know."

"I might," Vukoch said. "It depends."

Wulff had brought the doll in its brown paper wrapping. He unfolded the paper layer by layer, revealing the image to Vukoch, who took a long, concentrated look. He sat above the doll, coffee mug in hand, fascinated by its exactitude, its shiny tabloid colors, the head slightly too large for the body, the legs too small for the dress.

"Do you recognize the likeness?" Wulff asked. "Probably a female impersonator."

"Yes, certainly," Vukoch said.

Wulff rewrapped the doll. Wulff recognized the spider now. It was a poisonous brown recluse.

"What do you want with me?" Vukoch asked.

"Do you recognize the face?"

"May I ask what this is all about?"

"It isn't drugs."

Vukoch shrugged good-naturedly. "Without knowing, I'm helpless to assist you. You can imagine my position. If I help you without knowing why, my reputation suffers. People hear things. Soon, nobody trusts me."

"I can tell you this much," Wulff said. "This person isn't wanted by the police. She's done nothing wrong and she isn't involved in any crime or in any conspiracy."

Vukoch turned his hands upside down and tapped the table with his rings. "I'm sympathetic, of course," he said.

"She's in danger," Wulff said. "I just don't know who she is or where she lives."

Vukoch rubbed his chin. He pointed to the coffee mug. "It's real coffee," he said. "When's the last time you had real?"

"Six months ago," Wulff said. "At the Café Bauer."

"Really?" Vukoch said. "That long?"

"I'm in a hurry," Wulff said. "I'm serious about this person being in danger."

"What the fuck," Vukoch laughed. "I think I'll trust you. She calls herself Uli. They call themselves something, all of them. *She* called herself Uli. They all have a name."

"They?" Wulff said.

"Uli works the El Dorado on Matzstrasse, just off Jagerstrasse. It's an unusual kind of place."

"Unusual?"

"Transvestite. They don't play games at the El Dorado. Or that's all they do. It depends on how you look at it."

"And what does Uli do?"

"You are that naive?" Vukoch laughed. "That's pretty good! What does Uli do!"

"Perhaps you'll tell me," Wulff said.

"Uli shills drinks for the club. She gets the suckers to buy two-mark apple brandies. Then she goes home with the highest bidder. They look pretty good in the dark if I do say so myself."

"She's always a cat?"

"My dear Kripo," Vukoch said. "There are dozens of cat ladies on Jagerstrasse. And dozens more within six blocks of here. But the doll you showed me, I'd say that was Uli. It seems to catch her style pretty well."

"No question about it?"

"No doubt," Vukoch said. "Now I'm busy."

"Just a few more things," Wulff said.

"Make it quick." Vukoch cracked a knuckle, already having lost interest.

"Who runs the El Dorado?"

"Spitzer by name," Vukoch said. "Everybody knows that."

"And after him?"

"The Verein," Vukoch said. By Verein he meant the organized gangs of Berlin, the men who bought and sold women, drugs, and guns, who operated gambling dens, who brokered false identity papers, ran numbers, and sold protection. There were ten or so Vereins in Berlin, each with a slice of neighborhood pie. They drank real coffee in hard times, toasted themselves with French champagne, lived in expensive apartments, and drove luxury Mercedes touring cars.

"Would Uli be on salary?" Wulff asked.

"You must be joking," Vukoch said, bored. "They work for drinks and meals. They find a customer who takes them home. Otherwise they'd be selling ass on the street."

"Do you know where Uli lives?"

Vukoch dismissed the question with a wave of his hand. "Go see Spitzer. He might know and he might not. I'd bet he doesn't know and doesn't care. Who cares where these pathetic fucks sleep?"

— —

Sun washed over a work crew pile-driving a new Alexanderplatz station on the subway line. Wulff watched the crew work for a time, sweaty men digging holes for a tube line that would connect central Berlin with its vast suburbs, a conurbation of four million. Chestnut blossoms were falling on the work crews, covering them with white. Krause had brought potato salad, cucumber slices, and plates of smoked salmon. Weiss was drinking mineral water from a cut glass cup.

"This is very kind of you," Wulff told the deputy chief. It wasn't often that he ate fresh potato salad and rye bread just out of the oven. Wulff tasted a bite of bread with salmon and studied the workers covered in chestnut blossoms. "I have no special news about your termite," he confessed. "But I'm edging my way toward him. I've made some discoveries in Bruckmann's apartment. There is a certain photograph. It is a slight trail, no more than that."

Weiss smiled wearily. "I understand," he said. "But in the year since our investigation started, the political difficulties have multiplied. This situation is vastly different."

"I assure you—" Wulff began.

Weiss cut him off with a gesture. "I want you to take the Oberkommissar position at Berlin Mitte. I want you to be the chief inspector."

Wulff turned back to the window. He had dreaded this moment. "Are you certain of this?" he asked.

"More than certain," Weiss said. "I want you to take the position."

"I'll take the job," Wulff said. He walked toward Weiss and the two men shook hands, then toasted the occasion with mineral water. They ate together, plates on their laps.

"Begin today, why not?" Weiss said finally. "You move into Bruckmann's old office. Take over his staff or clean house, I leave that up to you. I warn you, there are Nazi sympathizers shot through Department IV."

"I know who they are," Wulff replied.

"Do all your own paperwork," Weiss counseled him. "Assign the detectives yourself and remain responsible only to me for this termite. There are leaks everywhere. We are sinking, Wulff. I must concentrate on keeping Stapo above politics. Once the Nazis infiltrate Stapo, we are finished."

"I'd like to maintain control of the Hirrenstrasse killing," Wulff said.

"I don't think—"

"A transvestite killed more than a year ago. Just near Alexanderplatz."

"Ordinarily it would be assigned out."

"May I keep this one case?"

"Do as you wish," Weiss said. "But I don't want you burdened with too many individual investigations. Perhaps just Bruckmann and this Hirrenstrasse thing. You're an administrator now! A man who eats fresh rye bread!"

"I don't wish—" Wulff said haltingly.

"I know, my friend," Weiss told him. "You wish to remain a simple Kripo. How often I've heard that tune!" Weiss speared a wedge of cucumber and ate it with gusto. He walked to the window and looked down at a flight of huge crows that had settled in the chestnut trees. "Do you have further information about the Bruckmann killing? Certain articles have appeared in the bourgeois press."

"I planted those articles," Wulff said.

"How very clever. You have a suspect?"

"Someone named Edgar Braun. If he is alive."

"Never heard of Edgar Braun," Weiss said.

"He was Bruckmann's henchman in the Freicorps. His specialty was the garrote."

"An amazing discovery. But why Braun? What's special about him?"

"I've accounted for most of Bruckmann's known associates and friends, what few he had. Some are dead, some assigned to other parts of Germany, and some have achieved a respectable coloring. They've grown old and fat and rich and taken mistresses in Koblenz. Braun is the only one unaccounted for."

"What does this man Braun look like?"

"The photo was made in 1923. Partial views, a profile. But he was a large man with big ears, a shaved head, and a little black goatee. He'd be very different today, I suspect."

"What brings you to Braun? The garrote?"

"Certain dossiers I've read," Wulff said.

Weiss turned back from the window. "Why would this Braun kill Bruckmann, his former associate?"

"I really don't know," Wulff confessed.

Adjutant Krause entered the room after a knock. "A message by telephone for the Kriminal Kommissar," he said. "I am asked to deliver it."

"He's a Kriminal Oberkommissar now," Weiss said.

"Very good, sir," Krause snapped. "Schloss Kaserne Precinct in Little Wedding reports a murder."

"Not now," Weiss said.

"But there is a specific instruction from Herr Oberkommissar Wulff," Krause protested. "He asked to be informed."

"What is the message?" Wulff asked.

Krause nodded stiffly. "The precinct captain begs to inform the Oberkommissar that there has been a sex murder in his district that involves strangulation. The captain was instructed to report to Herr Wulff any such activity. Apparently the body has just been found."

"Please forgive me," Wulff said to Weiss. "But I must go quickly."

"But you haven't finished your lunch!" Weiss said. "And you are an administrator now. You shouldn't be concerned with individual killings!"

"This is my Hirrenstrasse killer," Wulff said.

"Ah, well then," Weiss said.

Wulff hurried away.

⸺

Weiss sat at his desk, looked at the plates of half-eaten food. He went to the window and waited a few minutes until he saw Wulff bounding down the Alexanderplatz steps, taking them two at a time toward the square. Wulff crossed the square on a half-run, then climbed inside his small blue police Opel.

Weiss circled his huge mahogany desk and sat. He opened his day-book and wrote in large letters: EDGAR BRAUN, underlining the words twice in bold red. ENGAGE STAPO TO FIND THIS MAN.

18

A youthful Schupo Unterwachtmeister saluted Wulff grimly and said, "Upstairs, Herr Kriminal Kommissar, first on the right down the hall."

He had driven through Little Wedding, one of Berlin's neighborhoods in the eastern suburb of Charlottenburg, an otherwise upper-middle-class region of detached villas, semi-detached houses, expanses of park, tree-lined boulevards, and shops. On its eastern edge, however, stood rows of hovels, gray-faced Hinterhofs dominated by the Communist Party and their block loyalty system. From nearly every screenless window hung home-painted hammer-and-sickle flags, with antigovernment slogans whitewashed on every wall. Wulff returned the Schupo's salute.

"What's it look like?" Wulff asked a bit wearily.

On the opposite side of the street, a haggard woman with stringy gray hair leaned out of the Hinterhof and beat a dirty rug with a broom. Skeins of dust drifted down from the rug, and Wulff could hear the sounds of children crying.

"It's a little room with someone dead on the floor," the Schupo said. "Looks like a strangulation if you ask me." He told Wulff he'd answered a call from the woman who acts as a landlord's agent in the building. His captain at Schloss Kaserne Precinct told him to secure the scene and wait for Wulff.

"Is there a police telephone booth on the street nearby?" Wulff asked. He was in no hurry to see the dead body. He'd seen many bodies.

The Schupo angled an arm around the corner of the stairwell, indicating with a gesture "up the street." Wulff walked to the box about a hundred meters away, then dialed the number of Levitt's apartment in Lichtenberg.

When Levitt answered, he said, "Oh for God's sake, Wulff, I was sleeping."

Wulff suppressed a laugh. "I'd like you to look at something with me."

"I'm an autopsy doctor," Levitt said. "You are always dragging me into the daylight. It is quite unnatural. I live only at night, like the vampires." Levitt paused. "I conspire with the dead, and now you wish for me to join the living."

Wulff spent a few minutes explaining his need for immediate forensics and the unreliability of Schloss Kaserne's detectives, most of whom had gone over to Nazism. Levitt said he'd be along in thirty minutes.

Wulff returned to the alley where the Schupo waited. A flight of wooden stairs led to a second-story landing, an opening into a dark hallway where doors hid small flats. He climbed the stairs and ducked his head into an open door on the first right. Near a daybed lay a body face up, a thin and muscled white male leg delicately cast over an ankle. There was a shaved head covered by black stubble. The face was made up to resemble a cat face, complete with whiskers, arched eyebrows, and pink cat-mouth. The body was naked except for a sheet drawn tightly between the legs and a cheap bra stuffed with rags. Wulff walked back to the landing and called down to the Schupo.

"Have you talked to the concierge?"

"Only to get a name. The dead guy is Vincent. She didn't hear a thing."

— ⌐

Levitt found Wulff alone in the dead man's room, sitting on a daybed with his head not one meter above the head of a corpse. To Levitt, the Oberkommissar appeared overcome by a wistful discourse with the body itself, in a kind of trance that resembled a medium's attempt at telepathy.

"Wulff?" Levitt asked hesitantly. "Wulff, are you all right?"

The Oberkommissar sat back on the bed and crossed his legs. "The bastard shared a kiss with her before he strangled her," he said. He smiled distantly. "I could have prevented this, you know. This is partly my fault."

"Nonsense," Levitt responded sharply. "You're having what the Freudians call transference." He walked to the daybed and studied the corpse along with Wulff. It was the body of an undernourished but still well-confirmed male about twenty-six years old with a shaved head and wide-set black thyroid eyes. Levitt noted the room, its servile drabness. He clapped Wulff on the back. "Nonsense," he said softly. "How could you be at fault for this tragedy?"

"This was done by the Hirrenstrasse killer," Wulff said. "He killed at random last year. Now he's got a taste for it. He likes it. He's working his way up to a masterpiece. He wants me to know."

Levitt sorted through his memories, trying to dislodge one corpse from the hundreds of corpses he'd autopsied. Levitt finally remembered. A transvestite named Timkin Mueller, strangled in an alley.

"Timkin Mueller," Levitt said.

"Yes, Timkin Mueller. Strangled last fall. Nearly a year ago just off the Alexanderplatz."

Levitt remembered the naked body on a metal surgical table. He remembered opening the cadaver with a Y-cut, its organs spilling out. Levitt remembered discussing a last kiss. "I remember now. Is that why you got me here?"

"For your experience and for your expertise," Wulff said.

Levitt had spent considerable time on a field-forensic squad, but that was years ago. As a Jew, soon he would be forced into retirement. "But you're not at fault," Levitt chided Wulff. "As I recall, there were no real clues to the identity of the murderer. Apparently random, no? Very difficult to solve. How could you be at fault, my dear Wulff?"

"We'll see," he said to Levitt. "I want your opinion on this victim. You'll be my preliminary forensic team."

Levitt seemed to understand Wulff's growing isolation from those precincts which were coming under the influence of Nazis, his present association with Jews and socialists, making enemies of people he ordinarily would have relied upon for help. Levitt kneeled above the corpse, examining its eyes and the lacerated neck. He placed a finger on its damp skin.

"But I think you're off the hook, Wulff," Levitt said. "This one was killed by a garrote, not strangled manually. As I recall, your Hirrenstrasse victim was strangled manually."

"It's the same killer," Wulff said dully. "Hirrenstrasse was spur of the moment. He stalked this one and killed him with a preferred instrument."

"You can't be certain, Wulff," Levitt said.

Wulff glanced up at Levitt. He'd told only Johanna about the dolls. He'd told Barlach of course, but Barlach was still in the hospital struggling just to walk. "I am certain, Levitt. You'll have to take my word on it, but I have evidence it is the same killer."

Levitt roamed the room with his eyes, taking in every detail with the attention of a watchmaker. There was a bottle of schnapps and a glass on the floor. A few gold marks lay on the dressing table amid tubes of lotion and makeup.

"Your victim picked someone up on the street?" Levitt mused.

"Wearing her cat face! Think, Levitt, think!"

"Of course!" Levitt shouted. "How stupid of me. He worked on Jagerstrasse. The killer paid money to come home with her."

"Yes, of course," Wulff said. "And do you recall that this is the second garrote killing this summer. What do you think of those odds?"

"You're referring to Bruckmann, of course," Levitt said. Wulff was still sitting on the daybed. "And do you think this Hirrenstrasse killer also killed Bruckmann? What would be the logic in that?"

"It does seem unlikely," Wulff agreed. "But it is a pity. I could perhaps have prevented this tragic death."

"Ach, Wulff, you are not Jehovah."

"No, not Jehovah," Wulff agreed. Wulff sighed deeply, coming to grips with it all. "Please go over this victim carefully will you? Tell me what you think? Can you do it tonight?"

"For you—" Levitt shrugged.

"Your opinion on time of death?"

Levitt touched the feet of the corpse. Rigor had come and gone. The posterior showed signs of lividity. Levitt verged on a realization. The feeling Wulff held for this corpse was more than moral compassion.

"The time of death," Levitt mused.

"Just your best guess."

"I guess several days, then," Levitt said.

"Saturday night?"

"I'll need more data. Temperature, stomach contents, blood, and lividity. But Saturday is my first best guess."

Wulff rose from the daybed. "Thank you, my friend," he said. Levitt followed him out into the hall where Wulff lit a cigarette. On the landing there was a puff of breeze. It had been a warm summer in the city. The unemployed had taken to the streets in droves, sleeping in vacant lots and abandoned buildings, creating cardboard shelters beside highways. Crime had risen in the usual places at the usual hours. In the Scheunenviertel, at the Schleicher and Stettiner Bahnhofs, in the districts of Bülow Platz and Little Wedding, one was afraid to walk after dark.

"I want to congratulate you on your promotion, Herr Oberkommissar," Levitt said after they'd stood silently for a few minutes. "I presume you'll purchase a new automobile."

"I like my Opel," Wulff said.

There was a brick wall opposite them. Someone had painted the hammer and sickle on it in white.

"May I inquire about Johanna?" Levitt asked.

"She's well. Thank you for asking."

"She's a beautiful girl," Levitt said. "I knew her father. Perhaps you should consider a conversion!" he joked.

"I just might," Wulff laughed.

"Ah, what you would miss if you became Jewish! You would have to give up your beloved pork. Think of the hours you would waste learning *mitzvot*, studying the dry Torah. And yes, Wulff, you would appear quite ridiculous in the *kippa*!" Levitt approached Wulff and stood just off his right shoulder so that they could both see the street below. "And yes," he whispered, "you would have to be circumcised!" Levitt chuckled to himself and pretended to spit. He put an arm on Wulff's shoulder, the pair of them standing quietly in a narrow brick alleyway where one could hear the sound of children. "You love her, don't you, Wulff?" Levitt said. "It is none of my business, of course."

"Oh, I love her," Wulff said.

"So shit on them," Levitt said loudly. "Marry her then. In this country to think they make love a crime! Fuck them! Fuck them if they make love a crime!"

━ ━

Loos locked the boiler room behind him with a pass key, a key that opened every maintenance closet on each floor of Alexanderplatz

HQ, then swept his way down a long dark corridor toward the office of Bernhard Weiss, deputy chief of Berlin's Metropolitan Police. At the outer door of the office, he paused and listened for Krause. He'd made a key from a wax impression. Taking the key from his pocket, he listened again, concentrating on every silent nuance. Every six months, security would change the locks, and Loos would make a new impression. After all, he was a locksmith. He had learned his trade well. Child's play really, almost too easy.

For years, he had studied the comings and goings of security, of the Reichswehr guard cadres, the places they paused to smoke their cigarettes and eat their ham sandwiches, when they played dominoes and chatted, took their pisses and shits, when they slept on duty. For another instant, he listened at the door, then slid the key into its lock.

Inside, Loos walked through the outer office and used another key to open a second door. He walked quickly to a huge mahogany desk that stood before a stone fireplace. For a moment, he looked up at the portrait of President Hindenburg. On the desk was a daybook, a memoir and diary combined, a heavy leather volume embossed in gold with a lock one could pick in one's sleep. Loos opened the book to its final entry of the day and read: EDGAR BRAUN. ENGAGE STAPO TO FIND THIS MAN. The words underlined twice.

Loos snapped shut the book, his forehead damp with sweat. He hurried out of the offices and locked the outer door, pausing again to listen. He walked downstairs and into a basement hallway near the morgue where Levitt dissected cadavers. It was just before midnight, and he could hear voices from the laboratory.

Just then, Wulff came out of the morgue dressed in a gray suit, carrying a sheaf of documents under his right arm. Loos looked up, containing his surprise, but startled nonetheless to see the police detective at midnight in Alexanderplatz. Loos broomed down the hall, trying to hide his face. At the boiler room door, he paused and looked back in time to see Wulff watching him, head cocked, as if some thought had suddenly grown heavy in his mind.

Loos entered the boiler room and closed the door. The cramped, low-ceilinged enclosure was damp and hot.

"To hell with you, Kripo," Loos whispered to himself.

19

The August heat brought Berlin a drought. For weeks, the skies remained clear, and there was no hint of rain. Wulff had worked with his socialist investigators, blood and fingerprint men, records examiners and photographers, all from the Savigny Precinct, setting them loose to hunt for clues in the Vincent/Uli murder. Preliminary reports were discouraging in the extreme. There was no blood evidence; no hair, fiber, or fingerprint leads; no leads of any kind as to the identity of the killer, save for those clues Wulff alone knew.

Late one afternoon, Wulff parked in front of the El Dorado on Jagerstrasse at the corner of Matz. The stale odor of beer wafted from its open door. Inside, he wound his way around a dozen tables, across the dance floor, then found a door to the business office just to the side of the stage. In the light of day, the El Dorado was elaborately sleazy. Wulff knocked on a padded door. A deep bass voice from inside told him to come in.

Spitzer sat at a small desk in front of a pile of papers. He was a large, dark man with square shoulders. He wore an expensive, camel-hair belted sports jacket, his brown hair oiled to a high sheen. "You're Wulff?" Spitzer said indifferently.

Like Vukoch's, this office, too, was decorated with photographs of celebrities from sports, film, and theater, representing vaudevillian comics and jugglers, boxers, actresses and mimes, labor and political leaders of both shades, Right and Left. There were no windows in the room, the only light coming from two brass lamps. "Two questions," Wulff said abruptly. Spitzer remained seated and did not offer his hand.

"So you said on the phone."

"One of your girls is dead."

"Uli, you mean?" Spitzer grunted.

"I'm told she was a money-maker."

"Word gets around," Spitzer said.

"What can you tell me about her?" Wulff asked.

"Not a thing," Spitzer said coldly.

"Do you know his real name?"

"I don't care what his real name was," Spitzer replied. "She called herself Uli. She came every night and she went home every night."

"She'd been here a year?"

Spitzer nodded, picked up a fountain pen, and signed his name to a check.

"The man who killed her met her here," Wulff said. "Probably bought her some drinks and then took her home. He strangled her with a garrote."

Spitzer put down the pen. "You're breaking my heart," he said.

"All right," Wulff said. "I'm convinced you don't give a damn. I'm impressed."

Spitzer bounced the pen off his wooden desk once. "She worked here a year. She never gave me any trouble, but I don't know who killed her. I'm short-term partners with all the girls. They use my chairs to sit on their asses."

"Whose idea was the masks?"

"You don't get around much, do you?"

Wulff smiled. Irony was like rubble in war, part of the business.

"The murderer is a big, strong man. He's probably come to the El Dorado for weeks if not months, getting to know Uli, making himself comfortable. He spread around gold marks, which makes him unusual."

Spitzer tapped his pen again. "You got to be crazy to come into a place like this," he said. "Me and the old man who sweeps the floor are the only ones not crazy."

"I'm almost out of questions, I guess," Wulff said.

"You're six or seven over the limit."

"So you wouldn't mind if I talked to the chief waiter?" Wulff said.

Spitzer blinked once. "Go see Rolfe. He's probably near the kitchen folding napkins and watering gin. Tell him I said it's all right to talk."

"All right, thanks," Wulff said. He turned and touched the door handle, a knob of fake silver carved into a Satan's head.

"Broke her fucking neck?" Spitzer asked.

"A garrote," Wulff said on his way out.

He heard Spitzer say, "Uli brought in a lot of money."

Wulff skirted the stage and found the swinging kitchen doors. Rolfe was perched on a crate in front of a set of metal cabinets, polishing glasses and folding napkins into flamingo shapes. He was a small, compact man wearing a tattered black tuxedo. Wulff introduced himself and watched as Rolfe turned nearly dead white from shock. When Rolfe recovered, he continued folding and polishing, probably hoping that the tall Kripo was a bad dream.

"Spitzer says it's all right to talk about Uli," Wulff said.

"I heard she's dead," Rolfe said. He shook his sandy blond hair, showing Wulff his pox scars. Wulff told him the whole story of Uli's death, start to finish.

"That's terrible," Rolfe said.

"Did you know her?"

Rolfe finally turned up two saucer-shaped eyes. Wulff took out a pack of cigarettes and offered one to Rolfe, who declined with a sad smile. "I knew Uli," he said. "She was all right by me. She was a real person. She wasn't a freak. She gave me tips from her share. That's more than some of them do." Rolfe cleaned a small schnapps glass and wiped his hands with a linen towel.

"Did you know her real name?" Wulff said.

"Vincent Frommer," Rolfe said.

"Do you know if he had a family? Where he came from?"

"That's all I know about Uli," Rolfe said. For a time he seemed lost in thought. "I think I know who killed her. It happened on Saturday night, didn't it?"

"Yes. Did you see Uli on Saturday night?"

"Sure, I served her drinks."

"Crème de menthe and champagne?"

"We call it the Claudette Colbert. How did you know that?"

"There was an autopsy," Wulff said. "But what about the man who came in here on Saturday night?"

"Have you ever been here at night?" Rolfe asked. "Of course you haven't," he added quickly. "Well, it's very dark. There is a candle on every table and a few dim lights overhead. Everybody wears a mask. But there was a man who came in every Saturday night, and had been coming for two months or so. Maybe longer. That would make him a regular." Rolfe leaned up and began to concentrate. "This man wore a heavy topcoat and a watchcap. He was big and strong. You could tell it from his hands. He never took off his coat and hat and he wore the mask. He sat hunched over with the telephone to his ear so that it was hard to see him clearly. He would order apple brandy for himself and champagne and crème de menthe for Uli, and he would pay in gold marks. You don't see those much anymore, so I remember. That's how he paid last Saturday night. Uli gave me part of her tips."

"You saw Uli leave?"

"She left early. It was just after nine. I remember because she always stays until midnight on Saturday night. She left because of the gold marks. Is that the man who did this to Uli?"

"I think he did," Wulff said. "Did you notice anything else about him? Any habits, tattoos, birth marks?"

"Nothing," Rolfe said. "It was dark and he wore a topcoat, even in this heat. People are elbow to elbow and I have to serve drinks."

"Do you recall the table where he sat?"

Rolfe stood and gestured to a corner table. "Nobody likes that table because you can't see the whole stage and people mill about. You can't get to the dance floor. I guess that's what he liked about it. This man wanted to sit in a corner, didn't he? Uli was in the balcony, so he could see her and that's all he cared about." Rolfe sat down again and began to fold napkins nervously. "That bastard," he said quietly.

—◦—

The afternoon Spree-Tour launch puttered to a halt opposite the Comic Opera near Friedrichstrasse quay. From the starboard aft rail, Rom could see the spires of Kaiser Wilhelm Cathedral towering above the chestnuts on Dorotheenstrasse, where dozens of cabs and trams were speeding by. The high blue sky was specked with thin clouds after weeks of cloudlessness. With the high temperatures, Berliners were escaping to Luna Park for a swim or to Halensee for picnics on the lake shore. Those who could afford it trained to Grunewald and ate lunch in a shady beer garden.

Rom watched Loos buy a ticket. There were perhaps fifteen English tourists on the boat, most listening to a lecture about Wilhelmine history under the front glass canopy. Loos scrambled over the gangplank and came aft. He was a hulking form, wearing a ridiculous topcoat despite the heat.

The Storm Führer was drinking apple juice from a bottle. He walked to the opposite rail and sat down near Loos, who was looking at the dirty river water, the marble embankment beyond, and beyond that the cavernous maw of official Berlin, its massive classical stone buildings, department stores, and arcades. "You want some apple juice?" Rom asked.

Loos leaned over the rail and spit into the water. Flower sellers upriver had tossed their day-old gladiolas into the water and the blossoms were floating by. Some of the gladiolas had stalled in stagnant water, turning circles in the afternoon sun.

"I don't want any fucking apple juice," Loos grumbled.

"You sound angry," Rom said.

There was a knot of muscle in Loos' neck. Rom watched the knot quiver. "Yes, certainly I'm angry," said Loos sullenly.

"Perhaps I can help you then," Rom offered. "SA helps those who help the SA. We are benevolent beyond your wildest dreams." Rom smiled inwardly, besting now even his most ridiculous of boasts.

Loos looked at Rom from the corner of an eye. He wondered momentarily if he were being mocked, and decided against it. But he was in a game of hide and seek.

"Stapo has my scent," Loos said. "And that fucking Wulff as well."

"The new Oberkommissar?" Rom asked. "You mean *that* Wulff?"

"He looks at me," Loos said. "He has an evil eye."

"That's all?" Rom asked incredulously. "Wulff stared at you and gave you the evil eye?" The facts of the Bruckmann murder hung between them like smoke. Rom had never mentioned it to Loos, nor had Maikowski.

"Do not condescend to me, you minor functionary," Loos growled angrily. The knot in his neck rippled. "I am aware of other facts. Things you cannot know." Loos glanced up at some children who were playing tag in the stern. His eyes wandered to the blue sky. "I have other information," he added dreamily.

Suitably vague, Rom thought to himself. He wondered if he should mention the word "paranoia" in reports he made to SA staff. "What is this other information?" Rom asked. "Do you have a special report for me this week?" Many weeks had passed without a significant report from Loos. Maikowski was becoming anxious over the waste of SA funds, the needless connection to this unstable individual inside Alexanderplatz HQ. In some ways, Loos had become more of a liability than an asset.

Loos sucked his teeth. "There is nothing to report this week," he said.

Rom pondered the dirty river water, its gladiola garbage. The captain of the launch was powering its diesel motors, making a muck of the shredded flowers. Rom decided to chance a question. "Is there word on the Bruckmann investigation? Do you have any inside information?"

Loos worked the muscles in his jaw. "There is an unnamed suspect," he lied.

"An unnamed suspect?"

"I have his last name," Loos said finally. "The name is Braun. It is all very vague."

"Vague in what way?"

"It will be a dead end."

"So long as it does not dead end at the SA," Rom said.

"Impossible," Loos replied offhandedly.

"Nothing is impossible," Rom asserted. He turned from the rail, watching gladiolas wash along in the boat's wake.

"My hundred marks," Loos said.

Rom turned and handed Loos five twenty-mark gold pieces. "Your information is useless," he said.

Loos flashed a look of hatred at Rom. "My time at Alexanderplatz is almost over. I want another position inside the SA. For services rendered."

"What kind of position would that be?" Rom asked, almost amused at this clumsy blackmail.

"One with a uniform," Loos said.

"I'll talk to my superior," Rom said.

"Do you mean Herr Maikowski?" Loos said.

Rom drank some apple juice, then tossed the bottle down into the river. "Yes, Maikowski," he replied. "I'll speak to him."

Loos backed from the rail and headed forward. He sat at a seat under the glass canopy. Rom stayed aft with his hands in his pockets as the launch neared the cathedral and docked just behind the Imperial Palace. Rom watched Loos rise and trudge over the gang-plank, then disappear into the crowds of Burgstrasse.

"Piss on that shit," Rom said audibly. "How did I become involved with this lump of dog crap?" Rom knew it had been folly from the first. But now it had become dangerous as well, this tinkering with a psychopath, all without any noticeable quid pro quo. After a few minutes, he walked forward, crossed the lowered gangplank, and was himself swallowed by the crowds of central Berlin.

— —

Wulff walked slowly down the silent corridors of the hospital. He paused at the door to Barlach's room, afraid of what he might see inside. It had been a busy day, Wulff compiling forensic reports, sending out teams again to check and recheck witnesses, trying to glimpse the darkest corners of his case. He felt he was inching toward the monster of Hirrenstrasse, his bleak creature. And in the middle of all this muddle, Wulff was forced to attend to duties at Berlin Mitte, rounds of administrative toil, its endless speeches to new recruits, reviewing training reports, repositioning teams of homicide investigators. He had seen Johanna only twice during the week.

Wulff pushed timidly into the room. Barlach stood near a far wall dressed in blue hospital pajamas, pacing slowly back and forth, prac-ticing the walk he'd forgotten after eight weeks in a coma. Wulff watched quietly as the grim-faced man forced himself through pace after painful pace, every effort confirming an inner resolve. Wulff knocked softly on the jamb as Barlach turned to offer a wan smile.

"I can walk," Barlach announced proudly.

"In two weeks, you'll be out of the hospital," Wulff said. "You'll be marched through intensive physical therapy. You'll be fed like a calf, then tossed out into the world."

"You've become an Oberkommissar, sir?"

"Listen to me, Barlach," Wulff said. "In my new position I have certain privileges. I may nominate a certain number of Schupo for appointment to Department IV. If they pass the examinations, these new people become detectives. I've placed your name in nomination for one of these positions, and you have been inserted on the list of examinees. The examinations take place in November every year. While you recuperate, I expect you to study. I'll expect you to pass these tests."

Barlach sat silently, almost in shock.

"You approve of this course?" Wulff asked.

"Yes—yes, of course," Barlach said proudly.

"It's settled then," Wulff laughed.

"You'll not be disappointed," he told Wulff. "And is there any news of the Hirrenstrasse killer?"

"He's killed again," Wulff said. "In Little Wedding. He strangled a transvestite with a garrote."

"Bruckmann was killed with a garrote," Barlach said.

"Exactly," Wulff said, "and I've got a name in the Bruckmann murder. The suspect is called Edgar Braun. He is a former associate of Bruckmann's from the Freicorps. Why he would kill Bruckmann, I have no idea."

"But who is Braun?"

"I don't know *who* he is," Wulff said. "Right now he's just a vague photographic image. There hasn't been a trace of him since Munich in 1923." Wulff recounted for Barlach the search for Braun, his own patient examination of Reichswehr dossiers, and the photos compiled by Bruckmann himself. Edgar Braun was a violent man with a shaved head and a brutal-looking goatee.

Barlach walked to the bed and sat down. He picked up his cane and pointed to the wall. "Three hours a day, I walk this wall. Next week, I'll be allowed out into the hall for physical therapy. When I gain stability, I'll throw away this cane." Barlach raised his slightly withered left hand. He tried to twitch the fingers and failed. "What about this?" asked Barlach.

"You'll be a detective, not a watchmaker."

"The doctor says it will improve," Barlach said. "I'll probably be able to drive."

Wulff walked over to Barlach and put his hand on the man's shoulder. "I'll be back to see you soon."

Once outside the hospital room, Wulff paused. He could hear Barlach's shuffling gait. Outside the trees were singing high summer in Wilmersdorf.

20

From her window, Eva saw in double vision a spire of St. Michael's Church, tile rooftops, and a delft blue sky that shimmered furiously. She lay down on a recliner and watched a spider work industriously in one corner of the ceiling. After an unknowable interval, she rose to one arm and studied the blackened spoon she used to cook her morphine, the wooden table on which it lay, and an empty ampule. Eva got to her feet, licked clean the dirty spoon, and blew her nose on an edge of bedspread.

Merchants were busy in the square below, displaying vegetables and freshly baked bread, books, and iron tools, while a fishmonger followed his cart in fine summer weather. As always, the old Jewish tinker was humming to himself. In desperation, Eva lit a kitchen match and held it under the spoon until a white fizz appeared. She took a hypodermic needle and attempted to suck up the last thread of her morphine, then plunged the needle into her neck, just below the right ear. She sat down suddenly, smiled inwardly, and licked her lips.

The door to her apartment opened, then closed. Maikowski was looking down at her, arms folded, an unsubtle cynic's gaze in his eyes.

"Eva, you stupid bitch," Maikowski said, shaking his head a bit sadly.

Eva sat back up on one arm. The sun had gone behind a spire, great burning arms of light burnishing the rooftops. Placing two bare feet on the floor, she looked up at Maikowski, who was frowning. "Morphine will be your ruin, Eva," Maikowski laughed.

Eva pushed herself away and wiped her runny nose. She had a fever, and the scabs on her neck refused to heal. When she was able, she got up and walked to the sink and splashed cold water on her face. She counted her blessings as her mother had taught her: a two-room apartment in the Schwabing quarter of Munich, a small but select clientele of SA men, police, and a few corrupt priests who brought her wine and sacramental wafers. Subtract these sadists and masochists from her life and Eva would be on the street. She wiped her face with a towel. "That's quite humorous coming from you," she told Maikowski finally.

Maikowski grunted and took off his leather SA jacket, worn on a warm summer evening as the symbol of something Maikowski thought he symbolized, a movement toward the new Germany. Also symbolizing the movement were his light brown shirt, dark brown pants, a plethora of leather belts that crisscrossed his torso, a peaked cap with swastika pins, and a red armband. He sat down on a wooden chair, and Eva went to him, kneeled, and began to pull off his heavy black boots.

"I've had a long day," Maikowski said. "Relax me, Eva. You know how to relax me, don't you?"

She studied his teardrop-shaped head, the sharp features and coal black eyes, his thinning black hair greased back from a widow's peak, the pale white forehead. Eva felt like spitting in his face, but instead she smiled at him and said, "Am I your little boy today?"

Maikowski nodded his assent.

She stood and walked to her closet, stripped off her slip and bra, unsnapping the bra and letting it drop to her feet. She closed her eyes again, ashamed of her sagging breasts and scabby, bruised legs. She took from the closet a pair of schoolboy knee pants, a long-sleeve blue shirt, an English school tie. With her face to the window she donned her "English boy" outfit with shaking hands. When she had finished, she returned to her dressing table, tied her lank blonde hair into a bun, and cleansed her face of what little makeup there was on it.

Maikowski had taken off his clothes and was naked save for a pair of white socks. He was skin and bones, a nasty stomach scar disappearing into a small bush of pubic hair. Eva turned and advanced slowly, coyly, leaned down and pinched the man's nipples, twisted them, and bit him on the knee.

"I'll call you Robert," Maikowski said. His nipples were pink. He touched one of them reflectively.

"I'm your little Robert, then," Eva said.

"How old are you, Robert?"

"I'm only thirteen years old," Eva said. Her clients often preferred thirteen.

"Are you a good child?" Maikowski asked her. "Or are you a bad child?"

"I'm a very bad child, indeed," Eva said, standing now with legs straddling his, hands on hips.

"Then you must be punished," Maikowski said.

Eva circled Maikowski once. She sank to hands and knees and thrust up her ass, Maikowski already grasping his rhinoceros skin whip with one hand. The whip was an artifact from bygone days, but had become de rigueur in SA culture when Hitler began to carry one, a gift from one of his society-matron admirers. The first blow fell gently on Eva's right buttock, a soft mocking moth-kiss. Then Maikowski struck her twice more, harder.

"How delicious," Eva said.

Maikowski emitted an indecipherable noise.

Eva cast her glance back to see Maikowski in the throes of pleasure, his eyes rolled up inside his head, thin lips pressed together. Just like morphine, Eva concluded. And just then, with his eyes closed, Maikowski struck her quite hard on the back, spreading a warmth of pain through her shoulders. "And are you my schoolmaster?" Eva managed to ask him, despite the increasing severity of her pain. The morphine had made her somewhat impervious to Maikowski. In her real fantasy life, the life that was realer than real, she was floating above the tile roofs of Munich arm in arm with her lover.

"You must be punished, Robert," Maikowski managed to say.

"Oh, punish me, master," Eva laughed in barely disguised contempt.

A thin film of sweat was covering Maikowski's naked body. The room was rich with the scent of blood. Everywhere on the walls Eva had hung cheap reproductions of French art, some Fauves and a few impressionists. Days before, she'd picked a vase of tea roses in the park, and they were wilting on the wooden table. Eva could see a smudge of blood on one of her shoulders. She felt her head being pushed forward, Maikowski with one hand under her belly so as to lift up her ass and strike it with his whip. Eva saw his boots tucked neatly beneath the bed.

Maikowski's warm urine flowed down her neck. She smelled its sick acridity. It soaked her blue shirt and dampened her underarm hair.

"You'll be good, won't you, Robert?" Maikowski asked her.

"Very good," she said.

"You love your schoolmaster, don't you, Robert?"

"Very much, sir," she said.

Maikowski suddenly shuddered as if shot. Eva allowed herself to relax onto her belly and lay there panting as though she'd been doused with gasoline. Maikowski was putting on his boots, nudging her with one of its toes.

"Now me," Maikowski said without emotion. He lay down on the floor next to Eva, eye to eye. She rose, took off her pants, and pulled down her underwear, squatting over him.

Her legs trembled as she let herself go. A wet stream poured from between her legs, splashing down on the prone Maikowski. When she had finished, she pulled on her underwear and sat in the wooden chair, staring down at her SA client whose breath was coming in great gulping gasps. Maikowski lay there for a long time, naked except for white socks and black boots. After five minutes, he rose and walked to the sink. "For a whore, you're quite special," Maikowski acknowledged, examining his face in the mirror.

"Thank you," Eva said, exhausted. "Will you be long in Munich?"

"Don't you read the newspapers?"

Eva told him no. She never read the papers. She pissed on people and she took morphine.

Maikowski laughed. "Two policemen were killed in Berlin yesterday."

"This is news?" Eva said distractedly.

"Eva, please," Maikowski told her in a fatherly tone. "Don't exaggerate the evil in Berlin." Maikowski dried his arms and chest, pulled on his brown shirt and dark brown pants, and buttoned the fly. "Yes, two poor police captains were shot dead near Bülow Platz. The police and newspapers accuse the SA and the SA accuses the communists. Of course, we know the truth, don't we, Eva?"

"The communists are responsible," Eva said dully. "So, you must leave for Berlin in order to attend to business."

Maikowski grunted, puffed out his chest, and adjusted the red Nazi armband on his left bicep. "There is always business, Eva," he said.

"And when will you return?"

"October," Maikowski said. "You mustn't forget the big Hitler putsch march in November that we must plan. And after that, the party rally in Nuremberg. Think of it, Eva! Just think of sixty thousand marchers under torchlights! The stadium will be filled!" Maikowski laced his boots and turned back to the mirror, running a comb through his thinning hair. "Yes, that's better," he said. "Much, much better."

"I did hear about the death of Bruckmann," Eva said. "He was a pustule if there ever was one."

"Not to speak ill of the dead," Maikowski laughed. "And I thought you didn't read the newspapers."

"I said I *heard*," Eva replied. "In case you didn't know, Bruckmann was another of my distinguished clients." Eva had begun to smell herself, Maikowski's piss and her own blood. It was nauseating her, or else it was the morphine. "Rom imports me to Berlin. I thought you knew that."

"And Rom told you about Bruckmann's death?"

"He told me nothing. I have friends in Berlin."

"Your friends should mind their own business."

"And what exactly *did* happen to Bruckmann?" Eva said coyly. "Rom didn't tell me he was going to die."

Maikowski adjusted his peaked cap. He stood before the mirror preening like a simian. "Put Bruckmann out of your mind, my dear Eva. He is a dangerous topic."

It was nearly dark now. Flies sat calmly on the window screen. One of the flies licked its back legs as Eva watched. Eva remembered the spider. She thought to herself, what sort of despicable animals piss on each other for pleasure? "Will I be coming to Berlin any time soon?" Eva asked after a moment of reflection.

"That is entirely up to Rom," Maikowski answered. "Things are coming to a head in Berlin. As if you cared, the political situation there now favors the SA. Berlin's era of fun and games is almost over."

"You'll not discharge me," Eva said.

"Eva, Eva!" Maikowski laughed, clapping his hands. "Discharge you, my dear! Never!" He patted his chin, firming it with a sort of fey charm. "Whores like you are indispensable, Eva, don't forget it!"

Maikowski turned and stared at Eva who was watching the spider spin its web. "But Eva, I wish to give you a piece of advice. When the revolution finally comes to Germany, I would leave this communist shithole of Schwabing if I were you. As Hitler says, 'Heads will roll.'"

"Hitler will clean house?" Eva taunted him.

Maikowski frowned, detecting the sarcasm. He wet a finger and smoothed it along both of his eyebrows. He picked up his leather jacket and folded it over his free arm. "Sarcasm is a knife with two edges," he said.

"Oh, Otto, don't be angry with me!"

"I've asked you not to call me Otto," Maikowski said angrily.

"Otto, Otto, Otto!" Eva screamed. Her mood had taken a reckless turn, as it often did. "You're really nothing but a clod-hopper in a fancy uniform."

"Shut your slut's mouth," Maikowski shouted in reply, turning beet-red in the face.

Eva lowered her eyes, mimicking shame. "Oh, Otto, don't be so bloody fussy. Won't you have a glass of schnapps before you go? Just one glass, dear Otto!"

Eva poured him a schnapps, and Maikowski accepted the glass silently, then downed it in one gulp. "Can't you afford anything better?" he asked glumly.

"Be generous with me, Otto," Eva said.

Maikowski took an envelope from his leather jacket and spilled its contents on Eva's bed, ten ampules of white morphine powder and a few paper marks. He retrieved four of the ampules and returned them to his jacket pocket.

"You son of a bitch," Eva screamed. "You promised me ten ampules and fifty marks!"

Maikowski walked to the door and opened it. He stood in its entry, glowering happily. "You should never call me Otto," he said quietly.

From the stairwell, he could hear her screaming. "Son of a bitch! Turd and swine shit! Asshole! Nazi pervert!"

Oh, Eva had soul, she did. But Maikowski could do without her if he had to.

— —

Wulff rose early, put on a good blue suit, and taxied to Berlin Mitte. He spent thirty minutes reviewing reports, then assigned a detective to a new case, a beating and theft occurring in the Prenzlauer, probably not political. Schupo Control informed him that two police captains had been gunned down overnight, their bodies discovered near communist party headquarters. He signed Barlach's special application to take the November detective examinations, then looked over the Theodor Loos file he'd been compiling for quite some time. *Mother: Flemish. Father: German of good family. Educated in Catholic schools and at the local Freiburg gymnasium.* Loos had tried to enlist in the army during 1918 and had been assigned a training unit, though the armistice intervened and he was immediately discharged. Loos had contracted influenza in late 1923, then had made his way to Berlin where he was hired on at the Reich Ministry of the Interior as a boiler technician and janitor. Later, he found a job at Alexanderplatz. *Not married. Lives alone.*

Another dead-end for Wulff.

Wulff left his office and walked downstairs to an oak-paneled conference room to find that Weiss had arrived early and was sitting in one of the big oak chairs scattered around the table. Krause was unpacking the contents of a pasteboard box containing files, dossiers, and photographs. The conference table was partially covered with documents and reports already, and Krause was hurrying to unpack the rest. Wulff offered his apology. He glanced up at the wall clock and found that he was ten minutes early.

Wulff sat down heavily, feeling suddenly depressed and angry. The Hirrenstrasse killer, Bruckmann, and now this. He was being swamped by his administrative duties and had managed to hire only one trustworthy aide. He sensed his struggles coming to nothing.

"And what about you?" Weiss said, looking up with a hopeless smile. He wiped his glasses with a handkerchief and returned them to his nose. Krause had finished his work and was standing in one corner, arms folded.

"I am at my limit with the termite, with Hirrenstrasse, and with Bruckmann."

"The termite!" Weiss laughed. He stared at Wulff, eyes magnified by the thick lenses. "Let me tell you something in confidence, my friend Wulff. I have just made up a revised list of Nazi-dominated Schupo precincts." Weiss nodded, as if confirming to himself the results of a mental inventory. "Last spring, when I began to compile this list, it was nearly empty. At that time, only eight or nine precincts were infested. Now it is late summer. That number has doubled. I have some captains openly avowing the Nazi cause. And I can't fire them because the Ministry of Interior persists in calling the Nazis a legitimate political party. Even Hitler plays the game, proclaiming his allegiance to the course of legality. Therefore, I cannot fire a civil servant who advocates the downfall of the very government which employs him. What folly!"

"And the termite?" Wulff asked.

"The termite," Weiss said, whistling softly. "The administration is now riddled with leaks. My own Stapo force has its own problems, too. Our termite has become one among many. And now the Nazis have brazenly killed two Schupo captains in the street." Weiss thumped a fist on the table.

"Before our meeting begins, there's one more thing," Wulff said. "Something that might help."

"And that is?"

"It's about Edgar Braun," Wulff said. "I want to go looking for him."

"He does not exist," Weiss said. "What I mean is that I've had Stapo looking for him for three weeks and they can't find his track. Nobody has seen or heard of him since Munich in 1923."

"He's a devotee of the garrote."

"And this makes him a suspect in Bruckmann's murder?"

"I think it does."

"You have a hunch then," Weiss said.

Wulff shrugged. "I want to go to Juprelle near Liège in Belgium. Braun was born there and grew up there. I want to see if anyone has information that might lead us to him."

"His parents are dead," Weiss said. "Well, we presume his father is dead. The man is unknown."

"I'll be gone less than two days," Wulff pleaded.

"Ach," Weiss hissed. "And you need a requisition."

"Tickets and travel expenses."

Weiss laughed and shook his head. "You are Kripo to the core," he said. "Despite my attempts to indoctrinate you into the political police, you remain an investigative bulldog. Where have I gone wrong, Wulff?"

"It's my nature," Wulff said.

"Very well then," Weiss said. "Take your trip and I'll see you're reimbursed." Weiss sat back down. "But please delay it for two weeks. Give me at least that much time during our investigation of the murder of Captains Anlauf and Lencke."

"Yes sir, two weeks," Wulff agreed.

How many more would die in two weeks?

━ ━

They'd gone to the Grosspielhaus to see a new Brecht play that Sunday afternoon. Earlier, they'd gone swimming in Luna Park, splashing madly like children in the coolish water of the huge public swimming pool, just the two of them off in a shady corner where it was almost chilly, where the children and old people didn't venture, both laughing like thieves who'd stolen the czar's underwear. Wulff had gone underwater and kissed her belly, ran his tongue up and down her lovely legs, touching the delicate hairs floating between them while she ran her hands through his wet hair. That afternoon, Johanna had donned her red skirt, a white short-sleeved silk blouse, a light pink vest embroidered with crested peacocks in brilliant arrays of gold, green, and turquoise, and had tied a light crimson scarf around her neck. Wulff told her she looked like a sunset, and he meant it. That day they made love three times in all.

After dinner at the Romanishes Café, Wulff engaged a horse-drawn carriage for the ride to Adlon's hotel on Wilhelmstrasse, a trip of perhaps three kilometers through quiet Sunday evening streets.

The hotel was crowded with diners, Berliners who went for late afternoon tea and stayed to greet the symphony and theater crowds. Once inside, Wulff spotted Erwin Kisch at one end of the long mahogany bar holding a drink. Kisch waved at Johanna, then shook hands with Wulff.

"So, how goes it?" Kisch said gayly, giving Johanna a bearish hug. He was chewing an unlighted cigar and informed them that he'd only just begun to drink. "Have you heard that the Nazis broke all the windows in the Katakombe Klub last night? Apparently the anti-Nazi skits were too much for their thin skins. It's a pity, too. The Katakombe was about the last place left in Berlin to have a joke at Hitler's expense!"

Johanna kissed Kisch on the cheek. "You're an absolute fount of news," she laughed.

Wulff scanned the bar area, its gold-flocked wallpaper, round tables and spotless white linen, crystal ashtrays, and gold service. A long mirror behind the bar glowed with reflected light. Behind them, an entryway led to the ornate ballroom nearby, and one could hear an orchestra tuning its instruments for the evening's light entertainment of waltzes and divertimentos. Standing in the lobby was Louis Adlon. They nodded a greeting.

"We've been to see the latest Brecht," Johanna told Kisch.

Wulff ordered champagne cocktails, the latest rage in Berlin. In one corner at a table, Wulff saw Kurt Daleuge, the paramount SA chief in Berlin's growing SA movement. He also recognized Dieter Rom and Otto Maikowski, men who ran the day-to-day operations for the SA in the city.

"Have you heard the latest gossip?" Johanna asked Kisch. "Our friend Goebbels is going to marry his society lady. Apparently, they are formally engaged."

"This is different," Kisch interrupted. "Nazis usually impregnate their women and then abandon them."

"They are to be married in the Catholic Church," Johanna continued. "Wouldn't you know it! This good Nazi will go down on his knees to the Virgin Mary! I feel as though this country is being raped."

"Utterly predictable," said the suddenly glum Kisch. "Scratch the surface of a good Nazi and you will discover a petit-bourgeois in an ill-fitting linen suit."

Johanna smiled and sipped some champagne. Wulff knew that she had abandoned her written study of Goebbels, finding it both depressing and dangerous. "Herr Goebbels refuses to share his dreams with me," Johanna said. "Therefore my analysis is stymied."

"I can tell you his dreams," Kisch laughed. "He sees a long line of muddy Jews streaming out of Germany toward the east. He sees bare-headed communists starving in prisons while the trains run on time!"

Johanna blushed and held onto Wulff's right arm as though she might faint. Wulff loved her terribly just then, with her peach-colored cheeks and flashing green eyes.

"And just how many times have we jointly analyzed Herr Goebbels?" she asked Kisch. She finished her cocktail and put an arm around Wulff's waist. "Here we are always trying to didacticize his relations with women," she said. She paused, raised her eyes to Wulff, gazing at him with shy longing. "But the true focus of any scientific analysis of Goebbels must be his relationship to Hitler, and not to the society women he covets. The *awe* in which he holds Hitler, the utter devotion he shows to the man, the deference to his inane ideas and the blindness of his loyalty—really, it is quite remarkable psychologically. And his willingness to serve! Hitler says, 'We are stabbed in the back by November criminals! We are betrayed by the Jews in banking and finance! We are the true revolutionists of Germany!' Hitler says these things and Goebbels *believes*!"

Kisch grunted. "Are we to take it that Hitler is a father figure?"

Johanna's eyes seemed to blaze. "Let us think about it. Here we have a movement dominated by a single male, a male who is without a wife, a family, or children, whose whole existence is untouched by either hearth or home, and for whom life is peripatetic, rootless, disorganized. Here is a movement dominated by a male who distances himself from all human contact and intimacies, who apparently goes without either sex or friendship, who is, as the anthropologists say, without a kinship structure. And how his followers yearn for his love! How they hang on his every utterance! Truly remarkable."

"So Hitler is their father!" Kisch laughed.

"Not precisely," Johanna cautioned, warming now to her task. "He is the *absent* father. He is the father who intentionally withholds his love, who pats his child on the head at Christmas, who never writes a letter, who never bestows a kiss."

"Talk, talk," Kisch said.

"My dear Erwin," Johanna said, "haven't you noticed how much these Nazis talk about their problems? They have nothing but problems to solve! They have the problem of the Jew!" Johanna put down her champagne glass, her face shiny with petulance now. "They have the problem of the bourgeois and they have the problem of the workers and Bolshevism, the problem of the November criminals, nationalism, socialism, lebensraum." Johanna gave Wulff another squeeze. "They are the mightiest of talkers. Hitler sometimes talks for hours at a time. His speeches are interminable. And when he finishes a speech, he retires to his apartments and continues to talk. Talk without end."

"As I've told you before," Kisch said, "these Nazis have learned their tricks from Al Capone. They are nothing more than criminals in business suits and fancy uniforms."

Louis Adlon had walked to the bar. He put a hand on Wulff's shoulder and led him away a few steps.

"How are you, Harry?" Adlon whispered. "And how is your father, please?"

"We are both well," Wulff told him.

"Tell your father I miss him," Adlon said. "I miss both him and the old days."

Wulff said he would convey the message. Adlon seemed nervous to Wulff, not his old self. He tugged at his bow tie.

"The SA is here in force tonight," Adlon said at last.

"Yes, I've seen them in the corner," Wulff responded.

"At least it isn't that pig Göring," Adlon said quietly. He shrugged his shoulders helplessly. "I'm told Göring prefers restaurants where the portions are large."

Wulff laughed under his breath. He turned and took a quick look at the SA men, Dieter Rom, tall, blond, and sleek in his fitted brown uniform. Maikowski, short and thin with a perverse gleam in his eyes. Kurt Daleuge, hugely fat with a red drinker's face. "What are they doing here?" Wulff asked, turning back to Adlon. Wulff could hear Kisch laughing at something he'd said himself.

"They make themselves seen," Adlon replied. "They are like the scars of smallpox. They are not the disease, but they are evidence of it. Until now, the Adlon Hotel has avoided both the disease and the scars."

Rom had risen from his table, had thrown down his linen napkin, and was crossing the room toward Wulff. His uniform was impeccably tailored, pressed to hard creases and sharp angles, his leather accoutrements, the belts and boots, highly polished. Johanna was saying, "The father figure..."

Kisch laughed and ordered more champagne cocktails. From the ballroom, Wulff could hear a light waltz. Rom advanced toward them, his smile haughty, flashing his brilliant white teeth, his razor-cut hair without a strand misplaced. Rom nodded to Wulff.

"I believe you are Oberkommissar Harry Wulff," Rom said seductively, giving a sidelong glance at Kisch who had stopped talking.

"At your service," Wulff said.

"And this oaf must be Kisch," Rom said, suddenly jerking his head to the bar.

Kisch saluted Rom with his champagne glass. "I am not familiar with the formalities," Kisch said and smiled. "Do I say 'Heil Hitler,' or just vomit on your black boots?"

Rom smiled oddly. "You are writing false articles," Rom told Kisch. Wulff watched, expecting the worst.

"The Bruckmann articles, yes," Kisch said. "But they are not false."

"The SA is not responsible for Bruckmann's death," Rom said coldly.

"Don't be absurd," Kisch told him. "There have been rumors for years about Bruckmann, about his fondness for little boys and little girls. They even say he liked to bite people on the neck! Imagine it! Bruckmann as a vampire! That would put him in the same category as the leader of the SA, Ernst Röhm, would it not?" Kisch paused dramatically, grinned, and licked his lips.

"There will come a day," Rom said.

"Please, Herr Rom, I am asking you to return to your table," Adlon said quietly. "This is neither the time nor the place for politics."

Rom turned back to Wulff. "You are the investigator, are you not?"

Wulff nodded.

"You are aware," Rom continued, "that all this theory about Bruckmann's death is the merest kike spittle, are you not?"

"Kike spittle?" Wulff said.

"Kike spittle," Rom told him again. "The drool from a Jew's mouth. Filth and dreck."

Wulff felt a tightness in his throat. "I'll thank you to leave us," he said.

"See here, Wulff," Rom continued, "I want you to know that the SA holds no grudge against Kripo. We fight the same battle, no?" Rom looked at Johanna, who was watching the scene with barely disguised horror. "But beware of the old saying. If you lie down with dogs…"

Wulff slapped Rom hard on the cheek. Rom staggered slightly, then recovered after knocking over an empty champagne glass with his right hand. Where Wulff had hit him, the cheek was inflamed.

"Gentlemen, please!" Adlon called out.

Rom rubbed his jaw once. "I shall not forget this," he said.

"I don't want you to," Wulff told him. "And in my circle, this is an invitation to fight. Do you prefer the pistol or the saber?"

Rom studied the room, the ceiling, its gossamer light and reflected colors. The bar had become totally quiet save for the sound of a violin being tuned in another room.

"I will give you my answer at another time," Rom said.

"Perhaps you prefer ambush. Like Anlauf and Lencke."

"My weapons are patience and organization," Rom said, turning slightly to nod at Johanna.

Wulff bowed in mocking deference. Rom turned and crossed the room slowly. Wulff watched as the three SA men paid their bill and left the hotel. Johanna had tears in her eyes.

"I'm so sorry, Harry," Louis Adlon said. "This sort of thing shames me."

Wulff felt suddenly cold, his blood running with ice. For a brief moment, he would have denounced God for the chance to kill Dieter Rom.

21

Wulff parked his Opel in a cab zone. A barricade had been erected, blocking the street ahead, a haphazard stack of cast-off furniture, blocks of building concrete, paving stone, and empty beer barrels. Beside the barricade stood two Schupo, smoking cigarettes and chatting aimlessly, tapping their truncheons against the legs of their woolen uniforms. Wulff circled the barricade on the sidewalk and showed the Schupo his ID with its gothic German script and official photograph.

"What are your orders?" Wulff barked at the ranking Schupo, a hulking Wachtmeister. "Sergeant," Wulff asked again, this time louder.

"The order of the day, sir," the sergeant told Wulff. "We have no special orders." Wulff clenched his teeth in anger.

Two young Jewish girls ran along the street just in sight of Wulff and the two Schupo, their dark hair tied back with white ribbons. Wulff left the barricade in disgust and hurried down the street. There was a slice of moon above the apartment buildings and shops, barely visible in the gloom of early evening. Now the shops were shuttered, a few windows broken. There was an acrid odor and one could see smoke rising above the synagogue. On Fasanenstrasse, the Jews of Berlin had built their most beautiful temple facing the street. For hundreds of years, the Jews of Europe had not dared to place the front doors of their places of worship on the streets, instead facing them toward alleys, a token to the forbiddenness of their worship. Now, just across the street, Wulff could see the huge stone Torah above ornate doors, glass in shards on the steps, an elderly man with a long gray beard on his knees in the gutter, his hat crushed nearby. The smoke was yellow and the tiny sliver of moon bone white. Wulff drew his Parabellum pistol.

Down the street, an open green Opel passed slowly, two men in front, one large man in back with a foot on the passenger seat, carrying a walnut truncheon. As the Opel passed, the man screamed vile epithets and obscenities at a dozen or more Jews cowering on the front steps of the synagogue. The Opel stopped suddenly and a man in the passenger seat threw a stone.

Wulff could see a Stapo cadre nearby, all the men in dark suits, Weiss at its head. Wulff holstered his pistol and hurried down the street. Six of the cadre were carrying carbines and Weiss held a small revolver.

"What are you doing about this?" Wulff asked Weiss when he reached the cadre's position. Wulff had forgotten his protocol, the necessity for respect. He felt dully angry, almost sullen.

"Ah," Weiss grunted, "you've never seen a pogrom before?" Weiss spoke slowly, his voice a near-growl. "How did you hear the news?" he asked Wulff.

"One of the congregation telephoned Johanna," Wulff said. "We'd been at Halensee and had just returned to Berlin."

"You should go home, Wulff," Weiss said.

"How long has this been going on?" Wulff asked, ignoring the suggestion.

"They'd only just ended the *Selichot* service," Weiss answered. "Perhaps a hundred SA began this riot, although not all of them were wearing their uniforms. The majority were in brown shirts, but not all. They timed their arrival for the end of the service, surrounded the synagogue and wouldn't let the congregation leave. Some old men have been beaten and a few of the women frightened out of their wits, and there have been some broken windows."

"Who's that in the green Opel?"

"Count Wolf-Heinrich von Hellerdorf," Weiss told him.

"The Nationalist?" Wulff asked, having heard of this strangely political count, a crackpot on the fringe of the Rightist movement.

"One of the *volk*," Weiss said. "He's open enough about his pro-Nazi anti-Semitism that Stapo has stopped tracking his whereabouts. I suppose this is his little surprise in conjunction with the SA. A pogrom on the most holy day of the year."

"Have they burned the synagogue?"

Weiss looked across the street at the rabbi and his flock huddled on the synagogue steps. "The synagogue isn't on fire," he said. "Orpo has it surrounded now. In the alleys, the SA built bonfires during the service. Tires and garbage, some sticks of furniture and clothing. After the service, about sixty uniformed SA blocked the entrance. The women and children are inside now."

"What about Schupo response?" Wulff asked. "I've just now seen two Schupo smoking cigarettes and enjoying the show."

Weiss laughed shrilly. Wulff had never seen Weiss appear so manic. "The central precincts have largely gone over to the Nazis now. Some are merely indifferent. We're waiting for more Orpo troops to be trucked over from their barracks. When they come, we'll move on the SA and beat some heads to a pulp. The plan is to surround them as they surrounded the synagogue."

"How many Stapo have you here?"

"Perhaps twenty-five by now."

The green Opel sped by, Count von Hellerdorf standing tall in its back seat, pounding his truncheon against the metal skin of the car, screaming epithets.

"I want him off the streets," Wulff said coldly.

"We'll wait for Orpo reinforcements," Weiss said. "They have heavy weapons and armored vehicles. You'd best go home now, Wulff. There is nothing more to be done here. The entrances to the synagogue are being guarded, and nobody is going to set it on fire. Some of the windows are broken, but they can be repaired. When things calm down, I'll escort the congregation outside and get them on their way. We'll take care of the SA in our own time."

The smoke curled upward, thick and black now. Wulff could smell shit. "They're burning dung," he said.

"It's pig offal and guts," Weiss said. "They've trucked it in from butcher shops."

Wulff studied the synagogue in failing light, its broken glass, the huge stone facade. "Let me arrest the count," he pleaded. "I'm not afraid to do it right here and now."

"Of course, you're not afraid," Weiss said. "And I'm not afraid to do it either. None of my men are afraid to do it. But it isn't a question of being afraid. It is a question of practical politics now, and nothing more. Do you know what will happen if I arrest the count? Immediately he will be released by the magistrate on bail. His case will become a cause for the Right and he will be acquitted by the judiciary. The count will revel in his arrest. Perhaps he will receive a hero's ribbon from the Stahlhelm." Weiss shrugged and looked away distractedly. "My sole duty here is to protect the integrity of the synagogue until I have enough men to surround the SA. We will crunch a few heads and send them away."

At the far end of Fasanenstrasse, an Orpo armored vehicle stopped, disgorging a dozen heavily armed men in green uniforms. Wulff watched them deploy.

"Go home, Wulff," Weiss said gently. "You're Kripo. Remember?"

"I don't consider this political," Wulff said.

"What do you consider it, then?" Weiss asked him.

The Opel sped away, turned the corner, and disappeared. A few uniformed SA were leaking into the gathering dusk, making for alleys and side streets. Wulff watched as Weiss and his men hurried across the street and joined a few other Stapo on the steps of the synagogue. Weiss engaged in a short conversation with the head rabbi, calmed the people, and began addressing those who remained. Wulff turned and walked the two long blocks back to his automobile. By the time he arrived back on Lennestrasse, it was nearly dark and a bright moon gleamed down on the Tiergarten.

＞＝

The polka band began to play at seven o'clock sharp. Maikowski had taken a seat at a cedar-and-beech plank table of the Hunting Lodge lounge of the Kaiserhof Hotel, where there was a boar's head above the bar, a polished mirror where numerous beer steins hung, and a rack of ancient Meerschaum pipes on display. For at least ten minutes, the walls resounded with music, accordion, bass, organ, and a shrill harmonica, Maikowski despising every moment of its non-Prussian rusticity. He laughed contemptuously to himself and sipped some Black Velvet he'd learned to appreciate on a secret political junket to Ireland, one of the many times he'd gone off to contact political groups of the "other Europe."

Maikowski picked up the hand-printed menu and studied it reflectively: baby Elbe eels, smoked herring on a bed of fresh lettuce, candied sauerkraut and pig's feet, buckets of grilled oysters, Westphalian ham, sauerbraten, oxtail soup, a vegetable platter of beets, cucumbers, and leeks. To drink, there would be Rhenish wine, beer, ale, sherry for after dinner. And of course, there would be the obligatory Goebbels speech, titled "A Germany without the Jews."

Rom stood talking with a group of junior army officers across the lounge. Maikowski felt a little jealous of Rom just then, his square-jawed glamour, his trimly tailored blue suit with its wide fashionable lapels, his highly buffed shoes probably imported from Italy, even his fingernails that were polished like the mirrors of the Kaiserhof Hotel bar. Rom walked to the table and sat, unspeaking.

"You've seen the program?" Maikowski asked. Despite his spate of envy, Maikowski felt suddenly jovial, even companionable. The news of the day was excellent, and the prospects for a productive Nazi autumn exquisite on top of that. They had conducted a successful pogrom. "We're being favored by another Goebbels speech."

"A Germany without the Jews," Rom said sarcastically. "What a huge surprise. The party is distracting the masses with this asininity."

"You've heard about the pogrom?" Maikowski asked him. "After today, they'll remember us on Fasanenstrasse." Maikowski paused, waiting for a response which never came. "Do you want a drink?" he asked, just to break the moody silence. "We mustn't remain completely sober for a Goebbels speech. It is beyond human endurance."

Rom smiled politely.

"You were on Fasanenstrasse today?" Maikowski asked Rom after they'd ordered a round of drinks, another Black Velvet for himself, beer for Rom. When the drinks came, Maikowski fingered his cut-crystal glass and contemplated the boar's head, its pink tongue and vague glassy eyes.

"I was there, but not in uniform," Rom answered.

"What was the damage?"

"Broken windows, burned pig shit in the alleys. We herded some kikes around like cattle."

"What about the count?"

"He played the rabble-rouser in somebody's bad dream," Rom said. "Drove his open touring car up and down the street shouting slogans and pounding his truncheon like a tom-tom. I imagine he'll have to repaint the car. The ignorant ass thinks he's part of the movement."

"Pity," Maikowski said. "And the other activity?"

"Piles of pig shit at all the doors," Rom said. "Burning tires. I hear the synagogue was filled with smoke. Most amusing, don't you agree?"

Maikowski roared, a bit falsely Rom thought. "It was a luscious idea," he said. "Did you think of it yourself?"

"Actually, yes," Rom said.

"Anything else?"

"My men beat up some *Ostjuden*," Rom said. "Nothing too serious as of yet." Rom sipped some beer. "We surrounded the synagogue and kept the kikes penned up."

"Beat up some old Jews!" Maikowski laughed. A thin froth of Black Velvet lay on his lip like a moustache. Rom said nothing about it, leaving it there like a private joke on Maikowski, who always wished to appear above reproach, perfect in his manners and guises, even as he drank himself into a pissy mess. Even now, Rom could detect the first alcoholic flush on Maikowski, the slightly unfocused eyes and sugary phraseology, the damp forehead and nervous hands.

"We painted swastikas on the building," Rom said distractedly. His thought was elsewhere.

"Oh, how excellent," Maikowski said, placing two elbows on the plank table and leaning forward, Rom aware that he was about to become privy to something private and delicious. "Your termite is delivering nothing," Maikowski said. His words marched slowly across the table in single file.

"I'm aware of his uselessness," Rom said. "He thinks Wulff has his scent. It has become his *idée fixe*."

"The SA awards him one hundred marks a week," Maikowski said. "He's become a thorn in our side. I expect him to produce, or we'll cut him loose." Maikowski grinned and drank some of his Black Velvet. "When he murdered Bruckmann, he became an instant liability."

"So cut him loose if you dare," Rom said.

"If I dare?" Maikowski said, leaning back with a contemptuous leer on his face. "We can cut him loose if we wish. Who is he, anyway? I've had him checked out by security. His name is Loos. He's from Lille and has lived in Frieburg. He's a fucking janitor, for God's sake, with a German father and a Flemish mother. Beyond this there is nothing known about him. He is as blank as the far side of the moon."

"He is unstable, in my opinion," Rom said. "He'd never stand being cut loose just like that. He might do something damaging to the SA."

Maikowski drained his Black Velvet. He wiped away the froth moustache with a table napkin. "Have you read the articles that Kisch is writing about us in the bourgeois and socialist press? He is a one-man communist uprising right here in Berlin."

"I've read them," Rom said.

"So, what happens if we simply stop paying this termite of yours?"

Rom noticed the possessive shift—*yours*. "We could try it," he said. "But there would be trouble. Perhaps he should simply be killed."

"Ah, but dear Rom," Maikowski replied.

"He might simply find a new conduit."

"He might go to the army with this worthless information?" Maikowski said.

In truth, Rom was tired of the termite, weary of meeting him in transvestite bars and nightclubs, waiting alone in some dark cavern while men danced with men, the termite looking on in glazed fascination as Rom tried to wheedle information amid the stink of beer and piss. Week after week passed as the termite fed Rom useless tidbits, news that Rom doubted was even legitimate, much less helpful to the SA or party. "He fears Wulff," Rom said at last. "He thinks Wulff knows about his existence, or has the scent. Whether this is true or not, the idea is firmly fixed in his head. He wants to join the SA and wear a uniform. Can you believe this fellow?"

Maikowski and Rom shared a nervous laugh. In fifteen minutes, they were due upstairs in the Kaiserhof ballroom for a dinner and speech, a celebration of the first official Nazi pogrom of the New Era.

"And what about Wulff?" Maikowski asked. He glanced at his watch, just before eight o'clock. For an hour, he'd been drinking Black Velvet and was sensing a pleasant lack of feeling in the tips of his fingers. "Where does Wulff stand in his investigation of the Bruckmann murder?" Maikowski asked.

"Nobody knows," Rom said. "Wulff is neither a drinker nor a gossip. And he isn't influenced by money."

"An honest man!" Maikowski laughed.

"A Schleswiger," Rom said. "Half fucking Danish."

"He slaps hard for a Dane," Maikowski said malevolently. "We'll forget Wulff for now." He smiled again, showing Rom his little mole-like teeth.

Rom muttered something under his breath, something half-hidden by a new wave of polka music and the rising tide of conversation. "Wulff will get his," Rom said.

"They say he challenged you to a duel!" Maikowski smiled again. "Did it happen, Rom? I couldn't hear from that far across the Adlon bar."

"Unimportant," Rom said.

"You should fight him, Rom!" Maikowski roared. "I can see it now. A foggy morning on the Spree, north of Berlin in the dense forest. They stare at each other from across ten paces of wet fern and rhododendron. Then the silence is broken by a shot. A second shot! One of the men falls and there is dark blood on the dark forest floor!"

"Shut your mouth," Rom said.

"Ah, cheer up, Rom," Maikowski laughed, standing now and clapping Rom on one shoulder. "We're listening to Goebbels tonight! We're eating eels and smoked herring! And we've broken all the windows of the Fasanenstrasse synagogue, sent the kikes scurrying like cockroaches. It is a night to celebrate!"

— ⁓ —

She had been crying. The candles in the room had guttered out, and everything smelled of wax, honey-apples, and autumn smoke. Wulff led her to the ottoman and made her lie down. He went around the room closing drapes and turning on table lamps. He found a symphony on the radio. He kneeled beside her and said, "It's over now, darling. They've chased them away from the synagogue and everybody has gone home."

"I listened to the news," Johanna said, one arm over her eyes, trying to stop the tears. "But there isn't any news. They won't broadcast the truth."

"I suppose not," Wulff agreed. "But you mustn't worry anymore. Weiss was there with his Stapo men, and a large contingent of Orpo are guarding the synagogue tonight. The injured are being cared for. Orpo escorted the congregation to their homes. The smoke was only from garbage and tires. It wasn't the synagogue itself."

"They broke the stained glass windows, didn't they?" she asked Wulff.

"Yes, they broke the windows. I couldn't see everything."

"The big one in front?"

"Yes, I'm afraid so." Wulff was unable to lie. Lies were untellable now.

"What else have they done?" she asked him. She looked stricken, drained.

"They knocked down some old men," Wulff said. "Count von Hellerdorf drove around and around in his Opel shouting operatic slogans. Pounding his truncheon against the skin of his car. Childish really."

"Childish," Johanna muttered sullenly, holding Wulff's arm now, her fingers pink with strain. "What else? What else did they do?"

"They threw rocks and paving cobbles," Wulff said. He was committed to the truth now, wedded to its axioms. "They painted swastikas on the building."

Johanna choked back more tears, then suddenly began to sob in gusts. "These are the most holy days," she cried.

"Why don't you get into a hot bath?" Wulff suggested. "I'll draw the water and rub your back. Perhaps it will make you feel better. I'll stay with you tonight if you like."

Johanna rose and put her feet on the floor, kicked off her black shoes, and touched his face. "All my pretty theories are meaningless, aren't they, Harry? Just a lot of Jewish intellectual nonsense, talk and more talk. Theories mean nothing to these people. Reason is useless, talk is empty, my whole analytical stance is stupid!"

Wulff kissed her gently on the forehead, just a touch with his lips. "Don't let's think about it now," he said.

"Harry, Harry," she began plaintively, "you don't theorize about these people, do you, dear? You know deep inside that talking about their motives and their hidden thoughts is absurd, don't you? You've known this all along, haven't you, Harry? You and Kisch. You both know that talk is worthless, less than worthless."

"This will pass," Wulff told her. "Germany won't fall for their lies. There are too many good people here for that to happen. There are too many honest workers, too many honest police, too many ordinary folks."

"Erwin called," Johanna said. "He tells me that Schupo did nothing to stop the pogrom. He said they stood on the street and smoked cigarettes and did nothing while the SA had their pogrom. Is that true, Harry? Did they do nothing?"

Harry searched her green eyes, now wide with disappointment and longing. "The central precincts are full of Nazis now," he said. "And besides, they had no orders. You know how stupid they are without orders."

"Are you making excuses for them, Harry?"

"No," Wulff said. "They did nothing."

"You know, Harry," she said, "if enough people do nothing, anything is possible."

Wulff went to the bathroom and turned the taps. He shook bath salts into the hot water and added a capful of oil. He tested the water, then walked back to the ottoman where Johanna was busy unpinning her hair. He kneeled beside her again and touched her face.

"*L'shanah tovah tikatevu,*" Wulff said.

"*L'shanah tovah tikatevu,* my darling Harry," Johanna told him gently. "And after today, no more theories, Harry. I don't believe in theories anymore."

22

He changed trains from an Aachen express to the local, bound toward Liège with stops. For eight hours, Wulff had ridden through a tunnel of fog and steady rain, the countryside toneless, the elephantine hills somber, and the vineyards drenched in smoky silence. Crossing the Rhine, both banks rose up from water with a precipitous suddenness that thrilled and stunned Wulff, the apple orchards shrouded in a dank mist as a few lonely farmers drew water from wells or drove horses through the steamy distances. At Aachen, the station was like some lonely steel spider, its deserted tracks slightly melancholy in the first few rays of morning sun.

Wulff puffed a cigarette. He observed the miners on the station platforms with their glasses of beer at seven o'clock in the morning, life underground etched on each tired face. Wulff had begun his journey at midnight in Berlin. By eight o'clock, he was leaving Aachen in a trembling local coach, eating a stale sandwich as the miners drank their beer on the platform. When he finished his sandwich, he walked the length of the Belgian train looking for a club car, but concluded that there wasn't one. At Liège, he changed trains again, a local that stopped at every village and market town. In forty minutes, Wulff arrived at Juprelle, a village of perhaps five hundred souls set on a steep hillside. There was a parallel row of shops, two cobbled streets, and a green common. High on a hill was the Catholic church, stone gray against a gray background.

Wulff hauled out his overnight bag from beneath the seat, then walked uphill in light mist toward the church. He had worn his black raincoat but had forgotten an umbrella. In the morning it was cold, as dark as sin, his breath trailing him as crows squawked in the spice-scented air. He found the chancel empty, bare of ornamentation, with a row of windows above the nave. Wulff walked inside the church and found the vestry vacant as well.

From behind, he heard, "May I help you, sir?"

He turned abruptly and saw the priest, a frail Belgian wearing a dirty black cassock with a mane of white, disheveled hair, and a robust red drunkard's face.

"Do you speak German?" Wulff asked.

"Some," came the slow reply. "Yes, I speak some German."

Wulff returned to the door and stood beside the priest, who came up to Wulff's breastbone, no more. The priest had bushy eyebrows, an unkempt-looking face, and he smelled of unwashed socks. Wulff set down his overnight bag on one of the rough wooden pews nearby. Outside, the dank mist had transformed itself into a gentle rain, and Wulff could hear it patter down through the rhododendrons and ferns. He showed the priest his Kripo ID.

"A German policeman?" the priest said, surprised. "You've come a long way. You must be very tired."

"Yes, a long way," Wulff agreed.

"There is something you seek in this small village?" the priest asked. "Nobody comes here."

"There's been a murder in Berlin," Wulff said.

In Flemish the priest said, "I'm sorry," Wulff not understanding. "But how does this concern Juprelle?" The priest noticed Wulff's look of consternation, then repeated the whole sentence in German. "Surely, a murder in Berlin?" The priest stood there open-handed, a supplicant's pose.

"I need information about someone born in Juprelle," Wulff said.

"Someone in my parish?"

Wulff nodded. "I think so, Father," he said. The priest ran his hands through the wilderness of his white hair.

"Would you like some tea?" the priest asked Wulff. "Perhaps some bread and butter?"

Without waiting for Wulff's answer, the priest walked outside, Wulff following down a stone path to the chancellery and vicarage. The single-story stone house was divided into living quarters, a low-ceilinged kitchen that smelled of damp wood and coal, a small office crammed with books, a stamp collection, and several chess sets. The priest busied himself with tea.

"My German is not so good," the priest said, finally sitting as Wulff sipped hot tea.

"I must catch the return train to Liège," Wulff said, as if that explained his harried expression.

"Then—you must ask your questions," the priest said.

"I am here about Edgar Braun," Wulff began. "I believe he was born in this village."

The priest closed his eyes. "Poor soul," he said. "Has Edgar done something? Is he in trouble? Is that what you've come to say?"

"I don't know, Father," Wulff admitted.

The priest stood, repositioning a tin pot that caught leaking rainwater from the roof. He sat down opposite Wulff again. "I knew Edgar and his mother," the priest said.

"You called him a poor soul."

The priest frowned. "We must not cast stones," he said.

"I am not interested in rumor," Wulff said. "And I don't carry tales like a child. My business is official and very important. People's lives are at stake."

"Of course," the priest sighed. "I thought you'd say something like that."

Wulff leaned over the table. "But I do need to know something about Edgar Braun. It is possible he killed a man in Berlin. A policeman."

"Oh dear me," the priest muttered, lapsing into Flemish, which Wulff thought he could decipher. "That's quite terrible if it's true," he continued in German. "But you see, Edgar has not lived in this village for many years. Since the beginning of the Great War. When the Germans came, they took him away to camp. And he never returned. So, you see, I know very little about Edgar." The priest sighed again and sipped some tea. "I'm sorry to say the Germans took many away, and many, like Edgar, never returned."

"I should apologize," Wulff said.

"It was long ago," the priest said tiredly.

"Can't you tell me about him as a child?" Wulff asked quietly. "Before the Germans took him away."

"A most unfortunate child," the priest said.

"Unfortunate?" Wulff prompted, seeing that the priest had lapsed into a distracted silence. He glanced again at his watch, a purposeful gesture. He had three hours in Juprelle before the return train passed on its way back to Liège, Aachen, and Berlin. "This is really quite important, Father," Wulff added.

"Yes, I suppose it must be," the priest said. "Edgar's mother was quite devout in her own special way. But I'm afraid she heard voices that did not exist as you and I would speak of things existing. I'm sure they were very real to her. More's the pity. She would dress herself as the Virgin Mary and appear in the village that way, though I'm certain she had no thoughts of blasphemy. It rather created a scandal."

"And how did Edgar react to this?"

"He withdrew, of course. He was kept at home. His mother did not send him to school, although this was not unusual at the time. Many children went uneducated. The mother made a small income through sewing and taking in laundry. The mother kept a cow and some chickens for eggs. They had a summer garden like everyone else in the village as well." The priest looked away for a moment, gathering himself. "Edgar's mother could be found in the village on her knees, dragging herself through the streets, raising her voice on the common in some kind of prayer, calling on saints and the Virgin. She would roll in the grass and be laughed at by the oafs from the pub. So, you can see it was a most unfortunate life for young Edgar."

"And the father?"

The priest shrugged unhappily. "There was no father in the home," he said. "Some believed him to be an itinerant apple picker. Others thought he was a miner passing through to the Ruhr in Germany, looking for work. Some say he was a soldier, and others that he was a tinker." Here the priest shrugged again. "There is a sudden liaison and a girl is pregnant. The child is an unfortunate victim of circumstance."

"What was the mother's name?"

"Margaret Marie."

"And you're certain the father isn't known?"

"He was never known," the priest said. "In a small village like this, the slightest fact is always known. It is impossible to conduct a private life."

"Braun would have been about eighteen years old at the outbreak of the war," Wulff said. "Do you know what he was doing then?"

"My dear sir," the priest began, "he left Juprelle when he was sixteen to apprentice with a locksmith in Liège. At the outbreak, he returned to the village in order to be safe from the Germans."

Wulff tried to think of something to say. Rain was plinking into the tin pot. Webs of slime had formed on the interior walls of the priest's home. It was barely warmer in than out. "And so he returned and was taken away," Wulff continued with a helpless smile. "How were his mental faculties?"

"Oh, he was a handy boy," the priest replied. "One day, I locked myself out of the vestry, and he came up and in a moment he'd opened the door. Really quite clever, I thought. For a boy who'd been so elementally mistreated, he was remarkable in that respect."

"He had a facility with locks?"

"He wasn't dull," the priest said. "Has he done this thing of which you speak?"

Wulff was not distracted by the cold. "I wish I could ask him," he said. "Is there anything else you could tell me about Edgar Braun? His life as a child, his growing up, the way he was treated? Did he ever commit, shall we say, acts of violence in the village?"

"Oh, I couldn't say, sir," the priest said.

Wulff thanked the priest, who asked about a game of chess. Wulff declined, then walked downhill toward the village. He found a row of shops, a square shed used to house the village firefighting equipment, and a single pub that turned out to be nothing much more than a stall with a plank bar and a few plank tables. On one side of the wall was a dirty mirror and a few bottles of cheap wine and Calvados, the local drink. On a dreary Tuesday morning, two customers sat hunched over one of the plank tables, both of them smoking short clay pipes, sharing a game of dominoes. Wulff ordered brandy from a fat bartender in a dirty smock who looked as though he'd just sheared a sheep.

"Do you speak German?" Wulff asked the bartender.

"A little," he said coldly. "The Germans come through here often enough."

Wulff laughed politely, then put down a gold mark. The bartender stared at the coin in barely disguised disbelief. "I can't make change for that," he said.

"Change won't be necessary," Wulff said. "I'm here to make inquiries about Marie Braun and her son Edgar."

The bartender snorted abruptly. He wiped a beefy arm across his chest, picked up the mark, and bit into it. He laughed quietly, then put the mark into his vest pocket.

"Henrique!" the bartender shouted suddenly. "Do we know Marie Braun?"

The two farmers looked up from their dominoes and laughed rudely.

"You knew them both?" Wulff asked.

"I knew them both," he said.

"You'll have another brandy?" the bartender asked Wulff, who hadn't touched his first. He spoke imprecise German, laced with informalisms and improper grammar. Wulff finished the first brandy in silence and dropped a second gold mark on the table. The bartender refilled his glass. The bartender bit the second mark and slipped it into his dirty vest pocket.

"Crazy as church mice, both of them," he told Wulff at last. "Wasn't they crazy, Henrique? Crazy as church mice."

"Crazy how?" Wulff asked.

"Never seen nothing like it," the bartender said, warming to his topic. "Marie—the dirty sow. She traipsed all over the village in her blue robe and blue veil and fingering her holy beads, always praying and rolling her eyes like a witch, until a few of us would drag her back to the shack she shared with that dirty little bastard of hers down by the stream. Everybody shits in that stream and it runs to where Marie lived with her bastard." The bartender brightened, his face shiny with delight. "She talked to God, she did, said she loved God and that He talked back to her. Can you imagine that? Find her on her knees you would, crawling in the mud and wailing to God for this and that." The bartender dropped a hand on the bar and some glasses rattled behind. "Ain't that right, Henrique?"

Toothless laughter from the dominoes players.

"So she dressed up and prayed through the streets?"

"Piss in hell if that isn't all," the bartender said. "Used to make her own tallow candles and saunter around the village with a lighted one, dragging her bastard behind her by the scruff of his stinking little neck, all the while hooting about God and the saints." The bartender leaned over to Wulff, as though sharing a secret, his face sweaty and fat. "And with her damn face painted snow white like she was the Holy Ghost himself. She'd paint on big red lips and big black eyebrows, she would. She was a maniac! Claimed to hear Jesus, Mary, and Joseph. Can you imagine someone claiming to hear the voice of Jesus?"

"And what about Edgar?" Wulff asked.

"You fucking Germans took him off, you did," the bartender said, leaning back with a grin. "Good riddance for once, if you ask me."

Wulff sipped the terrible brandy. From far away there was a faint peal of thunder. "That's all about Edgar? The Germans took him away?"

The bartender leaned again into Wulff's face. "That Marie used to dress up her little bastard and make him wear long curly hair. Made him wear girl's clothes until he was almost grown. She put makeup on his face, too, like they were both whores. Big red lips and a white face, just like her. There they'd be, Marie and her little bastard traipsing around the village dressed up like whores with Edgar in a taffeta dress Marie made herself. Shameful and disgusting, if you ask me."

"Have you seen Edgar since the Germans took him away?"

"Hah!" the bartender laughed. "Ain't seen him since they took him off. Went to Liège as an apprentice then came back here with his tail between his legs fleeing your army. Good riddance to both of them."

"And Marie is dead?"

"She's up in the cemetery if you don't believe me. You can go up there and talk to her! Being dead and all, she'd probably answer you."

Wulff left his brandy where it was, then walked downhill toward the tiny railroad station. He sat under a wooden awning and lit a cigarette, smoking while rain poured down from drab skies.

Good for the priest, he thought. Good for the priest who kept Marie's secret. Good for the priest who refused to cast a stone.

‑ ‑

Eva had captured a corner table at the Café Dom, her haven from the perpetual chill and damp of late autumn in Munich, a coal fire warming her, that and a cup of tea she nursed for hours at a time, using her tea bag again and again until the waiter tired of bringing her hot water. Tonight, in thin fog and pressing cold, she was being served by a youthful blond waiter named Hans.

"You look like shit," her dissolute friend Kruger said. "You are an absolute walking scar."

Eva stuck out her tongue at Kruger, then fingered the open abscess on her lower neck, a wound just below the ear, where she'd broken off a needle. "How nice of you to say," she told Kruger, who was nursing a tiny cupful of schnapps, holding the cup with his permanently chilblained fingers.

"You should take better care of yourself," Kruger said, genuinely concerned.

Kruger was a fine-boned oafish sort of fellow with a round head surrounded by a puckish dish of blond hair. Kruger dressed entirely in black and affected a beret. For now, he made his living smuggling penicillin from Switzerland, buying it there on the black market and selling it to clinicians in the Tyrolean Alps who catered to rich patients with a touch of TB. Otherwise, he hawked pornographic postcards on the streets of Munich, waylaying pimpled English students on sabbatical from their homosexual-ridden universities, opium dens, and gambling casinos. "An abscess like that is dangerous," he told Eva.

Eva watched Kruger sip his schnapps. He would take a deep breath of the alcoholic liquor, inhale it once or twice, roll his eyes with pleasure, dip the tip of his tongue in the liquid, then spit it back into the glass. "Broke again?" she said sarcastically.

Kruger smiled happily and shrugged as if to say, *Isn't everyone?* "You are a master psychologist, Eva," he said. In an earlier time, Kruger had desired Eva. In those days, she had been studying dance and was being squired around Schwabing by a Tyrolean boy named Leonardo. Now all Kruger really desired was an ampule of morphine and a cozy place to warm his stinking feet.

"Exactly how hungry are you, Kruger?" Eva asked him with a look of serious concern.

Kruger narrowed his rheumy little blue eyes. "We mustn't sentimentalize hunger," he said. "It is much too serious a topic."

"This is not a joke," Eva said flatly.

Kruger considered Eva an old and valued friend, a suitable philosophical companion, a foil for his joking nature. "I'm afraid I don't engage in serious conversation these days," he complained.

"You're hungry and you've got consumption," Eva said cruelly. She remembered the old Kruger as she remembered the old Eva—which meant the young Kruger and the young Eva—a brash youngster with a set of pure delft blue eyes and blond hair that glistened like Rumpelstiltskin's golden straw. He had been a lithe and serious boy who enjoyed painting and music as well as the company of actresses from musical comedy. "You'd probably take the penicillin you smuggle if you could afford to, wouldn't you?"

Kruger waved her away. He wanted to drink schnapps, leave the café later for someplace quiet and noncompetitive, a veritable opium den of the soul. "Piss off, Eva, will you?" he said with no ill will.

"Kruger, please," Eva said. "I know where I can get us two thousand marks." Her eyes were bright now. "There is a garden basket full of morphine ampules, Westphalian hams the size of beer barrels, buckets of oysters and eels. Even deviled kidneys and calf liver."

"You have finally lost your mind," Kruger concluded. He rolled his eyes exaggeratedly, trying to subtract from the earnestness of the moment.

"Think of it!" Eva half-shouted. "Two thousand marks."

Kruger failed to respond. Talking about money was nearly as awful as talking about food.

"I am prepared to offer you the chance at an annuity, my dear friend," Eva said brightly.

Kruger sat there half-frightened and half-amused. "What are you talking about?" he asked stupidly. In truth, he'd developed a sudden interest in this fantasy of Eva's, her self-styled confidence.

"One of my clients has real money," Eva said.

"Don't lie to me, Eva," Kruger told her. "You're down to the dogs again."

"This dog doesn't fuck me," Eva said. "He likes to pee on me and he likes me to pee on him. He's very influential and he's got money to burn. If anyone ever knew…"

"Very amusing," Kruger said.

"One rich client," Eva said. "Think of the possibilities! A rich client who likes golden rain and who likes to stripe me with his rhinoceros-hide whip, and who likes pain. What do you think of him?"

"A common enough sort of chap," Kruger said blandly. "If you're thinking of blackmail, Eva, it will never work. For one thing, these rich pukes are *all* perverse, and most of them don't care who knows they're fruity. And for another, their families are used to this kind of business, and almost expect it. It is a way their wives and mistresses have of keeping them on a short leash. They indulge them in their peccadilloes."

"Not this rich client," Eva said. "He's a political official."

Kruger sat up suddenly. "Tell me he's not a priest," he said. "Those shits don't have any real money. And besides, they've got the Church looking out for them."

"He's *political*," Eva hissed.

"Even so," Kruger said. "You could never do it. It's too damn complicated and dangerous."

"But I've seen it done," Eva said. "I was in Berlin when I saw it done. I've been part of the scheme. It can't fail."

"It can't fail!" Kruger howled in delight.

"Listen, you idiot," Eva said. "This client comes to my room alone. He doesn't want anyone to know that he sees me. He brings me money and morphine. If it were known that he likes the golden rain, he would be expelled from his group. And he is a high official in Berlin, believe me. He can pay and he can pay. Without end, as it should be."

"I'm listening," Kruger said.

"He comes to my room and drinks a glass of schnapps," Eva said. "Just to get warm. The next time he comes to my room, suppose this schnapps is laced with chloral hydrate. He becomes very tipsy, then a bit nauseated, and then he can barely control his motor functions, but does not lose consciousness. He is malleable, Kruger! As malleable as putty!"

"Malleable, eh?" Kruger said.

"We take his photograph in compromising positions. We send him these photographs with a simple demand for two thousand marks. He pays us the money."

"And as for me?"

"What a fool you are, Kruger!" Eva laughed. "You are my photographer, of course. You burst into the room like some mountebank in French farce and you emulsify this rich shit." Eva sipped some lukewarm tea and grimaced. Outside, the streets were damp with fog. The blank barrier of winter faced them. "I admit," she said, "it is a bit of a desultory little scheme. But it works. I've seen it work."

"And who is this rich client?"

"SA from Berlin."

Kruger pretended to spit. "Oh shit," he said a bit sadly. His face had deflated like a child's balloon. "Just wonderful, the SA. Why couldn't you have picked Satan himself? It would have been less dangerous."

"What do you care?" Eva asked. "He'll never even see you, never know who you are, never even remember you being in the room. Your job is to round up the chloral hydrate from your medical student friends, and a camera. The noose is around my neck, not yours."

Kruger considered this line of reasoning and found it somewhat compelling. After all, he was quite hungry and could eat neither his pride nor his fear. "Well—" he managed to say.

"Come on, Kruger," Eva pleaded. "We can retire to Greece and bask in the sun."

"When?" Kruger asked simply.

"The client will be in Munich at the end of the month to plan the SA march in honor of Hitler's putsch. He will come and see me then. He always does."

"Soon, then," Kruger said trepidatiously.

"You can locate the chloral hydrate and the camera?"

"That's the easy part," Kruger said.

"Do it then. Sooner rather than later. Are we agreed?"

Kruger licked his chapped lips and coughed once gently. Fever was a message from the microbe in his blood, and he understood the message well. "An SA prick," he said, staring at the schnapps in front of him, its pale opalescent color. The SA terrified him, caused him nightmares. He hated them on principle, of course. "We're agreed then. What about the money?"

"We're partners then, aren't we? Half and half."

"I suppose we are," Kruger said.

"You'll have your penicillin," Eva assured him.

"And you'll have your morphine," Kruger replied.

Schnapps to teacup, they toasted the future.

⌐ ⌐

Wulff took off his damp suit coat and pants. In the kitchen, he made himself a cheese sandwich from stale bread and Gouda, then ate it quickly standing at the counter alone. He went to the bathroom and brushed his teeth, then tiptoed to the bedroom where Johanna lay curled under an enormous goose-down comforter, the windows wide open, and cold air from the Tiergarten pouring in.

"Oh, Harry," she sighed. "I'm so glad you're home."

"Go to sleep, darling," he said.

She turned to face him. Her breath smelled of warm milk and honey. "It was a long, terrible trip, wasn't it?" she said. "Did you find your Edgar Braun?"

"I don't know who I found," Wulff said.

"Are you telling me a riddle?" she said.

"Yes, a riddle."

It was after one o'clock. The Berlin streets had been swept by sleet.

"What kind of riddle?" Johanna asked.

"I've found someone unexpected," Wulff said. "Someone I wasn't looking for, but someone who was there all along."

"Braun, you mean?"

"Braun grew up a bastard in Juprelle. His mother was a schizophrenic who fancied herself in communication with the saints and with Jesus."

"How terrible for the boy," Johanna said.

"That's not all," Wulff whispered. "She dressed Braun in taffeta like a girl and kept his hair long. She applied heavy makeup to his face, lipstick and eyebrow pencil."

Johanna rose to one arm. "Harry," she said quietly. "You *did* find the wrong man." She kissed his cheek. "This sounds more like the killer of Timkin Mueller than the killer of Bruckmann."

"That's just what I thought," Wulff said.

Johanna lay back down. "Such a childhood would produce a tremendous ambiguity over sex. There would be anger at the absent father and an ambivalent sexuality. And clearly an identity problem. Here is the play between hetero- and homosexuality. The strong animus toward suffocation."

"But if Edgar Braun killed the transvestites, that lets Theodor Loos off the hook."

"And who killed Bruckmann?"

"Indeed," Wulff said.

"Harry," Johanna said, "the man who sent you those dolls had a childhood like the one Edgar Braun had."

"I thought you'd say that," Wulff told her. "The element of make-believe and dress-up. The cream base and the lipstick and all the rest. The suffocation by the mother and the anger over an absent father. It all fits. But I don't know which puzzle it belongs to."

"And Bruckmann?"

Wulff closed his eyes. "Let's let it go for tonight," he said.

He listened for rain and finally slept before it came again.

23

Maikowski sat in the grainy half-dark of a winter evening holding the brown envelope in his lap. The envelope seemed to possess malevolent heft, its hasp bent, his own smudged fingerprints on the flap. For the fourth time that day, Maikowski opened the envelope and shuffled nervously through its contents, hoping that by some kind of black magic they somehow might be whisked to another dimension or altered by alchemy.

He looked at the first photograph of the series, a shot badly composed and poorly focused, but just as certainly one of Maikowski himself, his unmistakable little mole teeth and smirking leer, his narrowly beaded eyes and pasty white skin, Maikowski on hands and knees with the woman above, whose fully nude body had already accepted a number of stripes from the rhinoceros-hide skin which Maikowski then held outstretched in one hand, the whip posed in mid-air as the woman smiled in obvious pleasure. Maikowski was bleary-eyed and drooling, training his gaze head-on at the camera as though he were a Pavlovian dog. Visible too was a slice of worn carpet, the edge of a bed, some French art on the walls. There in the half-dark of Alexanderplatz in winter, Maikowski touched the shiny surface of the first photograph and thought back to Munich, that one stormy night he'd visited Eva for the last time. Nothing crossed his memory of the visit at all, only a faint but fragrant whisper of himself plunging into a nauseated dive from consciousness.

Maikowski placed his forehead on the cold glass of the passenger window and stared out at Alexanderplatz and its bizarre and barren chestnut trees, a few hobos and bums stomping their feet near barrel fires they'd built to ward off the gathering cold. The great sixteen-cylindered Gau Mercedes hummed contentedly, its combustion cycle flexing like a gray python.

The second photograph was well-composed and clear. And there was Maikowski, again dressed ridiculously in underwear at his ankles, Maikowski on his back with a woman who was unmistakably Eva squatting above his face, losing a dribble of piss on his forehead as

Maikowski struggled to right himself. And more of the same in photograph three, Eva balanced above Maikowski as he stretched one hand in supplication toward the invisible camera, a rare combination of pathos, comedy, and horror. And photo four: Maikowski posed utterly and completely nude in a chair. Someone had put a red swastika armband over his head. And four more photos expressed variations and covariations of the same theme, Maikowski this and Maikowski that, emphasis on humiliation, subjugation, submission, power to Eva as she rode, throttled, whipped, pissed on, postured, and beat.

Maikowski replaced the photographs in their envelope and examined the postmark: Munich. Outside, a flare of light dominated the square, Wertheim's gigantic neon sign now flickering on as the sun set. Through the gloom, Maikowski saw Loos walking purposefully across the square beneath the chestnuts, his shoulders hunched forward, the big man trundled in an overcoat and watchcap. Loos halted at the sight of the construction for a new subway and paused there as though he'd forgotten his way, then nodded in Maikowski's direction, walked to the Mercedes, and climbed into a passenger seat in back beside Maikowski.

"I have to go to work soon," Loos said.

"You know who I am?" Maikowski asked him. It was not so much a question as an introduction.

Loos cast his gaze outside to the square. Maikowski noted how large a man he was, his knuckled hands and unruly black hair beneath the cap. What did he smell of? Was it cabbage and smoke? But everyone in Berlin smelled of that.

"Everybody knows who you are," Loos said at last. "This isn't smart," he continued. "Meeting like this on the square. Wulff has my scent, I tell you. What if someone is watching?"

"We'll take care of that," Maikowski said.

"All right then, what do you want? You don't like my information?" Loos had discontinued his operation some weeks before, suspending his daily examinations of the daybook Weiss kept. It had become too dangerous.

"I don't care about that any longer," Maikowski replied. "You've proven useful to the movement. Now I'm thinking that a man with your special—how shall I say?—talents, can be put to better use by the SA. A better use at any rate than snooping in the Jew's business. Besides, now we have so many informers in the police it hardly matters. We are drowning in information."

Loos made a sucking sound, a quick intake of breath. "I see," was all he said.

Maikowski tapped on the glass separating the driver's compartment from the rear. The sleek Mercedes swung away from the curb and began to drive in circles around the square.

"You interest me greatly," Maikowski said.

"In what way?" Loos replied.

"You're a fighter for Germany, aren't you?" Maikowski said admiringly. For this occasion, he'd worn his full dress uniform, black leather jacket over brown shirt and pants, black boots, a series of leather belts and straps, an entire regalia of swastikas and pins. Maikowski could see his own reflection in the partition glass, a premonition in blue and green. "You are part of the movement, aren't you? You know how you fit into the new Germany, don't you?"

"And that makes me interesting?" Loos said.

"Oh yes indeed," Maikowski said, smiling.

They left the square according to Maikowski's prearranged plan with the chauffeur, and drove past the Red Town Hall, where squads of Schupo were patrolling. Since the pogrom of September, there had been dozens of deaths in Berlin, a few communists actually shot down while peddling their worthless propaganda and smutty news sheets, one Nazi pelted to death with cobbles on his way home from a drunken evening at the local pub.

"I have to go to work," Loos said.

"You have a higher calling," Maikowski assured him.

For the first time, Loos stared at Maikowski, a stare that brought chills even to the local SA leader. Maikowski had lunched with Göring and Goebbels, and had shaken hands once with Hitler when he'd been invited to a tea at the Brown House in Munich where cake and oolong had been served to Germany's industrialists and financiers. But nothing compared to the light in Loos' eyes, the sinister vacancy there that transfigured everything. It was the look of blood and iron, a kind of German fugue.

"I have a higher calling," Loos parroted sarcastically.

"You are part of our spiritual rebirth," Maikowski pressed on. "A renaissance of German destiny."

The Imperial Palace loomed up on their left. In the background, figures paraded like ghosts. The Mercedes crossed the Spree in light traffic. Yellow lamps glowed on the bridge.

"I am a janitor," Loos said. "I maintain the central boiler system at the Alexanderplatz police station. I sweep floors, and, when asked, I clean windows. I empty garbage and polish furniture, replace light bulbs, and do minor repairs to electrical fixtures and outlets. I am not required to clean the toilets. Junior janitors are compelled to perform those tasks. I hold a senior rank on the maintenance staff."

Maikowski pondered the black river below as a queasy feeling spread through his body. Loos was like a machine who drooled oil and discoursed in laminated rhythms. It awed Maikowski a bit. Göring joked and Goebbels admired pretty women, both human attributes. Hitler, of course, was another story.

"The SA has studied your past service," Maikowski said, undeterred. "It is odd that a man such as yourself could have come to maintenance work. Fine parents, good education."

"You think it odd?" Loos said without expression.

"I am informed that you came to work at the Ministry of Interior from Freiburg. You received a transfer to Alexanderplatz some years ago."

Loos put his hands into the pockets of his overcoat. "I did it for the money," he said.

"Rom has been sniffing into your past like a bloodhound. There isn't really much there, is there?"

"That is correct."

"It isn't what you might think," Maikowski said, trying to be careful and not lose his fish. "We aren't so much spying on you as convincing ourselves that you would be a useful colleague."

"Is that so?"

Maikowski leaned back on the plush seat of the Mercedes. He could hear the sound of his own leather accoutrements creaking.

"Listen to me," he said with a hint of anger. "You want to save Germany? Do you want to get out of that boiler room and stop sweeping the goddamn floors while your country goes down the drain? If you have a higher destiny, then you must act. Only through action can you reach your own potential. Otherwise, you remain a boiler maintenance man."

"Who are these bloodhounds?" Loos asked, apparently indifferent to Maikowski's speech.

Maikowski felt anger now. He smiled and tapped the glass once. The chauffeur made a long swing south on Oberwallstrasse.

"You're a young man from Freiburg," Maikowski began again. "Your father was a good German. You're a man who tried to join the army when you were just seventeen as the war was ending. You wound up in Freiburg with pneumonia. And then—*voila*—you appear at the Berlin Interior Ministry. And you remain under Bruckmann's tutelage. Extraordinary! Such a sudden and complete transformation!"

"So much tripe," Loos said.

"Join us, Loos!" Maikowski said feverishly. "I am ready to enroll you as a sergeant in the Storm Troop. You will wear a uniform like the one I'm wearing and your men will obey your every order. Exchange this stupid overcoat and cap for the uniform of an SA fighter. Toss away your old self and enroll in the SA. Think of it, Loos! Wear the brown of the movement and lead Germany to something better than the shit she has now. Cleanse the body politic of these leeches and vermin who masquerade as bankers and financiers. Bathe in the ethnic purity of Germany, a Germany risen from ashes, a Germany free of this parliamentary crap!"

Loos mumbled under his breath. The streets were stained with steam now, dark buildings row upon row. The full winter moon was like a stone in the sky.

"Why me? Why now?"

Maikowski raised himself ever so slightly. "May I call you Comrade Theodor?" he asked.

Loos failed to respond. They neared Jagerstrasse.

"Ah, but we know that you're a killer, don't we?" Maikowski said quietly. "And killers should do what comes naturally for them, shouldn't they? Think of the panther in the jungle. Where would it be without killing? Would you expect the panther not to hunt? What would it be without blood?"

"It would be another thing," Loos said, expressing a minute interest in this reasoning.

"Exactly, Comrade Theodor!"

"So you propose that I become what I am."

"And even more," Maikowski said, now intrigued by this strangely robotic man.

"How shall I become more than I am?" Loos asked.

"Some men are only what they fear. You shall become what you dare to dream. Think of prompting your innermost desires into reality. What kind of man dares do that?"

"Gibberish," Loos said.

"But you must listen, my friend," Maikowski said, feeling his moment slipping away now. "There is a woman in Munich who represents a present danger to the movement. She is an enemy of the German people, a bohemian and whore, probably a communist in the depths of her slutty whore's cunt. She must be eliminated, and the SA is willing to pay two thousand marks to the man who will do that job. Think of the opportunity, Theodor!"

It struck Maikowski as ironic, this sprightly offer of two thousand marks for Eva's death, exactly the sum she had demanded from Maikowski for the suppression of the photos. It troubled Maikowski that he didn't know who'd taken the pictures, but he would deliver a stern warning to whomever it was.

"You want me to kill a woman in Munich?" Loos asked.

"You will enjoy it. Admit that you will enjoy it."

"And what about my job?"

They turned into Jagerstrasse, its bright neon facades and gaudy arcades.

"You will work for Germany," Maikowski said.

"Just leave Alexanderplatz?"

"We will provide you with a new apartment, someplace in Kreuzberg near Precinct 12."

"A new apartment?"

"A new apartment and a new identity, something fitting your status as a sergeant in the SA. On your new salary, I'm certain you will be quite comfortable." Maikowski rubbed his hands together. "I have the complete particulars of your Munich target. At the end of this month, there will be a march through the streets of Munich in honor of Hitler's putsch. You will travel to Munich during that time and there will be many other SA enlisted men and officers present. You will change your identity and you will change your looks and you will become part of a great Brown Shirt mass, sharing your goals and ambitions with thousands of others like yourself. In a sea of uniforms, you will be only one more. A dot. It is the perfect time." The chauffeur stopped in front of the Residenzkasino, another of Jagerstrasse's nightclubs featuring telephones at the tables, grotesqueries, and fantasy. "Now go and enjoy yourself, Sergeant Loos," Maikowski said, handing Loos one hundred paper marks. "You are permanently finished with Alexanderplatz. You will be provided with papers to establish your new identity, and you will be moved into your new apartment this weekend."

Loos put a hand on the door. "I'll want a uniform as soon as possible," he said.

"That is taken care of already. Your name will be inscribed on the rolls tonight. I've taken the liberty of paying your dues six months in advance. You are a new man. Congratulations."

"What about my two thousand marks?" Loos asked.

"But, Herr Loos," Maikowski said. "I'll give you a packet of information about the woman, along with one thousand marks. You'll have a train ticket and lodging in Munich. When the job is done, you'll get the rest. Just kill the whore and let nature take its course."

Maikowski watched as Loos departed, trudging up the Jagerstrasse toward the Residenzkasino. Outlined in neon, he had become a magical aspect of the street itself. Once he had been Bruckmann's creature, and then Rom's. Now he belonged to Maikowski.

━ ━

A light snow had dusted the street. They sat at a window table, Wulff still in his black leather trench coat, Barlach in a new tweed suit. A dispirited waiter had brought them potato soup sprinkled with paprika.

"Here's to the new Kriminal-Assistant," Wulff said gayly, raising a glass of dry sherry. That afternoon the Adlon Hotel was nearly deserted. Waiters hovered like hungry crows in their black uniforms. "You are to be congratulated most heartily."

Barlach lifted his glass shyly. The sherry caught some pale light and distributed it. Barlach had passed his Department IV examinations and had been certified by police surgeons for duty. He could grasp objects and squeeze a trigger.

"I owe you a great deal, sir," he said to Wulff.

"Speaking of which," Wulff said,. "I wonder if you've been looking into this fellow Loos?" Wulff had been swamped by work. The detective force was constantly busy with crimes, even political murders now that they had become so common. The Prussian judiciary was trying the Nazis accused of murdering Anlauf and Lencke.

"It's strange," Barlach said. "But Loos has left his job at Alexanderplatz. I checked with his supervisor when I came back to work, and I was told he simply walked away and disappeared. Didn't come to work one night."

"Just walked away from a good job?"

Barlach replaced his glass on the damask tablecloth. "Failed to come to work one Friday night. Didn't offer a resignation or speak to any of the supervisory staff."

"But you spoke with them?"

"The head of maintenance is named Froeb. He told me he hadn't spoken ten words to Loos during the past six months. Loos came to work and he went home after eight hours on the job. He maintained the boiler and swept floors. He didn't fraternize with his fellow workers and he didn't attend any of the labor union meetings. He earned his pay and kept to himself."

"It is strange to quit a job with six million unemployed," Wulff said.

"That's what I thought," Barlach agreed.

"But certainly not illegal or criminal."

Frost lay in the corners of the windows. Above the diners, chandeliers hung like stalactites.

"He could have gone home to Freiburg," Barlach ventured.

Wulff signed deeply. "In truth, there's no reason to believe he killed Timkin Mueller. You saw him one night on the Hirrenstrasse, and we know he rides the tram to Lichtenberg. Like hundreds if not thousands of other men."

"That's true," Barlach said.

"I'm more concerned with Edgar Braun now," Wulff concluded. "Did you check the apartment where Loos lived in Lichtenberg?"

"I spoke with the old woman who was his landlady," Barlach said. "She said he moved out one day without notice. He didn't have much to take. A few boxes of clothes. A naval retiree has moved in already. I searched the room, but there was nothing much."

Wulff smiled. "At any rate, congratulations to you, Barlach. And congratulations on your new baby and your speedy recovery."

"I'm indebted to you, sir," Barlach said.

"You're deserving."

They finished their potato soup and their salad, but refused dessert. Wulff paid the bill, and together the two men walked through the empty formal dining room to the marble-floored lobby, where Barlach retrieved his topcoat and hat. As they passed the entrance to the bar, Wulff noticed three men, Daleuge, Rom, and Maikowski, sitting at a table in back. Rom lifted his eyes and seemed to stare at Wulff, then nodded and smiled warmly.

Outside, it had stopped snowing.

—◦—

When Daleuge had gone, Rom said, "What the fuck are you doing making Loos a sergeant and giving him an apartment?"

"I outrank you, Rom," Maikowski said. "And besides, a man like Loos has his uses." Maikowski wiped his mouth with a linen napkin. "Was that Wulff?" he asked.

Rom stabbed a pickled carrot with his fork. They had eaten goulash, discussing plans for the Munich march in honor of Hitler's putsch. There would be fifty or sixty thousand SA men under torchlight, banners, flagons of beer, gusts of patriotic sound, devotionals to the New Germany, and of course, speeches. A march along the old putsch trail where Nazi heroes had fallen nearly a decade before.

"That *was* Wulff," Maikowski said after a time.

"Loos is quite mad, you know," Rom said, ignoring the comment.

"Oh, mad as a hatter," Maikowski agreed.

"The newspapers have forgotten about Bruckmann," Rom said. "But what Loos did was stupid."

"I couldn't agree more," Maikowski answered.

"But making Loos a sergeant in the SA…" Rom said.

"I'm responsible for Loos now."

"I hope you know what you're doing," Rom said.

Maikowski grinned. "Don't I always?"

PART FOUR

1932

"I am neither a German, nor a European, nor even perhaps a human being, but a Jew."
—Arnold Schoenberg,
letter to Kandinsky, 1923

24

The convent lay on a wooded hill facing the horseshoe bend of an unruly stream. From the shelter of a café where he'd taken refuge from a downpour, Wulff regarded the building, drank a cup of oat-coffee and smoked a cigarette while his shoes dried. He finished his coffee, picked up his umbrella, and paid a sour-faced French waitress, who pointed him toward a wooden footbridge that crossed the stream. Wulff trudged six hundred meters and was met in the foyer of the convent by a young novice in black. Two stained glass windows allowed in a gray light at the head of the stairs. After a ten-minute wait, he was led by the novice to the uppermost floor, consisting of two corridors leading to cubicles where older nuns lived. Wulff waited outside one of the doors, leaning on a windowsill where he could watch the hillside change color from gray to pearl and back to gray again. A few moments later, the novice led him inside one of the cubicles where he saw Sister Marta sitting alone on a stiff-backed wooden chair in front of a wooden writing table.

"You'd be the policeman from Berlin," Sister Marta said to him in a gravelly voice. Wulff had wired ahead and had been given permission to speak to Sister Marta, who had operated the Freiburg Clinic during the early 1920s, who had tended the sick through several epidemics of influenza.

Wulff introduced himself formally, bowing from the waist, then displaying his identification card, at which she barely glanced. The nun asked him to sit on the bed, but he declined. "I'm afraid that's all there is to sit on," Sister Marta said.

"I'll be brief, Sister," Wulff said. "I don't want to take up your time."

Wulff had caught the midnight Berlin Express to Frankfurt, then changed trains after a forty-minute wait. The Freiburg Express had arrived just after eight o'clock in the morning.

"Time is my friend," Sister Marta said jovially. "I have all the time in the world," she added. Geese were going over the hills now. Wulff could hear them honking to one another. "I'm afraid I have nothing to offer you to eat or drink," the sister was saying. "It's Friday, and it is my practice to fast until supper. I eat a bit after evening prayers. Forgive me."

"It's all right, Sister," Wulff said. "I'm going back to Berlin this afternoon and I'm in a bit of a hurry. I'm here to ask about the influenza clinic you operated during the early 1920s."

"Mother Superior told me," she said. She folded her hands on a Bible.

"I wonder if you remember a boy named Theodor Loos," Wulff said abruptly. "He would have been ill about this time of year in 1923. I know it's a long time ago, Sister."

"There were many ill during that year," she said.

"You were in charge of the critical care ward?"

"Yes, I was," she said.

"The Mother Superior told me you were very familiar with the clinic and all its operations."

Sister Marta closed the Bible and glanced at Wulff as if she were reluctant to go on. "But I remember Theodor Loos very well," she said.

Wulff felt a rush of excitement. His nerves were electric with the scent of a madman. "Can you tell me about Loos?" Wulff asked calmly. "How is it you remember Loos from all the others?"

"May I ask you something?" Sister Marta said.

Wulff nodded. "Yes, of course."

"Why is it you seek him?"

"Well," Wulff began hesitantly, "there is a man in Berlin who goes by that name. He might be Loos. He probably is. On his work application and other documents, he says that he hails from Freiburg, that his mother was Flemish and his father German, and that he was educated in a Catholic boy's school here in Freiburg before the war, and at the gymnasium later. I wonder if this man in Berlin is the Theodor Loos who was ill with influenza during November of 1923. I wonder if he was treated here at the clinic."

"It sounds like him," Sister Marta said. "What does he look like?"

"He is rather large, with large hands and black hair. He has big ears and moves slowly."

"Lived for a time in Lille?"

"In Lille," Wulff said.

"It may be the same boy," Sister Marta said. "But his hair was rather lighter. He was rather fine-boned, as I recall. I remember him well because he was in my mathematics class at school."

"He was at the clinic? What happened to him?"

"He left the gymnasium to join the army. But the war was ending, and he was discharged. He attended the institute in Freiburg for several years, then was infected with influenza. His mother had died, as had his father, poor boy."

"But—" Wulff managed to say.

"He wanted to be a civil engineer," Sister Marta continued, not giving Wulff a chance to speak. "What did the poor boy do in Berlin?" she asked a puzzled Wulff. "And why are you asking about him? Has something happened to him?"

"A policeman has been killed," Wulff said. He was aware of having told a half-truth.

"How does this concern poor Theodor?"

"Sister, please," Wulff pleaded. "Can you tell me about Theodor Loos and his stay at the clinic?"

"This will help Theodor? Or hurt him?"

"I think it will help."

Sister Marta looked out the window. "I remember it as though it were yesterday," she said. Outside the narrow mullioned window, a hillside was swept by rain. "There had been thousands of influenza cases in the aftermath of the inflation, when people had no coal to burn. Nor was there much food. Theodor was brought to the clinic from the institute because he was my student and had studied at the boy's school. His condition worsened steadily, his fever becoming dangerously high. We had no penicillin to give him. Of course, drugs could be purchased on the black market, but the church had no money for such things. Despite our efforts, I'm afraid Theodor's condition became quite desperate."

"Did he recover?" Wulff asked, still puzzled.

"He was taken away from the clinic," Sister Marta said. She fixed Wulff with her gray eyes. "Yes, just taken away."

"Taken away?" Wulff repeated.

"The Freicorps operated in this area," Sister Marta continued. "Both the Freicorps and the French would come and go from the clinic, asking us to treat their wounded and sick, taking our drugs when we had them. One day, two men came to the clinic in some kind of staff car. They pulled up on a lane outside the building and sat in their car for a long time. I sent out some nuns to see if they could tell what they wanted. But the two men just came inside and asked to see Loos. They told me he'd been a member of their company and they wanted to see him. I found it impossible to believe that Theodor Loos had been a member of the Freicorps, but I could not refuse these men. They were very threatening and demanding. And they seemed to know everything about Theodor. They went upstairs and spent a long time with him."

"Did they give their names?"

"They did not, nor were they asked," Sister Marta said. "It would have served no purpose. These were not human beings in the ordinary sense of the term. They had become something beyond human. They were neither Christians nor husbands nor fathers. They had no regard. No concern."

"What did they do?"

"There was a young treating nurse on the third floor where Loos had a bed among many others. They told her they had drugs with which to treat Loos and that they were bivouacked in a village not far away. They let it be known that they were taking Theodor away, whether we agreed or not, and that they would treat him with penicillin. One of them went downstairs for a gurney they had brought with them. I saw them carry Theodor out the door under a blanket. He was bundled up head to foot. I didn't have time to speak with Theodor. Not a single good-bye. They wouldn't let us come near him, and they both had guns. One of the nurses wanted to take his temperature, but they became very angry and threatened even her."

"And they drove him away?"

"Yes," Sister Marta said. "And I am glad that he is alive and well in Berlin. They must have helped him recover, but I'm surprised he was one of their company."

Wulff juxtaposed the young Loos with his recollections of the jan-itor at Alexanderplatz. "I know it's been a long time," he said. "But could you describe the two men who took him away?"

"Oh, that's quite easy," Sister Marta said. "One of the men wore an eye patch. He was very much smaller than the other and had a scar down the left side of his face."

Bruckmann—Wulff acknowledged inwardly what he'd always known. "And the other man?" Wulff asked.

Sister Marta shook her head. "He was bundled up," she said softly. "An overcoat and a wool hat. I think he had long black hair, but that's about all. Wire rim glasses, I suppose. He was covered with mud."

"Did he have a goatee?"

The sister placed a hand on the side of her cheek. "Why yes, I believe so. How do you know that?"

Wulff bowed again. "Thank you for your help, Sister," he said.

"You must go?"

"Back to Berlin."

"But who is this policeman who was killed? And what does young Theodor have to do with it?"

"Theodor is not involved, I assure you," Wulff said, smiling gen-tly. "On my word of honor as a gentleman."

"I'm so glad," Sister Marta said. "And forgive me. On Friday, I stay in my room all day. Otherwise, I would walk with you downstairs."

"It's all right, Sister," Wulff said.

"You're not Catholic, are you?" she asked Wulff.

Wulff smiled painfully. "No, Sister, I'm not," he said.

"Theodor was a good Catholic," she said. "Has he done something bad? Has something happened to him?"

"No, Sister," Wulff said. "He has done nothing bad. He was a good man, I'm sure of it."

"I'm so glad," Sister Marta sighed. "He was such a nice little boy. Not like some of the boys. Some of them can be quite monstrous."

"I'm sure they can," Wulff said.

"Some of them grow up to be monsters, too," Sister Marta said. "It is a way of the world. Like those two in the Freicorps."

"I suppose that's why there are policemen," Wulff said.

Sister Marta smiled, a sweet, forgiving smile. "Please tell Theodor that Sister Marta thinks of him. That Sister Marta prays for him. Perhaps he will remember me. I will pray for him this morning if you think it will do good."

"I'm sure it will do good, Sister," Wulff said. He stood at the door, one hand on the latch.

"There are many monsters in the world, aren't there?" she asked Wulff.

"There are some," he said.

"I will pray for them, too," she said.

Wulff nodded in agreement, closed his eyes, then stepped out into the silent hall.

━ ━

The chestnuts had lost their leaves. Pretending to look at them with interest, Maikowski stood at the window, arms crossed. Below him lay the deserted suburban street, a few parked cars, a gray afternoon between autumn and winter. Behind him, Maikowski could hear his monster preening, examining himself in the mirror and emitting tiny paw-print murmurs. To break the ice, Maikowski cleared his throat once with a short guttural cough. After a week of looking, he'd found his monster a small flat in Wilmersdorf, a partitioned manor house that had once been a prosperous bourgeois manse. They were five kilometers from central Berlin. It was costing Maikowski and the SA a combined five hundred marks a month. "And so," Maikowski said. "How does it feel to be a sergeant in the SA?"

The window glass was dirty. Maikowski could see the reflection of his monster on the glass as the monster studied his own image in the mirror. They were a three-part fugue, Maikowski at the gray window in the gray light, the monster in dirty yellow light at the mirror in his brown shirt, dark brown pants, a labyrinth of leather belts and black copper buckles, a red swastika armband, a swastika pin on his peaked cap. Maikowski opened an envelope he had been holding. "Your new identification," he said. "I've chosen to make you Albert Huebner. From now on, you're Albert Huebner, sergeant in the Storm Troop, Berlin Division, Charlottenburg Squad. You will work exclusively for me at this time, and take orders only from me, and you will take orders from nobody else. Do you understand, Sergeant Huebner?"

Huebner looked at his passport. "Of course I understand," he said.

"And here is your driver's license and your worker's identification card and your SA membership card." Maikowski offered these to Huebner, who made no move to take them. Finally, Maikowski left them on an end table near the mirror. The flat was as yet sparsely furnished with an old Victorian couch, two end tables, and a single chair. There was a small kitchen in the back, and to one side, a bedroom containing a mattress-less bed and a chest of drawers.

Huebner continued to study himself in the mirror. He ran an index finger down one of the leather belts that circled his chest. "Albert Huebner," he said quietly.

"It is a good German name," Maikowski said. "Not at all like Theodor Loos."

"It will do," Huebner said.

The anniversary of Hitler's Munich Beer Hall Putsch was to be celebrated in just two days. Maikowski had purchased a first-class train ticket in the name of Huebner. He took it from his wallet and made the man take it. "You leave early tomorrow morning for Munich," he said. "You are aware of your assignment?"

"I'm aware," Huebner replied.

"Nevertheless," Maikowski continued. "When you arrive in Munich you will take a room at the Ludwigshof Hotel near the Isar Bridge. After the march, you will go to the Café Dom near the Bridge itself. Eva can be found at a table in the back near a coal fire. She is blonde and not unattractive in a whorish sort of way. You will see her immediately if she is there."

"I've heard this all before," Huebner said in a voice eerily empty of emotion.

"Please attract her," Maikowski said. "It doesn't take much to attract Eva, but you must try. You will engage her in conversation. She will, perhaps, ask you what you like to do, and you will offer to share morphine. You must suggest that you have morphine, and a lot of it. In this way, she will be irresistibly attracted to your charms. I've given you some ampules. I assume you've got them."

"Of course, I have them," Huebner said. "Do you think I would use this morphine myself?"

Maikowski shrugged, hiding his anger. "Your room at the Ludwigshof is at the back. Offer to take her there. There will be hundreds of SA men registered at the hotel. After you've done your work, take her out the back and put her in the alley. She will be found eventually, after the rats have had a chance to work on her. Nobody will notice in the rush of festivity."

"Are you finished?" Huebner asked.

"Just be careful," Maikowski said.

"And what about my vehicle?" Huebner asked. "You promised me a vehicle."

Maikowski walked to the window. "Down there," he said, gesturing to the street.

Huebner was standing behind Maikowski now, a head taller. "That's a Russian Renault," he said.

"Did you expect a Mercedes?"

"I did not expect a Russian Renault."

"It was available and cheap. After being on foot for years, I thought you'd be pleased."

"Something better," Huebner said. "I expected something better." There was a pause as Maikowski sensed Huebner peering over his shoulder. "What is this Eva to you?" Huebner asked. "Why is she so important that she must be killed? She is not a Yid. She is a whore."

"Be reasonable," Maikowski countered.

"You think I'm stupid, don't you?" Huebner said, turning away.

"Not in the least," Maikowski replied, suddenly cold in the room that had no heating. He sensed that his monster—whoever he was—now peering in the mirror again, was a kind of ticking time bomb. "Look at this from my perspective," Maikowski continued mildly. "You have been made a non-commissioned officer in the Berlin SA, Charlottenburg Squad. You have a flat in Wilmersdorf and money in your pocket. You have a vehicle, *albeit* a Russian Renault. And not three months ago you were sweeping floors and spying on a little kike for one hundred marks a week. And the man handling your affairs was stealing from you. Your rise in the world has been spectacular. Don't you agree?"

Maikowski turned and watched Huebner adjust the top button on his brown shirt. "The fucking car is *Russian*," Huebner grunted.

"Ach, never mind that now," Maikowski said jovially. "You have a first-class ticket to Munich tomorrow morning. Stay in the room I've reserved for you in the Ludwigshof. You will march in the putsch parade, you will share the enthusiasm of thousands of other young Germans. You will meet a not bad-looking whore named Eva Vollheim, known by everyone in Schwabing as a morphine addict and prostitute. She will lick your scrotum for an ampule of morphine, if that's what you wish her to do. It is said she has a fondness for uniforms."

"What if I am recognized?"

"Who would recognize you?"

"The police. Somebody in the café."

"There will be sixty thousand SA in Munich next week," Maikowski said calmly. He felt as though he had regained an initiative of some sort. "There will be more than ninety thousand SA in Nuremberg the week after that. Southern Germany will be filled with marching men in uniform. It will be a delightful sea of brown in which you will be nothing more than another dollop of foam. And who notices a dollop of foam in the ocean?" Maikowski folded his arms and looked down at the street again, its barren chestnuts, gray apartment buildings, and empty sidewalks.

Huebner picked up a pair of wire-rim spectacles and put them on. He examined himself in the mirror again for a long time, his newly grown black goatee and shaved head. Maikowski waited, expecting nothing in particular. In his monster's presence, Maikowski sensed an imminence to disaster, an openness to mayhem that saturated the air like methane. Reluctantly, Maikowski admitted to himself that fear was an interesting and original concept. "I see you have a minor disguise," Maikowski said, knowing that the spectacles were of clear glass.

Huebner turned his head. "I am taking a great risk doing this for you," he said.

"You are being well paid."

"Two thousand marks and a Russian car."

"When the thing is done, return to Berlin. You will be paid a second installment."

Huebner extended an index finger and touched his own image on the mirror's surface. Maikowski was both fascinated and repelled by the gesture. He buttoned his suit coat and made purposefully for the door. He had had enough of his monster.

"What has Eva Vollheim done, then?" Huebner asked.

"Sergeant Huebner," Maikowski said officiously, "I've told you she is a communist whore." Maikowski felt an involuntarily flutter in his right eye. He opened the door and smelled the damp hallway. "And in the SA, one takes orders and does his duty. Do you wish me to locate another willing to perform these duties?"

Huebner contemplated Maikowski. "Is your mother alive?" Huebner asked.

Maikowski might have blanched had he not been already unnerved by his monster. "Why do you ask?" he said.

"Is she alive? Just answer me."

"In a village in Pomerania."

"Go now," Huebner said.

Maikowski hurried downstairs and walked down the block to where he'd left his chauffeur with the Gau Landauer. Once he'd climbed in the back seat and was alone, he glanced up at the second-story window where he'd left Huebner. He saw Huebner looking down through a double image of reflections, his face a wedge of colors distorted in the autumn gloom. Maikowski discerned a strange otherness emanating from Huebner, passing through the glass, dropping down to Maikowski himself, a kind of electric current. He ordered his chauffeur to drive to the nearest tavern.

⟶ ⟵

Rom was following Maikowski in a Mercedes borrowed from a local party hack who'd gone to Munich for the Putsch march. Rom intended to go to Munich himself, even though he was not enamored of drunken revels, song fests of Storm Troop tunes, their boozy camaraderie and romantic sentimentalism. As he sat in the black car, he watched Maikowski, a Storm Colonel, second in command of the Berlin SA, leave a rather dreary suburban manor house that looked as though it had been subdivided into many flats, as had most in this part of town. Maikowski paused at the front gate, seemed to shrug, then walked half a block and got into the back seat of his big black Landauer touring car. For some reason, Maikowski sat in the back seat for a long time, until the car finally pulled slowly away from the curb.

It was a dreary late afternoon in fall, and Bibi had been whining at Rom for about half an hour. "This is just so stupid, Dieter," she said in her high-pitched little girl's voice. "I'm bored, baby, just bored to death."

Rom liked his new mistress enormously. He valued her stupidity, an ignorance that made her completely transparent. And she was wonderfully maladjusted, unable to take much sun or sea air, certain kinds of food and drink. And of course, she was spectacularly willing in bed. "We're leaving now, dear," Rom told her, patting her knee, then sliding his hand up her dress, where she allowed it to rest on an inner patch of thigh, just beneath her garter belt. Rom had given Bibi a largish bottle of real Chanel perfume for her birthday, and she'd drenched herself with it. In the confines of the Mercedes, with the heater running, Rom could hardly breathe for the stench.

"I'm hungry," Bibi cried petulantly.

He started the car and pulled away. At this time of day, the suburbs were deserted. He had watched Maikowski for nearly half an hour, and had seen perhaps two people passing on the sidewalk. Now that Theodor Loos had been taken over by Maikowski, Rom had more free time. It amazed him to what lengths Maikowski had gone to mollify this pitiful little termite—apparently an apartment in Wilmersdorf, a ridiculous Russian Renault, and the rank of Sergeant in Storm Troop 33, Rom's own unit. There had been considerable expenditures on false documentation for Loos, a passport, worker's identification, even a driver's license.

Rom reached the Kaiser Alle and headed north in light afternoon traffic. The sky was gun-metal gray, and Rom sensed the ominous smell of snow in the air. Rom had it in his mind to become a colonel, and to replace Maikowski.

Bibi nuzzled him just below the collar. Rom could feel one plump breast on his chest. She was bundled into a fox coat. "What were we doing back there?" Bibi asked nonchalantly.

"Spying on an SA colonel," Rom said.

"Don't tease me," Bibi chided him. "You know how I hate to be teased."

Rom knew it was impossible to become angry with Bibi. And he could tell her anything plausible. "I'm telling you the truth," Rom said.

"Come on really, baby," she said.

"It's the truth," Rom said. "I'm plotting to overthrow my superior officer and replace him in the SA. It could mean a great deal to my career. I would have more money, a larger automobile. I might even deserve a huge Landauer."

Bibi giggled.

"But don't tell anyone," Rom continued. "If you tell anyone, I'll have you throttled."

Bibi laughed and looked away, her hand on Rom's right leg. She had painted her fingernails blue and she was wearing blue lipstick.

That night, they attended the theater, then ate a late supper at an out-of-the-way café near Jagerstrasse. The following morning, when Rom checked the SA rolls, he discovered that Maikowski had enlisted Sergeant Albert Huebner as his personal adjutant. Then, before noon, Rom taxied to the Potsdamer Bahnhof just in time to catch his train to Munich.

25

Through track steam and diesel exhaust, the dawn was a blue-green filter. In the cold air, Wulff's breath carved a slipstream path behind him as he walked along the busy track. He retrieved his overnight bag from a porter, and when he looked up, he saw Johanna running toward him from the Potsdamer lobby. He dropped his bag, was able to take two steps toward her, and then her arms were around him.

"I told you not to bother coming," he whispered to her as she kissed him.

"I couldn't help it, darling," she told him, almost in tears.

"Has something happened?" he asked. She was smothering him with kisses.

"No, nothing," she managed to say.

All around them, porters were hustling with luggage. Several conductors had gotten off their cars and were smoking cigarettes or sharing jokes. Arm in arm, Wulff and Johanna walked down the track, then through the Baroque lobby where men were drinking beers at stand-up kiosks.

"Johanna, tell me," Wulff asked her in the taxi going home.

"I missed you, that's all."

"I was gone only thirty-six hours," Wulff laughed. He put his arms around her.

"I've the shakes," she said before he could comment. "It isn't anything in particular. I read the newspaper yesterday, and Herr Goebbels is going to marry Magda Quandt at Christmastime. Their photos were in the society section, and they looked quite happy and normal."

It was dawn on Sunday in central Berlin, the streets empty, long gray lines of shops and stores. On one corner, a Schupo stood alone. "Please let me put you on a train to Switzerland," Wulff said, a plea he'd made a hundred times before.

"Let's not talk about that now," Johanna said, drying her tears with a hankie. "Harry, dear, I don't know if I could ever go, and if I did, if I could ever go without you. But please, let's not talk about it now."

"All right, darling. Whatever you want."

Wulff rolled down the window. The air outside smelled of industrial city grit. There was a threat of snow.

"What did you find out?" Johanna asked him.

"It's as I thought," Wulff told her. "The man we know as Loos isn't Loos. Bruckmann and Braun were in the Freicorps, and they came to Freiburg and got Loos, took him away from the clinic. They killed him, and Braun assumed his identity. Braun had been living as Theodor Loos for the past nine years. It was Braun who was the janitor at Alexanderplatz."

Johanna made a small sound. She put her head on Wulff's shoulder and they rode silently for several kilometers. "And do you think that Braun killed Timkin Mueller? That he killed the person who called himself Uli? That he killed Bruckmann?"

"It has to be," Wulff said. "It can't be any other way."

"And where is Braun now?"

"I haven't the slightest idea," Wulff confessed.

"But that's terrible, dear," Johanna said.

Wulff held her face in his hands. He looked at her, studying her green eyes. "Going to Switzerland isn't a speculation now," he said. "I think Braun is a very dangerous man. I think he wishes to kill me, and he will undoubtedly try. He's sent one of his dolls to your apartment, and that means he's watched both of us. He may be watching us together. It has become part of his passion. I want you to go to Zurich. I'll send you money. You have friends. Do this for both of us."

Johanna closed her eyes and pulled away. She dabbed at her final tears. "It isn't me who's in danger," she said. "We've discussed this before."

"But you represent an obstacle," Wulff said. "To get to me, he may have to get to you. Be reasonable, darling. This situation is quite dangerous, even for bystanders, if that's what you're trying to argue you are. I am putting in long hours at Berlin Mitte. And my hours will only get longer as time goes by."

"I just want us to go home," Johanna said, folding herself inside a lambswool coat fastened in front by half a dozen large black buttons. "I want to go home and have Sunday with you absent any talk of Edgar Braun. Then we'll decide what to do."

"I think that would be fine," Wulff said.

Wulff watched the city pass, its overbearing stone surfaces. He wondered where in its four million Braun had found to hide, where in the vast overlay of apartment blocks, Hinterhofs, suburban villas, and detached houses, the monster had constructed his new lair.

⌐ ⌐

Huebner stepped off the train at Munich's North Bahnhof. He had left Berlin at mid-morning on a darkish day, though now in Munich the sky was clear blue with only a frosting of cloud on the distant, mountainous horizon. Before dawn, he'd driven his filthy Russian Renault to the Jewess's apartment on Lennenstrasse. He was surprised to see her leave dressed in an elegant black lambswool coat and hail a taxi. He had followed her to the Potsdamer Bahnhof and trailed her inside the train station lobby, where he bought a glass of beer and waited near the entrance to Track 55. Huebner looked up— FRANKFURT. The train had arrived from Frankfurt. Huebner had thought for a long moment, regarding the workers nearby with their hang-dog faces, wondering where Wulff could have gone over the weekend. Frankfurt? It occurred to him that Wulff might have gone to Freiburg—after all, the eastern trains for France all routed through Frankfurt. Huebner performed a quick mental calculation. He imagined Wulff departing overnight Friday, arriving in Frieburg in the early hours of the morning, then catching an afternoon train on Saturday, returning to Berlin at dawn on Sunday. It was more than possible. When the couple appeared at the tunnel entrance, Huebner abandoned his beer and walked behind them for a way. Wulff was wearing his black leather trench coat and carried an overnight bag; the woman was clutching him as though he were a lifeboat, her eyes filled with imminent tears. Just then, he hated Wulff more than he hated his mother, more than he hated the villagers of Juprelle.

And now in Munich, Albert Huebner, dressed in his full SA uniform, caught a taxi to the Ludwigshof Hotel near the Ludwigstrasse Bridge over the Isar River. He was given a third-floor room at the back near a stair exit to an alley, not a good room by anyone's standards. Just a plain room with a lumpy mattress, dirty drapes, a brick wall across a narrow well. It was, of course, the perfect room. Huebner lay for a long time on the bed, staring at the ceiling and thinking of Wulff, the man's dead blue eyes.

— ‑

Weiss sat with arms folded, Wulff and Barlach opposite him in the cold office at Alexanderplatz. Krause had brought them tea, which nobody touched. "Hitler will run for President," Weiss said, apropos of nothing. "Yes, Hitler will run," Weiss continued to muse. "I suppose Hindenburg will oppose him."

"He cannot win," Wulff said. "Hitler cannot win." Wulff had been up much of the night thinking about Edgar Braun. More than anything, he was afraid for Johanna.

Weiss picked up a leather-bound diary, unlocked it with a small key, then opened it. "Even the thought of Hitler makes me physically ill," he said.

Barlach was looking for something to do with his hands.

"I know the identity of the termite," Wulff said suddenly, seizing a moment of silence in which to make his point. He wished for some way to approach the subject, a way to soften the blow. But he thought of nothing. "It is a complicated story, but I believe it is true."

"How very interesting," Weiss said. Weiss was confronting almost certain political oblivion. His proposals to curtail the Nazis had fallen on deaf ears at the Reich Ministry of Interior. More and more, the centrists were becoming isolated. Rumors had circulated Alexanderplatz of a coup d'etat, a palace uprising in which Weiss would be sacked, perhaps arrested. "I'm sorry," Weiss said finally, distracted, glancing down at his diary. Wulff could see the diary, its blizzard of inky handwriting. "Please tell me what you've concluded in this matter. It's been so long."

It had been more than a year. Too long, by Wulff's estimation, to make much difference. "The termite is a man who called himself Theodor Loos," he said. "This is the name under which he was employed here at Alexanderplatz for six years as a boiler maintenance man and janitor. He worked downstairs and roamed the halls. His shift was the night shift. He was a very adept and clever person, with skills as a locksmith."

"And how have you discovered this?"

"My written report is being typed as we speak," Wulff said.

Weiss snapped the diary shut. He sighed and said, "But you're here now and we have tea. Perhaps you wouldn't mind telling me in person."

Wulff explained the killing in Hirrenstrasse, its connection to Loos and his tram rides from Prenzlauer. He guided Weiss through the Uli murder, his own trips to Juprelle and Freiburg.

"But this does not make Loos our termite," Weiss concluded.

Wulff spent some time explaining Edgar Braun, his past, and his connections to Erik Bruckmann. "So you see," Wulff said, "Edgar Braun was an expert locksmith. He was given the identity of Theodor Loos by Bruckmann. The murders of Mueller and Uli had nothing to do with his role as a termite." Wulff had said nothing about the dolls. He produced a photo of Braun with Bruckmann. "This is Braun," Wulff said. "He's a tall, hulking fellow with black hair and a goatee, though in this picture he's shaved his head. He began to feed information to Bruckmann, who sold it to the army and the SA."

"And you have proof of this?" Weiss asked.

"Yes, for the most part."

"And do you have proof that Braun also killed the two transvestites?"

"Only circumstantial proof."

"Stapo has been searching for Edgar Braun," Weiss said. "They have failed to turn him up."

"Braun is now somebody else," Wulff said. "He's taken on a new identity, I'd wager. But I sense he is still in Berlin. And that he has a new sponsor."

"A sponsor?"

"How else could he exist now?" Wulff asked. "He existed because of Bruckmann for many years. And now he has no secure position at Alexanderplatz. Where could he go, what could he do without a sponsor?"

"You mean the SA or the army," Weiss said.

"It is not the army," Wulff said. "I am certain it is not the army."

"The SA then," Weiss said.

"It is a logical conclusion," Wulff said. Wulff looked at Barlach. "Tell the deputy chief what you discovered that day."

Barlach coughed nervously, clearing his throat. "I followed Bruckmann the day he was killed. It was Loos, or as we now know, Edgar Braun."

Weiss sat up. "They had a falling out? But why?"

"We've been giving this some thought," Wulff said, saving Barlach, who looked pale. "Chloral hydrate was discovered in Bruckmann's bloodstream. It was in minute quantities, but it was there nonetheless."

"And what does this mean?"

"We have given this much thought as well," Wulff said, nodding to Barlach. "According to Levitt, there is no known use for this compound in regular pharmacology. It is quite simply a knockout drop. It can render one unconscious in large enough doses, and induce disorientation. I conclude that someone administered this to Bruckmann days before he was killed."

"And what has this to do with Braun?" Weiss began to polish his glasses.

"Yes, indeed, what," Wulff mused. "After Bruckmann was killed, Loos continued to work at Alexanderplatz for a period of months. Perhaps he continued to collect secret information. I conclude he had another handler, probably someone in the SA directly. Perhaps Bruckmann was being blackmailed. Why else would he give up control of his termite?"

"And so Loos believed he'd been betrayed by Bruckmann," Barlach said.

"We don't know exactly why," Wulff added. "But we think he did and we know that now he's disappeared into Berlin. He's out there somewhere."

"Has he changed his appearance?" Weiss asked.

"More than likely," Wulff told him.

"And what do you propose to do?" Weiss asked. "And how did Loos manage to discover so much about Stapo operations? You've investigated every possible angle, as I understand it, and there are no stolen staff notes, copies of orders, or memos. You spent more than a year on this."

"I'm developing a theory," Wulff said. "But for now I need to see your SA files. We'll begin to search them to see what we can find out about Rom and Maikowski. If anyone knows about SA operations in Berlin, it is those two."

Weiss opened his diary again and seemed lost in thought. "This is all very disappointing," he said. "For a long time, we thought we were involved in an investigation of a loyal police captain. Now we discover that Bruckmann was a traitor. And that he was murdered by a man who has been stealing secret police information right from under our noses."

"At least we know," Barlach said sheepishly.

"Yes, there is that. You've both done good work." Weiss smiled gently and began to write in his diary. He looked up. "My memoirs, gentlemen," he said wistfully. "Perhaps someday my children will read and learn."

The three men stood and shook hands. Barlach followed Wulff through the reception area and into the ornate corridor. Wulff stood at the window and lit a cigarette.

"I think I know how Loos did it," Wulff said.

"But how?" Barlach asked in astonishment.

"Weiss keeps a diary," Wulff said. "You saw him writing down the happenings of the day. I imagine Loos broke in and read the diary. Loos didn't steal orders or break into safes. He simply read the deputy chief's daily diary."

"Shouldn't we mention this to Weiss?"

"It doesn't matter now, does it?"

"Perhaps not," Barlach said.

"We can wait a bit," Wulff said. "Perhaps after we've got Braun in custody."

"How do we find him?"

"A better question—who is he?"

Deep in his soul, Wulff knew that Braun would come to him, would emerge from the shadows where he lived. At the end of the day, it would be Braun and Wulff, as Wulff knew it had to be.

— ‑

Eva eased the needle from her neck. Across the room, Kruger lay on a couch, his eyes glazed. When Eva could, she lifted her head and looked out the window of her new apartment on Frauenstrasse, a spot from which she could see the progress of the brown shirt marchers celebrating Hitler's failed putsch, long lines of men appearing at the approaches to Ludwigstrasse Bridge.

"How many of those fuckers are there?" Kruger asked languidly. He had taken the last of the morphine, and licked his dry lips in subtle anticipation of future need. "I didn't think there were that many idiots in all of Germany."

"Thousands and thousands and thousands," Eva intoned, enjoying the soft sound of the words. "It is enough to make one sick, even now."

"That's the last of it," Kruger said, referring to the morphine. With Maikowski's two thousand marks, they had purchased morphine and rented a new apartment for Eva. She had spent the money quickly, on good Sekt and fresh salmon, a dozen ampules of dope. "Eva dear," Kruger added mournfully, "you've squandered the money and taken all the morphine. You're a silly cow."

"I've mailed another demand to Maikowski," she said. "We'll have another two thousand soon enough, little man."

"Little man!" Kruger laughed rudely. Suddenly, he felt light as a feather, a warm pleasure better than sex. One could expound the virtues of morphine and never even approach its truth. Kruger examined the ceiling, the molded sconces. It was the first time in years he could remember being warm in November. "You won't feel so feisty when your goose stops laying his golden eggs."

"My goose will lay," Eva said. She put her chin on an arm and watched the march. Newspapers were reporting twenty thousand, though right-wing papers said sixty. "My goose has a lot to lose," Eva continued. "He's second in command of Berlin's SA. He won't want to jeopardize that."

"When did you mail the demand?" Kruger asked. He licked his lips again. "It's been a week or two, no?"

Eva blinked, now desiring a hot bath to cure her cramps. The Brown Shirts looked like so many spiders, a wave of arachnids. In fact, she was out of money and her rent was due and her morphine supply was finally gone. She needed cash desperately and was beginning to worry about Maikowski. What if he failed to send the two thousand marks? She would expose him, of course. But that alone would not solve her problem.

"Eva?" Kruger said quietly. He had lain his head down and was about to drift away. He felt as though he'd entered an enormous womb. "Eva, you have no money? Isn't that true? We are out of money?"

Eva studied her own reflection against the Brown Shirts. "Go to sleep," she said.

"Correct me if I'm wrong," Kruger continued.

"Shut up, will you, Kruger?"

"I do love your style," Kruger said. "You know, I was just thinking. Perhaps we should switch to opium."

"Why is that, my dear?"

"One needn't speak during an opium high. It has a tragic sort of silent beauty."

"You've always been a poet," Eva told him.

"Yes, a poet," Kruger said, eyes closed. "But you're going to have to find another golden goose."

"We have some chloral hydrate and a camera," Eva said. "It is always possible we can discover another trump in our hand."

"Well put," Kruger said.

Another band was marching past downstairs.

"Stupid polka music," Kruger said.

"They dress in brown and march like boy scouts," Eva said. It was late afternoon, and the sky had turned mauve. She wondered how long the march would continue, how many of these fascist playboys would go marching by. From early morning, they had swarmed out of the train station, taken over the streets, manhandled some Jews and socialists, even wrecked a newspaper office. And the town government seemed happy to host them. "Just like boy scouts, don't you think?" Eva said.

"We'll be back on the street," Kruger said.

"We'll go to the Café Dom tonight," Eva told him, trying to adduce some cheer. Once Kruger passed into melancholy, Eva knew he was hard to rouse. "We'll find a pigeon and dose him with chloral hydrate. You'll see. We'll have us another goose."

"Another goose," Kruger lamented.

Eva pressed her nose to the glass. "Oh, look," she said gaily. "There's a fat Nazi playing a tuba. I don't believe I've ever seen anything so stupid in my life!"

Kruger had gone to sleep. Eva dreaded returning to her former life. But it was the only way to survive.

26

He hated crowds, loathed the hordes of marchers and the bands. And despite his new uniform and his new identity, Huebner found himself revolted by the spectacle of the Putsch march. Amid the clamorous throngs, he marched, tubas braying, the Storm Troops singing their songs, wild cheering as they neared the famous Burgerbraukeller, then milder chants as they passed beyond the river across the Ludwigstrasse Bridge, then down the Tal, through the cobbled plaza of the Marienplatz, north toward Odeonsplatz where there were speeches, music, and more chanting. By the end of the march, he had fallen to the rear, and could hardly hear what was being said by Party leaders.

Huebner left Odeonsplatz and taxied to Schwabing, about a ten-minute ride. As darkness fell, he found the Café Dom on a corner near Kemmerstrasse, just as Maikowski had described it. Its windows were brightly lighted, and the place seemed jammed with young people, bohemians, artists, and musicians. He was wearing his uniform, and there were only one or two other SA present. There were some SA men on the street in front of the café, and a few more nearby, some filtering away from the festivities. There had been isolated fights, some small riots, and the windows of a few Jewish stores had been broken. Just inside the door to the café, Huebner paused, noticing the woman named Eva, a dirty blonde who was sitting at a back table with a dwarfish fellow who wore a black beret.

Huebner went through the café and stopped at their table. "May I sit down?" he asked Eva. If nothing else, the uniform provided a sense of power and authority. It had become his new skin.

"What do you think, Kruger?" Eva said, eyeing the stranger suggestively, running an imaginary finger over the uniform with its gaudy array of belts and buckles, its red swastika armband and pins. "Shall we let this German sit at our table?"

"If I may," Huebner said.

An SA standing at the bar smiled and raised a glass. Huebner nodded, then sat without saying anything further.

"I suppose we should let this SA sit down," Eva said, winking at Kruger. Kruger was nursing a small schnapps, fearful of finishing it.

"It's all the same to me," Kruger said sullenly.

Huebner put his hands on the table and let them lie there, fingers outstretched. Eva smiled at her stranger and began to see herself in his apartment, filching paper marks from his wallet. A warm glow spread through her body, signals from her sixth sense.

"I'm called Eva," she said. "And I like to drink good Sekt. You look like a prominent citizen who could buy a girl a good glass of cold Sekt."

"A glass of good Sekt for the lady," Huebner said. His confidence was growing. It had been years since he'd been in a lighted café, in the presence of others, years since he'd spoken to a human being in confidence. "And an apple brandy for me," he added.

"I'll bring the drinks," Kruger said. He shooed the waiter away. "I have to go take a piss anyway."

When they were alone, Eva said, "You've been on the big march, huh?"

"It just ended."

"Marching for Germany, for the Führer."

"For a better life for all of us," Huebner parroted.

"Aha, ha," Eva chuckled. "A better life! I'll drink to that, certainly. A better life!" There was a puddle of Sekt in her glass, and she drained what remained, then licked the rim, smiling at Huebner, who was growing warm inside his heavy uniform. His face felt flushed, and the tips of his ears were tingling. "And tell me, friend, what's your name?"

Huebner thought for a moment. "Harry Wulff," he said. "My name is Harry Wulff."

"Wulff," Eva repeated. She could feel the absence of morphine, a throb of anxiety and desire. The pain had made her irritable. "An interesting name," she said to kill time.

"Do you think so?" Huebner said.

"But tell me," Eva said. "What is this better life you talk about? What does this new Germany look like?"

"It is clean," Huebner said.

"How interesting," Eva laughed. "Who does the cleaning?"

Huebner now felt disoriented, unable to go on. He had ways of expressing himself, but they were not with words. "Let us not talk about politics," he said.

"Should we talk about money?" Eva asked.

"Money is never boring," Huebner said.

"Not if you have it," Eva laughed. "I love money, don't you?"

Huebner paused, trying to think. "Money is—" Huebner gasped, surprising Eva.

"Are you all right?"

"Of course," Huebner said. "But I have money," he said.

"Yes, I thought you might," Eva said. "Did you know that some people will do anything for money?" Eva leaned close to Huebner, revealing to him the abscesses on her neck, the sour pallor of her skin, her breath fetid with alcohol. Huebner thought of her as a cadaver rotting from the inside out.

"That is plausible," Huebner said.

"What a lovely way to put it," Eva said, touching the man's hand.

"I'm glad you approve," Huebner said.

"I am one of those people," Eva laughed quietly.

"You are one of those people," Huebner found himself saying.

"Ah, why not? Why not come to the point?"

"We will have a drink," Huebner said, suddenly very terrified of the woman leaning close to him, pouring her alcohol breath over his body.

"Do you think I'm pretty?" Eva said. She was irked by the simple transparency of her work, its fraudulence and stupidity. Even now she sensed the patent ludicrousness of seducing this hulking SA sergeant with his belts and buckles, his wads of paper marks. "Do you think I'm just a little pretty?"

"Of course I do," Huebner said.

"You like me, then?"

"I would say so."

"Tell me about yourself while we wait for our drinks to arrive."

"There is nothing to tell." Huebner caught a glance of himself in the glass windows of the café. Faces surrounded him, dark questioning stares.

"From where do you come?" Eva asked. "Your accent is not German."

"I live in Berlin," Huebner said.

"You must have a life story," Eva cooed. "Tell us your life story. It is a way to pass the time. With the bartender as slow as he is and the café as crowded as it is, it may be a long time before our drinks come."

"I have no life story," Huebner said angrily.

Eva shushed him, growing impatient. She'd had enough of this life. Perhaps, she thought, she'd leave Munich, flee Germany altogether. Perhaps she would go to Greece. "Never mind, my dear," Eva told her sergeant tenderly. This one was more immature than most, a baby. And she'd had SA men by the score. This one was putty.

╌ ╶

They listened to Louis Armstrong as it rained. At the opposite end of the ottoman from Wulff, Johanna sat reading a liberal newspaper.

"Goebbels is to be married next week," Johanna said. Wulff had been looking at the rain-filled windows, the trees of the Tiergarten wet with rain, the sky a dull-grained gray. "They will have the ceremony at St. Olaf's."

"I'm so happy for them," Wulff said sarcastically.

"Another article says that there are thirty thousand Brown Shirt marchers on the streets of Munich."

That day, Wulff had spent hours studying the SA files maintained by Stapo. If Edgar Braun was a new recruit, it was unlikely he'd appear on intelligence reports so quickly, or under that name. Still, it was work that needed to be done. "Will you come to Poel for Christmas?" he asked.

"Would your father approve?"

"He wants to meet you."

"We'll talk about it," Johanna said, unfurling the newspaper to hide from Wulff. "There have been riots in Munich, and pogroms as well. Hitler addressed the crowds."

"I want you to leave Berlin now," Wulff said. "At least until this thing with Edgar Braun is over."

"I've told you, Harry," she said, "he is interested in you, not me."

"Even so," Wulff said. "He's going to kill again. Somewhere, sometime."

"That's probably true," Johanna said.

"And I'm going to place more articles about him," Wulff told her.

"I wish you wouldn't," she said.

"I want him to come to me," Wulff replied.

The record ended and began to scratch. Wulff rose and lifted the needle. He stood at the window looking down at the street and the Tiergarten, the forlorn park, men and women scurrying in the rain.

Johanna said, "They say that Goebbels and Magda Quandt are taking a posh apartment in Stieglitz. They say Hitler is attending the wedding. Won't that be lovely, Harry? Adolph Hitler as the best man at a church wedding? I can see it in my mind's eye now, the bride and groom with Hitler handing Goebbels a ring. It will be the social event of the winter season, won't it, Harry? Do you suppose I'll receive an invitation? Do you suppose Goebbels will invite a Jewish doctor to his lovely wedding?"

"Please, darling," Wulff said.

"Your father is well?" Johanna asked.

Wulff sighed and looked at the Tiergarten again. It would soon be 1932, and things were getting worse. Worse and worse, worse by the minute.

"Father is well," he said.

"I'm so glad," Johanna told him.

— ~

Kruger filled his cheap tin-cork flask with apple brandy and added four drops of chloral hydrate from a medicine-bottle dropper. He swished the apple brandy, smelled it just to make certain, and stoppered the flask. Leaning against the bar with the flask in his pocket, he felt a sudden shudder of morphine pain, a kind of physical longing that was like learning someone you love has died. He took a sip of schnapps, rendered the memory of morphine into a scrap of nostalgia, and began to see the poor SA sergeant as a kind of Savior. What would he carry in his wallet? Several hundred marks, perhaps?

They would drug him gently, let him fall asleep, then steal his wallet and his watch, perhaps some of his pretty swastika pins.

Kruger left the bar, carrying a glass of good Sekt and the flask. He stood near the table, where he could overhear a shred of the conversation between Eva and her sergeant.

"Never mind, dear," Eva was saying, patting the sergeant's hand as though he were a child. Kruger admired Eva's make-believe tenderness, her way of soothing the beast. And then there was the framework of her over-large sense of lust, the lucidity she brought to what would otherwise be a very dull game. "You're lonely, aren't you, lonely and looking for a little company on a cold night in the big city?"

"Yes, just a little company," the sergeant said.

"Where are you staying?" Eva whispered.

"My hotel, then," the sergeant said.

Unlike most of Eva's clients, this one didn't pretend excitement, nor even mild interest. She recalled that even Maikowski expressed a thin horse-faced smile or an annoying eye twitch when Eva played her little games. But this sergeant was definitely a dull boy. "It's the Ludwigshof near the bridge," he was saying.

"I'd prefer to go there separately," Eva said. "Just as a matter of propriety."

"You'll come, though?" the sergeant said.

Kruger detected pathos. Perhaps the sergeant was not so dull. Perhaps his marks were burning a hole in his pocket.

"Don't worry, dear," Eva said, patting his hand. "But really, do you know what kind of games we'll play?"

The sergeant pondered Eva's question. Kruger waited patiently for the right moment to deliver his chloral hydrate. Eva's Sekt was going flat.

"I like to play with morphine," the sergeant said.

"You are a naughty boy," Eva said. "I think we're going to get along just fine. I'm going to make you happy, as happy as you've ever been."

"I have morphine," the sergeant repeated.

Kruger sat down at the table and poured a glass of apple brandy into the sergeant's glass. Eva took her Sekt eagerly, spilling some of it on the table. The sergeant picked up his brandy and drained it in one gulp. Kruger was pretending to look for his gloves. He poured another glass of brandy for the sergeant. The sergeant took the glass and lifted it to his lips and drank.

"What room are you in?" Eva asked.

"Can't we go together in a taxi?"

"Please, my dear," Eva protested childishly. "You wouldn't want to be seen going into your hotel with me, would you? You checked in alone. Your reputation will be ruined. I'll just join you."

The sergeant studied her, his jaw muscles taut. Eva began to wonder if she was destroying her chance. Kruger poured the sergeant another brandy.

"Drink up and we're off," Eva said brightly. She offered her client a puckish smile. He drank only half the brandy.

Eva made a move to get up, then whispered something into the sergeant's ear. The sergeant stood up stiffly, then walked out of the café.

"Give me the flask," Eva said to Kruger. "He's in room 315 at the back of the hotel. It sounds perfect, with an exit to the alley."

"I know the dump," Kruger said.

"Did you hear about the morphine?" Eva asked him. "This must be our lucky day. I'll give him a drink when I get there. He'll be sick by then and won't give us much trouble. Think of it, Kruger! Tonight! Money and morphine! It's like a beautiful dream, Kruger!"

"Just be careful," Kruger warned.

"He's a pussycat," she said. "He's scared to death."

"He looks dangerous to me."

"Kruger, you're an alarmist."

Eva put on her cloth coat. Once she'd gotten this sergeant's German marks, she intended to buy a decent winter coat. It would be wool with whale-bone buttons. "Let's ride together," she told Kruger. "You can get out a couple of blocks away and walk over."

"All right," Kruger said anxiously.

"Just wait outside the door. I'll signal you when it's time to come in. By the time he gets to his room, he'll be disoriented. One drink more and this baby is in his crib."

"Eva, you are amazing," Kruger told her.

— —

Bibi had outfitted herself in a ridiculous black-and-white polka-dot dress, two-toned shoes, and real silk stockings with seams. She was wearing a cup-shaped hat adorned with duck feathers. Rom had decided that, if nothing else, she provided him protective coloration, a point of focus that diverted attention from Rom and delivered it to Bibi's big breasts. Together they had been sitting in the lobby of the Ludwigshof Hotel for twenty minutes, Rom reading a newspaper, Bibi beginning to whine.

"I'm bored, Dieter," she said.

Rom had spent a morning studying SA requisition forms in Berlin, finally discovering that a reservation had been made for Sergeant Albert Huebner at a cheap hotel just near the river, a not-quite-nice address where hundreds of other non-commissioned SA officers were lodged. The lobby was crowded with them, the bar jammed, the streets clogged. Rom found it all faintly absurd, a throwback to Gymnasium or worse, summer camps in the Schwartzwald where adolescents cavorted naked in their cabins and diddled one another in the dark.

"Why don't you buy a bar of chocolate?" Rom suggested.

"I don't want chocolate," Bibi whined. "I want to go somewhere and do something. I'm tired of sitting here. What are we doing, anyway?"

Rom decided then and there to tell her the truth, knowing that it would go in one ear and out the other. They were waiting for Albert Huebner or Otto Maikowski, though he could have told her they were waiting for the second coming of Christ for all the difference it would have made. That afternoon, during the big march, Rom had caught sight of Huebner at the back of the procession, but he'd been swallowed by huge throngs on the Odeonsplatz, then had disappeared from sight altogether.

And so—what was Albert Huebner doing here in Munich? What trick was he performing for Maikowski?

"I'm going to buy you a trout tonight," Rom told Bibi by way of appeasement.

"I don't want to sit around a tavern full of your brown-shirted friends," Bibi said. "I want to go somewhere gay."

"We'll go someplace elegant and quiet," he said.

Rom had taken a room at the Odeon Hotel, a first-class suite in a good hotel with roses on marble tabletops and a view of the Tal. It was expensive, but worth it for the privacy alone. And Maikowski was on the floor below, making it easy to follow him to a meeting with Huebner at the Ludwigshof. But later, Rom hadn't counted on losing the sergeant in crowds. Now he was stuck waiting in the lobby of a second-rate hotel with Bibi whining interminably.

Then suddenly, Rom caught sight of Huebner, the man slightly rumpled and red-eyed. He was standing in the glass doorway of the lobby, swaying slightly as though he'd had too much to drink. He proceeded across the marble floor, then caught an elevator near a pot of browning palms. Rom glanced at his watch and waited. Five minutes later, the Schwabing whore named Eva came through the glass doors, paused for a moment to orient herself, then caught the elevator as well.

"Bibi, I feel wonderful," Rom said. He tickled her ear playfully.

A curious dwarf-like man came into the hotel wearing a black turtleneck sweater, a black leather jacket, and a black beret. He was not quite five feet tall and almost bald, except for a fringe of graying white hair. He turned a corner by the front desk and climbed some stairs.

Bibi nudged Rom. "Will I get to meet Hitler?" she asked. Rom felt annoyed. They all loved Hitler, didn't they? The runty little bastard and his fastidious ascetic ways. Was it simply the aura of power?

"As of today, the chances are better," Rom said.

"I'm so anxious," Bibi was saying. "But how much longer do we have to sit here?"

"I want to tell you something," Rom said, grasping her left forearm and squeezing it. Bibi flinched, but said nothing. "We're going to sit here for fifteen minutes or so. Then I'm going upstairs to a brief meeting. I want you to sit here quietly and say nothing more. And when I'm gone, I want you to say nothing to anyone else. If you say something to someone and I find out about it, I'll break your arm Bibi, and then I'll put you on a train for Berlin. So help me God."

"Dieter?"

"Shut up, Bibi, please."

Bibi affected a pout. Rom had seen it before. "At least let me have a bar of chocolate while you're gone," she whined.

Rom handed her a paper mark. She beamed and kissed his cheek.

27

Wulff drove south on Kaiser Allee to Schoenberg, a distance of five kilometers. He had spent the night with Johanna at her Lennestrasse apartment, where he kept sets of business suits. He found a place to park on a side street, then walked four blocks over to a row of down-at-the-heels flats fronted by wrought-iron gates, gaudily painted porticoes and gables, great barren hydrangea gardens. He located no. 57 at the end of a row of six or seven and rang the buzzer.

Kisch answered the door in disheveled work clothes. His hair was standing straight up on end, and his white shirt was stained by starburst-shaped blots of spaghetti sauce. With one hand on the jamb, Kisch leaned forward as though he might topple onto his face. He staggered back slightly when Wulff pushed on the door.

"For God's sake, man," Kisch muttered. "Do you know what time it is?"

"Let me in, damn it," Wulff said.

"You're a very annoying friend," Kisch said. "And being up so early makes you a moral shit."

Wulff swept inside on a gust of what could only be cigar smoke emanating from Kisch. A narrow hallway led to a larger bachelor room stuffed willy-nilly with an odd assortment of mismatched furniture, the furniture in turn piled high with books and newspapers, filled and half-filled ashtrays, beer bottles, and magazines. Even the windowsills had been crammed with nameless junk, ledgers, political tracts, a stuffed owl, a goldfish bowl that had gone dry, a desiccated fish on its bottom. In the midst of the clutter were two sedan chairs, several footstools, a sofa, and a plaster-of-paris model of the new Tempelhof Airport. Kisch stumbled into the room after Wulff, and kicked at the model of the new airport, then collapsed in a heap on the sofa.

"Do you want a schnapps?" he asked Wulff.

"I have to go to Mitte in a few minutes," Wulff said. "I want you to wake up and talk to me."

"What if there had been a young woman here?" Kisch said. "Would that have made a difference to your German mentality?"

"But there's never a woman with you," Wulff said.

Kisch rubbed his chin. "I beg to differ," he said.

Wulff sat opposite Kisch on a chair from which he'd swept some newspapers. He put his hands on his knees and leaned toward Kisch, who had begun to yawn.

"I need your help again," Wulff said.

"Harry, please," Kisch said. "Can't it wait until morning? I've only just gotten in."

"No, it can't wait," Wulff said imperiously. "I want you to write a series of articles."

"Now see here…" Kisch burbled. The journalist rose and walked to the tiny kitchen. Wulff heard water running from a tap, the sound of Kisch gargling. Kisch returned to the sitting room with a towel and began to rub his face and arms. "All right," he said. "I suppose I'll have to listen. What's it all about?"

"I'm just a breath away from our Hirrenstrasse killer," Wulff said stonily.

"Ah yes," Kisch said. "Your monster. Your bleak creature. Whatever in the world became of this fellow?"

"It's quite simple," Wulff said. "He's loose in Berlin. He's out there somewhere."

"So he is," Kisch said, shaking his head.

"I want you to profile the case," Wulff said.

"Ah, Harry," Kisch lamented, "people have lost interest. The country is falling apart. The public are not compelled by your bleak creature."

"But this will interest your readers," Wulff said. "I want you to profile the case yourself. I want you to discuss these killings and highlight their political dimension."

"These killings do not have a political dimension, Harry," Kisch said. "A bleak creature strangles an unfortunate transvestite. It is pap. Worse than pap. It is maudlin."

"No," Wulff said simply, "These killings profile the history of Germany from after the War. I will give you information that will shock and titillate your readers. But more importantly, this story is critical to an understanding of our country."

"If you say so, Harry," Kisch said, yawning again.

Wulff stared at Kisch until the man stopped yawning. "If you could write a history of the Freicorps, the Black Reichswehr, and the SA, and connect it with the personal history of a single bleak creature who is killing transvestites right here in Berlin, would that interest you?"

Kisch seemed suddenly alert, like a fish that has found a hook in its mouth. "I would say," Kisch remarked. He had dropped the towel. "But Harry," he continued, "are you certain you wish to pursue this matter now? Christmas is coming, as well as the presidential elections. They say that Hitler is going to run against Hindenburg."

"Now," Wulff said dryly. "No later than the first of the year, I suppose. But now."

"These matters you can substantiate?"

"More now than ever."

"How so?"

"I can connect the SA to Bruckmann's murder."

Kisch sat up as if electrified. He ran a hand through his wild hair and smiled. "How very marvelous. But what about the Hirrenstrasse killer? I thought you said this would profile him."

"It is the same person," Wulff said. "And here is the plan. The man who killed both Bruckmann and Mueller works for the SA. I know his real identity, but he is living life as someone else now, though here in Berlin. I want you to write his history. His history is the dark side of German history. I want you to feature me in these stories. I want you to give my home address, my office location. I will provide you with everything you need. The articles will be sensational. You will win prizes, Kisch. You will be covered in socialist glory."

"Your bleak creature," Kisch said, musing.

"Whatever you wish to call him."

"Why a series of articles? Why not a single exposé?"

Wulff was silent. "He must be drawn out and baited."

"Wulff, Wulff," Kisch said. "You've played this dangerous game before, and he was not drawn out. But now, isn't it even more dangerous than before?"

"But drawn out he must be."

"But you assume he is stupid."

"Oh no, he is not stupid."

"Then why would he be drawn out now?"

"Because he has lost his identity," Wulff said. "He is in danger of becoming nobody."

"Ah—what do you mean?" Kisch said, puzzled.

"Now the threat to expose our killer is also the threat to destroy his new false identity. And to stop me from exposing his new false identity, I think he will seek me out. He cannot be deprived of his secret because the truth of his life is simply too terrible to bear."

Kisch rubbed his chin again. "You're fucking mad," he said. "You'll expose yourself to danger and me along with you, not to mention Johanna. Why not wait and let him make a mistake?"

"Others will die," Wulff said. "We've been through this before. And look around you. Everywhere the Nazis are triumphant. If political conditions change, and they will, our killer will become an ordinary German."

Kisch was rubbing his hands together for warmth. For the first time, Wulff noticed the cold in the unheated rooms, their aura of chill. A small black kitten wandered into the room and began to rub its back against Kisch's leg affectionately. "The whole story," he said. "Beginning to end."

"Installment by installment. The story begins in Freiburg and Liège, small villages near there. It ends in Berlin."

"My editors will shit their pants."

"Let them," Wulff said.

Kisch went to the kitchen and returned with a bottle of schnapps. "I think I need a drink," he said.

"One story a month?" Wulff asked.

"It won't do," Kisch said, waving a hand. He tipped up the bottle and drank. "That's too much interlude. People would lose interest, if they had an interest at first. My editors will never authorize a single installment once a month. Their stories must move. But *Vorwärts* has a Sunday political section which is illustrated quite nicely. You could provide illustrations? The pieces run every two weeks. It would be the perfect place if there is enough copy."

"There is enough copy."

"Ah, but how can we know?"

"I told you this story begins during the War and continues through the period of the revolution. It involves political intrigue, political torture, murder, betrayal. It dovetails with the political disintegration of Germany itself. And you ask me if there is enough copy!"

"Oh all right," Kisch said. "I accept your word."

Kisch found two dirty glasses and poured some schnapps into each. Wulff accepted one of the glasses and drank a tiny toast with his friend. He felt remote from the alcohol, detached from its fumes. Kisch wiped a dirty sleeve of his shirt across his mouth.

"It's your bloody neck," he said wryly.

— —

By the time Eva and Kruger reached the corner of Marienplatz, it was almost dark. Pigeons were roosting on the statues, and neon signs were blazing.

"I have a bad feeling about this, Eva," Kruger said.

"You and your feelings!" Eva laughed, clapping the dejected Kruger on his shoulder.

Eva opened the taxi door and looked at Kruger one last time. The sky was clear and cold and one could see the winter stars over distant mountains. Kruger handed Eva the flask of brandy laced with chloral hydrate and offered her a wan smile of encouragement. "I'll walk to the hotel," Kruger said, getting out.

Eva put the flask in a pocket of her cloth coat. After she bought a nice new coat with the money she would steal from her sergeant, and when Maikowski's two thousand marks arrived, she would go to Greece.

Eva watched him trudge away, and then she paid the taxi driver who had stopped in front of the hotel. She went inside, located the elevator, and rode to the third floor. In the lobby, she was amazed, never having seen so many SA in one place before. Was her mind playing tricks? The world was flooded with brown shirts.

Eva knocked softly on the door of 315, just at the end of the corridor and near a window with dirty lace curtains. She knocked again loudly and called the sergeant's name. When the door opened, she was not surprised to see her sergeant standing there with his tie half-undone, his eyes red and barely focused, an unhealthy green pallor to his skin. When the sergeant said nothing, Eva whisked her way past him and gently closed the door herself.

"So you've come," the sergeant said. He licked his lips and scanned the room as though a thousand images had gathered on his retina. "So, you've come," he repeated dumbly.

"Of course I've come," Eva said cheerily. She took off her coat and threw it over the arm of a nearby chair. It was a simple room with an obviously lumpy mattress on a double bed, a few prints of Bavarian mountains on the wall. "You didn't think I'd miss a night with you?" Eva asked coyly. "I hope we can have a little drink together. Dear, I've borrowed a flask of apple brandy from my friend. I'm sure he would-n't mind if you had a nice drink."

The sergeant staggered and fell back slightly, dropping to the bed. Eva found a glass on the night stand, opened the flask, and poured a drink. "Dear, you need a drink," she said. "Why don't you have a drink?"

"I don't need a drink," the sergeant told her.

Eva sat down next to him. She could sense his great power, the strength of his body. She lifted the brandy glass to his lips. He opened his mouth and took a sip.

"I hate to bring this up," Eva said. "But we need to talk about money. I think it's always a good thing to get that out of the way so we can have fun without worrying. Don't you think that's a good idea?"

"I have money," the sergeant said.

Eva stood, walked to a dresser, and stood for a few moments observing herself in the mirror. Behind her, she could see the sergeant in the mirror as well, the man sitting on the bed, staring at his hands. He seemed ready to collapse, barely able to support the weight of his own head. Just then, the sergeant stood groggily and approached her from the rear. Eva decided she would allow the sergeant a single kiss, just one before she made him drink a second brandy and went to work. As the sergeant stood behind her, she understood his naked and revolting power, a sense of how large he was in comparison to her.

The brandy glass fell at her feet. She could see a pool of liquor spreading beneath her, and when she raised her head again, she felt a noose being tightened around her throat as her body was hoisted off the floor in a great crescendo of strength. The breath gushed out of Eva in a grand biblical wave.

"Oh God!" she cried weakly. The effort of trying to breathe was causing her enormous pain. Bright red stars streamed into her consciousness. Opening her eyes briefly, she could see herself and the sergeant in the mirror, both of them red-eyed and caught in a daze of disbelief, the sergeant's huge face just over her right shoulder as he squeezed, making a fist with the rope that was cutting into her shoulder.

Eva managed to raise a hand and scratch, digging her nails deeply into the sergeant's cheek. He twisted away, trying to tighten the noose. Eva screamed, choked, and caught her breath. Then she kicked backward from the dressing table, sending both of them spiraling to the floor. Something snapped sharply in Eva's arm. A wave of hot vomit splashed on her cheek. Suddenly she could breathe and she closed her eyes, rolled slightly to her side, and encountered a terrible bleating pain in her shoulder and left elbow, an electric pulse that was nearly unendurable. "Kruger, Kruger!" Eva managed to shout. "Oh God, Kruger!"

Just to her right, the sergeant was moving. He made a grunting animal noise.

"Oh God, Kruger, please come and help me!" Eva shouted again. There was blood on her blouse and blood on the worn carpet and a petal of blood collecting in the pit of her right ear. She could smell its iron-like bitterness, and when she glanced down at the bodice of her blouse, a circle of blood had formed where the noose had kissed her skin.

⁓ ⁓

Rom left Bibi in the lobby of the hotel and took the elevator to the third floor. He stepped out, sniffed the dusty, closed-in aroma of the corridor, then spied a dwarfish man at the end of the hall, his mouth wide in a kind of horror movie pose. Rom glanced at the other end of the corridor and saw nothing save for a dimly lighted passage, doors, tattered carpet, a dead-end of wall about fifteen meters away. He hurried toward the dwarfish man, who began to back toward an exit. Rom halted him with a stare. It helped that Rom was wearing his full-dress SA officer's uniform and that he towered over the man.

"What's going on here?" Rom demanded. "Tell me quickly."

"There's been an accident," Kruger said, holding his hands like shivering birds. He looked as pale as a corpse. "Something terrible has happened."

"Does this involve Eva Vollheim?" Rom asked. He put an ear to the door of 315 and listened. He thought he could hear panting and a faint crying sound. "Hurry up and tell me what happened."

"Please, please be quiet," Kruger begged. "Yes, something has happened to Eva. How do you know her?"

Rom tried the doorknob. He turned it and opened the door. He could see Eva and Theodor Loos on the floor at the foot of the bed, Loos sitting back with a glazed look on his face, Eva nearby staring at the ceiling and moaning. The woman's hair was matted with blood and Rom could see a terrific open gash on her left arm. Rom grabbed Kruger by the coat collar and pulled him inside the room, then closed the door. Loos was looking up at Rom with vacant, sun-blasted eyes. He forced Kruger back against the door and locked its latch, put a finger on his lips to indicate that Kruger should keep quiet. Taking two steps across the room, he kneeled above Eva, careful not to stain his uniform pants-leg.

"Eva, you stupid whore," Rom said. "What have you gotten yourself involved in?"

Eva looked at Rom. Her skin was gray, and a ring of blood circled her neck, starting at the collarbone. Rom saw a knot of bone protruding from her left arm just above the elbow. Turning his head, he studied Eva's bloody neck, then lifted a hank of her matted hair and discovered a huge, broken bruise just above the left ear. So—she had tumbled backward, struck her head on the bedstead and broken her arm in the fall. Rom stole another glance at Loos. "Eva, quickly," Rom said. "If you can speak, tell me what you've done here."

"Help me, Rom," Eva gagged.

"You've badly broken your arm, darling," Rom told her, smiling.

"It hurts, Rom," Eva said. She tried to move the fingers of her hand but found them frozen. The thought of death did not move her, but the thought of being paralyzed terrified her badly. Her skin felt clammy and her head quite light. "Rom, please," she said.

Rom threw a thumb at Loos. "Do you know who this is?" he asked Eva in a whisper. Loos was breathing heavily now, trying to move. "Tell me, Eva, do you know who your playmate for the evening works for?"

"He's just another sot client," Eva said angrily.

"You've been fooled, Eva," Rom said.

"I don't understand," Eva muttered, now feeling a spread of numbness throughout the entire left side of her body. Even her lips felt numb. Perhaps this was what it was like to die.

"You honestly don't know," Rom laughed.

"Shit, you prick," Eva said angrily. "Can't you give me some help, you Nazi prick!"

Rom shushed her. "Eva, please," Rom said. "This fellow belongs to Maikowski. Did you know that this fellow belongs to Maikowski? Does that surprise you?"

Eva tried to lift herself. Rom placed a finger on her chest and kept her down.

"Help me out of here for, God's sake," Eva said.

"She's got to go to the hospital," Kruger pleaded softly.

"Shut up," Rom told Kruger, giving him a quick angry glance. "Now, Eva," Rom continued, "you're going to have to tell me what you're doing here, or there will be consequences. Do you hear me, Eva? Consequences."

"Oh shit," Eva said.

"Those SA beasts in the lobby would flail you, Eva," Rom said. "You know they would."

"All right," Eva said.

"And make it quick. This smell is making me sick."

"I was going to steal his money," Eva said. "Steal his watch and his money."

"Oh Eva!" Rom said. "You've drugged this fellow with chloral hydrate, haven't you? You learned this trick from me! How unique!

But if you're still here when he wakes up, he'll strangle you, Eva. Isn't that clear to you, Eva? Even in the state you're in?"

Eva nodded, pitying herself all at once. Her arm had stopped bleeding, but just seeing the white nub of bone protruding above the elbow, its elegant structures and blue nerve endings, and the white-gray-purple mesh of marrow, was making her faint.

"So Maikowski sent him to kill me," Eva said.

"Now we're getting somewhere," Rom said. "Eva, if you tell me the whole truth, I'll get you out of here and to a hospital. I'll see to it you're taken care of. But you must act quickly, or your chance will disappear."

"Tell him, Eva," Kruger said breathlessly.

"He's right," Rom urged her.

"Yes, yes," Eva gasped. Rom lifted her head. She winced in pain and sat upright a moment before she could begin to speak. "I drugged Maikowski, too," Eva admitted. "We took photographs. Just like the photographs of Bruckmann. That's the whole story. It is really quite simple, you prick."

"And where are the photographs?" Rom asked.

"Show him one," Eva said to Kruger.

Kruger took a photograph from his jacket pocket. He handed it to Rom who studied it with a smile. An out-of-focus document, Maikowski naked on hands and knees, staring at the camera in unmodulated disbelief, Eva squatting above him like a scornful harpy, her face masked.

"Oh but this is wonderful," Rom said. "Eva, you are a comic genius."

"Please help me now."

"To be sure," Rom said. "How much did Maikowski pay you?"

"Two thousand," Kruger said. "But now we've got to take her to the hospital. Can't you see how badly she's hurt?"

"Ah, so she is," Rom said. "Listen to me, both of you." Loos had lifted an arm. "I'm going to give both of you five thousand marks for the photographs and the negatives. I'm going to take Eva to the hospital and see that she's taken care of by doctors. And when this is all over, I want both of you to forget this ever happened and leave

Munich. If you don't, you'll be killed. Maikowski will kill you, and I'll tell him where you are and how to do it."

"But Rom," Eva said.

Rom put an arm under her right shoulder and helped Eva to her feet with Kruger's help. They stood above Loos who looked at them vacuously. A burble of vomit-spit hung from his lower lip. Eva spat on him and whimpered.

"This is your lucky day," Rom said. "We'll go outside to the alley. I'll call from the lobby and we'll take a taxi to the hospital. But I want those photographs."

"I have them," Kruger said.

"When I get them, you'll each have your five thousand marks."

Rom held Eva by the waist, Kruger opening the door. The three staggered outside over the prone body of Theodor Loos. Eva had turned white with shock. Even Rom, who had an iron stomach, was sickened by the sight of bone protruding through skin.

28

They were reading the Sunday papers at Johanna's flat. Now more than ever, he stayed with Johanna at night. In the back of his mind, he knew he was subjecting her to danger, but he couldn't help himself. They had visited Poel Island during Christmas, just Wulff and Johanna, spending the languid snowy afternoons playing dominoes with Wulff's father. They had candlelight suppers and took evening walks across the frosty fields as crows flew. Once he returned to Berlin, Wulff worked like a dog.

"Hitler is in Berlin," Johanna said, looking up from a Sunday *Beobachter*. "He is visiting Goebbels at his fancy Stieglitz apartment and giving a few select speeches to industrialists and Party faithful."

Wulff was listening to a Charlie Christian record. A languid gypsy guitar solo resonated as snow fell outside. Wulff sipped some ersatz coffee and snuffled one toe into the caftan Johanna was wearing. She had opened the drapes so that they could see the snow, huge drifts of it falling in the Tiergarten, covering the barren trees. Wulff heard Johanna say, "There was a party last night. Goebbels and his movie-star wife, Göring and his Swedish girl. The paper calls it a 'glittering affair.'" Johanna smiled, then rumpled the paper in disgust. "We were not invited, Harry. Does this make you sad?"

Wulff chuckled. For some reason, he felt momentarily content. "There are persistent rumors in the paper that Hitler will run for president," Wulff said. "And no, I wouldn't care to go to that party." Wulff was wearing a bulky cable-knit sweater and old flannel pants. They had made love in the afternoon.

"Surely he will lose," Johanna said.

Alone, they had lost track of the hour. Wulff looked at the clock and saw it was almost midnight. He was due at Berlin Mitte early for meetings about the murder of two communists by Nazis. And for weeks, he'd been busy composing a series of articles on the Edgar Braun case while at the same time trying to track down the man without success. "My father is head over heels for you," he said.

"I'm so glad," Johanna said. During the holiday, she had cooked for them and had listened to the old man's war stories. "He's really quite nice beneath that exterior of leather and iron."

"He's not a Prussian, you mean?" Wulff laughed. He nudged Johanna with his toe.

"No, he's not a Prussian," Johanna said.

The downstairs buzzer rang. Wulff stopped the record and punched a button to listen.

"Wulff, I know you're up there!" said a voice. "Johanna, let me see Wulff. I don't care what you're doing in there, I must see Wulff!" It was Kisch. Wulff shrugged to Johanna and pressed a buzzer releasing the downstairs lock. Wulff opened the door to the flat and waited. In moments, Kisch came bounding down the hall in an ochre-colored woolen sweater, a green muffler around his neck, a Russian-style hat pulled over his ears. His pant cuffs were crusted with snow and his cheeks were red with schnapps and cold. He fled past Wulff into the sitting room and stood huffing, stamping his feet while melted snow dotted the carpet.

"It's almost midnight," Wulff said.

"Hello, beautiful woman," Kisch said to Johanna.

"Erwin," Johanna said. "You have a sense of the dramatic, I'll give you that much." Johanna smiled at him, waving a hand to offer him a seat. Kisch waited a few moments, then dropped into a chair near the coal fire.

"Do you want a drink?" Wulff asked him.

"Not now, thanks," Kisch said. "I need to talk to you, Harry. It is rather private."

"So talk," Wulff said. "I have no secrets."

"About the articles?" Kisch said in surprise.

"I've told Johanna our plan. She doesn't approve."

"Frankly, neither do I," Kisch said laughing. He took a newspaper from beneath his sweater and unfurled it. "This is tomorrow morning's edition of *Vorwärts*. I thought you'd like to see it before it hits the street."

Wulff took the paper. In bold print, the headline read, HITLER TO CHALLENGE HINDENBURG. In small print beneath: *Nazis threaten control.*

"This is no surprise, Erwin," Wulff told him.

Kisch seemed feverish, his face splotched. "Wait until you read the article."

Johanna took the paper from Wulff and began to read.

"He will lose," Wulff said.

"Hitler will lose? What if he doesn't?" Kisch shook the last of the snow from his boots and sat warming his hands. "You know what Hitler had promised us? Heads will roll. Yes, heads will roll, Wulff. Those heads belong to people like me."

"He will lose," Wulff reiterated.

"Those heads belong to people like you, too," Kisch told Wulff. "And those heads belong to people like Johanna." Johanna lowered the paper. "I'm sorry, Johanna," Kisch said. "I shouldn't be so blunt. My stupid mouth is a liability sometimes."

Johanna smiled gently. "No, Erwin," she said, "you're absolutely right. It will be your head and it will be my head. I've finally abandoned my silly theorizing. There is no question that heads will roll."

"Why won't people believe it?" Kisch asked himself.

Johanna had crossed her legs, cradling the newspaper in her lap. "People long to believe the best," she said. "This is a truism. Despite all the Nazis say, people believe life will improve. They believe in their hearts that the Nazis will better the country. It is all they contemplate when they scream for Hitler. They are good people, all of them."

Kisch shook his head. "*You* are a good person," he told Johanna. "But you delude yourself about Germans."

"I don't think so," Johanna insisted. She lifted the newspaper and continued to read.

Wulff had been listening. Kisch caught his glance with one of his own.

"The presidential elections are in March," Kisch told Wulff. "I've discussed your series of articles with my editors at *Vorwärts*. They will not devote such space to a murder until after the elections."

"For God's sake," Wulff exclaimed. "Lives are at stake. The monster may kill another innocent person. Can't you get them to change their minds?"

"They're dedicating the paper to Hitler's defeat," Kisch said. "Every Sunday supplement will be filled with election articles, stories about Brown Shirt violence, the Nazi program. They must convince left-socialists to vote for Hindenburg and not waste their time on minor candidates. Can you imagine a socialist voting for Hindenburg?"

Wulff leaned forward, his voice hushed. "I've been looking for Edgar Braun these past six weeks. Much of my free time is spent in this search. Barlach and I work overtime. And there are other murders, my administrative tasks, political riots, all of which take up my time. There are perhaps twenty-five officers I trust in my own command at this point. Precinct after precinct is turning Nazi. If I don't catch Edgar Braun soon, he'll disappear into the Nazi horde. And he will kill again. I am convinced of it, Erwin."

Kisch sighed. "I understand, Harry," he said. "Believe me, I understand. And I've spent days arguing with my editors. But they consider your problem with this killer minor when compared to the problems confronting Germany. I've begged on your behalf for space, but none is to be had right now. I'm sorry, Harry, but you have to accept that I've done all I can do. You'll have to wait until after the March elections. I don't agree with your need, but I have argued your case as the best lawyer would argue it. I've lost, Harry."

Wulff leaned back. Johanna put the newspaper down in her lap.

"The situation is serious," Johanna said. "Perhaps Erwin is right, Harry. You should read the articles."

"What is it, dear?" Wulff asked her.

"Hitler is flying to every state in Germany," Johanna told him. "He will visit all the major cities, speak to millions of people, spend hundreds of thousands of marks. Goebbels will run the campaign and flood the radio with messages. Hitler vows to win, and he is risking his entire party to do so."

"Is this true, Kisch?" Wulff asked.

"I'm afraid so," he said.

"Your intelligence is that good?"

"It is no particular secret, Harry," Kisch said.

Wulff had to look away. His disappointment seared like physical pain. Kisch rose and wrapped the green muffler around his neck.

"We'll publish in March," Kisch said. "All your articles. The whole series. It will be spring then, and Hitler will be defeated, and then perhaps some rational course for the country will emerge. These are critical times, Harry. One must think of the common good."

"Can you ask again?" Wulff said.

"No, Harry," Kisch replied. "I happen to agree with my editors. It is only because of my respect for you that I argued with them as I did. Your Hirrenstrasse killer can wait. Hitler must be defeated first. When he loses, he will fade from the scene. Then we can fight your battle."

"All right," Wulff said. They shook hands, and Kisch went through the door to the corridor.

"Hitler will lose, won't he, Harry?" Johanna said. "He'll lose, and then he will fade from the scene, won't he?"

"He will lose," Wulff said.

Rom parked his Mercedes six blocks from the Fischerhof Hotel in Alt-Köln. The streets were wet with snowmelt, the cobbles slippery and gleaming with reflected light. Rom had chosen not to wear his uniform for the meeting with Maikowski. Instead, he dressed deliberately in a coal-black, double-breasted suit with matching vest, a red tie, one red carnation in the left lapel, and a black-and-red swastika pin on the other. Because it was so cold, Rom wore a woolen topcoat with a beaver collar. The coat, which he'd just purchased, was far too expensive for his captain's salary, but he had purchased it anyway, already looking forward to the wage of Colonel. Despite the purely speculative nature of his plan, Rom felt well-heeled, expansive, almost superhuman in his prescience. In the SA, it was common knowledge that somehow Maikowski had "misplaced" his adjutant who had disappeared after the Nuremberg rally. Too, there were embarrassment about the promotion Maikowski had granted to this mysterious sergeant. But as yet, Maikowski was still a colonel, still drove a massive Landauer touring car, still gave orders.

Rom opened the door to the Fischerhof. Seeing Maikowski in one corner of the bar, he raised a jaunty hand in greeting.

"Ah, Rom," Maikowski said jovially.

Rom halted for a moment and allowed his shadow to fall on Maikowski. What a wonderful gesture—allowing his shadow to fall on the man's horse-face, his ticking eye. Rom wondered if the shadow produced a chill in Maikowski, if Maikowski knew the legends surrounding vampires, how vampires did not produce an image in the mirror, nor a shadow. In that context, Rom thought of Edgar Braun now living in a cheap one-room bed-sitter in the Kreuzberg near Tempelhof. What a dreary existence! Like being buried! Rom could hardly wait to tell Braun—Huebner—of his plan to liberate the man at Wulff's expense.

"Good evening," Rom said. He sat down across from Maikowski, who was dressed in his SA best and drinking a Black Velvet. When a waiter came, Rom ordered beer.

"I'm in a bit of a hurry," Rom said.

"This won't take long," Maikowski answered. "I just want to ask your help with something."

"More than happy," Rom laughed.

The waiter brought Rom's beer, and he sipped some. Rom felt a twinge of sexual desire. For weeks, he'd been on the lookout for a suitable mistress, someone to replace the irreplaceable Bibi, who'd run off with a putative Hungarian count. He had spotted an actress or two, one chorine from Jagerstrasse who had promise, and a party secretary at Gau headquarters.

"Do you remember that Schwabing whore?" Maikowski asked innocently.

"Let me see…" Rom said quietly. He rubbed his chin in mock puzzlement.

"What was her name?" Maikowski huffed. "The one you used on Bruckmann? I can't recall her name."

"Yes, what was her name?" Rom asked himself. Rom pursed his lips expressing deep thought. He feared himself in danger of overacting.

"Ah, it was Eva!" Maikowski exclaimed. "Yes, Eva."

"Poor Eva," Rom muttered, as though he possessed some profound secret in regard to her life. "What about Eva?"

"Have you seen her, Rom?" Maikowski said. "Do you know where she is?"

Rom broke a grin. "My dear Maikowski, what have you got up your sleeve? If I didn't know better, I'd think you have an urge for the little bitch. And here I thought you were some sort of ascetic."

Rom detected a slight twitch in Maikowski's left eye. "This is the Eva you used on Bruckmann, yes?" Maikowski said eagerly. He looked away, feigning disinterest. Maikowski had been searching for Eva and Albert Huebner, but he could not find them. And now he had received another demand of two thousand marks from the whore. The stress was keeping him up at night and had robbed him of his desire for girls dressed as little boys. "I have need of her services," Maikowski continued, laughing self-consciously. "Of course, not for myself, but for someone in the party. If you know where she is, I order you to tell me."

Rom drank some beer. "You wish to use Eva for political purposes again?"

"Don't quibble with me, Rom," Maikowski demanded. "I think you understand me perfectly. The whore will serve the party. She will be well paid. So, if you know where she is, please tell me. I order it."

Rom drank a long draught of beer and thought about Bibi again. She was as expendable as a pair of socks to Rom, but he regretted the absence of her cunt. "Tell me," Rom said after a moment, "do you wish to photograph another unsuspecting client like you photographed Bruckmann?"

"You directed that operation," Maikowski said impatiently.

"Under your orders."

"Don't quibble with me, Captain," Maikowski said angrily. He sipped his Black Velvet and faced Rom squarely.

"Photographs are such wonderful tools," Rom said. "Now I would like to show you a photograph which recently came into my possession. Consider it part of my private collection of erotica. Pornography, if you wish. Imagine it on Christmas greeting cards."

"I am not interested in pornography," Maikowski snapped. "Have you lost your mind, Rom?"

Rom dug into his suit coat pocket and extracted a single photograph. It was the one with Maikowski lying on his back, naked save for a pair of white socks. Eva was squatting above him while loosing a stream of urine on Maikowski's chest. Rom slid the photo across the table where it came to rest at Maikowski's fingertips.

"Such a remarkable likeness," he said dryly.

Maikowski blinked once, then closed his eyes. When he opened them, his face had blanched white. Rom noticed a second twitch in the left eye.

"What is this, Captain?" Maikowski said haltingly.

"Isn't it obvious?"

"I demand that you tell me how this came into your possession."

"Nonsense," Rom snapped.

"What? What are you doing, Rom?"

"I'm blackmailing you," Rom said flatly.

Maikowski's shoulders sagged and he seemed to shrink as his left eye twitched madly.

"Blackmailing me?" he repeated.

"I have dozens more like this. None much worse, but some very bad indeed. Do you want to see them?"

"No," Maikowski said. "What do you want?"

"I want you to resign from the SA effective immediately. I want you to write a lengthy letter of resignation citing your bad health, and stating that you believe that I could better handle the position. You must insist to Daleuge that I take your place. You must insist that I take your apartment, your Landauer, your salary, and your travel budget. Your staff." Rom sat quietly, smiling intently at Maikowski, who seemed to have collapsed. "And if you refuse, these photographs will be released to all the appropriate newspapers, to the Party leaders, and to the SA in both Berlin and Munich. You can imagine the scandal. But, of course, if you resign and promote me in your place, you will salvage your dignity. Otherwise, you will be utterly destroyed and will have nothing. Go quietly, Maikowski. Go quietly."

"You have made a deal with the whore," Maikowski said.

Rom shrugged.

"And you are hiding Huebner, aren't you?"

Rom shrugged again.

"You've seen Eva, no?"

"Eva is my friend, Otto," Rom said. "Eva understands and admires me. It is you she despises, not the least because you planned to have her murdered. Of course she has betrayed you, Otto. You are finished."

Maikowski said nothing.

"You have five seconds to decide," Rom snapped.

Maikowski raised his hand. "What choice do I have?"

"Say it, Otto."

"I surrender."

"Ah, there's a good boy," Rom laughed. "But before we go, you must tell me something. What pleasure is there in being pissed on by a woman?"

— ◦ —

By four o'clock in the afternoon, Huebner had counted seventeen take-offs and thirty-one landings at Tempelhof, a modest number by normal standards. His hair was growing out, and he had shaved the goatee. In transition, his was a face that had lost all individuality. He took his meals in a workman's café down the street, bathed once a week in cold water under a dribbling shower-head in the tiny grime-splattered closet at the end of the hall, sat at the window, and watched airplanes come and go.

Entering the bed-sitter, Rom interrupted Huebner in mid-thought. Huebner ran a hand across his face, but failed to move.

"Counting airplanes again, eh?" Rom asked him.

It was a single gloomy room without a kitchen or bath. More than anything, it resembled a cell.

"Thirty-one arrivals today," Huebner said.

"We'll have you out of here soon enough," Rom said encouragingly.

Huebner turned to face Rom. He wore his uniform all day, every day. It was both his fetish and his totem, a symbol of everything disconnected in his universe.

"I've been here two months," Huebner said.

"Don't exaggerate," Rom laughed. "It's been six weeks."

"I want out of here."

"Your time is coming," Rom said soothingly. He sat down on a wooden chair. When Rom had installed Huebner in this tiny bed sitter, there had been no dressing table or mirror. Huebner had insisted that they be brought in, so Rom purchased both at a used bazaar in the suburbs. "We've not had much time to talk since Munich," Rom continued. "Don't you think it's time we had a nice long talk?"

"Why not?" Huebner said. "But why am I here? I want to leave this place."

"I've told you," Rom insisted patiently. "The police are looking for you in Berlin. Herr Wulff is on the lookout for you everywhere. And first, Maikowski must be dealt with. And after Maikowski, then Wulff. After all, it was Maikowski and his blunders that landed you in hot water, wasn't it?"

"Bring him here then," Huebner said.

"Like Bruckmann?" Rom said.

Huebner turned his attention to the window, its gray glaze of indistinct light. In the distance was a series of concrete runways, a brick conning tower topped by glass, brick buildings, two cavernous storage hangars. Huebner had memorized each structure in the field of structures. He had walked the neighborhoods thereabout in search of magazines, finding nothing. He was without either cosmetics or a wig. "Yes, yes," Huebner whispered to the window. "Why not just like Bruckmann?"

"But really," Rom said, "you'll be delighted to know that Maikowski is out of the picture. He's been taken care of. Are you not pleased?"

"Yes," Huebner said laconically.

"Maikowski will tender his resignation from the SA. He will return to civilian life." Rom paused, studying the room, its drab, featureless walls and dusty rugs. He marveled that anyone could sit at a window and watch airplanes day after day.

"Am I on the SA roll?" Huebner asked.

"Assuredly," Rom replied. "You will return to active duty in the near future."

"Active duty?"

Rom sighed heavily to emphasize his coming point. "Let me ask you something," he said. "When I spoke to Eva about your mutual situation in Munich, she said you'd introduced yourself to her as Harry Wulff. I found this detail quite fascinating. Would you mind explaining to me why you did that?"

Huebner folded his arms. "Is it important?"

"Perhaps not," Rom said. "And then again."

"Wulff has caused certain articles to appear in the press," Huebner said. "They offend me."

"Yes, certainly," Rom said quietly. He remembered the Bruckmann stories. Something about a bleak creature.

"They offend me," Huebner said again. Rom could see a halo of breath on the windowpane. Huebner respiring, Huebner standing stock still in cold-gray light.

"I want to explain something," Rom continued. "I hope you will listen carefully. SA intelligence is certain that you are being investigated on suspicion of murder. Our sources say that you have been identified as the termite at Alexanderplatz already. I hope this interests you. I hope it explains to you why I have been hiding you in this flat in Kreuzberg. It is for your own benefit."

"And you?"

Rom smiled knowingly. "Of course. We will benefit one another mutually. It is the way of the world."

"Yes, the way of the world," Huebner said vacantly, his back to Rom. A twin-engine passenger plane glided to earth. Huebner followed it with his gaze.

"Back to Harry Wulff," Rom said. "You've not told me why you chose his name as yours in Munich."

"He investigates me," Huebner said. "He wants to take away my life."

"Would you like to see him dead?" Rom asked. Rom clapped his hands together for effect and sniffed the carnation in his lapel. "Treat this as a theoretical question, if you like."

"What do you suggest?" Huebner said. His SA uniform was filthy, full of slept-in creases.

"I suggest we murder him," Rom said. Rom recalled the slap given him by Wulff at the Adlon Hotel. "I suggest we give in to our needs in this matter."

Huebner turned and smiled. "I want to leave this place."

"You want Wulff dead. I want Wulff dead. You will only be safe when he is dead."

"And after Wulff dies?"

"You become an adjutant to a colonel in the SA."

"Meaning you?"

"Of course, meaning me."

"And how do we do this thing?"

"You garrote him."

"He is a policeman," Huebner said. "He is surrounded by his detectives."

"He lives with a Jewess on Lennestrasse," Rom said. "Kill him in his love nest. It would be fitting."

"You have thought this through?"

"You have experience with locks?"

"Yes."

"And you have experience with disguises?"

"Yes."

Rom stood and moved to the door. "Surely you can handle a simple lock on a front gate?"

"I can make a wax impression," Huebner said.

"Of course you can," Rom said. "But we cannot hurry this project. Hitler is running for president. It is important that this operation to kill Wulff wait until after the election. Nothing is more important than the election of Hitler, and I have many duties in connection with it. Goebbels is heading the propaganda section of the Party, and Berlin SA figures prominently in marches and demonstrations. I am much too busy for Wulff until after the election. And besides, you must change your appearance. But after the election, we will kill this kike-loving detective."

Huebner breathed out deeply. He could see patches of old snow on the Tempelhof grounds, puddles where snow had melted during the day. "I must have my automobile," he insisted.

"I've told you," Rom said. "You must not be seen in public."

"I want magazines," Huebner said.

"Magazines," Rom huffed. "Rubbish and nonsense."

"Bring me my car."

Rom shrugged. It was not worth an argument. "You must promise not to leave the vicinity of Tempelhof."

"I will buy magazines at the airport," Huebner said. "There are newsstands inside."

"But do not leave the area," Rom told him. "Wulff looks for you everywhere. Soon enough he will be dead and the Nazis will control the Berlin police. At that point in time, my dear Huebner, everything will be permitted to you."

"All right," Huebner said.

"Good then," Rom said encouragingly.

"One more thing."

"Yes what is it?"

"My name is Edgar Braun."

"Shall I call you that?"

"Yes."

Rom walked back to the window and clapped Braun on the back in a show of solidarity. He left the bed-sitter hurriedly and went outside, getting into his Mercedes. In the pocket of his jacket, he carried a letter of resignation from Maikowski and a second letter directed to Daleuge recommending Rom as colonel in the Berlin SA. As Rom drove away, he caught sight of Braun at the window, his reflection blurring itself against dirty glass.

29

A gray scrawl of rain lay on the soot-black monuments. April was said to be a month of rain in Berlin, days of steady gloom punctuated by suddenly bright skies, dank leaves underfoot in heavy weather. Out walking one day during lunch, Wulff had seen crocuses poking through the black earth, a few hydrangea buds, even pale strokes of green in the chestnuts. Hitler had received 30 percent of the vote, and Hindenburg was president again, the eighty-year-old soldier hanging onto breath, prescribing Germany death in small doses.

Barlach had finished his morning coffee. "I'll retrieve the early intelligence reports," he said to Wulff. They were meeting in Wulff's corner office at Berlin Mitte. Wulff was sitting on a windowsill. "We can review them here," he said. The streets below were jammed with black cars, people carrying black umbrellas. The world was a black circus, and the ringleader a small, dark man with a Charlie Chaplin moustache. "Have you had breakfast? We could have something sent up."

"My wife fixed me porridge," Barlach said, heading off to collect the day's interdepartmental mail.

Once alone, Wulff performed a mental inventory. Department IV had failed to solve the latest political murders. Edgar Braun was still at large. Hitler had lost the election, but had vowed to fight on until he became chancellor. Day by day, Bernhard Weiss was losing control of Stapo, and the socialist government of Prussia was crumbling in the face of Nazi pressure. Rumors circulated through the ministries that there would be a coup d'etat against Prussia led by the aristocratic no-account von Papen—who had the president's ear—and was supported by the Army. If that were to happen, Wulff would probably be *persona non grata* in his own department.

Barlach knocked lightly on the door, pushed it open slowly, and entered holding a sheaf of documents bound by a red ribbon. On its front was an official stamp: HIGHLY CONFIDENTIAL.

"They say Hitler demands the chancellorship," Barlach said.

"The Nazis have no more money," Wulff told him, still perched on the edge of his desk. The rain continued to fall. "He has worn out his party in this futile election effort."

"Goebbels argues otherwise," Barlach said.

"They live in a fool's paradise."

Barlach shrugged and placed the documents on Wulff's desk, a mound of densely typed words. Wulff reviewed intelligence every morning, looking for word of Braun. "Oh, by the way," Barlach said, "Oberwachtmeister Kraft at the front desk says there is a lady who demands to see you. She says it is urgent and is quite important. She won't say what it's about."

"I don't have time for a lady," Wulff said. "Direct the sergeant to take a report."

"The first sergeant already tried that route," Barlach said. "She is insistent, and she won't leave."

"Nobody knows what it's about?"

"He doesn't know. She says it is a matter of life and death."

Wulff sat down behind his desk. He didn't have time for a mystery woman. Everything was a matter of life and death in Berlin. Didn't people know that?

"Anything on Braun this morning?" Wulff asked, shuffling some of the documents.

"Nothing obvious. Stapo has nothing again."

"He's bloody disappeared," Wulff said angrily. "What's he doing?"

"He'll try to kill again. Perhaps he'll fail and we'll catch him."

Barlach started to leave. "What shall I tell the sergeant?" he asked Wulff. "I've got to tell him something. He's been pestered for thirty minutes. She won't go away."

"Usher her out of the office," Wulff said. "She can give a written report to the first sergeant or she can leave."

Barlach nodded, buttoned his jacket, and left Wulff alone. Wulff sat for a moment and watched the rain streak his windows, thought of Johanna, then thought of his father alone on Poel Island with a bad cold. Barlach knocked again, opened the door, and came inside. "Perhaps you should see the woman," he suggested quietly.

"What do you mean?" Wulff asked.

Barlach approached the desk as Wulff looked down at the intelligence reports. "I spoke to this woman," Barlach said. "She said only one thing to me. She said 'Erik Bruckmann.'"

Wulff glanced up at Barlach. "Have her come up," he said. "Show her in and leave us alone, would you?"

Barlach left the office. In a few minutes, there was a soft knock. When the door opened, Wulff could see a woman framed in it. She was of medium height, dressed in a long navy blue woolen coat clasped in front by large gray whalebone buttons. Her hair was cut into a short, boyish style. Her gray-blue eyes set off the blonde hair, and she had plucked her eyebrows. The thinness of her face and her ashen complexion gave her a haunted look. In places, her skin was marred by blemishes that had turned dark blue. The left sleeve of her coat was empty, giving Wulff the impression that her left arm had been injured. As she stood in the doorway, she caught Wulff in a piercing gaze. In her good arm, she carried a black umbrella. Wulff stood, bowed slightly, circled the desk, and offered the woman a seat, which she took. When Wulff offered her coffee, she declined politely.

"My name is Wulff. Harry Wulff. I believe you wanted to see me."

"I am Evaline Vollheim," she said.

Wulff nodded imperceptibly. The name meant nothing to him. The woman looked as though she had lost a great deal of weight in recent weeks and months.

"Have we met?" Wulff asked.

"You don't know me," she said.

"But you wanted to see me specifically?"

"I read an article about you in *Vorwärts*."

Wulff pursed his lips. The first Kisch-sponsored article had been published only a week before in the socialist Sunday supplement. It had described the facts of a series of murders taking place in Berlin, how the series would telescope German history into the history of one bleak creature. To Wulff's chagrin, the article had been titled NAZI ROBOT KILLER—A GERMAN MORALITY TALE. Wulff had complained to Kisch about the tabloid sensationalism of it all, but Kisch had responded that he was not responsible for the title.

"How can I be of service?" Wulff asked.

"I knew Erik Bruckmann when he was alive." The woman remained expressionless. Wulff tried to place her and failed. There was a lengthy silence during which Wulff sensed something unfathomable at the center of this strange woman.

"Bruckmann was killed by garrote at the Capitol Cinema in Berlin," Wulff said, buying time.

"I know who did it and I know why it was done," the woman told Wulff in cold, unrelenting tones.

The words shocked Wulff, shocked him as much as if he'd touched an electric wire. "I see," Wulff said calmly. "And who murdered Bruckmann?"

"The man who murdered Bruckmann called himself Harry Wulff."

Wulff smiled faintly. "I assure you, I did not kill Erik Bruckmann."

"Nevertheless," the woman said. "The man who murdered Erik Bruckmann also tried to murder me. It was he who told me his name was Harry Wulff. Of course, when I read the article in *Vorwärts*, I knew that was not his real name. I knew then that I must speak to the real Harry Wulff."

"Perhaps you should explain," Wulff said.

The woman bit her upper lip. She looked out the rainy window and thought for a long time. One could hear the sound of traffic. Wulff could see tears at the corner of each eye. Wulff pitied her for unknown reasons.

"I was once a prostitute," she said. "I worked the streets of Munich. I was also a morphine addict. I am neither of those things now. At times, I was asked to come to Berlin to service special clients for the SA. They would be politicians or party hacks. I sometimes serviced Erik Bruckmann. Sometime later, I became certain that the SA was blackmailing Bruckmann."

"And who arranged this? How was it done?"

"It was arranged that Bruckmann was drugged with chloral hydrate. Certain photographs were taken of Bruckmann in a room in the Fischerhof Hotel in the old quarter. These photographs were used to blackmail Bruckmann. I have no idea why Bruckmann was being blackmailed. I only know that it was happening."

"And who put you with Bruckmann?"

"A man named Dieter Rom." The woman dried her tears with a hankie. Despite the tears, she remained expressionless.

"You are sure of this?"

"Yes. I saw Dieter. I worked for him. He is the man who drugged Erik Bruckmann. I don't know the man's name who killed Bruckmann. It was said in the newspapers that a garrote was used. The man who tried to kill me used a garrote as well."

"You saw this man?"

"Yes, in the Ludwigshof Hotel in Munich just after the Putsch march."

"Can you describe this man?"

"He was a tall man. As tall as you. His head was shaved and he wore a goatee and wire-rimmed glasses. That night, he was wearing the uniform of an SA sergeant."

"And why would he try to kill you?"

"I was blackmailing Otto Maikowski."

Wulff sighed. "Chloral hydrate and photographs?"

"I learned from Dieter Rom."

"Why have you come to me now?"

"I was very nearly killed."

"That's all? It could be dangerous for you. I might even ask you to testify."

"But you won't," the woman said. "And besides, you know I will not testify." Eva Vollheim sat primly, a black umbrella balanced on her chair.

"How did you meet this man who tried to kill you?"

"I was sitting in a café in Munich," she said. "He sat down at my table. I did not know then, but I know now that it was not an accident. He was looking for me. At that time, I was a creature of habit. When he introduced himself, he told me he was Harry Wulff. I had no reason to doubt him. To me he was just another of thousands of SA men in Munich over that weekend. Do you know his real name?"

"He is called Edgar Braun," Wulff said.

"I hope you will not attempt to detain me," the woman told Wulff.

"There will be no attempt to detain you."

"Good then," Eva Vollheim said. "I must go now. I've told you everything I know. It is dangerous for me in Berlin."

"Would you give me one minute more?"

"One minute I can give you. I must catch a train."

"How did you escape your planned death?"

"Dieter Rom saved me. I am certain the killer was sent by Maikowski. Some chloral hydrate was put in his apple brandy."

"He drank apple brandy?"

"Yes, apple brandy."

Wulff thought of Uli, her killer's preference for apple brandy.

"Go on," Wulff said.

"We struggled," the woman said. "I tumbled backward and broke my arm. When I regained my senses, Dieter Rom was above me, whispering in my ear. Rom helped me get to a hospital and gave me some money. I am grateful."

"Do you know why he would do this?"

"Of course," she said.

"Would you tell me?"

"There were certain photographs taken of Maikowski. I had taken them." She took out a hankie and blew her runny nose. "Everyone in Berlin has a cold," she remarked. "I gave Rom the photographs of Maikowski. He warned me to keep quiet or he would have me killed."

"I see," said Wulff. "What will you do now?"

"I'm going to see my mother," she said. "I haven't seen my mother in ten years. And then if I am lucky, I will visit Greece."

"I wish you that luck," Wulff said, standing.

"You will not try to stop me?"

"I'm grateful to you. Why would I stop you?"

"Because you are Kripo."

"It hardly matters anymore," Wulff said.

"You will catch this killer?"

The woman rose. Wulff circled the desk and stood near her.

"He will be caught, one way or another," Wulff said. Wulff looked at the woman, thinking that she could have been pretty given half a chance. They walked toward the door.

"I am not a prostitute," she said.

"I hope you enjoy Greece," Wulff said, smiling.

"Germany is an insane asylum, you know."

"So I've heard," Wulff told her.

Wulff opened the door and watched Eva Vollheim wander down the empty hall. Barlach, standing outside, raised his eyes, then came inside the office. Wulff closed the door.

"Was it important?" Barlach asked.

"Dieter Rom is now sponsoring Braun." Wulff stood beside the window looking down at rainy Berlin. "If we follow Dieter Rom, he will eventually lead us to Braun."

"I'll do the work," Barlach said. "Do you suppose that Rom is hiding Braun? And if so, why would he do that?"

"He will eventually find a use for Braun." Wulff turned and faced Barlach. "Rom was blackmailing Maikowski. The woman became involved."

"Well, that explains Maikowski's resignation from the SA. We've been wondering about that. And it explains Rom's good fortune and advancement."

"Yes, it rather does."

"But why is Rom so quiet?"

Wulff shrugged. "Patience is his weapon," Wulff said. "He told me that once."

— —

Braun parked the Russian Renault and walked a block over to the workman's café he'd frequented for more than two months. For once, it was an afternoon without rain, and there was a whiff of spring in the air. Braun found himself hating the seasons for themselves, their predictability, their way of becoming a topic of conversation. At the café, he could see faces in the windows, a dozen or so people hunched over steaming cups of oat coffee, Rom in the back sitting alone in a booth. Braun caught a look at himself reflected in the dirty window, a clean-shaven fellow in a new topcoat. He had been out most of the night prowling the Jagerstrasse, strictly against Rom's order. He had driven by the Lennestrasse apartment, seized an impulse to park, then had rushed up to the stoop and had made a wax impression of the outer door lock. It had been child's play to have a key made.

Braun went into the café and hung his coat on a rack near the booth. When he sat down, Rom said, "I've been waiting half an hour."

"I'm here, aren't I?" Braun asked haughtily. Despite being awake for twenty-four hours, he was lucid. He felt as though he were balanced on a high-wire with no net.

"Sit down then," Rom said. Rom was wearing civilian clothes. Braun had noticed the Landauer parked across from the café, a woman in the back of the long black automobile that had once belonged to Maikowski. It had begun to drizzle again. "You've been leaving your room, haven't you?" Rom said.

"What of it?" Braun said. "The election is over. You said that when the election was over, we would kill Wulff."

"Keep your voice down," Rom demanded.

Braun ordered coffee from a disheveled waitress. It was chilly in the café, and the floors were filthy. Braun ate here every day. He often saw cockroaches and silverfish. If one looked closely enough, they were everywhere.

"Did you read the Wulff article in *Vorwärts*?" Braun asked Rom.

"Of course I read it," Rom replied. Rom had ordered coffee, but it was obvious to Braun he hadn't touched it.

"Wulff will reveal my identity," Braun said. "And so we must eliminate him. He will connect me to the SA."

"Of course he will," Rom said. "Perhaps you should make a key to his apartment."

"He spends most of his time with the Yid," Braun said. Braun smiled and took a paper envelope from the inside pocket of his jacket. He took a single key from the envelope and slid it across the table. "This is the key to the front door of the Yid's place."

"I thought we would kill him at his own place," Rom said.

"He is hardly ever there."

"You have been watching him, then?"

"Of course," Braun said. "Did you take me for an idiot? A robot

Nazi killer?" Braun tasted the weak coffee. "You should not make the same mistake as Maikowski and Bruckmann."

Rom fingered the key and deftly slipped it into the coat he was wearing. He thought of his impatient mistress and the cockroaches he'd seen scuttling on the floor of the café. "Don't be ridiculous," he said.

"We must kill Wulff."

"You must be patient," Rom said.

"This is double suicide," Braun said angrily.

"Hindenburg has banned the SA and SS," Rom said. "Don't you read the papers? There will be huge riots. They are now in the planning stage. I am too busy to kill Wulff now. But in another month or two, the Prussian government will be broken. So when we kill Wulff, there will be nobody interested enough to investigate. Would that not be a good joke?"

"And what about the articles?"

"They appear every two weeks. We have time."

"You speak freely of time," Braun said. "I am tired of the flat, tired of living at Tempelhof, tired of that fucking one-room bed-sitter."

"You should be more grateful," Rom said.

"And you sound just like Maikowski."

"We should not quarrel. We want the same thing."

Braun laughed glumly. "I have been following Wulff and his Yid lover for weeks now. She is alone in the apartment, she sees a few patients. Wulff works long days. He arrives every night and seldom goes to his own flat. When he does, it is to pick up mail. They are clay pigeons."

"Wulff might surprise you," Rom cautioned. "You should be careful with him."

"It is Wulff who will be surprised."

Rom pulled on a pair of kidskin gloves he'd purchased on a holiday in Vienna. He loved Austria. Its Nazism was so much more refined than the German brand.

"We must not meet after today," Rom said. "There is a phone box one block away from here. Every night at eight, call me at my apartment. You have the number. You may continue to watch Wulff and his

Jewess so long as you do not run risks. But above all, we must not meet. Use the telephone. When I give the word, we will meet at the woman's apartment, and you will go inside and wait for Wulff in the hallway."

"And my money?"

"You will receive a package by messenger tomorrow morning at ten." Rom put a paper mark on the table. "Don't be stupid, Braun. I have matters in hand. We will kill Wulff, but we'll do it in our own good time. I'll name the night. You will not be disappointed. But if we wait a month or two, our chances of success will be that much greater. The police will be under SA control. Try to be patient."

Braun said nothing. He glared at Rom as Rom rose, walked out of the café, and got inside the Landauer. A Nazi Party secretary named Monika was in the back seat, dressed in a black wool skirt, white blouse, and a brown beaver stole Rom had purchased for her at a furrier in Vienna. Rom put his arm around her, cupped her black hair, and kissed her lightly on the ear.

"You promised ten minutes," Monika said gruffly.

Her figure was like an hourglass, her legs as lithe and muscled as a skater's. In fact, Rom thought she resembled the Olympic Champion Sonja Henie. Despite her beauty, despite the pallid luxuriousness of her skin and her pert tits and her comely bottom, she had drawbacks. She was a devoted Nazi. Rom considered ideology in a woman unbecoming, almost unforgivable. But for now, he had decided to ignore such considerations in favor of long lunches in bed at the Adlon Hotel, where he would eat oysters from her bellybutton. "I have to go to work," Monika said, prickly with impatience.

Rom covered her tight little mouth with a kiss. Her lips were cold, and he loved probing her reluctance. When he had finished, Monika busied herself with makeup and lipstick as Rom instructed his chauffeur to deliver Fraulein Tietz to Party headquarters on Hedemanstrasse near the Reichstag. Rom glanced outside, seeing Braun emerge from the café, topcoat over one arm. It came to him that he could kill two birds with one stone, Wulff and Braun in a package, tied with a nice bow.

After weeks of searching, Braun found the perfect head in a fashion supplement to the periodical *Tagebuch*. It was a male modeling swimwear whose clear Aryan features, blond hair, and sharply chiseled bone structure closely resembled Wulff. In bright light at the dressing table, Braun carefully glued the face to a cardboard body he'd constructed—a tall, dashingly elegant man in a tuxedo with red cummerbund, brightly polished black shoes, and black bow tie. Braun wrapped the doll in tissue, dressed himself in a suit and tie, walked outside to his Russian Renault, and drove across central Berlin. After driving around the block twice, he found a parking place a few meters from Lennestrasse and walked over.

He sat on a bench in the park for two hours, alone except for pigeons and a few elderly people. He would watch the apartment, get up and walk through the park, around the block, then choose another seat some distance away from the first. Just past seven o'clock in the evening, he bought a bar of chocolate at a kiosk, then walked around the block again, and returned to an even more remote bench. For months, he had followed this and other routines, seeing Wulff and the woman come and go, noting other tenants. He had begun to put faces and names together with routines and was making a list of people who lived in the building, their personal and professional characteristics, their schedules, their habits, friends, and visitors. He would sit and wait, spy a tenant collecting the mail, then casually stride across the street and check names on mailboxes. Herr Mueller, Herr Rohr. A thin, ungainly, rheumatic man who dressed in black and white named Diehl, an elderly couple with the unlikely name of Schopenhauer. That night, just before eight, he watched Frau Krull come home, retrieve her meager mail, and hobble upstairs. Braun felt as though he knew her—a stout war widow who dressed in black and gray, heavy overcoats and shawls, a tight flannel hat pulled low over her face. She lived on the third floor, just down the hall from Wulff's Yid.

Braun drove to Jagerstrasse, where he bought an admission ticket to the Residenzkasino and found a table in back. He ordered apple brandy from a waiter dressed in white, then picked up a heavy black telephone on the table and began to talk to a mystery woman whose voice was like silk and smoke. She called herself Kitty because of certain stylized characteristics—stylishly arched black eyebrows, kohled eyes, garish pink lips, and whiskers on each cheek. She drank good Sekt, which did not surprise Braun because it was the most expensive wine on the list. Braun did not pay in gold. When he thought back on his career, Braun believed that paying in gold had been his sole mistake.

— —

It was after midnight when Wulff returned to Lennestrasse. He paused in the sitting room to take off his topcoat, poured himself a glass of mineral water in the kitchen, then went to the bedroom to find Johanna propped up in bed reading a newspaper.

"There are riots," Wulff said disgustedly.

"There was something on the radio," Johanna said. She put down the paper. Wulff thought she looked tired.

"The SA is building fires all over central Berlin," Wulff continued. "Weiss has Stapo out, and Orpo is cordoning off the streets."

"My patients didn't come today," Johanna told him.

Wulff sat down on the edge of the bed and unholstered his 9mm "08" pistol.

"Something happened today," Wulff said.

"I know," Johanna said. "I know about the riots and how the Nazis have taken over the city."

"It isn't just that," Wulff said quietly. Johanna pulled up her knees and held them. Her face showed expectant fear, an almost-emotion. "A woman came to see me today," Wulff said. "A somewhat courageous woman. She'd been attacked in Munich and nearly murdered. The man who attacked her used a garrote."

"Braun?"

"She survived, but it was Braun. I'm sure of it. Dieter Rom is sponsoring him in Berlin."

"Oh Harry," Johanna said. "It's Braun. In Berlin."

"Yes," Wulff said, loosening his tie. He took off his suit jacket and sighed.

"You'll find him, won't you, Harry?"

"Barlach is following Rom. He'll lead us to Braun sooner or later."

"Yes, of course he will, darling."

"It is a question of patience."

"I'm so glad," Johanna said.

Wulff walked to the French windows and opened the drapes. In the Tiergarten were huge trees, chestnuts and feathery lindens showing a furze of green. "Now I want you to go to Switzerland," he said. "Until this thing with Braun and Rom is settled. Will you do that for me, Johanna?"

"I want to be with you," she said.

"Be reasonable, dear."

"I won't go, Harry."

Wulff returned to the bed and sat next to her. He touched her hair gently and kissed her cheek. "I'm going to put this gun in the table drawer near the door. Tomorrow morning I will teach you how to fire it. You must use this weapon if you have to defend yourself. You must tell me you will use this weapon if the need arises. I can't work thinking you are in danger."

"Harry, I'm not in danger. It's you who is in danger."

Wulff thought for a moment. "I do not wish to minimize these dangers, of course. The man who attacked the woman in Munich used my name. He called himself Harry Wulff."

"Oh God," Johanna said quietly.

"These men are capable of anything."

"I'm behind lock and key, Harry."

"Braun is adept at lock and key. Do not answer the door for anyone you do not know. Is that clear, darling?"

"I hate guns, Harry," Johanna said. "They make me physically ill. You know that."

"Promise me," Wulff asked her.

"All right, Harry, I promise," she said haltingly.

Wulff lay down at her feet. He remembered he hadn't eaten since noon, and then only a plate of day-old, dry ham on rye bread and a single pickle. But for some reason, he did not feel hungry. He thought of Barlach, who was dogging Rom's every move. Where would Wulff be without Barlach now that every man's sympathies were suspect?

30

Central Berlin was in chaos. Police and Orpo units were besieged. For weeks, there had been sporadic riots and pogroms conducted by SA and SS combined units. Nazi cadres roamed at will, setting barricade fires, beating socialists and communists, shrieking their demand that Hitler be made chancellor. Through it all, Wulff and Barlach had worked nonstop searching for Braun.

Now, both were in Wulff's office reviewing the early intelligence reports, creating a personnel list of administrative employees loyal to the Nazis. These days, whole precincts had gone over to the Right. It was early morning, a hazy day. On his way to work, Wulff had smelled smoke. When there was a knock on the door, Barlach opened it. They saw a frowning adjutant first sergeant standing there.

"Sir, I'm sorry to interrupt," the first sergeant said.

"It's all right," Wulff told him.

The first sergeant took a single step inside. "There has been a coup," he said. "Last night."

"A coup?" Wulff said, surprised. It had been rumored for weeks. Longer. Now that it was a reality, Wulff could not believe it.

"Yes, sir, a coup," the sergeant repeated.

"Do you know the details?"

"They've come over the wire," the sergeant told Wulff. "Von Papen has become a presidential chancellor. Officials from the Reich Ministry of Interior have taken Weiss and Grzenski into protective custody. I thought you should know," the sergeant said stiffly.

"Yes, thank you, sergeant," Wulff replied.

Barlach sat down. The sergeant closed the door. Wulff looked out the window to a beautiful summer day without a cloud in the sky. He had risen early, leaving the sleeping Johanna before dawn. He hardly slept four hours a night anymore. Johanna's patients were drifting away, one by one, frightened by the inevitable political news, the riots, the threats of pogroms and beatings. A band of thugs had brought central Berlin to its knees, brown-uniformed oafs who carried black truncheons and set fires like children. Standing by the window, Wulff made a few quick mental calculations. Who should he telephone? What could he do to help Weiss? In mid-thought, his own telephone rang. When he picked up the receiver, he heard Louis Adlon's voice.

"Wulff? Is that you, Wulff?" Adlon said breathlessly.

Wulff assured Adlon that it was he.

"There's been a coup," Adlon said.

"I've just been told."

"They've held Weiss overnight," Adlon said. "He was under some sort of house arrest. But they've released him. I thought you ought to know."

"Yes, I'm glad you called. I was just thinking about Weiss. About what to do."

"Harry, there is nothing to do. It is the beginning of the end. We knew it was coming, didn't we?"

"Who will replace Weiss and Grzenski?" he asked.

"Colonels Poten and Heimannsberg," Adlon told him. "Weiss has told me. He's sitting here in my office."

"They are corrupt puppets," Wulff said.

"Of course they are, Harry," Adlon said with a faint laugh. "Would you expect something else?"

"Weiss is with you?" Wulff asked.

"Sitting right here. He is fine. And how are you? Is everything all right with Johanna?"

"She's at the apartment. I was just about to ring her."

"Call her, Harry," Adlon said. "She's a fine girl."

"Is that all?" Wulff asked. He sensed another agenda, something that Adlon wished to say that had been left unsaid.

"Is this line secure, Harry?" Adlon asked quietly.

"I imagine so," Wulff answered.

"Then I must tell you something that is highly confidential. I am making arrangements for Weiss and his family to leave for Vienna tonight. They are in danger here. I am handling the matter of documents, bank transfers, the sale of personal and real property. I think you understand the urgency of these affairs. Weiss would like to see you before he goes. Can you come to my office at the Adlon?"

"I'll leave right away," Wulff said.

"Good, Harry. I thought you might want to."

Adlon rang off, and Wulff sat immersed in thought. Barlach thumbed through the morning intelligence. An eerie silence had descended on the streets.

Barlach grimaced and looked up. "There is no more Prussian government," he said. "The elected officials have been deprived of their posts by the Reich. What does it mean? Who do we work for now?" Barlach dropped his document in a heap. "And who are Poten and Heimannsberg?"

"They are figureheads," Wulff said. "When there is no legal government, we work for the strongest man."

Barlach joined Wulff at the windows. They looked down at the nearly empty streets. "I have to go," Barlach said. "I must pick up Rom's track before he leaves his apartment."

"You've been invaluable to me," Wulff told him. "I want to thank you."

"Is this the end?" Barlach asked.

"Very nearly," Wulff said.

"What shall we do?"

"Continue on one more day. Tomorrow morning we will meet here, assess the intelligence, decide what to do. Your job is quite safe, I think."

"What about you?"

"I am a different story," Wulff answered.

"Perhaps today will be the day," Barlach said. "The day that Rom meets Braun." Barlach turned and walked briskly out of the office.

Wulff spent a few minutes signing authorizations and organizing his desk. He assigned a squad of detectives to a murder in the suburbs, one unconnected to politics. He walked outside into the sunshine, hailed a taxi, and rode ten minutes down Unter den Linden to the hotel. Down side streets, Wulff could see squads of Orpo blocking access to the thoroughfares of central Berlin, men in uniform bunched around armored vehicles, the remnants of broken glass and bonfires. A thought entered Wulff's mind—What was keeping Braun?

Wulff paid his taxi driver and went inside the deserted lobby. On a mezzanine floor in back, Louis Adlon maintained an elegant business office. Wulff walked up a flight of carpeted stairs and tapped lightly on the door. Adlon opened it, and Wulff saw Bernhard Weiss sitting on a chair, legs crossed. Wulff walked over and shook his hand warmly.

"I've been sacked, arrested, held overnight," Weiss said with a slim, ironic smile.

"I'm sorry," was all Wulff thought of to say. It seemed pitifully inadequate.

"I asked Louis to call you," Weiss said. "I want to say a few things to you before I go."

"So, you will leave Berlin?"

"It is necessary for my family." Weiss took off his glasses and commenced to polish them with his handkerchief. Wulff had seen the gesture a hundred times. Weiss was dressed as he always dressed, a tight-fitting brown suit, polished black shoes, a curiously offbeat yellow bow tie. "You must keep this a secret. I am leaving tonight for Vienna with my family. I did not want to leave without telling you how much your friendship and support have meant to the department and myself. Please do not think of me as a coward. I am not running away from a fight. But I have a wife and I have children, and they are more important to me now than the fight ever was. Can you understand this? I hope you understand. Others must resist. Perhaps you yourself will resist, although I would not blame you if you didn't. Our association has made me proud of the Berlin Metropolitan Department."

"The feeling is mutual, I assure you," Wulff said, nodding in deference. "I wish you Godspeed."

"Perhaps God will make the trains run on time."

Wulff turned to Adlon. "Louis, what have you heard?"

"It will be government by decree," Adlon replied.

"What of the police?"

"There is no longer an independent police in Berlin," Adlon said. "The police are now a political force being run at the behest of whoever controls the government of the Reich."

"And if Hitler becomes chancellor?"

"You know the answer to that question as well as I," Adlon said sadly. "But, Harry, there is another reason I called you here. I can help you leave Berlin, Harry. There is a lot of confusion now. You and Johanna have a chance to leave without scrutiny. It may be your last chance. Will you talk to Johanna? You know how much I think of you both."

Wulff thanked Adlon. "I'll speak to Johanna tonight," he said. "We'll telephone tomorrow. Is that soon enough?"

"Tomorrow," Adlon said. "And by the way, have you spoken to your father?"

"I've just had a letter. He has a summer cold. Otherwise, he is well."

"Give him my best," Adlon said.

Weiss stood and straightened his bow tie. "I must go home now," he said. "My family is worried. I wish you the best, Herr Kriminal Oberkommissar."

Adlon and Wulff sat together after Weiss had gone.

"A courageous man," Adlon said. "He was never given a chance, Harry. As a Jew, he was hated and mistrusted from the start. Those he worked most closely with despised him secretly. All save for you, Harry."

"I didn't do him much good," Wulff admitted.

"You were loyal," Adlon said. "That is quite a lot."

"But he's lost after all," Wulff said.

"We've all lost," Adlon said.

━ ━

Rom was awakened by the persistent sound of the telephone. It seemed to be ringing inside a dense invisible fog. He opened his eyes and glanced at the bedside clock. Just before seven o'clock in the morning. Beside him, Monika was snoring like a cat, her mouth half-open, on her back under silk sheets, one leg exposed. Rom fumbled for the phone and answered it.

"It's seven o'clock," he growled into the receiver. Monika moved, coughed once.

"It is Braun," a voice said.

He'd instructed Braun to telephone precisely at eight o'clock every evening. And had the man obeyed? Of course not. Sometimes he called and sometimes he didn't. Sometimes it was eight o'clock when he telephoned, sometimes later, although Rom had to admit, he never called early in the morning. Rom smoothed back some hair from his forehead. With the Nazis so close to victory in Berlin, perhaps it was actually time to liquidate this monster.

"Telephone me tonight, dammit," Rom growled.

"No, not tonight," Braun said. "Tonight we are going to kill Wulff."

"I said call me tonight," Rom demanded. Monika moved again, snuffled, rolled onto her left side. The line of her rump made a contour under the sheet. "At eight o'clock. Call me tonight."

"I kill Wulff tonight," Braun said. "With you or without you. It will be dark around six-thirty or seven o'clock. It must be done then. And it must be done tonight. I will wait no longer. I am tired of this dismal flat, and I am tired of your delay."

"Don't be stupid," Rom said. "You can wait another night."

"Tonight," Braun said.

There was silence. Rom was afraid that Braun might hang up the phone. If that happened, he'd have to drive out to the flat near Tempelhof and talk to the crazy lout. What an annoyance he had turned out to be, just like Maikowski had said. Rather than killing Wulff, Rom had decided it would be much easier to wait a few months, have the man arrested and placed in the cellar of the Ministry of Interior, where Rom could visit him. With the aroma of political victory in the air, Nazis would soon control every ministry. What a joy it would be to confront Wulff, see him in chains, and perhaps put a boot to his face.

Rom squeezed shut his eyes and thought. "All right, Braun," he said reluctantly. "Go to the Lennestrasse apartment precisely at seven o'clock. I'll be across the street in the Tiergarten watching. I'll back you up if something goes wrong. But I don't want anything to go wrong."

"Nothing will go wrong," Braun said. "I'll go inside with my key. There is a widow named Krull who lives in the building. I'll be dressed as she dresses. I will go inside and wait for Wulff. The Yid will keep me company."

Rom hung up the phone. Monika made another noise and turned again, pulling the covers up to her neck. Rom opened the nightstand next to his side of the bed and checked the police-issue 9mm "08" pistol he kept there. He closed the nightstand drawer, stretched out his hand, and touched Monika's shoulder. Rom lifted the sheet and put his hand on her naked stomach.

"Don't you ever get enough?" Monika said angrily.

Rom removed his hand and let the sheet drop. After tonight, he would find a new mistress, someone more like Bibi. He'd had enough of women with ideology, bright ideas, and full-time jobs at Party headquarters. There were plenty of women in the world who would open their legs for money. Like Edgar Braun and Harry Wulff, Monika had become a thorn in Rom's side.

➤ ➤

Johanna sighed and began to close the door.

"Good night, Frau Bierbaum," she said gaily.

"Thank you, Doctor," said Frau Bierbaum.

Johanna stood with her back to the door, eyes closed, her breath coming in self-conscious spurts. She could hear Frau Bierbaum trudging down the corridor with her heavy footsteps. Johanna walked to the kitchen and fixed herself a cup of tea. She took off her beaded Peruvian vest and her shoes, then sat at the kitchen table staring at the tile work on the floor while her tea cooled. And so there had been a coup d'etat in Prussia! The government was in the hands of a silly top-hatted aristocrat and his army general foil! Could one imagine anything more absurd?

She finished her tea, then wandered to the bedroom and pulled open the drapes, unlatched one of the French windows, and opened it as well. She allowed a soft summer northern light to drown her senses, light that shimmered in the summer trees outside, the huge chestnuts of the Tiergarten, light that fell and dipped through the leaves like schools of fish. For a long time, she resisted the urge to telephone Harry at his office, but finally submitted. His line rang three times before he finally answered.

"I'm sorry, darling," Johanna said reluctantly. She told Harry that she was genuinely sorry, that she was a crybaby and a waif. That she loved him and longed for him and that her feelings were the result of transference and self-hate.

"Don't be silly," Wulff laughed.

"I know you're busy," she said.

"Yes, yes," Wulff told her. "There's been a coup. Weiss has been sacked, and I'm trying to find out who I work for. Isn't that stupid? Weiss was under house arrest last night, but he's been released. He's going to Vienna with his family."

"I'm glad for him," Johanna said. "I know how you feel about his work." Johanna stopped talking only to discover that she was physically trembling.

"Are you all right, dear?" Wulff asked.

"It is the rioting and the coup," Johanna said. "It is taking its toll on my nervous system." Johanna could hear the trees singing in the park.

"I'm going to say this only once more," Wulff told her in a stern voice. "I want you to think about it. Adlon has ways of seeing people across the border with their papers and their money. He can handle selling their personal property and their real estate. He wants you to think about this offer. But dear, you can be in Zurich in a week, perhaps less if we really work on it. You must think seriously about this. I've heard from Kisch. He's gone already to Vienna. It is rumored that Levitt will lose his job as well. I've telephoned him about leaving."

Johanna could hear Harry breathing into the phone. "But what about you, Harry?" she asked him.

"Don't cry, darling, please," Wulff said in anticipation. They knew each other. They had traded skins.

Johanna steadied herself. Across so many kilometers of wire, her lover could foretell her moods. Johanna brushed away a tuft of hair that had fallen across her forehead. "I won't cry, Harry," she said uncertainly. "When are you coming home?"

"I have to work late tonight again," he said. "It is unavoidable. I'm clearing up old business. And I have to see some people."

"You've worked late for months," Johanna said, not wanting to complain, but unable to help it. She had made up her mind that she would not cry. That was the least she could do for Harry.

"It won't be long, darling," he told her reassuringly. "Around seven or eight o'clock."

"Not before?" she said almost childishly.

"Sleep for a couple of hours," he said. "When I come home, we'll go out and eat."

"What about the riots?"

"That's just in central Berlin. You know that. We'll go to Adlon's hotel and have dinner in the dining room. We can try to dance. We'll drink some Sekt."

"While Rome burns." Johanna regretted saying it the moment the words left her mouth. She was disappointed and lonely and couldn't help being petulant.

"I love you," Wulff told her gently.

"Oh, Harry, of course you do," she murmured.

She told him good-bye. She took off her clothes and went into the bathroom and ran a tub of water. For nearly an hour she sat in the tub reading a newspaper, burning a candle on the porcelain edge of the tub. She tried to listen for lions at the zoo far away, but heard none. All she detected was the faint sound of traffic, the sibilant trees in the park. Once or twice she drifted into slumber, only to awake. Finally, she dried herself with a towel and went into the bedroom and lay down on the bed.

Some time later the door buzzer woke her. She put on a robe and hurried through the sitting room and into the hallway. For a moment, she thought about opening the table drawer near her right hand, finally deciding against it. She was more afraid of guns than anything. At the door, she looked through the peephole and saw Frau Krull outside, the hulking stoop-shouldered woman dressed in a drab overcoat and slouch hat, misapplied lipstick, wisps of gray hair falling down around her shoulders.

Johanna chained the door, opened it a crack. "Frau Krull?" she asked. "Is something wrong?"

"I was going out—"

"I'm sorry?" Johanna said, still half-asleep.

"I've locked myself out," Frau Krull said in a low voice.

Did that make sense?

Johanna peered through the opening. Frau Krull took up most of the space in her view. Johanna sensed that the corridor was empty. It was dark out there, as timeless as a tunnel.

Johanna smelled apple brandy and had time to mutter to herself, "Oh, my God." When the door chain snapped, a wood splinter struck her forehead.

— ⁓

Barlach always varied his routine. Did that make it less than a routine, or was he only fooling himself?

The thought occurred to him that Rom knew he was watching, that the last two or three months had been an unsubtle charade, with Barlach himself at the center of a joke. Now, sitting in the police Opel only fifty meters from Rom's Stieglitz apartment, Barlach entertained a sudden weariness with his job that felt surreal. In his mind's eye, he saw a scene as he'd seen it dozens of times before: just after eight o'clock at night, Rom would go out to his Landauer that was parked in a garage just down the street. He would drive across central Berlin and pick up his current mistress. They would spend time at expensive restaurants, nightclubs, pubs where party hacks and SA officers gathered to talk, drink beer, sing songs. Barlach would maintain a healthy distance. Barlach would follow Rom back to his apartment in Stieglitz and another night would end as the nights always ended. Tonight Barlach was surprised when Rom left his apartment well before seven o'clock. He walked to the parking garage and retrieved his Landauer. And another surprise. He was driving the Landauer himself. No chauffeur.

Sitting in the Opel had made Barlach sweaty and uncomfortable. "You're a little early tonight, Herr Rom," he said to himself. They went west, then south, then west again in light traffic. It was dusk, but the Landauer was simple to follow, a huge black car with large, red taillights.

On Lennestrasse, the Landauer slowed, Barlach back about a block. He followed Rom around the block twice, the Landauer stopping once in a bus zone, then moving on. On the third time around, Rom found a place to park two blocks away, got out of the Landauer, then walked a block back and found a bench in the Tiergarten, just across the way from Johanna's flat.

Barlach parked the small Opel. He rolled down the window and looked at Rom, who was reading a newspaper in the failing light. It was too dark to read, wasn't it? From where he was sitting, Barlach could see Johanna's stoop, a row of purple hydrangeas in front, an iron gate. Rom was directly opposite the building, about twenty meters inside the park boundary, languishing quietly on a green park bench surrounded by a wire fence protecting some flowers. Barlach opened his notebook and jotted down his observations, the date, the time, Rom sitting on a park bench opposite Johanna's apartment.

At seven o'clock, Barlach noted that an old woman with white hair and a slouch hat pulled low had gone up to the stoop. She stopped, searched her purse for a key, then opened the front door and disappeared inside. At eight o'clock, Wulff arrived in a taxi. Barlach touched the eight-shot Parabellum pistol on the seat beside him. The metal was warm to his touch.

As Barlach watched, Wulff went into the apartment.

31

Wulff focused his mind and entertained the question: Could he have behaved differently? Could he have anticipated this future, the riots, the coup d'etat, the nearness of chaos? The gloomy hallway stretched before him, and he suffered the absence of Johanna, the mornings they'd had together now like so many tombstones. Wulff walked up three flights of carpeted stairs, paused at the landing to take out his key, then shuffled to Johanna's door. He listened at the door for a brief moment, wondering if she'd taken his advice and gone to sleep. He turned the key in its lock, opened the door, and began to close it when he noticed a sliver of wood cracked from the jamb just above the chain. He turned halfway around when he felt a noose slip around his neck and discovered himself being lifted and carried nearly off his feet by a quick burst of energy from someone behind.

He relaxed, allowing himself to be lifted and arched rearward. His mind raced violently, but he resisted the urge to claw at the hemp noose, resisted the urge to struggle for breath, to kick his feet and scream, all of which he'd been trained would merely intensify the drama of death.

Wulff touched his toes to the floor. Braun's breath reeked of apple brandy, his body of sweat. Wulff heard a low growl just behind his right ear. He arched himself against Braun, lifted his arms, touched the back of the man's head, found eye sockets with his thumbs, and pushed them down hard. With all the strength left to him, Wulff tipped backward and drove his thumbs into Braun's eyes.

Wulff heard a low scream. The door to the apartment stood open, and Wulff could see the corridor, one light bulb burning weakly in a sconce, and a slice of striped wallpaper. He could feel Braun moving back, trying to avoid Wulff's own effort, the thumbs he was working into Braun's eyes. Something sticky lay on Wulff's fingers. Braun shook his head, and Wulff lost his purchase. The noose loosened momentarily, and Wulff grabbed a precious breath, circled his fingers around Braun's head again, found the eyes, and forced his thumbs into their sockets with all the strength he could muster.

Braun hurled himself backward again, the noose dropping to Wulff's collar bone. In the time it took Wulff to right himself, Braun had regained his balance and thrust the noose around Wulff's neck, lifting him again off the floor a centimeter or two. Wulff relaxed again, giving his muscles space. Braun was breathing heavily, exhaling apple brandy odors into Wulff's face as Wulff searched again for the eye sockets, placing a thumb into each. Wulff dug in each thumb deeply as Braun screamed and fell back.

Wulff dropped to his knees, panting. In a moment of panic, he grabbed for the nightstand drawer to search for the gun as Braun kicked Wulff in the stomach, knocking him sideways against one wall of the hallway. Wulff tried to stand but stumbled instead, sending the nightstand to the floor, the pistol just out of reach. Wulff's vision was blurred, his heart pounding. He noticed a spot of blood on his own tie, Braun on hands and knees groping for the noose, which Wulff felt looped again around his neck in an awkward drag against his own body weight. Wulff jabbed a thumb at Braun's eye and found his target.

Braun uttered a scream of pain, tumbled down with his back to the wall. Wulff, on hands and knees, scrambled forward, found the police "08", and managed to grip it tightly in his right hand. Two meters at most separated Wulff and his bleak creature, the man dressed as a woman in a dark slouch hat and heavy woolen overcoat, some kind of gray wig, faintly ridiculous lipstick, and misapplied eye shadow. The eye shadow was smeared where Wulff had gouged Braun's eyes. Wulff raised the pistol, held it poised for a moment, and thought of Johanna before pulling the trigger.

A great rose-colored wound appeared at Braun's throat, just above his Adam's apple. Braun seemed to gasp and relax, then slump against the wall, blood flowering down his chest. Wulff caught his breath, put down the gun, and rose to his hands and knees again. On the floor beside Braun was a doll that looked exactly like Harry Wulff himself.

At that moment, Wulff sensed someone in the open doorway behind him.

"I'm aiming a gun at your head," Wulff heard someone say. He turned to see Rom. The pistol remained on the carpet. In Rom's right hand was a police-issue "08".

"You've killed your nemesis," Rom said. "You've saved me the trouble."

Wulff was finding it hard to breathe. His vision was blurred. Perceptions of Rom were daggering at him from dozens of angles. Wulff coughed twice, trying to dislodge whatever was choking him. The front of his shirt was covered in blood.

"What have you done?" Wulff managed to say, looking up at Rom.

"We don't have much time," Rom said. "People in the apartment building will surely have heard the shot. They'll be peering out their doors."

Wulff thought of Johanna again, his mind a blur of panic.

"Don't hurt Johanna," Wulff said.

"The Yid, you mean?" Rom laughed quietly. "I wouldn't think of it."

"What do you want then?" Wulff asked.

"Do you remember the Adlon?" Rom asked. "I wanted only this moment as a recompense."

"You've been hiding Braun," Wulff said. He looked at the creature, trying to catch his breath, wondering if it were remotely possible to make a stab at the gun he'd dropped and get a shot off before Rom could react. Braun's body lay between Wulff and the gun, the gun itself angled grip-away. It wasn't likely.

"Braun means nothing," Rom said. "He was a means to an end, as you can see."

"Then why use him?" Wulff asked, stalling for time.

"He's really quite insane," Rom said.

"Unlike yourself."

"Quite unlike myself," Rom said, delightedly. "The accepted police theory—the one in the record books—will be that you and Braun shot each other during a struggle. Braun attacked you, but you fought yourself free and shot him with the '08' on the floor. But not before Braun managed to shoot you as well with his own gun. Besides, it hardly matters how rigorously the facts are scrutinized because the police are already partly under our control."

"Someone will have heard shots separated by time," Wulff temporized.

Rom glanced at the hallway, still deserted. He looked back at Wulff shaking his head. "People will not come forward to testify," he said. "I assure you this case will be closed quite rapidly."

"It's about me then?"

"Of course it's about you," Rom said. Rom took a step back into the hallway and let one hand drop to the doorknob. He listened carefully, tuning himself to silences as yet unbreached. Again he looked at Wulff. "You had your chance, Wulff. You could have joined us. You were a fool not to come over to our side. I've often wondered what you were doing over there with the monkeys and the kikes and the vermin socialists. You are a smart man and a German. The wave of the future was before you, and you let it wash over you, drown you. I pity you, Wulff. I pity you sincerely." Rom raised the pistol and pointed it at Wulff.

In a parody of slow motion, Rom's head exploded in a blizzard of bone, blood, and tissue. Wulff heard the gunshot, a single roar and a single echo and then a silence that pulsated into nothing. He managed to tuck one leg beneath his body in an effort to rise. Halfway up, balanced with his back to the wall, he saw Barlach's face in the doorway.

"Herr Oberkommissar," Barlach said. "Rom was going to kill you."

"Barlach!" Wulff grunted. "Get me up, can you?" Wulff felt dizzy and nauseated. "We've got to find Johanna."

Barlach holstered his pistol and helped Wulff slide up the wall and stand. Wulff was poised there, balanced above a pool of blood that was spreading from the back of Braun's head. The creature lay there on his back, the slouched hat to one side revealing a cruel, distorted face. The blood moved down the hall, Braun and Rom in death together. Wulff realized that the buzz inside his mind was the sound of Rom's intended bullet.

— —

They discovered Johanna in a bedroom closet. Braun had covered her with a goose down quilt after tying her hands and feet, stuffing handkerchiefs in her mouth and binding them. Wulff sat with her on the bed, Barlach on a chair near the open French doors. Summer light was falling into the room, a soft blue glow that vectored itself against the lace curtains. Wulff found that he was covered with blood. Barlach was holding Rom's gun as though it were a crucifix. Johanna had not cried. Wulff put his arms around her shoulders. They could hear other voices in the corridor outside.

"Did he hurt you, dear?" Wulff asked Johanna. Wulff's hands were bloody and he could not touch her face.

"He hit me with a truncheon," Johanna said. Her voice was distant. "I don't remember very much expect waking up in the closet and being afraid. It was terrible, Harry. But not so terrible as for you."

Barlach was sitting slouched forward, hands on knees now, his face white with shock. He looked to Wulff as though he might faint.

"Braun is dead," Wulff said.

"Harry?" Johanna asked, looking up at Wulff.

"I shot him," Wulff said. "Rom wanted to be rid of both Braun and me. And so Rom sent him here and he would have shot me, too, except for Barlach."

"I watched Rom for an hour," Barlach said to the floor. "When he went inside the apartment here, I had to follow. I didn't have a key, so I broke the door window and reached inside. I didn't know what else to do."

"We owe you everything," Wulff said.

Wulff could feel Johanna's cold skin against his cheek. He found a sweater and put it around her arms.

"What shall we do now?" Barlach asked.

"I want you to call the forensic crew at Savigny Platz Precinct. They're the only reliable crew left in Berlin. And I'll telephone Levitt and see if he'll stop by. If we have Savigny Platz and Levitt work the case, we'll be able to control the investigation. If Poten or Heimannsberg interferes, it will be too late."

Barlach left the room. Johanna put her head on Wulff's shoulder and pretended to look at the trees in the park. A yellow moon had risen. The chestnut trees were catching its light.

"You must leave for Zurich," Wulff whispered to her.

"You'll come, Harry? You'll come with me?"

"Not just now," Wulff said. "Perhaps later. Yes, surely I'll come later."

"Don't stay here, Harry," Johanna said. "What good would it do to stay here now?"

"You'll be safe in Zurich," Wulff said. "That will give me the space to think clearly." Wulff kissed her tenderly. "You'll go to Zurich in a few days. You'll go see Louis Adlon tomorrow morning and make the arrangements?"

"Yes, Harry, I'll go," she told him.

"You'll be well and safe. You'll have professional friends and you can begin a new practice."

"It will be lovely, Harry."

"We'll exchange daily letters."

"And you'll follow? You'll come to me?"

"We'll go see Louis Adlon tomorrow morning. We can decide about us later."

Wulff could hear Barlach in the next room talking on the telephone, summoning a forensic crew from Savigny Platz Precinct. Six good detectives and technicians, no Nazis among them. They were perhaps the last policemen Harry Wulff could trust in Berlin.

"I love you, Harry," Johanna said.

"Of course you do," Wulff told her.

Wulff looked down at his blood-stained hands and blinked once. When he opened his eyes, the blood remained.

EPILOGUE

<hr>

FEBRUARY 1933

Wulff sat on the porch of the lodge wearing his father's heavy field coat. He had arrived on Poel the night before, taking the overnight North German Express. In Berlin, he and Barlach had watched the ghastly torchlight parade celebrating Hitler's appointment to the chancellorship, Hitler, Göring, and Goebbels on a third-story balcony of the Kaiserhof Hotel while crowds cheered them madly, raised their hands in the "Heil" salute, as SA battalions and SS squads marched past. The next day, Wulff had closed up his apartment.

It was still and cold. Wulff could tell that his father had come out of the door and was standing just behind him. Morning frost lay on the moor, and there was a line of crows leaving the spruce trees at the edge of the village, borne on a chilly wind.

"So, Hitler is chancellor," Gunter Wulff said.

"Hindenburg appointed him two days ago."

"And what will happen?"

Wulff thought. Kisch had gone underground in Vienna, pursued by Nazi death squads. Levitt had been forced to retire weeks ago and was living on a pension. Wulff had heard that Freud was ill, refusing to leave Austria despite the anti-Semitic situation. He'd had a telephone call from Adlon informing him that Weiss and his family had disembarked in England and would move to London. Grzenski had gone to New York to give speeches.

"They'll come for me eventually," Wulff said.

Gunter Wulff grunted and moved forward toward the porch steps where Wulff was sitting. Wulff could feel the touch of his father's hand on one shoulder. A church bell was being rung in the village.

"Then you must go," Gunter Wulff said.

"They'll come for you, too," Wulff told his father.

Gunter Wulff laughed. "They wouldn't dare. I am a hero of Germany's Great War." Gunter Wulff sat down on the porch step beside his son.

"You know they'll come for you," Wulff said again.

"What if they do?" Gunter Wulff rubbed his hands for warmth.

"I'm an old man."

"I can't leave you, Father."

"But you must."

"I'm a German as well."

The road to the lodge was a single dirt lane running between gorse fields bordered by two thick hedges. They were kilometers from the village. Gunter Wulff pointed at the road. "There is a clear field of fire here to the road. I am a good shot, Harry, a damn good shot. If they come for me, I'll take a dozen of them with me."

"You think you could kill a dozen?"

Gunter Wulff laughed again. "But you must go to Zurich and not worry about me."

"You will come with me?"

"Never," Gunter Wulff said. "I live here now, and I am an old man. But you are a young man, Harry."

"I'm sorry I brought this to you, Father."

"I do not associate with cowards."

They sat quietly together watching the morning.

"Who will come, Harry? Do you know?"

"SS, most likely," Wulff told his father. "Do you think you could kill a dozen?"

"If that many came."

"We could kill a dozen each, then."

"Yes, a dozen each. But they wouldn't send so many, would they, Harry? They might send half a dozen. I could kill them all. It would make a headline in the Berlin papers."

"With both of us here they would have to send a platoon," Wulff laughed.

"But you really must join Johanna, Harry."

Wulff looked at his father, the old man's face gray with age. "I'll make us some breakfast," Wulff said. The servants had fled long ago. Wulff stood up, helping his father rise as well. Wulff gazed toward the sea which was obscured by fog. "If they come at night, we couldn't kill a dozen each," he said.

"They would come at night?"

"I think they would come at night."

"Yes, of course," Gunter Wulff growled. "They might come at night. I will not let them take me from my bed. It wouldn't do."

"We must not let that happen," Wulff agreed. "Now, I'm going to fix fresh eggs."

For a while, they watched the crows stream from the forest to feed. And then Harry Wulff prepared them both a good German breakfast.

ABOUT THE AUTHOR

Gaylord Dold is the author of fourteen novels, many of which have received starred reviews in *Publishers Weekly*, *Booklist*, and *Library Journal*. He has written four travel books and many works of criticism. In 1988, he cofounded Watermark Press, and as managing editor published books such as *Leaving Las Vegas*. Educated in San Francisco and London, he has traveled widely in Europe, Africa, and the Caribbean. He makes his home now on the plains of southern Kansas.